I would like to dedicate this book to all my students: past, present, and future, who inspire me to write.
Keep reading and follow your dreams!

Southern Charms Publishing

Ordering Information
Quantity sales: special discounts are available on quantity purchases by corporations, associations, and others. For details, contact the publisher below.

Publisher's Cataloging-in-Publication data
Wilson, Tracy
The Final Aeon

ISBN 979-8-9912384-4-1(Paperback)
ISBN 979-8-9912384-3-4(Hardback)
ISBN 979-8-9912384-5-8(ePub e-book)

Library of Congress Control Number: 2024918258

First Published (2024)
Southern Charms Publishing
inquiries@southerncharmspublishing.com
www.thelastgardener.com

THE FINAL AEON
Book 2 in the Last Gardener Series

TRACY WILSON

The puzzle box. Made of metal and depicting the Seven Fires Prophesy weaved through intricate carvings

Writing this book has been such an awesome adventure and it would not have been possible without the support of my best friend and husband, Joshua. Thank you for always supporting my crazy ideas. I also want to give a special thank you to my three incredible children for listening to my wild stories and helping me bring them to life.

Table of Contents

Chapter 1

A New Reality

(Present day)

*T*he incessant beeping pierces my eardrums like a persistent pickaxe; slowly, but rhythmically, chipping away at my sanity.

> *I should be the one hooked up to those machines, not Jaxson!*

My eyes, like magnetic hazel hematite, are drawn to the monitor as I watch Jaxson's heartbeat form small, continuous peaks. I silently pray that his heart continues beating as the hopeful summits blur from the tears puddling in my eyes. Forcing down the lump forming in my throat, I inhale a cleansing breath of bravery and attempt to be strong for my parents' sake. They sit hunched over Jaxson's shrinking frame, lying perfectly motionless under a layer of pressed white sheets and blankets. I glance at Dad's wrinkled stare, and his distant gaze greets me. I can't discern what is running through his mind.

> *Are the creases between his brows deepening with the thought of his son's life hanging on the line, or is he concerned about the deals he might be missing out on with his new company, Elementerprise?*

My eyes shift to Mom's grey-streaked, undone hair as a stray strand frees itself from behind her ear and falls to frame her worried expression. Her reassuring words telling me *this isn't my fault* seem so superficial. I know deep down inside they blame me for Jaxson's fragile condition.

If only I hadn't taken Jaxson down to the cellar in the first place, none of this would have happened!

The unexpected knock on the hospital room door causes my body to jerk as a dark-haired doctor slices through the dense silence like hot metal gliding through butter. We all stare at him with gut-wrenching anticipation.

"Excuse me, Mr. and Mrs. Gardener, may I please have a word with you?"

His almond-shaped, deep-set eyes shift in my direction like lasers.

"Privately," he adds, gesturing for me to leave the room.

"Why don't you go grab yourself a snack from the vending machine," Mom suggests.

"I want to stay and hear what the doctor has to say." I plead with every fiber of my being.

"I think I have a few dollars in my purse." Mom's eyes double, clearly informing me that she is too tired for an argument.

My teeth dig into my tongue, and I stomp out reluctantly, not even bothering to get the money she offered. I feel I owe it to Mom to obey, but I don't have to be happy about it.

The doctor thrusts the heavy door closed behind me as I exit, but luckily, it isn't a very forceful shove. The latch in the door acts as a doorstop and slightly ricochets against the frame to push the door open just a crack. Hopefully, it is open enough for me to hear what the doctor has to say about Jaxson.

The busy hustle and bustle of the nurse's station in front of me are going to be problematic for eavesdropping. In their matching royal blue scrubs, three nurses laugh and talk obnoxiously as if this is just a typical day and my little brother's life isn't hanging by a thread. I feel my legs weaken beneath me as my back slides down the wall just outside Jaxson's room door. Crouching into a sitting position, I pull a small fidget gadget out from my jeans pocket. It is another one of my creations containing a knot of twisted metal loops and gears that will come apart if I manipulate them in just the correct sequence. A man in the same blue scrubs rushes by and hesitates upon seeing me squatting next to the door. I shoot him an innocent, coy smile and then proceed to fiddle with my gadget, running the warm metal between my fingers. Realizing he has more important things to do than question me, the man scurries on to his patients. Squeezing my eyes tighter than a vice, I strain to focus my attention on the doctor's voice inside Jaxson's room. Unfortunately, due to the chaos around me, I can only make out bits and pieces of his diagnosis.

"…in a coma…

…resting peacefully…"

Dad's voice isn't as soft-spoken as the doctor's, and I hear him blankly ask,

"When will he wake up?"

"…unknown…

…brain damage…

…only time will tell."

*Only **time** will tell? How ironic is that?*

11

*Me taking Jaxson through **time** is what put him in this predicament.*

The large wooden door swinging open causes an overwhelming aroma of Bleach and Iodine to sting the inside of my nostrils like a swarm of unwelcome wasps. Almost stumbling over me at the base of the wall outside the door, the doctor glances down at me and nods professionally and apologetically as he slowly pulls the door back toward the frame behind him as he exits. Raising his head and looking onward, he exhales and walks away rigidly down the hall. My eyes follow his pristine white tennis shoes as their methodical squeak grows too faint to hear. The muffled concerns exchanged between Mom and Dad behind the door beckon to me and draw my attention back into the sterile hospital room where Jaxson lies hooked up to wires and machines like one of my inventions. It takes every ounce of energy I contain to push myself to stand. My legs feel like rubber from the strenuous journey in time they have been through. They nearly give out as I turn to look through the window cut into the door of my little brother's hospital room. The weight of the situation punches me in the gut. This isn't a movie or hospital drama I'm watching on TV. This is my reality.

Shoving my gadget back into my pocket, I slowly push the door open and shuffle my aching feet into the room. I watch as Mom wipes her tear-stained cheeks and paints a fake smile on her drained, pale face as if she is a Kabuki. But she isn't a very good actress.

"The doctor said Jaxson is resting peacefully as his body is healing." Mom wraps her frigid fingers around my hand and attempts to sound optimistic. I don't have the energy to ask about the details right now, and I don't want to make Mom relay them to me. That might break her. I force a synthetic smile of my own.

"Visiting hours are over, and no one under the age of eighteen is supposed to be on this floor. The doctor also stated they are limiting guests to one at a time due to health restrictions. Honey, why don't you take Dameon home? I want to stay with Jaxson tonight. I don't want him to be alone if he wakes up."

*If he wakes up? Why didn't she say **when** he wakes up?*

"Please call me if there is any change. I will be back tomorrow." Softly kissing Mom on the forehead, Dad lovingly wraps her slumped shoulders with a white hospital blanket that was folded on the back of her chair.

"Try and get some rest." Dad barely utters the words to Mom before getting choked up. I painfully watch every muscle in Dad's jaw twinge and flex tight. He is obviously doing his best to be the strong husband and father we need him to be. Dad purses his lips together even tighter and totters out of the room with heavy shoulders.

"Goodnight," Mom whispers to me with tears pooling in her eyes.

My heart fills with pain, knowing that I can't stay here with Jaxson and Mom.

"Goodnight, Mom.

I love you." I add hesitantly.

I'm not one to openly tell Mom or anyone *I love you*, but I just feel it needs to be said tonight.

"Goodnight, Jaxson. Love you, buddy," I whisper as my cheeks burn. I swallow hard as I force my feet to walk briskly to catch up with Dad's worrying pace.

∞   ∞   ∞

Dad stares blankly at the barren road ahead of us. I watch as the two columns of light extend from our car into the darkness and blur together to make one orb, guiding glow. I suck in a big breath of Dad's artificial "new car" smell. I never understood why he always buys that same air freshener. He isn't fooling anyone into thinking this Honda, which is older than me, is in any way new. Up until Dad inherited Great Granddad's company, everything about Dad was just as artificial as the chemical scent wafting from the cardboard cutout dangling from the steering column. He always posed as having money and success. When, in actuality, he was just another drone in the hive. He wore the same fancy suit every day; its fading fabric was freshly pressed to cover our true mediocrity. His phony smile and satisfaction with life seemed just as synthetic.

The screaming silence inside the car is too much to handle, and I slowly reach up to turn the knob on the dash.

"Is it ok if I turn on the radio?" I search Dad's face for a reaction, unsure of how to make this car ride less miserable.

"You look exhausted. It's ok for you to go to sleep." Dad's reply is more like an excuse to continue the silence rather than concern for me and my exhaustion.

"I don't think I can sleep right now," I retort but decide against turning on the radio for his sake. Instead, I decide that I can use the hour-and-a-half car ride to perhaps get some information about Elementerprise from Dad.

"So, how is the new business going?" I ask, crossing my fingers hidden under the sides of my legs. I hope that Dad is willing to open up.

"Uh, it's good. It's already very successful and growing every day."

14

Another agonizing minute of silence ticks by despite me leaning in toward him, signaling I would love to hear more details.

"What is this new company? What will you be doing there?" I do my best to sound interested, not interrogative. However, Dad still seems hesitant to talk, and his gaze stays focused on the stretch of road ahead.

"Who knows, maybe one day I will want to follow in your footsteps and help out with the family business." I even throw in a proud smirk.

No father can resist their son wanting to be like them, right?

Dad's face whips toward me like I said a curse word or something.

Maybe that wasn't the right thing to say.

But then, as if for the very first time in my life, Dad truly looks at me, and I see a hint of a sparkle in his sapphire eyes as his shoulders relax a bit with his exhale.

"Well, I think Elementerprise is a company you would really enjoy. It is very progressive and ahead of our time."

You have no idea!

"All the advanced technology and ideas came from your Great Granddad's ingenious inventions.

You two are so much alike. You have a brilliant mind, just like his."

Wait, did Dad just compliment me?

Dad has never seemed to approve of me tinkering around with my gadgets and inventions.

"Really? You think so?"

"Absolutely! You will love all the things Granddad has invented that will change the world. The fiberoptic capabilities he came up with are incredible. He discovered how to harness energy from Earth's elements, which are found everywhere. There are enough elements to power the entire world a million times over."

A genuine smile spreads across my face as Dad describes Elementerprise. I love seeing the excitement in his eyes returning the more he speaks.

"Just a minuscule amount of the right elements could make our military the most powerful in the universe."

"Wait, are you saying your company makes bombs, weapons, and things that could destroy the planet?" The upward edges of my mouth instantly drop. I recall Great Granddad stating that nuclear bombs and great wars lead to the destruction of the Earth. Surely Great Granddad didn't create such weaponry.

Dad, reading my current disapproval, quickly changes the topic.

"It's not like that at all. Wow, I never knew you were such an Earth activist. We are currently working on many of his inventions which are going to help the world. For example, did

16

you know that he was the one who discovered using Cobalt for electric engines?

We are mass-producing these new Eco-engines that I hope will be used in cars all over the world. Can you imagine the positive impact on the Earth if everyone drives electric-powered cars instead of gas-powered cars? All our new advancements are leaving the other companies and countries begging for our secrets."

Dad is doing his best to make everything sound appealing to me. But thoughts of the great nuclear war Great Granddad told me about keep replaying in my head like a hard-to-watch war movie.

This is it. This is the reason the world gets destroyed, and Dad is now leading it.

How can I get Dad to force Elementerprise to not move forward with weapons of mass destruction? And not use all this advanced technology since it sounds like that is the reason all the wars start in the first place. Pretty much everything Dad is ecstatic and rambling on about is everything I need to stop. If only it were that simple. I need to devise a plan to shut down this advancement of technology and get all Great Granddad's invention ideas away from Dad and Elementerprise. Or is it too late? How many people have already seen the inventions? Dad stated they are already mass-producing many of his ideas.

"Have you heard of quantum computing? Dad's eyebrows jump near the top of his forehead like wiry springs. The excitement in his voice resembles Jaxson's when he is talking about his latest video games.

"Oh, ummm, quantum computing? Sure." Perhaps I should have been paying closer attention to what Dad had been rambling on about instead of getting lost in my thoughts about saving the world. He clearly senses my lack of concentration and interest in his rambling.

Dad's eyes shift from one side of the road to the other as if he is searching for his next words with great caution. The car fills with a palpable growing cloud of anxiety.

"What exactly happened down in the cellar with Jaxson? What caused that "explosion" you told the doctors about?"

And there it is. The question I had been dreading was just flung at me like a ninja star, and Dad expects me to play along like it is a friendly game. I contemplate jumping out of the swiftly moving car to avoid Dad's question. I feel Dad's gaze burn into the side of my face. His eyes don't waver.

If I don't answer, will he keep staring at me instead of the road?

My eyes try to keep up with the rushing haze of road whizzing by into the darkness outside my window, and I decide I better formulate an answer sooner rather than later if I want us both to survive.

"Uhhhh, that was it. There was a blast of light and then everything went dark. As soon as I found Jaxson's body, he wasn't breathing. He was just…"

My heart suddenly pounds more rapidly and pumps a burning acid of guilt and rage up to my flushing cheeks. My chin quivers uncontrollably, and I slam my eyelids closed before I will allow them to overflow in front of Dad. The exhales pulsing through my flaring nostrils rush with great haste, and it takes everything I have to keep from exploding. Out of instinct, my hand shoots up to push the little blue down arrow on the dashboard to turn down the temperature of the passenger side of the car, and I twist the knob to turn the AC fan to full blast. I inhale the sudden rush of cooler air, and I focus my thoughts on the hum of the engine. I strain to hear the gears shift from one to another and intermingle with the purr of the tires rotating steadily on the asphalt beneath us. Picturing the mechanics of the automobile methodically dancing together steadies my heartbeat.

After a painful bout of strangling silence from Dad, I let out a long, drawn-out yawn.

Glancing over at my exaggerated display of fatigue, Dad states,

"Why don't you close your eyes and get some rest? We can talk more about the company tomorrow. I can even show you some of the plans for the business if you're interested," Dad adds.

I can't even mutter a sound or nod my head in agreement as the gentle motion of the car is already rocking me to sleep, and I don't put up a fight.

Chapter 2

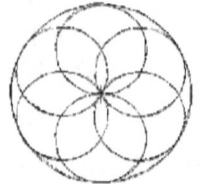

The Secret in the Closet

Falling through the air with my arms flailing aimlessly proves unsuccessful in slowing down the pull of gravity all around me. Slamming into the lava surface below me is inevitable. Neo, clinging to the cliff with one hand, tries desperately to grab hold of me with his other hand as I whiz past him just out of his reach. Bracing myself for a scorching impact, I squeeze my eyes tightly and fill my lungs with my last full breath.

The powerful hypnic jerk jolts my body awake and violently sends me crashing to the wooden floorboards below my bed with a thud.

Ouch!
Few, it was just another nightmare.
Although, it would be good to see Neo again.

Instant pain shooting down the right side of my body is a harsh awakening. Scanning the scene around me, I am reassured by the familiar view of my bedroom back at Great Granddad's estate – well, I guess it is our estate now.

I must have been super tired last night.
I don't even remember getting home and coming up to bed.

My snug pair of jeans make their presence known as they squeeze into my hips as I stand.

> *Obviously, I didn't take the time to change into my basketball shorts before crawling into bed.*

Glancing down at my gadget watch, the numbers 3:56 glow back at me.

> *Well, I can try to go back to sleep, or I can take this opportunity to do some investigating while Dad is still sleeping.*

Dad always gets up around 6:00 a.m., so I don't have a lot of time. The choices of where to search for information flood my thoughts.

> *Should I look around in Great Granddad's study first or in Dad's office to look over Elementerprise's plans?*

Realizing that I will most likely have other opportunities to search Great Granddad's study, I opt for Dad's office since he will most likely spend the majority of his time in there once he wakes up.

Glancing down at the nightstand next to my bed, the wristband I found down in the cellar gleams up at me, beckoning me to put it back on. It is the same wristband that cradles many secrets and recently aided me through battles and adventures you only read about in books. Lifting my watchless, empty arm, the weightlessness doesn't feel right. I yearn for the heavy, comforting pull of the wristband that somehow makes me feel invincible.

> *I guess it would be nice to have an extra light on hand while investigating.*
> *Having an attached laser is comforting, too.*

Reaching down, I affectionately run my fingers over each leather and metal detail on the wristband. Feeling the tiny metal bumps and grooves of the music box drum, the plinking melody chimes in my mind. Memories of Great Granddad's funeral dance through my thoughts and fuel my emotions. I do my best to suppress the aching in my heart for Great Granddad, Lan, and Jaxson. However, it is like trying to stop a powerful geyser with a small cork. The flow of water is too powerful as pent-up tears force their way down my cheeks. One can only be strong for so long.

A groan from a floorboard in the closet of my room reverberates off every nerve in my body, causing me to freeze suddenly mid-sniffle.

> *What was that?*
> *Is someone there?*
> *I know this house makes strange noises in the night, but that was the sound when someone, or something much larger than a mouse, moves off one of the floorboards. And it most definitely came from inside my closet.*

Holding my breath, I concentrate on every sound around me as I quietly grasp the wristband and buckle it around my wrist. Clicking on its light, I shine the beam toward the closed closet door. The stream of light magnifies every crack and timeworn imperfection. Each cog clicking from the downstairs grandfather clock ticks nervously in my ears like the countdown of a bomb.

"Hello?" My whispering voice cracks as I slide my socks across the wooden floor and carefully shift my weight from my left foot onto my right.

> *I'm sure it was all just my imagination.*
> *This house always gets the best of me.*
> *It was probably just the wind.*

Turning my head to glance out the window, the statuesque trees laugh and mock me motionlessly. There isn't even a hint of a breeze.

Okay, maybe it wasn't the wind.
But then what was it?
Perhaps an animal got into the house.

My heartbeat surpasses the ticking clock and doubles as I near the closet door.

Curling my sweating fingers around the intricate closet knob, I slowly twist and pull ever so gently. Screeching out into the silence, the door doesn't open without making its presence known. Freezing and holding my breath as if to put the closet door out of its misery, I tilt my wristband light toward the small open crack in the door. Shifting my weight in silence, I peek in to see a slight movement in the huddled mass on the floor of my closet.

Either my dirty laundry is alive, or there is definitely
something under there.

Squatting down like a secret agent, I aim my wristband laser at the mass, preparing myself to pull the dirty shirt off the clothes pile and reveal whatever creature lies beneath.

Ok, Eon, you can do this.
It's probably just a raccoon or something.
One…
Two…
Three.

Simultaneously swinging the boisterous closet door fully open and pulling up the soiled clothing, the lump springs to life with a blood-curdling *SCREAM*.

Before I can comprehend what or who it is, it springs up like a jack-in-the-box at a horror house and wraps its arms around me. Instinctively pushing the stranger away, I stop mid-shove when the glow of Lan's face flashes in the light of my wristband.

"Lan? What are you doing here? How did you…"

"Dameon, is everything okay up there? I heard a scream." Dad's trailing voice interrupts my thoughts, and my reunion with Lan, as he clumsily pounds his big feet up the creaky staircase.

Oh no, Dad is coming!

"Hurry, get back down and cover up. Don't make a sound."

Forcing Lan back down to the floor of my closet, I throw some dirty clothes back over her and slam the closet door closed. Sliding across the floorboards on my belly toward my bed, I concurrently snap off my wristband light. Dad bursts through my bedroom door to see me sprawled out on my floor, flopping around like a fish out of water.

"Are you okay? I heard a scream!" Dad huffs breathlessly, searching my room with his eyes darting from one side of my room to the other with concern.

"Yah, sorry. I just had a bad dream and fell out of bed." I only partially lie nervously through a grimace since I had honestly woken up on the floor from a nightmare earlier.

"You are sure you're alright? You were screaming like a girl." Dad jokes through a lion-like yawn.

"Yep, all good. Sorry for waking you." I flash my dad an all-clear thumbs-up and an embarrassed sideways grin.

"Okay, I'm going back to bed to try and get at least another hour of sleep before my alarm goes off. Goodnight, or morning, or whatever time it is…" Dad's mumbles waft behind him incoherently as he shuffles his way back down the old stairs.

Impatiently waiting a few minutes, I hold my awkward position on the floor and listen intently to ensure Dad is back in bed before daring to move. Once I feel satisfied with the situation below, I tiptoe over to the closet and open the door as slowly as possible. I am not sure if one quick squeak would have been less painful than the drawn-out *SCREECH* the door creates as I attempt to open it carefully. The moonlight illuminates Lan's perfect face, peering up at me. Her golden eyes glow like familiar embers.

"So, that was your dad?" Lan questions as if everything is normal. Like she didn't follow me here from the future and sits hiding in my bedroom closet under my dirty clothes.

Stepping toward her, I pinch myself to make sure I'm not still dreaming. Afraid to take my eyes away from the mirage of Lan's face, I slowly slump to sit next to her on the floor of my closet. However, a crinkled stash of wrappers noisily crinkles underneath me. Reaching my hand to remove the pile of questionable trash, a smile spreads across Lan's food-smudged lips, forming a small dimple on one side of her cheek.

"I take it you found the food?" I can't help but smile and stifle a small laugh as I stare at the adorable, guilty face reflecting back at me.

"You have an entire room full of the most delicious treasures!" Lan boisterously explodes, rescuing an empty fruit snack wrapper clinging to my pants.

"Shhhhh," I lean toward Lan and signal for her to remember to whisper.

"You can have whatever food you want, but first, you must tell me how you got here."

"Well, I couldn't let you leave me without hugging you and saying goodbye. So, I ran to you and tried to grab hold of you before you could go, but all I could grasp was the back of your shirt. The next thing I knew, I was blinded by an unimaginably bright light, and I woke up alone on the ground of the cellar. I kept calling out for Einstein, Erb, Neo, or you, but no one answered. I followed the underground tunnels and climbed up through an old mineshaft, that I know doesn't exist in my time. I knew I had come back in time as soon as I smelled the bizarre scent of wet wood. I have only ever smelled that scent when the guys and I found our underground well, except this smell

25

was above ground. The smell got stronger and stronger the closer I got to the opening of the mine. I checked my oxygen gauge, and it was green. I could see a bright light pouring in from outside the mine, and I didn't need an oxygen tank to breathe, which was good because I obviously didn't have one with me when we were down in the cellar. I couldn't help myself, and I ran toward the light and the fresh mossy smell."

Tears of pure elation begin to sparkle in Lan's stunning eyes as she pauses speechlessly. I breathe in Lan's joy and feel I could listen to her tell her story for the rest of my life, as if she is the oxygen that I need to survive.

"Once outside the mineshaft, there were towering columns of green as far as I could see. And above them was a sky so blue I thought it was fabric. It was the most beautiful thing I have ever seen. Well, second to the sparkling mass of water I witnessed down at the bottom of the mountain once I made it to the top."

"That is the ocean," I relay with excitement, living vicariously through Lan's recount. I try to imagine seeing all these miraculous things for the first time.

"I almost ran all the way back down the mountainside to the… *ocean*, but then I saw this amazing dwelling and knew instantly that it was Dr. Awkward's, and that I had made it back here to the past, and hopefully to you. I had to know if you were here. Much to my surprise, the door was unlocked and unguarded, so I came inside to search for you, but you weren't here. After discovering much of the delicious food in that glorious food room,"

"The kitchen."

"The kitchen. I came upstairs to look for you, and I instantly knew this was your room. It smells like you, and I found your wristband on that little table. So, I decided to wait here for you and hoped that you would return. I must have fallen asleep in here while I was hiding and waiting. And well, you know the

26

rest of the story." Lan's babbling slows and halts as she stares deeply into my eyes, waiting for a response.

"I'm so glad you're here." I sputter as I throw my arms around her into an explosion of an embrace. I never want to let her go again.

"Where is Jaxson? Did he make it back?" Lan whispers.
The hug halts suddenly, like a car slamming on its brakes.

"He's at the hospital. He wasn't breathing when we returned from your time. He's in a coma, and we don't know if he is going to wake up." I whisper back regretfully.

Saying it out loud is as painful as it crosses my lips as if I were spitting shards of glass.

Lan's eyebrows scrunch together. She is struggling to digest the rotten information I just fed her.

"Then what are we doing sitting here on the floor? We need to go and help him!" Lan spouts as she stands, yanks me to my feet, and begins dragging me toward my bedroom door.

"Hold on," I stop her and turn her around to face me.

"He is already at one of the best pediatric medical facilities in the country. There isn't much else we can do but let the doctors do their job. Not to mention, he's an hour and a half drive from here, and I don't even know how to drive yet. Dad promised me he would teach me this summer. He would be furious if I took his car." The thought of getting caught stealing Dad's car and driving, or probably crashing, it down the steep winding mountainside makes me shutter.

"So, what? We just stay here and wait?" Lan's words fling back at me like daggers.

"You know Dr. Awkward wouldn't sit around and wait for someone else to cure Jaxson.

He would go to him and give him one of his special life elixirs and save him."

"You're absolutely right. The last time Jaxson was sick, I was able to get the medicine that helped him get stronger. We need that medicine. What was it called?"

27

Scurrying over to where my satchel lies heaped on the floor, I snatch out both Great Granddad's journals and jump onto my bed to search them. Lan plops onto the bed next to me like an excited puppy.

"Ok, what are we looking for?" She asks, grabbing one of the journals and flipping it open to scour the pages.

"The name of the medication Erb sent us to get from Elementerprise. Erb wrote the name of it in the back of this journal." I eagerly flip to the back of the journal and look at my *To-Do List*. Amongst the list, I see the name of the medication:

Epilanthdopram Injection.

"I don't even know if this medication exists today," I say to Lan questionably.

"Wasn't there a recipe for his *Life Elixir* in here?" Lan's left eyebrow skitters upward.

I flip through the pages of Great Granddad's journal, searching for the recipe for the special Elixir. Lan sits impatiently at my side, her typewriter eyes moving back and forth, trying to take in all the remarkable information in this precious book of knowledge.

"Wow, Dr. Awkward really did know everything. He was a genius!"

"Here it is!" I shout more loudly than I should have, placing my finger on the title of the page, revealing the extraordinary recipe.

The Elixir of Life

Treats ailments such as leaky gut, organ failure, and hypoxia.
Crush and combine the following ingredients into the sieve strainer:
tea leaves (green or black),

eucalyptus

garlic cloves

juniper berry

reishi mushrooms

rosehips

ginger root

echinacea

lanthanum

Allow ingredients to seep in hot water until it becomes dark in color.
Remove the sieve. Add a generous amount of honey and serve warm.
Make the patient drink as much as possible.

In an EMERGENCY situation, combine the above ingredients with .3 ml
(for an adult or person that weighs at least 66 pounds) of
EPINEPHRINE. Place into injector pen or syringe and inject directly
into the patient.

*I created a supply of EPILANTHDOPRAM INJECTIONS for
convenient medical use.

"Well, I think the only two ingredients we might have access to are garlic and ginger." I finally spout in a defeated manner after reading the recipe.

"It uses lanthanum?" Lan straightens her back with pride.

"Yes, and luckily, I do know how to get more of all the elements, thanks to Great Granddad's brilliance. His journals taught me how to separate the elements with one of his inventions in the pumphouse."

The hours tick by like seconds with Lan sitting by my side.

The sound of thumping pipes and a whirring flow of water rushing through the wall behind us forces Lan to startle and stare at me for an explanation.

"Sounds like Dad is up and getting into the shower. We are going to need to keep you hidden. But where to hide you? I could sneak you up to the observatory or down to the cellar. But I'm not sure Dad will stay away from those places for long. I already saw him looking over the blueprints of the estate he found in Great Grandad's study, and they include every room and passageway. I know because I have studied them meticulously. Which reminds me, I still need to explore the unlabeled hidden space connected to Great Granddad's study."

"I will just hide in here." Lan glides back toward my bedroom closet.

"Are you sure? Hopefully, it will just be for a little while. I know Dad is planning on going back to the hospital at some point today, and then we can start looking for these ingredients. That is, if I can convince Dad that I need to stay home."

"Wait, is he going to see Jaxson? Can we go with him?"

"How am I supposed to explain you? I don't even have friends at our other home, let alone a girl… that is a friend. Besides, where would I have met you in this measly town?"

Lan's eyes look down to the floor as her shoulders slump with the realization that she is from a completely different time, and she doesn't belong here.

"What are we going to do? Will I have to stay hidden here forever? Will I ever see Einstein, Erb, or Neo again?" Lan's chest begins to rise and fall more quickly with panic.

"Don't worry, we will figure all that out together." My gaze at Lan intensifies.

"I promise." I hold both of Lan's hands in mine and squeeze them with reassurance.

The rattling pipes stop with a thud, causing us to jump with alarm.

Steadying the sudden race of my heart, I assure her.

"It's ok, but Dad is done in the shower. You wait up here, and I am going to go down and talk with him to see what his plans are for the day."

Lan nods with understanding and makes herself comfortable on the floor of my closet.

"I will try to hurry back up here." I beam and carefully close my closet door. Pausing for a moment, I think about the mind-boggling event that is occurring.

I, Dameon Gardener, Geeky Gadget Boy, have a gorgeous girl from the future hiding in my bedroom closet!
No one will ever believe this!

Chapter 3

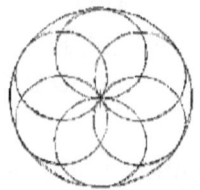

A Gourmet Breakfast for Two

Skipping two stairs at a time, I bounce down the glorious staircase. It is hard to believe that this extravagant piece of architecture belongs to my ordinary family. I ping off the railing like a pinball. I pause on the bottom step to gain my composure and clear my throat. I don't want Dad to see me smiling this early in the morning, or he will definitely know I am up to something. Listening to him getting ready in his bedroom, I quickly decide to plop myself on the couch in the living room and pull a blanket over the top of me. I lay my head back and pretend to be asleep as Dad walks into the room. Acting as though his presence has woken me up, I pick up my head with false grogginess.

"Oh, hey, Dad," I mumble through a forced, fabricated yawn.

Clearly, my dad had not seen me lying on the couch and is thrown off-step. He catches his balance by placing his hand on the eloquently papered wall.

"Dameon. What are you doing down here this early? You about gave me a heart attack."

"Sorry. I couldn't go back to sleep." At least I wasn't lying to him. There was no way I would have been able to go back to sleep with Lan hiding in my closet.

"You have a lot on your mind, don't you?" Dad notices as he ruffles my already messy head of hair.

You have no idea!

32

I nod pathetically instead of giving a verbal response.

"Do you want me to make you some eggs or anything?" Dad asks, as if that will solve all our problems. My shocked, tell-all face reacts to Dad's offer before I can even think. I have never seen Dad cook, other than when Mom makes him grill for us on holidays. Not to mention, Dad usually grabs his mug of black coffee and heads to his office to work in the mornings without any breakfast at all. It also seems way too early to even be thinking about breakfast.

"What? Don't look so shocked. Yes, I know how to cook eggs. Just because I usually don't, doesn't mean I can't."

Closing my gaping jaw, I respond with, "Sure, I guess eggs sound good."

"How do you like your eggs? Fried, scrambled...?"

Still surprised that he knows how to make different kinds of eggs, I respond hesitantly.

"Scrambled?"

"How many do you want? One, two?"

Thinking of my stowaway upstairs, I blurt out,

"At least a couple. Do we have orange juice, ohhh, and toast?"

Dad gawks at me like I am a ravaged beast.

"Sorry, I'm starving," I utter.

Dad just shakes his head at me and states,

"Wow, no wonder Mom asks me to stop by the store all the time on my way home from work. You must be going through another growth spurt."

"I'll help," I add, letting all my teeth show like in a toothpaste commercial.

I search the entire kitchen, looking for the pitcher so I can make some orange juice. We only have the frozen concentrated kind, where I mix it with water, but I'm sure Lan isn't going to know the difference between that and freshly squeezed. I humor Dad and act astonished as he explains every step of scrambling the eggs like he is the master chef with his own cooking show. With a pathetic French accent, he expresses,

"First, zu svirl ze eggs in ze pan, like zis.
Next, zu add a dash or two of ze salt seazoning.
Last, zu sprinkle in ze finest of cheeses,
ze stinkier - ze bet-tair."

An uncontrolled chuckle rolls off my lips as I shake my head in disbelief. But despite my embarrassed disapproval, he continues his ridiculous charade. I act like I want him to stop, but I don't. Cooking with Dad in the kitchen is amazing. We rarely do anything together. This is a really nice change.

Then, I hear the vibrating buzz of his cell phone. It is like a familiar stab to my heart that has grown numb to this all too familiar interruption. His silly antics stop immediately as he pulls his phone out of his pocket.

"Good morning, Mr. Fieldman."

And.... Dad is back to himself again. I knew this moment was too surreal. All I can think about is how much Jaxson would have been rolling with laughter at Dad's previous comedy act.

Dad motions for me to keep scrambling the eggs and finish up on my own. He quickly grabs the coffee pot and pours himself a tall, travel-size mug of black coffee. Then, he rushes off to his makeshift office down the hall as if all this was just a silly make-believe hallucination that played out in my mind.

Turning off the stove, I whirl around to grab two plates and cups out of the cupboard.

At least I can still share this breakfast with Lan.

I carefully scoop a cheesy glop of eggs onto each plate. I butter the toasted bread, spread a thick layer of raspberry jam, and place the toast on the plates next to the eggs. To be extra fancy, I even find a few sprigs of parsley in the fridge to garnish the eggs. I guess watching a few cooking shows with Mom has come in handy after all. Although, I definitely prefer Dad's "show" to any of the ones on TV.

While pouring the orange juice into two glasses, I am forced to stop suddenly as Dad rushes back into the kitchen. A splash of juice sloshes onto the white and grey swirled marble countertop.

"Hey, kiddo, that looks perfect. But I'm afraid I can't stay to eat with you. I just told my new team that I would meet them at the office building in the city."

I just stand motionless, watching as the orange juice puddles into a stream at the rim of the counter and drips off the edge like suicidal lemmings.

"Do you want to come with me? We could both take a tour since it will be my first time in that building, too.

It is only about thirty minutes from the hospital, so I am going to swing by there after my meetings and tour to check on Mom and Jaxson. What do you say? Do you want to spend the day with your old man?"

Wait, Dad wants me to come to work with him? This is definitely a first. Dad didn't even let me go with him to his old job when it was bring your child to work day. Who is this guy, and what did he do with my dad?

Under normal circumstances, I probably would have jumped at the chance to spend the day with Dad. But, scanning the two delicately decorated plates of breakfast, all I can think about is sharing this masterpiece with Lan.

"I haven't even showered yet, Dad. You would be embarrassed to meet your new team with your smelly teenager tagging along."

I grab a paper towel and mop up the spilled orange juice on both the floor and the countertop.

"If it's okay with you, I am looking forward to eating these eggs, showering, and catching up on some much-needed sleep."

"Are you sure you just want to hang out here all by yourself today?"

"Yes!"

Oops, I think I responded a little too quickly.

"I mean, you know I haven't had any time to myself to make any new gadgets lately. And I was kind of looking forward to a lazy day. I know Mom said that only one person can be with Jaxson at the hospital at a time anyway, and I am not even supposed to be in his room as a minor, so I will just be waiting in the waiting area or the car. That will be total torture. At least if I'm here, I can keep my mind busy with my gadgets."

"Okay, if you are sure that you would rather stay here. But eat that plate of eggs for me. It looks and smells delicious."

Releasing a silent sigh of relief, I realize that now Lan and I can freely search for the ingredients we need for the elixir without having to sneak around Dad.

"Oh, and don't mess with any of these appliances. I don't want Mom coming home to the toaster taken apart again. Make sure your cell phone is charged and connected to the mobile hotspot. The password is $Money$. I will call you in a while after I talk with Mom, and we make a plan for tonight.

And no blowing anything up." Dad spouts off his list of rules for me to stay home alone and adds a wink to the last stipulation.

"I promise, Dad," I cross my heart with my fingers.

"Besides, I haven't blown anything up in years."

"Not funny, Dameon. Call me if you need anything."

"If I don't answer when you call, I'm probably sleeping. Just leave a message, and I will call you back.

And let me know if there are any changes with Jaxson." I add as he walks out of the kitchen.

"I promise." He states while turning around to look at me as he crosses his heart.

"Take it easy, sport."

After pausing for a moment to give Dad time to get in his car, I dart to the window in the entryway to watch him drive across the overgrown stone roundabout and out of the front rickety, iron gates. Before the dust cloud from his car completely disappears, I am already sprinting back to the kitchen.

Little did Dad know, these two plates of food weren't for *us*; they are for me and Lan. I was planning on taking them up to my room, but since Dad is gone, I might as well set them at the table in the formal dining room. I haven't eaten in there yet. I gingerly place the plates of eggs, the glasses of juice, and silverware on the shiny, dark wood dining room table.

Somehow, the breakfast of scrambled eggs, toast, and juice looks so much more elegant in such an impressive dining room. The elaborate silver candlesticks inside the rich wood and glass of the China hutch situated along the wall catch my eye.

> *What am I thinking? That would be too much. This isn't a date, and Lan would probably think it is weird using candles for light when we have electricity.*

As if struck by lightning, a thought pops into my head. I run into the kitchen, grab the porcelain fruit bowl off the counter, and dash back into the dining room. Placing the glorious bowl of fruit in the center of the table, a smile brought on by brilliance sweeps across my face.

> *Perfect.*
> *She is going to love this so much more than drippy candles. Besides, Dad would kill me if I burned down the estate.*

Dashing toward the stairs, I am unable to contain the permanent grin staining my giddy face. The sock partly dangling from my toes causes my foot to slip on the first wooden stair tread, sending my arms squirming about like an octopus. Half-crawling, half-sprinting, I conquer the massive mountain of steps as I begin calling for Lan.

"Lan! Lan! You can come out!" I pant excitedly as if playing a wild game of hide and seek.

The propulsion of my run toward my bedroom is turned into a powerful *SPLAT* into Lan's approaching body. Our ungraceful collision in my bedroom doorway is beyond embarrassing.

"Sorry, are you okay?" Politely taking a step back, I try to sound genuinely concerned. However, the situation is quite comical, and we both share a mortified titter while rubbing our matching, pounding foreheads.

"Come on, I have something for you." Taking her by the hand, I quickly, but much more cautiously, guide her down the grand staircase. Lan's eyes double as she gasps at the grandeur of the house.

"This place is huge. I can't believe only one person lived in something like this."

Leading her into the dining room she lets go of my hand to gawk more closely at an impressive painting of an awe-inspiring, colorful fall setting.

"I thought trees were green?"

"The leaves change colors when the weather starts getting cooler. Then they fall off the trees."

"And then they grow back green?"

I nod and watch her astonished face try to make sense of the seasonal phenomenon.

"Here, take a seat. Our breakfast is getting cold." I attempt to bring her attention back to the perfectly set table as I pull out her chair for her.

Lan wanders over and plops onto the silk-cushioned armchair, screeching it forward across the tile right out of my hands.

Ok, so much for trying to be a gentleman.

"This smells amazing!" Lan inhales animalistically as she begins devouring the eggs before I even have a chance to sit.

"Do you like the eggs?" I question, enjoying watching her eat them more than I will ever enjoy eating them myself.

"Eggs are so good!" She spouts as she bites into the toast and jam.

"Ohhhh, this is even better!" Her eyes roll back in her head as if she is in heaven.

The food around her vanishes like magic, and I am too dumbfounded to even twitch. Noticing her staring at the bowl of fruit, I pluck a few grapes off a vine from inside the bowl and hand them to her. I watch her toss one into her mouth jovially. A chorus of *mmmmmms* and *ahhhhhs* proceed with every chew.

Finally, I attempt to eat a bit of egg; however, they instantly spit their way back out of my mouth as I involuntarily try to shout the word, "wait", and reach to snatch the unpeeled banana Lan grabs from the bowl and savagely bites into.

Scrunching her nose at the initial tough skin and bitterness of the peeling, she eventually gets to the sweet, soft center.

"A bit hard to chew, but still good." She beams with banana goo lingering in her otherwise perfect teeth. She then proceeds to take a sip of her orange juice, grimaces like the Cheshire Cat, and chugs the remainder of the glass's contents.

"Wow, do you always eat like this?" She asks, stretching against the back of her chair to help the mad dash of food make its way down to settle in her stomach.

"Well, not quite like *this* all the time." I stutter, trying not to let her know that her previous display was reminiscent of the dinner scene from Beauty and the Beast. And, although she resembles Beauty, her ravage eating was much more Beast-like.

"So, what do we need to do first to make that elixir for Jaxson?" Lan questions through a loud, rumbling belch, as she brushes an army of crumbs off her lap onto the floor.

This girl is great!

Rising to stack the dishes and clean off the table, I express,

"Let's start with researching that medicine first. I don't want to waste our time if it is something the doctors have already given to Jaxson."

"Great idea," Lan utters, stuffing the pockets of her filthy jumpsuit with an apple and an orange from the fruit bowl.

As soon as she eyes me snickering at her, she immediately ceases her fruit heist and flashes a self-conscious smile.

"Just in case I get hungry later."

Honestly, could she be any more adorable?

"Come on, I'll clean this up and see if I can find you some of my mom's clean clothes. Then, we can start researching the medication."

Chapter 4

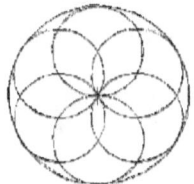

The Investigation Begins

Rolling on the wheels of the large leather computer chair from where Jaxson once sat playing a retro computer game, I glide closer to Lan, seated in the plush office chair directly in front of Dad's laptop computer. She almost doesn't look like Lan with her freshly washed, auburn hair swirled into damp tendrils, draping down one of Mom's plain, violet t-shirts. And Lan in jeans, especially faded Mom jeans, just doesn't quite seem right. However, the bulging, fruit-filled pockets are a dead giveaway that it is still most definitely Lan.

"Of course, Dad put a password protection code on his computer," I complain, rubbing my chin in deep contemplation. Millions of password possibilities churn through my thoughts like debris in the winds of a murky tornado.

> *Maybe Mom's name and or birthdate? Nope.*
> *Perhaps, Dad's name and or birthdate? Hmmm*
> *My full name? Jaxson's full name?*
> *I know, I'll try all our names put together. No.*
> *What about Dad's password for the hotspot?*

I pound out the keys *$Money$* and bite my lip as I nervously click enter. The black password screen flashes to an artsy array of colors, including various icon symbols.

"Yes, we're in!" I shout, nearly jumping out of my seat.

A clueless Lan anxiously picks at her freshly cleaned fingernails as her left leg bobs up and down uncontrollably. The constant leather scrunching sound from the bouncing chair pulses at my side.

Refocusing my thoughts, I click on the search engine and type in *Epilanthdopram*.

Your search: Epilanthdopram does not have any matching results.
Are you looking for Epinephrine?

"NO, I'm not looking for Epinephrine!" I bark at the laptop screen, banging my fists on the solid cherry wood office desk. I try to swallow in my bellow, but I'm too late as I watch Lan's worried face search mine for an explanation for my outburst. She slowly shifts to the side of her chair, inching away from me.

"Sorry, let me try a few more searches, but it doesn't look like that is a medication that is used today." My lips utter the apology as my fingers keep desperately trying to find a similar matching keyword.

As my failing search attempts continue, Lan stretches to her feet and wanders around the office curiously, observing all its bizarre contents. Glancing over at Lan, I watch her lean against the ornately carved window casing as she disappears into wonderment.

"Something out there just moved!" Her body stiffens up straight.

Jumping out of my chair I leap to her side to survey the intruder and gaze toward the movement to which her finger is pointing.

"That's just a squirrel," I chuckle, allowing my tense body to ease.

Her eyes follow a small robin gliding across the sky; then a bumblebee buzzes back in the opposite direction. Like pinballs, her small pupils zig and zag inquisitively from creature to creature.

"Your time is so full of life. And the creatures are so cute and small. I could fit them into my pockets." She manages to mumble through her intense gawking.

Perhaps if they weren't full of food.

"Erb and Einstein would love it here." The edges of her mouth droop. She turns slowly away from the window and heads back to the large computer desk. She collapses into the chair as her shoulders slump.

Quickly changing the subject and sudden somber tone, Lan comments on the document lying open closest to her hand.

"Is this the map of this house?" She asks, leaning down to study the large, yellowing parchment more closely.

"Yes, these are the original blueprints," I respond, briskly shooting to her side.

Pointing my spindly finger at an unexplainable opening behind Great Granddad's study, I add,

"This is the only place I haven't figured out how to get to yet. It is much too large of a space to just be a closet or opening for ductwork. The way this wall isn't even with the hallway makes the space back here quite a large room, but it isn't labeled. There must be a hidden door in Great Granddad's study, but I haven't been able to find it yet."

Lan, turning into the Grinch, conjures a sinister sneer.

"You haven't found it... yet."

"Do you want to help me look for it then? We might find other useful things to help Jaxson in Great Granddad's study during our search."

"Absolutely!" Lan spouts, her cheeks rising.

"There has to be a door or passageway somewhere along this wall behind his desk."

I relay, tracing the ebony line separating Great Granddad's study and the void on the blueprints.

"What are we waiting for? Let's go." Lan blurts as her feet spring off the worn floorboards.

"Hold on," I suggest, holding up my pointer finger and bounding over to Dad's laptop.

"I need to hide my search history and log off. I don't want Dad getting suspicious." I explain as I make the few necessary clicks of the mouse.

Then, grabbing Lan's calloused hand, I fling her through the mouth of Dad's office toward the magnificent staircase.

As if tickling the banister for the duration of our climb, Lan delicately runs her fingers over the finely carved woodwork. Dragging Lan through the long, upstairs hallway is like pulling an art enthusiast through a museum. She wants to stop and gaze at each sophisticated detail and touch every sparkling, carved glass doorknob.

My antsy feet hesitate in front of the heavy beacon door of the study at the end of the hall. Slowly, with guarded breath, I open the large wooden door to reveal Great Granddad's menagerie of intrigue. We saunter in respectfully as if entering the deepest thoughts and secrets of the mind of a true genius. A swirl of dust hurricanes around us as we enter. Clearly, Mom and her cleaning supplies have not made it up here yet.

Surveying the number of footprints pressed in the floor dust, it is evident that only Dad and I have been through here with little rummaging, but it's hard to tell without the lights.

Those are just summer storm cloud shadows scurrying across the floor and not something living, right?

Flipping on the light switch quickly, the two sconce lights on both sides of the oversized portrait of Great Granddad flicker him to life.

"That's Dr. Awkward, isn't it?" Lan gapes in awe. It is difficult not to get drawn into his striking, blue stare.

"Yep, and the secret door must be somewhere on that picture wall. Since the room we are looking for is on the other side of it." I inform her, karate chopping the cobwebs draping ahead of me.

Realizing I probably look like I'm combating air with a wimpy dance, I stand up a bit taller to square my shoulders in a more macho demeanor and proceed to walk through them like they don't bother me, even though they give me the heebie-jeebies.

"Let's check to see if there is an opening,
 a seam,
 a keyhole...
 anything."

Making my way around Great Granddad's massive mahogany island in the form of a desk, I run my eager fingers over the impressive, rich wood, judge-paneled walls.

Ok, where would I hide a keyhole or trigger for a secret passage?

Eyeing the oversized brick fireplace directly under the portrait of Great Granddad, I guess this would be the most obvious place for a secret door or passageway. Squatting down like a chimpanzee, I spread my scrawny arms forward to push every brick inside the fireplace like playing an oversized push-button game at an arcade. Disappointment troubles my nerves. None of the bricks I push on so much as wiggle. I save my nose from a tickling cobweb as Lan stifles a laughing snort.

"What's so funny?" I ask.

Looking down at my soot-stained hands, I realize I must have just given myself a dog-like black nose. Hunching over, I use the bottom of my clean t-shirt to wipe the gook off my nostrils, make myself appear human again, and proceed to wipe my ebony hands on my jeans. As my face parallels the floor, I notice the outline crack on one floorboard is wider than the others. Dropping to my hands and

45

knees, I urgently use my nonexistent fingernails in an attempt to pry up the seemingly out-of-line board.

> *Ah man, why did I just clip my fingernails? I guess I did have some extra time to kill while I waited for Lan to get showered and cleaned up, but they would come in handy right now with this stubborn board.*

Skimming the room for anything that can double as a pry bar, I blurt to Lan,

"Quick, hand me that fire poker," I direct, pointing to the long black iron stick ornamented with gold scrollwork hanging with the other fancy-looking fireplace tools.

Using my fisted knuckles to knock on the surrounding floorboards, my suspicion is solidified as the hollow thump of the askew floorboard triggers my heart to beat faster.

Snatching the fire poker from Lan, I hastily prod the tip into the widened crack and force the shaft downward. The loosened floorboard jumps up as if finally freed from its unwanted confinement. A camouflaged piece of parchment, thinly raised higher than the subfloor in the opening, beckons to be rescued. I free it from its dusty grave. The antique parchment crackles like a dried leaf as I unfold each tri-folded flap gingerly. Lan drops to peek over my shoulder to see the message of the hidden document.

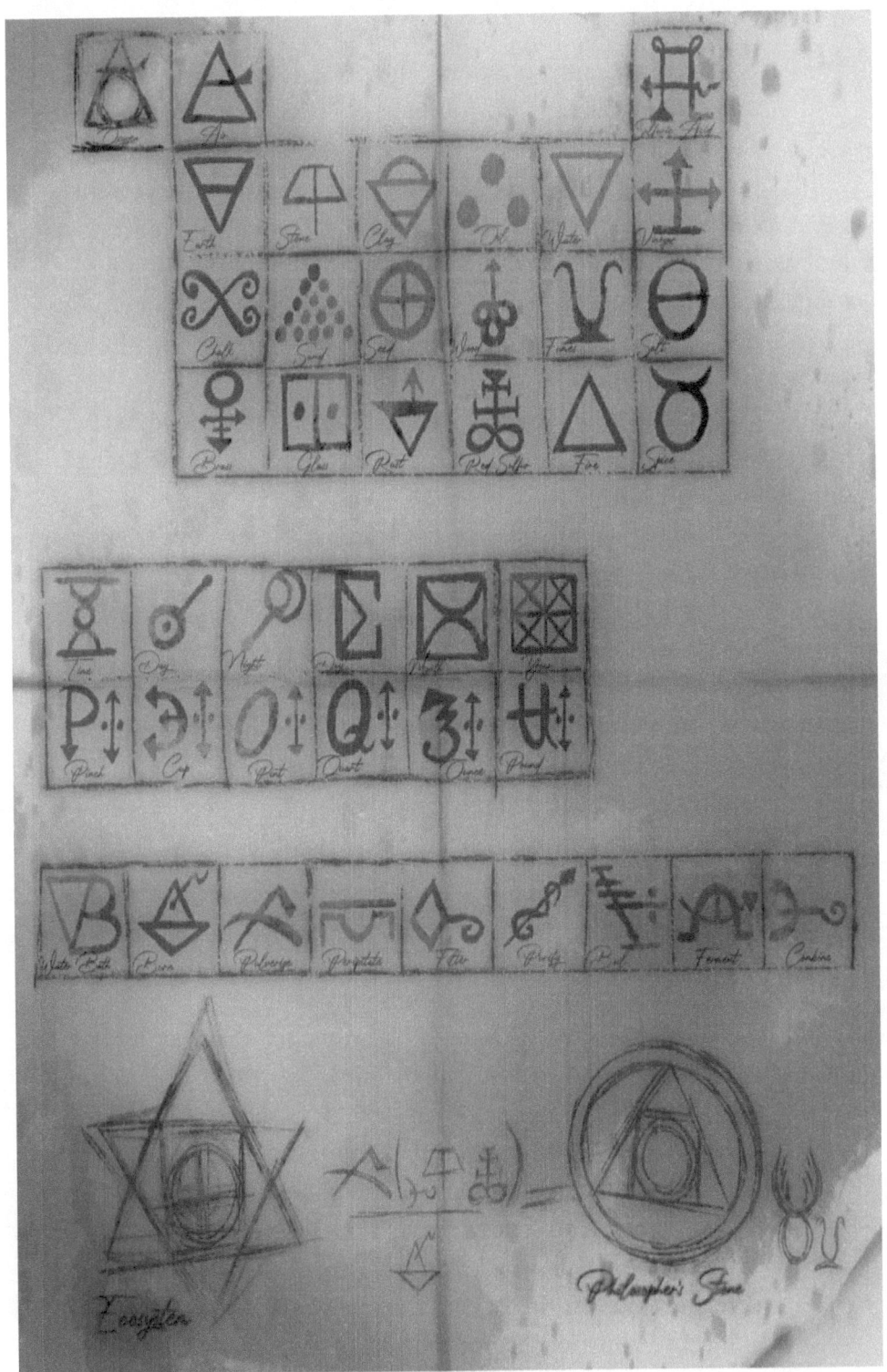

"They're alchemy symbols. The same ones Great Granddad drew many times in his journals. So why hide them under the floor? They really aren't much of a secret. I've seen them plenty of times before."

With great confusion ailing my brain, I stand and place the alchemy parchment onto the desk amongst the mountain of other unidentified documents.

"Let's keep looking for a way into that secret room," I breathe out heavily.

Lan continues to search the adjoining wall for a door as her eyes pause on the map in the detailed frame hanging beside Great Granddad's portrait.

"What is this a map of? Is it important?" Lan's eyebrows raise in question.

Studying the map, I reply, "it looks like it is a map of the world, but what happened to it?"

I observe that all the continents are mere islands where the oceans have grown to devour all the coastal cities like a swollen blob. Noticing the date toward the bottom of the map where Antarctica used to be, the number 2079 shocks my brain.

"Wow, I guess global warming is inevitable. In about fifty years all the world's ice will be melted, and the oceans will invade the lands like in a Sci-Fi flick.

Do you know how to swim?" I joke with Lan, attempting to lighten the despairing thoughts poisoning my mind.

"Wait, all this area is water?" Lan runs her shaking finger over most of the map.

"But in my time, there isn't any water. None of this makes sense." Lan shakes her head in disbelief.

"In Great Grandad's journal that he gave to me, some of his entries describe how after numerous nuclear wars, radiation, and rampant fires spread over the world, excess smoke and gasses get trapped in the atmosphere. This causes angry skies and terrible hurricanes and storms as the Earth grows hotter and more humid during the day. Even though the nights are frigid, the overall constant temperature elevation in the Earth eventually makes all the glaciers and ice melt."

"Glaciers and ice?" The perplexity on Lan's face deepens.

"Frozen water. The more water that forms from the melting, the higher the oceans rise, and apparently cover a majority of land according to this map. I recall him explaining that the more water there is, the more quickly it absorbs CO_2 and smoke particles into the atmosphere. The world may have been saved and balanced itself back out if it weren't for the continuation of nuclear wars, fires, and volcanoes. The oceans weren't able to keep up with all the greenhouse gasses, and eventually, the oxygen levels kept dropping, and the Earth's temperatures kept rising. Ultimately, over time, all the water dries up, and we are left with a barren desert, a nearly uninhabitable world. It's amazing that humankind survives at all."

Watching the color drain from Lan's face, I realize she only understood my last comment as her eyes begin to glisten.

"But there are survivors, and we need to help them before it's too late." Lan manages to express with a quivering chin, referring to her *family*.

"We will… I just have to figure out how." The familiar burden of needing to save the world comes crashing back down onto my frail shoulders like a planet-sized meteor.

Great Granddad, help me!
How can I save the world and the future like you said I would?
And how can I help save Jaxson?

My thoughts scream out in prayer.

I begin to maniacally sift through the documents, invention models, and strange objects scattering the overwhelming desk in front of me, trying to avoid tears from forming in my own eyes. I tug the beaded chain attached to the colorful glass Tiffany lamp on the desk for more light.

My arm instantly reflects a strange purple hue as my glowing arm hairs stand at attention.

"Blacklight. Why would Great Granddad put a black light in his lamp, unless…

Lan, go turn off the light switch on the wall. This blacklight must be here for a reason, and we can't have the overhead light on if we want to find out what that is." I spout with a new surge of enthusiasm.

As soon as Lan flips the switch, everything white, or lightly colored, in the room illuminates in energetic neon; including Lan's revealed toothy grin.

"Wow!" She utters with her glowing eyes growing.

Looking down at Great Granddad's desk, I notice that certain Alchemic symbols on the parchment we discovered hidden in the floor also illuminate to life.

"Lan, look, there are five symbols on this document that are glowing!"

"So, what exactly does that mean?"

"Look around the room and see if you can see anything with these same glowing symbols," I demand, searching the room frantically like a kid on Easter morning, searching for a golden egg. But nothing out of the ordinary is revealed other than the symbols on the parchment.

"It's too hard to see with just that one strange purple light," Lan squints.

Memorizing the words below the five glowing symbols on the document, I flick the light switch back to the on position on the wall next to the door. Our eyes protest the instant brightness but resume searching. After scouring what must have been every inch of the study, Lan squeals with excitement.

"Are these those same symbols, like on that paper?" Lan's voice echoes off the bricks inside the fireplace.

Dashing to where she is squatting, I witness her discovery. Wherever I previously pressed on a brick and smudged off the soot, glimpses of Alchemic symbols peek through bashfully.

"Yes, this must be it!" I yell, clapping my hands.

Ripping off my favorite flannel I had on over my t-shirt, I sacrifice it to scrub the bricks on the back wall of the fireplace. My heart pounds in my ears as every pore on my body tingles.

With a deep cleansing breath, I exhale, looking over the brilliance of the etched symbols displayed before us on each brick.

Attempting to deliberate amongst the prodigious symbols staring me in the face, I struggle to recall which one came first.

Earth, water, oxygen, seed, ecosystem.

I recite the memorized order of the glowing words in my mind like a broken record.

Searching for the first symbol from the parchment, my eyes scan every brick until they freeze on the symbol that matches. With trembling fingers, I clench my teeth as I press on the brick in the bottom left corner depicting an upside-down triangle with a line going through the tip. The faint clunk of a ball-bearing dropping causes Lan and I to look at each other with hope. Quickly, my predatorial finger races over the symbols on the bricks, hunting for its next prey.

"Water." I gush, my fingers attacking the upside-down triangle on the brick just above my head. Our bodies solidifying in suspense, Lan and I pause to hear another thump inside the wall.

Referring to my parchment guide, I relay to Lan, "Now we need oxygen; it is an upward-facing triangle, with a line through the top peak and a circle in the center."

Lan lunges with excitement, pressing the described brick. Another low click deep in the wall forces blood to rush through my veins with great force.

"Seed - a circle with a plus in the middle," I spit with eagerness.

Lan reaches to her right and enthusiastically presses the etched circle symbol.

I already found the last symbol. It is the brick directly in the center of the fireplace wall.

Tracing the two triangles filled with the same seed circle, a warm glow bursts through my body as it dawns on me that all those previous symbols combined create this symbol of a fully functioning ecosystem.

Grabbing Lan's hand with my free hand, I fill my lungs with as much oxygen as they can hold. Scrunching my eyes tight, I press the last brick. Loud rumbling spits dust and falling debris onto our heads as we duck out of the fireplace. We embrace each other in a huddle. Slowly opening our eyes, we lean in, too impatient to wait for the dust to fully dissipate. As if by magic, the entire back wall of the fireplace has vanished. It completely slid open to reveal an ominous opening.

"We did it!' Lan and I shout together.

"What do you think is back there?" Lan finally whispers after our elation settles with the dust.

I lean my head down toward the obscured, thick air. The stench is impregnated with a plethora of unfamiliar herbed scents and poignant vinegars that sting my nose.

"There is only one way to find out."

Chapter 5

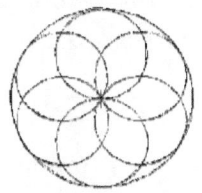

The Apothecary

My heartbeat flutters like a hummingbird's wings as I crawl on my hands and knees through the revealed opening behind the fireplace in Great Granddad's study. Breathing in through my mouth with shallow breaths, I try to avoid smelling the foul air. Instead, my tongue tastes like I licked the bottom of a sewer. I motion for Lan to follow me with a wavering limb.

"It smells horrible. I think an animal got in here and died." I relay cautiously as my eyes begin to burn and fill with water.

Pushing my weight onto my haunches, I stretch my legs into a standing position and pull Lan up at my side. With her nose buried in her shirt, her shoulder presses against me as she trembles closer. Clicking a button on my watch, the flashlight feature irradiates a particle-filled beam of light. Tunneling the light to various strange objects around us, I search for a more efficient means of light. Maneuvering our way around a large stone table in the center of the mysterious room, I attempt to make sense of the various objects sprinkled across its massive surface. A microscope, eye droppers, a mortar and pestle, test tubes, beakers of all shapes and sizes, burners, and other inexplicable inventions are amongst the dusty items resting peacefully.

My astounded eyes jump to the oil lamps affixed on each of the walls.

"Let's see if we can get some more light in here."

Of course, this secret room was never hooked up to electricity when the rest of the house was modernized since it wasn't listed as a room on the blueprints.

Shuffling my feet toward the wall to my left, Lan remains glued to my side. Peeling my arm from her dagger fingernails, I search near the oil lamp for a way to light it. I twist the brass knob on the side of the oil well, and to my surprise, it lights up without me having to provide a flame. Not only does this one oil lamp light up, but the other glass vase lamps in the room spark simultaneously. With mysterious flames dancing on each wall, the peculiar room flickers to life with its glow.

"Wow, this room is way bigger than the small space it showed on the blueprints," I utter.

Panning the room, I am unable to take in each overwhelming, surreptitious detail. The wall where I just brought life to the secret laboratory houses a display of rather large jars and metal canisters. Upon stepping back, I recognize the shape of the shelving unit as the outline of the periodic table, spanning the length of the wall. Each squared shadow box cradles what can only be sizable samples of every discovered element. I think there are even elements added on that I have never heard of before, displayed beyond the usual periodic table outline. But then again, I am obviously not a master of science. That was evident when I was forced to learn about the element Neon while imprisoned at the Elementerprise Facility in Lan's time. Gawking at the curious gallery of elements, I observe that the name and Alchemic symbol are painstakingly etched into each wooden shelf for all the elements.

My fluttering eyelashes entice my robotic feet toward the back wall to get a closer look at those contents. Unlike the last display, these containers don't have individualized compartments but are lined like soldiers along extensive horizontal shelves. Squinting at the labels tied or stuck to each container or bottle, I am familiar with only a few of the substances.

Aloe Vera, Ginger, Lavender, Turmeric, Garlic, Sage,
Green Tea...

"So, that wall to our left contains earth elements, and this wall appears to house different herbs and plants."

Lan's eyes bulge as she positions herself behind my back.

"Why do things on that wall appear to be moving?" Lan's head tilts to gesture to the next adorned unexplored wall to our right.

"Because those things are alive," my quivering voice informs, as I observe eerie aquatic creatures, rodents, and reptiles as they squirm and slither about in their containers.

Allowing my curiosity to overpower my hesitation, I force my legs to amble in the direction of the writhing wall.

Stretching my head as close to the terrariums and aquariums as I can without gagging, I focus on the unpronounceable labels.

Deinococcus Radiodurans?
Tardigrades?
Heterocephalus Glaber?
Alvinella Pompejana?
Spinoloricus Cinziae?
I'm not entirely sure these aren't the names of
dinosaurs.
Finally, one I recognize, an axolotl. It is labeled
Ambystoma Mexicanum.
That must be the scientific name.

"I am going to guess that this wall is different types of organisms and creatures."

The creepy wall is too much for Lan, and she backs away deliberately. Studying the plant wall, she asks, "Aren't some of these the ingredients we need to make Jaxson the *Elixir of Life?*"

"We don't need to make any. We have lots of Epilanthdopram Injections right here!" I shout, rushing to my discovery. My

55

feet are barely able to keep up with my racing brain.

On both sides of the fireplace entrance, we just crawled through, sit shelves full of premixed elixirs, potions, and medications labeled for every possible ailment.

"Wow, he truly was a magnificent doctor," Lan stammers taking in all the miraculous mixtures.

"And this is his secret apothecary!

Imagine how many people we can help with all this." My head shakes in disbelief.

"If only we had all these recipes, we could make more medications with the ingredients along the walls."

"You mean recipes like these?" Lan delicately brushes the cobwebs and grime off an ancient book, open on an altar on the stone table in the center of the room.

Sprinting to her discovery, my overexuberance fuels my socks to slide through the soiled floors like ice skates. Grasping the warm, rough edges of the rocky tabletop, the upper half of my body freezes as my legs continue sliding. Nearly teetering Lan off her stance, we steady each other with our goofy laughter echoing freely through the room. Controlling my rapid breath, I carefully blow the excess dust from the holy grail of books.

The familiar scratchy handwriting sings to my memories. Reminiscent of the *Elixir of Life*, written in Great Granddad's other journal, this recipe harmonizes each ink stroke.

"This must be another one of Great Granddad's journals." I carefully flip through the pages, sending particle specks dancing aimlessly.

"But, unlike the rambling explanations and invention diagrams like in the other books, this one is mainly filled with elixir and potion recipes."

"How does he know so much about everything?"

"He has clearly been through and seen a lot over the ages," I murmur in admiration.

"How can we use this information, and all his inventions, to save the world?" Lan's gilded eyes broaden with intensity.

"I wish I knew." My shoulders slump forward.

"But I am afraid there is only one person brilliant enough to know how to do that. And unfortunately, that person isn't me." A herd of elephants parades against my chest.

"Then why don't we ask him?" Lan's epiphany lights up her face.

"What…. he…" I stammer, unable to find a response.

Rubbing the back of my neck, the painful kink lingers and tightens.

"He's…. dead, remember?" I'm afraid to look up from the table, not sure if I can contain the emotion burning in my throat.

Lan drops to her hands and knees and scurries through the fireplace opening like a mouse into Great Granddad's study.

What the…

Rolling my eyes, I mimic Lan's maneuver powerlessly like one of Charlie's Angels. After all, I would probably do something much more embarrassing if she asked me to. She's hard to resist.

Before I can finish grooming the dust off the knees of my now filthy jeans, Lan's frantic voice floods the room.

"We know that Dr. Awkward died in my time. But he was clearly alive when he was here, or when he was here, or here."

Lan's finger shoots like lightning bolts from several photographs and hand-marked maps hanging around the room.

"All we have to do is choose one of these times and places. The dates are on all of them."

Lan studies my face intensely, searching for a reaction. But the grandfather clock echoes through the house long before I can respond.

As if every electron in my body pulses at once with realization, I spout, "You're absolutely right!

I am sure we can coordinate one of his journal entries with these maps and pinpoint his exact time and location, or at least get within the correct vicinity.

Let's look through his journals to figure out where, and when, we are going."

Comprehending that I might get to see Great Granddad again, I spring to life.

Cocking my head back in cynicism, a thick fog rolls over my thoughts like poison.

"So, do we need to go back in time from the entry to make sure Great Granddad is here at the estate?

Or are there other portals, or whatever he talks about in his journals, and we might end up in Timbuktu? There are so many unknowns. What if we can't get back to your time, Lan?

What if we can't get back here to Jaxson?" My voice trails off into incoherent rambles of doubt.

Lan violently shakes my shoulders, attempting to shake out my negativity.

"What if we don't try?

What if we just stay here and do nothing?

The world isn't going to save itself, and you said yourself that only Dr. Awkward is brilliant enough to help us save the world and Jaxson."

My grimace snakes its way to a crooked smile as I respire a chortle.

The vibration in my pocket launches me like a rocket toward the wooden, coffered ceiling. Pulling out my phone, as if drawing my gun in a western shootout, I see Dad's picture pop up on the screen. Signaling for Lan to hang on one second with one hand, I slide the green squiggling phone icon to answer the call with my other.

"Hey, Dad." I scramble quickly into the hallway, not risking Dad hearing Lan in the background.

"Hey, kiddo. I hope I didn't wake you up."

"Nope, I'm just... hanging out, you know."

"Well, I had a minute between my meeting and the tour, and I just got off the phone with Mom. She sounded exhausted and said that there isn't any change in Jaxson. I'm going to head over there as soon as I finish up here in an hour or two. I will try to get Mom away from the hospital and take her to dinner somewhere, but I'm not sure she will agree to that."

"Yah, that would probably be good for her." I agree out of concern for Mom, while simultaneously trying to buy me and Lan some extra time.

"She insists on staying with Jaxson again tonight, but I will do my best to change her mind. I want to be there with him just as much as she does."

Silence on the other end lingers longer than it should have. I'm not quite sure what to say to that. I mean, I know Dad loves us and cares about us, but it has always been Mom who wiped our fevers with a cool cloth or rubbed our backs when our bellies ached.

"Either way, one of us will give you a call when we are on our way home. Are you okay on your own for dinner tonight? I'm not even sure if anything around there delivers."

"You know I usually live on cold cereal and Pop-Tarts," I reply, thinking of all the times Mom has tried out a new experimental healthy recipe that tasted like…. well, the Elementerprise ration bars.

"Ok, Sport. I'm pretty sure Mom brought some of those with us. They're probably in the pantry.
Call or text if you need me."

I don't know why he calls me Sport. I don't even play a sport. I am the opposite of anyone who plays a sport.

"Will do, Dad. Bye." I press the red phone hang-up button eagerly while pirouetting to rush back to Lan.

Making my way through the door to Great Granddad's study, I pause to relish in watching Lan perched on the bayed window seat. Her body jerks as the thunder rolls but doesn't break her concentration, as her finger traces the trail of a raindrop down the windowpane. The creaky floorboard beneath my step, however, is more unexpected. Her hair whips around, and her rigid flinch softens when her eyes lock onto mine.

"There is water falling from the sky." Lan's eyes sparkle in

59

amazement.

"It's called rain." I forget that all this is new for her.

I sit next to her, just watching her observe the rainfall.

"I'm used to dangerous lightning storms in my time, but there is never any… rain." Her head tilts up toward the sky, desperately trying to figure out what is causing the dark clouds to cry.

"Rain has always been my favorite type of weather. But do you want to know the best part?"

Noticing a small metal hook rusted into its locked position, I pry it to the side.

Pulling up the ledge of the bottom of the window my knuckles turn white as my face grunts to crimson. Lan, realizing my weak muscles could use some assistance, tugs alongside me. Instantly, the paint splits away from the bottom of the windowsill and it jiggles up its track rigidly a few inches before it gets stuck again.

> *Show off.* I giggle to myself.
> *In my head, that window-opening scenario played out much differently.*

As the warm, humid breeze blows outside the window, the waft of wet earth oozes into the room. Closing my eyes, I harmoniously fill my nose with as much petrichor as it can inhale.

> *Petrichor. I'm impressed that I remember the term for the smell of rain from Chemistry class.*
> *It's probably one of the very few things I do remember.*

Lan must have seen my big inhale because she begins inhaling repeatedly. So much, in fact, to make herself feel as high as a kite.

"It smells so good," she finally bursts into an exhale.

"That's it. My favorite part of rain is the smell it emits." My geeky giddiness exudes.

"It does smell amazing. But my favorite part is the fact that there is water falling from the sky. If it weren't for the lightning, I would just sit out there all day and drink the rain."

"Well, perhaps we can make time for that today. But first, we need to decide on our best chance for meeting up with Great Granddad."

The damp section on my pants soaks through to my leg, informing me that the rain is coming in quite fervently through the opening.

"Let's close this up tightly before the rain ruins any of the furniture," I muster through a clenched jaw. With all my weight forced down on the window, it slowly wriggles into its closed position. It takes some joggling and convincing to slide the locking clasp back into place to secure the window.

"Whew," I whisper as my Jello-filled body squishes down onto the viridescent cushioned bench. Taking a few rejuvenating breaths, I finally state,

"I'll go get the journals so we can look through them to figure out our best chance of finding Great Granddad."

Unable to hide the audible gurgles and churns of my stomach, I add,

"I'll make us some lunch, too."

I didn't get to eat much of the breakfast. I was too busy absorbing the scene of Lan devouring it.

Lan's sudden erect posture and raising eyebrows communicate that she totally agrees with the plan including food.

I better hurry before she starts salivating and drooling, or that pillow is going to become even soggier.

I whiz out of the room, sniggering to myself, my demeanor bubbling over with exhilaration.

Chapter 6

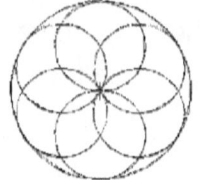

To When Should We Go?

"Okay, Great Granddad, where and when should we go, to make the biggest positive impact on the future?" I spit aloud, still chomping my way through a bite of a ham and cheese sandwich. Lan pays little attention to my question as she thoroughly relishes in a sandwich of her own. Scouring through Great Granddad's journal, my heart pulses with the hope of finding a time and location where we can travel to find him. These two leather-bound books have become my scripture, my solace of information. Hoping for a prophecy, I allow the pages of the Seed of Life journal to fall open as my eyes scrunch closed, relying on fate to show me the way. Slowly prying them open with hesitant slits of optimism, my eyes behold that the book is open to an equation of Alchemic symbols. My fingers pulse with recollection as they just pressed against those same five symbols on the fireplace bricks.

Earth + Water + Oxygen + Seeds = Fully Functional Ecosystem

"This has to be a sign!" I express to Lan, who nonchalantly humors me by peeking over at my breakthrough.

"Aren't those the same symbols used to open the secret door to that creepy room?" Lan questions, as a piece of a potato chip flies from her mouth to freedom through her continuous crunching.

"They are. Let's see, in the future, we need all these things to sustain life. The Earth is already present, at least hopefully it is, so we don't need to focus on that one. We found the seeds, and they are safely sustained for now, but we need to make sure there's plenty of water and oxygen for them to survive. Plants supply the oxygen, and in order for plants to grow, they need water. Therefore, I guess we need to focus on ensuring there is water in the future. That is much easier said than done." I sigh in frustration, thinking back to the dry desert wasteland of Lan's time in the distant future.

"What about that map on the wall? You said something about how the world was still at a point where it could heal itself when it was covered with water if the nuclear wars and whatever else stopped."

"Yes, but how are two teenage kids supposed to stop nuclear wars, rampant fires, and volcanoes?"

"Maybe Dr. Awkward will have some ideas he wasn't able to try."

Shaking my head, reservations pulse through my veins.

What is the year on that map when water was
abundant?
2079?

Thumbing through the dense pages of the journal, my eyes scan for entries with the same year. It is challenging to navigate through the hundreds of entries since they all jump around in time. There is no rhyme or reason to help me understand the sequence of events in the journals.

Suddenly, the sun reveals itself from its dark, cloudy hiding place through the window and reflects off the abruptly illuminating pages. My pupils scream, forcing my eyes to squint as they adjust to the sudden invading brightness. As if the heavens were reacting to the open pages like a *hallelujah*, my heart joins in the praise.

"I found it!" I shout as I crack my knuckles in preparation. I begin reading the entry aloud, my voice full of fervor.

Today, I had a successful wired call from my office with Kao Chin. Although we were unable to come to an armistice nuclear agreement, he did state that a hiatus in the war, and a brief joining of our forces, may be necessary for the world to focus its efforts on global communication. Even if his reasoning is to clear the atmosphere long enough to regain his rehabilitated satellite transmissions, I feel it was his last rogue nuclear missile backfiring and hitting too close to home that solidified the deal. Now, if I can just get Russia on board. They are the ones that started all this mess in the first place with their anti-satellite missions. As soon as most of the satellites were destroyed, they blasted mass EMP bombs all over the world. That is why the nuclear bombs that followed fell blindly and undetected. Why is it that all major countries want to outdo the others and join in on using weapons of mass destruction? Do they not realize they are only destroying themselves and our planet? Hopefully, I can convince them to let the Earth heal itself for a season. Only then can the abundant, yet dying, oceans have a chance to reoxygenate and reverse some of the greenhouse gasses and radiation fallout plaguing the World.

Lan's astounded face finally musters a stuttered response, "I'm not sure that sounds very inviting. Hopefully, Dr. Awkward successfully convinces everyone to stop the nuclear war. Perhaps we need to go a few days after this entry to give him some time to complete his mission and make sure it is safe."

"I'm afraid if we don't go on the date written on this entry, we can't guarantee that we can find him. He has access to a time machine, remember? It says that he is writing this from his office. I'm hoping that means his office here at the estate, or maybe it's the office in the city, where Dad is – which wouldn't be impossible to get to. It's our best bet." I'm not sure if I'm trying to convince Lan or myself.

"At least we are going to a time when there is water. I don't think I can handle any more endless dry heat." Lan forces the edges of her mouth toward her ears.

"That is the whole point. We need to do everything we can to make sure the Earth retains at least some water for it to have a future." I announce matter-of-factly.

"I guess we are heading to May 12, 2079, then?" Lan's hairline raises, and small creases appear on her forehead as she reads the date at the top of the journal entry.

"I guess we are," I reply. "But first, we need to close up the apothecary."

I stride back over to the fireplace and gaze down at the open wall where the back of the fireplace used to be. My hands feel around the sidewalls for a lever or latch to close the door, with no luck.

"Do you have to push the symbols to close it like you did to open it?" Lan asks, joining me in my search.

"I can't press the symbols because they are on the bricks that slid into the main wall when it opened."

"No, I mean from the other side. There are matching symbols on the backside of the bricks." Lan expresses, realizing I hadn't noticed them. I was much too busy looking at all the other contents of the mysterious room to notice them.

Crawling back through the fireplace door into the apothecary, I hold my breath wisely this time, knowing the stench of the room is nauseating.

> *I will need to come to clean out these cages and aquariums when I get back, or Mom and Dad, and the entire town of Coalville, will surely come to know of their pungent existence.*

Once on the other side of the opening, I stand and turn around to look at the backside of the fireplace door, where it slid in front of this apothecary wall. Sure enough, the backside of the fireplace looks identical to the front. Each of the bricks is etched with the same symbols. Before my fingers can press the symbols, the Epilanthdopram injectors stand out amongst the other vials and bottles on the eye-level shelf. Thinking of Jaxson's critical state, I decide to grab two injectors and slip them into my pocket.

> *Better to be safe than sorry.*

Hunching over, I press the five symbols in the correct sequence.

> *Earth*
> *Water*
> *Oxygen*
> *Seeds*
> *Ecosystem*

I throw myself through the opening just as it rumbles and slides closed behind me.

"Good observation. You are so smart." I compliment Lan and watch as blood flushes to her cheeks.

I rush back to the window seat and grab our empty lunch plates.

"Come on, let's go fill my backpack and satchel with some food and supplies before we go."

Lan's blanching face flashes a smile, causing her freckles to jump upward as she follows me out of Great Granddad's exhilarating study.

Chapter 7

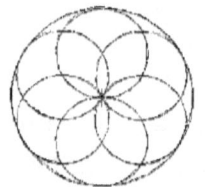

Blasting to the Future

Lugging my backpack onto my back, my shoulders tense in protest against the weight.

"Do you think we have enough food?" Lan asks with worry painted on her face.

"I don't think we can fit one more can into this bag, so this has to be enough. Besides, we aren't going back to your time, remember? Hopefully, there will still be plants, animals, and food available where we are going. But at least we are prepared if there isn't." I slip her quaint hand into mine and lead her toward the hidden door panel in the hallway at the top of the grand staircase.

Reaching into my jeans pocket, I fish out the old ring of skeleton keys and find the one that opens the secret door. With a faint *click,* I slide the door open, and the small ascending staircase is exposed. We fly up the stairs with our hearts racing. The refreshing sunlight cascading down the stairs beckons to us as we bathe in its light. The dark summer storm we just encountered while in Great Granddad's study is now nothing but a distant dream-like memory. Azure blue skies as far as the eye can see flood the encircling cupula windows in every direction. It blurs into the blanket of emerald trees until they fade into the ocean, sparkling like millions of turquoise sapphires in the distance.

"Wow!" Lan exhales a hypnotized utterance as her brilliant eyes reflect the glow of the awe-inspiring scenery. "It's… I had no idea the world was this…" Her lips utter silence, she can't find a word worthy of the landscape.

"Now do you understand why I was out of my mind when I came to your time and saw what the world becomes?"

Lan's head bobs, but her focus remains glued to the incredible panorama.

I allow her to bask in the beauty of the world around us while I unlock the trap door in the center of the floor of the observatory. I clasp my fingers around the pull handle and use my legs to help me heave it open. The heavy door clunks open, causing Lan to jump out of her trance.

"Are you ready to go?

Are you sure you want to do this?

I have the injectors with the medicine to try on Jaxson.

We could just stay here and see if it helps him. We can save the future another day."

"I would love to stay here forever, but I can't just leave Einstein, Erb, and Neo to fend for themselves and hope they have enough oxygen, water, and food to live in the future.

So yes, I need to do this. If you want to stay, that's fine. But I'm going with or without you." Lan inflates her chest with courage and steps down onto the first stair below the trap door. I hand her a flashlight from our freshly packed backpack and follow closely behind her down the tight staircase. The familiar stale stench plucks the strings of my memory of taking Jaxson down these steps for the first time. I hesitate for a moment, unable to force my foot down to the next step.

What if something goes wrong?
What if we can't get back here to Jaxson?
What if something happens to Lan?

The poisonous thoughts inflict my muscles, causing them to flinch and form a pirouette to launch me back up the stairs to the safety of the perfect world, where, at least for now, Lan and I can enjoy being together blissfully. Lan, sensing my hesitation, wraps her fingers around my hand. As if by magic, her small squeeze of my fingers sends reassuring optimism and warmth that flows up my arm and spreads through the rest of my body like a heartfelt hug passing from cell to cell. I continue to follow her down into the musty cellar, where the air is thick and difficult to breathe.

Stepping onto the dank ground, I reach up to pull the link of chains of the lightbulb hanging from one of the exposed beams. The cellar zaps to life as odd silhouettes form monstrous mounds of odd machinery around us.

Instantly, as if by instinct, I run to the vault door guarding the Seeds of Life, and peer in through the small round hole window in the thick metal door. The amount of light pouring in overhead makes the rows of plants appear to be glowing heavenly. Lan strains up to her tiptoes to peer in the circular viewing hole next to me.

"Breathtaking," she mutters.

"Come on, the sooner we go make sure the future has water, the sooner we can get back here to these plants and Jaxson."

I open Great Granddad's journal to the page with the instructions on how to turn on the boiler time machine. One would think I would have it memorized by now, but I don't want to accidentally forget a step. First, I grab the containers of elements I separated with the machine in the pumphouse. Lan helps me sprinkle a small amount of each needed element onto the earthy ground in front of the machine. Next, I twist the metal wheel to open the boiler door. It squeaks open with rusty resistance. Scraping the bottom of the wheelbarrow, I scoop as much coal as possible. However, there is more ebony dust than actual clumps of coal.

"I hope this will be enough coal." I pray through gritted teeth.

Next, I run over to the hose coiled up on the crumbling brick wall and tug with all my might. I drag it over to the opening on the boiler. Lan waits patiently with her hand on the knob, waiting for directions on when to turn on the water.

I force the nozzle end into the open drum of the boiler and hold it in place carefully.

"Ok, turn it on." I lick my lips with anticipation. My mouth instantly feels dry as worry fills my mind that the water may not come.

The whooshing sound of water approaching softens the creases on my face as I watch the oncoming water fill the hose like a creature scurrying to find a way out of the tube. Spraying with great force, the water causes the lava rocks lining the bottom of the drum to launch against the backside of the boiler.

"Ok, that's enough," I yell. "Turn it off."

Small ricocheting fragments of coal dust and blackened splashes of water drip down my face as I turn to Lan, blinking debris out of my eyes.

She presses her lips together tightly to hold in the laugh bubbling inside her.

"Perhaps it doesn't need to be turned all the way up next time." I sputter as I wind the hose back up onto the peeling wall.

"Sorry," Lan's chuckle spurts out with her apology.

I wipe my face with the back of my hand and attempt to make sure there aren't any particles left clinging to my cheeks as I make my way back over to the massive boiler machine. Pushing my shoulder into the door, I force it closed and twist the metal wheel with all my might to guarantee it is closed tightly. I turn the dial so the date reveals 05, 12, 2079.

"What time of day do you think it should be when we go? I ask Lan, randomly twisting the numbers as if gambling on a time.

Lan's shoulders shrug. "Whatever time you think we can find Dr. Awkward."

"It sounds like his journal entry was written that evening, so perhaps we can get there earlier that day to get our bearings and make sure we can find him?" I say, as more of a question than a suggestion. Lan nods her head in agreement. I twist the nob to 1200 for noon because I don't really know what other time to put into the machine. I flip open the journal to the page in the back where I write my own notes and write down the exact time of when we are leaving today so that we can come back to this exact moment.

Pressing the large button, the heat in the cellar instantly begins to rise. Sweat skitters down my back like a thousand dispersing spider legs. I secure the journals in the satchel and wrap the strap around my body. I pick up the backpack of supplies and swing it up onto my back. Grabbing Lan's hand, I squeeze it as we watch the needle on the temperature gauge move quickly up the scale of numbers. The air in the cellar is heavy and burns our throats like liquid fire. With the temperature needle hovering near 212 degrees, the red button begins buzzing. Lan's eyes shoot to investigate mine as her hand gravitates toward the glowing button. I nod at her, letting her know it is okay to push it. The instantaneous blast of red stones getting sucked up into the machine pelt and scrape against our pant legs, causing Lan to jump and dance around, trying to avoid blocking the rocks from flying into the boiler. Her flailing body, jumping around aimlessly, is impossible not to smile at. She instantly realizes my entertained gaze and immediately ceases her jig.

"I just didn't want to be in the way of the flying rocks." She states as if she needs to explain her actions to me.

I would pay money to watch that again.

A helpless smile takes over my face.

Just then, the blue button begins flashing right next to me. I press it without hesitation and turn to watch Lan's reaction.

Disappointingly, there is no dance to accompany this stage in the process. Lan walks around the outside perimeter of the piles of rocks to join me at my side. I look down at her as her face begins to flash yellow, and the yellow button begins to signal its readiness.

"Lanthanum?" she asks with a giddy grin.

Before I finish my nod, she pounds the button with great enthusiasm. Her entire aura glows with pride as she watches the golden flecks of dust and rocks fly into the machine. She turns her beaming face toward me, and I feel like I could melt into a puddle at her feet – and not because of the extreme temperature pouring from the boiler. However, the instant buzz accompanied by a purple flashing light refocuses my attention on the important process of setting up the time machine with exact precision. Upon pressing the purple button, the cellar commences its unnerving hum as every loose item and rock begins to bounce around aimlessly with unnerving vibration. This is the part when it feels like every electron in the room is free and separates from every previous bond. Lan wraps her arms around me, anchoring her body to mine. I freeze, not wanting the moment to pass by, until I notice Lan staring at me blankly, waiting for me to proceed. I quickly snap the pieces of the music box on my wristband into place. I almost forgot that I need the Terbium key, and the only way to get it out of its safe resting place at my wrist is by the magical tune of the little music box attached to my wristband. Winding the drum, I watch as the comb plucks over each raised bump rhythmically. However, the sweet melody is overpowered by the clanking of the machine and the ear-piercing alarm of the large silver flashing bulb. I squint my eyes and lean my head down to see when the secret compartment opens and allows me to extract the necessary key. As the Terbium key slides out into my waiting palm, I smile at Lan, indicating that we are all set. I feel Lan's fingers dig into the sides of my abdomen as she squeezes the breath out of me. However, I allow her to continue squeezing because I, too, want to make sure nothing goes wrong and that we get to the same portal together. I relish in her fierce grasp. She scrunches her eyes tightly together and buries her head into my sweat-soaked chest. Slowly, I drag in a long, drawn-out breath through my nose and prepare myself for the painful journey ahead. My trembling hand is nearly seizure-like as I focus on getting the old skeleton key into the keyhole. As soon as the Terbium teeth find their way into the hole, a blasting light overtakes the cellar. Lan and I are hurled to the ground in one massive heap.

Chapter 8

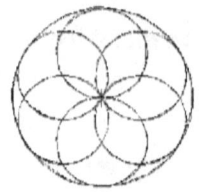

Treading Water

$\mathcal{I}$' feel Lan's arms wrapped around my torso, still squeezing the life out of me.

The pain in my head is excruciating and I contemplate just lying here on the ground until the agony subsides.

"Lan, are you okay?"

I watch the tight wrinkles around her eyes relax and her eyelids open nervously, one at a time.

"Did we make it?" She asks, removing one of her arms from around me to shield her confused eyes as they survey the cellar around us. This time, the lightbulb is lit, and I can see the surrounding cellar.

We both instantly notice the unmissable water leaking into the cellar from the doors and barricades that lead to the tunnels.

"Oh no, the blast must have weakened the…" but before I can finish my sentence, a once nailed board skids across the dirt ground toward us and water begins spraying into the cellar at a faster rate.

I quickly slip the Terbium key, which fortunately I still hold tightly between my shaking fingers, back into the secret compartment in my wristband and close the flap with a *click*.

"Quick, grab those boards over there," I bark to Lan as I search the nearby wooden table of tools for a hammer and nails.

Leaping into action, we do our best to seal up the openings which are now spewing water. However, the pressure of the outside water in the tunnels has proven to be much greater than the rusty nails and broken boards we can't seem to attach fast enough. The loud creaking and groaning behind the blockade increases, along with the number of new waterspouts releasing their fury. The pent-up water pressure is too much, and a geyser bursts through the barricade all at once, sending wood, and us, flying toward the back wall of the cellar near the stairs head over heels, tumbling, as if in a riptide current. I crash against the wall first as pain shoots through my body. I dive furiously, trying to place my body between Lan and the brick wall. Luckily for her, I soften her landing, but unfortunately for me, I get sandwiched between a forceful incoming bony body and the backpack full of cans impaling my back. Instantly, my breath is ripped from my lungs as I wince in pain.

"Are you okay? I finally manage to mutter to Lan through shallow breaths and chattering teeth.

"Yep, you?" Lan questions as she wades her way to the steps to get above the frigid, rising water. All the color has been drained from her cheeks, and she looks as pale as death.

Together, we manage to clamber up the narrow staircase with our heavy, drenched clothes clinging to our bodies, squeezing out shiver after shiver. The sodden backpack is weighing me down and making each step I climb more rigorous as my muscles and tendons tighten stubbornly. Lan heaves herself one last time and sits huddled on the top step with her arms wrapped around her body, shaking uncontrollably with her head as close to the trap door above us as possible.

> *I wish I had something dry and warm to wrap around her, but I'm sure everything in my backpack is as soaked as we are.*

I struggle past Lan's crouched body and reach up desperately to open the trapdoor to the observatory. But of course, it is locked or stuck. My shuddering breath begins to quicken as panic poisons my movement. Frantically, I pound on the trapdoor to loosen it from its hinges. I throw my rigid body against it to hopefully get it to budge. For a moment, adrenaline overtakes me, and I forget that I am freezing. All I can think about is getting this door open and getting me and Lan to safety. Clearing the muddled worry from my thoughts, I try to think with reason. Realizing the trapdoor might just be locked, I begin searching the door for a keyhole on this side of the door. Sliding my shaking fingers across every sliver and crack of the door, I can't feel anything. My fingers are numb from the iciness of the encroaching water. Lan tugs on my arm to get my attention and points to the rising waters sloshing around the soles of her boots. Lan's eyes, full of terror, burrow into my heart as the dark grey water begins to swallow us whole, starting with our feet. All the adrenaline I had moments ago is now pumped out of my body, and I can focus on nothing but the freezing waters billowing around my ankles, soaking through every eyelet hole and poorly sewn seam in my boots and piercing my feet like shards of ice. Lan's desperate eyes lock onto mine.

> "I don't want to die, not like this. I thought the water was the answer for survival, not our death." Her words are as choppy as her quick and shallow breaths, as if the glacial waters are slowly squeezing the life out of her lungs.

> "Hang on, I just need to get this door open," I grunt, thrusting my shoulder upward against the trapdoor.

> My fingers continue their desperate search for the...

> "The keyhole! I found it!"

> I fish my hand into the pocket of my jeans, which are practically sealed to my body under the water, now pressing against my hips. My numb fingers can't feel the metal skeleton keyring, but they know that they are touching something familiar. Grasping them, I wriggle the keys out of my pocket. I jiggle them from side to side to free them from their own drowning demise.

> *They are almost free, just one more stubborn key must be caught on a thread or pocket lining.*

> I tug on the keyring with great desperation, but in doing so, they fling from my pocket and out of my hand. I reach down,

scrambling through the dark waters, but my fingers only swish through the cold, empty fluid. My arm shoots out of the water, now puddling around my chest as my other hand meets it in front of my face. I switch on the flashlight on my wristband, squirm out of the straps of the backpack, and slip the strap of the satchel up over my head.

"Here, hold the backpack and satchel."

"Wait, where are you going? We are almost out of breathing room. Don't leave me!"

"I dropped the keys.

I need to go find them.

I'll be right back up.

I promise!"

I can't bear to watch Lan's eyes fill with tears of fear, or her chin quivering, and not because of the cold water lapping around it. It's motored by pure terror.

Breathing in anxiously, I inflate my lungs with as much oxygen as they can hold. Diving under the frigid water, I know that I need to find those keys quickly; our lives depend on them. I use the stairs to help pull me down faster, kicking my numb legs with every bit of energy I have. Bubbles furl around me like a tornado as the water pushing up the stairs creates a strong current against my struggle to swim downward. My eyes, frantically searching through my watch's beam of light in the murky water, sting and beg for me to close them and give them relief from the arctic water. My hands feel every square inch of each stair in hopes of feeling the metal keyring. I swim my way deeper and deeper toward the cellar floor.

Surely, they couldn't have fallen too far.

My lungs begin to burn like fire, screaming for me to fill them with oxygen again. My chest begins to convulse as if trying to breathe for me, but I squeeze my lips together tightly and refuse to let them fill with water. I can't help but flood my thoughts with Lan and Jaxson and how I need to hold my breath longer for them and for the rest of the world.

77

Just then, my hand brushes over something hard and metallic. Shining my wristband light to the discovery, my heart explodes as my eyes make out the shape of the skeleton keyring. Grasping the keyring tightly in my hand, I summersault my body to face the opposite direction and spring myself upward through the water. I kick my feet like a madman until I can't help but notice how suddenly my body no longer feels cold. In fact, it feels as though I have been wrapped in a warm blanket. The water that surrounds me is suddenly comforting and welcoming. I have the sudden urge to stop kicking and just let the congenial water cradle me into a warm, blissful slumber.

Sleep, that sounds so nice.

My eyelids, like heavy weights, close out the water around me, and my body relaxes and floats freely in the water like a feather drifting in a warm summer wind.

Lan's hand reaches down and yanks me upward. The instant jerking motion is like flipping an energy switch, making me abruptly aware of the desperate spasms in my lungs and the metal keyring still clenched in my hand. Kicking my legs hysterically, my head finally reaches where Lan's head is now completely submerged underwater. I shine my wristband light onto the bottom of the trap door, wading in water. There is nowhere to even attempt to catch a small relief breath of air. My other hand begins urgently thrusting the sun and moon skeleton key into the keyhole and twisting it with my fingers rattling like castanets. The sound of the clicking lock disengaging echoes through the water around us in waves of reprieve. Lan's pleading eyes are bulging as she helps me push the heavy trapdoor open. I am grateful Lan is here to help me push it open because I don't have much strength left in me to do it on my own. We both spring our heads up out of the water and take in a long, welcome breath of sweet oxygen. I never knew breathing could be the best feeling in the world. We both tug the backpack and satchel of supplies up onto the floorboards of the observatory with a violent *sploosh*. Then, with shaky arms, we drag ourselves out of the bitter waters and flop up onto the floor, panting.

Knowing that we can't rest until we close the trapdoor, we painstakingly swing the door closed, and it clanks into place. With great satisfaction, I lock the trapdoor, as if that will keep us safe from the rising waters below. However, to our surprise, the trapdoor acts like a watertight sealed hatch on a submarine. We stare down, just waiting for the water to seep up through the cracks in the floor. My excess breathing does little for my frayed nerves. The cogs tick by as water trickles down my arms and escapes off my fingertips.

"I think… the water…is subdued for now," I pant.

We collapse onto the withering floorboards, heaving and grateful for the welcome breaths. Pure exhaustion sets in, and I am too tired to even think about moving. The only thing I have energy for is rolling my head to the side to look at Lan. Her head rolls toward mine, and we look into each other's eyes. A hurricane of emotion brews inside me. I don't know whether I want to laugh, cry, or close my eyes and sleep forever.

"We made it." I pant weakly.

"Barely," Lan's teeth chatter, and her body retracts.

"We need to find some dry clothes. Maybe Great Granddad has something we can put on for now until ours dry out. Let's hope the main floor isn't full of water."

My stiff body protests and disagrees with my attempt to stand. I nearly fall backward, but Lan and I steady each other warily. The first step feels as though my feet are blocks of ice shattering under the pressure of my heavy body. Lan and I are instantly drawn to the angry stormy skies brewing outside the bayed windows, and we hobble closer for a view out into our new world. Turbulent waves beat around the house like a dark entity coming for us in every direction, stretching their dark grasping fingers closer and closer. Unsure if it is the thought of being surrounded by fierce, angry water, or that I'm freezing to death, but a shutter starts in my toes, works its way up my spine, and up through my whole body.

"Come on, let's go get warm and dry." I lug the water-logged pack and satchel onto my back.

I pull Lan toward the steps downstairs and away from her frightful trance. Stumbling, she huddles close to my body as I put my heavy, dripping arm around her shoulders. The staircase is too narrow for us to both descend side-by-side. I gesture for her to go first, like a gentleman, while still holding on to her back, just in case she becomes unsteady. I reach around the side of her torso with the key in my hand as my head rests on her shuddering shoulder to unlock the secret door into the upstairs hallway. She turns her face to mine, inches away, and I feel her warm breath on my cheek as it flushes with fire.

We both look forward awkwardly as the secret door slides open, interrupting our moment of closeness. Helping the door slide open fully, we both burst through the opening simultaneously, nearly getting ourselves wedged in the frame.

"Great Granddad?" I holler, shattering the uncomfortable silence.

"Dr. Awkward?" Lan yells as we both begin running, as fast as our frozen legs will allow, toward Great Granddad's study at the end of the hallway.

Twisting the ornate knob and allowing the familiar heavy door to screech open on its own, the study is just as though we recently left it. Perhaps a few documents and things are different on the large mahogany desk, but everything else is eerily reminiscent. Except for one major distinction, it is free from years of dust. The study looks as though it has currently been used and dusted. The lingering smell of aftershave and pomade still hangs in the air.

"He's got to be here!" The words blurt from my heart. "I can smell him. Great Granddad?"

I spin around and rush toward the grand staircase. Once again, my legs are buzzing with newfound energy. I dart down the rich wood stairs, leaving a trail of water spilling behind me. I dart from room to room, my blood pulsing with the anticipation of seeing Great Granddad again. I end up in the kitchen as the last place to search. The large, empty room's aroma of rotting food horridly attacks my olfactory senses. My heart begins to sink as I scurry to open the fridge, which seems to be the culprit of the stench permeating the air. My still-wet, wrinkly fingers tug open the door, and the disdainful stench intensifies. My burning eyes scan over the hairy assortment of blues, greys, and greens of the rotting milk, cheese, and I am not entirely sure what the other items used to be.

I hear the sloshing of Lan's boots as they squeak onto the tiled kitchen floor. But I can't seem to turn around as I allow the pungent mold spores to fill my nose and blur my vision, or maybe that is from the tears forming in my eyes.

"He isn't here." The words finally escape my lips in a whisper. The words are daggers to my heart and disappear into the pungent refrigerator.

"I honestly thought that when we arrived, Great Granddad would be here to greet us, help us figure everything out, and tell me how to save the world." I finally allow my piercing feet to turn around to face Lan.

Lan's hunched body stands quaking, surrounded by a puddle oozing outward around her shoes. Her blue lips are unable to utter a response.

"I'm sorry, come on. Let's find you something dry to put on. Then I will build us a fire in the sitting room."

Chapter 9

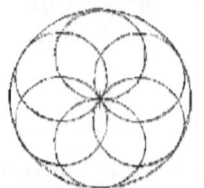

The Brewing Storm

Watching the pulsing red glow of the crackling firewood is just mesmerizing enough to keep my eyes from drifting closed. The log's sudden pop sends embers chasing each other around like a swirling waltz inside the fireplace. Lan's deep prolonged inhale signals she is sleeping peacefully as she burrows in closer at my side under the blanket. The canvas pants and wool shirt of Great Granddad's that drape her body feel itchy against my arm, yet it is comforting to have her snuggled into me safely. I can't help but relax and allow my eyes to slowly fade out the perfect moment as my breathing syncs in time with Lan's. I drift peacefully to sleep.

Pounding at the front door, followed by the doorknob rattling, jolts me awake suddenly. Lan's eyes snap open and she stares at me. Her eyes are full of discombobulation. I quickly scan the sitting room for anything I can use as a weapon if the hammering stranger intrudes. I jump up from the couch forcefully, causing Lan to tip over in my sudden absence. Darting over to the fireplace, I snatch the rod iron fire poker and hold it up-right in front of me like a swordsman ready to fence. Lan follows suit, grabbing the matching coal shovel. She stands behind me ready to fight if necessary, and not a moment too soon. A large, bearded man bursts through the front door with the harrowing rain and wind billowing behind him.

"Who's here?" A deep voice booms, shaking the windows as violently as the thunder roaring outside.

Lan leans into my back and peeks around my shoulder as the gnarly-looking man's silhouette takes form in the doorway of the sitting room.

"Get out, ya squatters!

Ya don't belong here!"

The leather glove protruding from his black, tattered slicker comes barreling toward us as if we are pesky flies. I step backward onto Lan to avoid the backhanded blow as we both stumble into a heap near the fireplace, trembling.

"Who are you?" I squeak, shoving the tip of the fire poker up toward the invader with the little bit of bravery I can muster.

"Someone who knows ya ain't s'posed to be here." He barks back through his yellowing teeth, resembling those of an old dog. His breath is just as foul as he reaches down and snatches us up to our feet.

"Wait, we just came to visit my Great Granddad. He owns this house." I plead like a child as I wiggle my feet dangling beneath me, desperately trying to stand on my own.

The man's grip on the back of our shirts loosens, releasing an aroma of old salty brine and rotten fish. Lan and I drop back down to the warm floorboards.

"Doc told me he ain't got no more family."

Leaning in closer to inspect my face, his bloodshot eyes squint to scan my features.

"I know yer lying. Get out'a here!" His unwelcome spit lands on my cheek.

"Please, he's telling the truth. He is Doc's Great Grandson. Doc wasn't expecting us, but I know he will be happy to see us." Lan valiantly retorts.

"Zip it, Las. I saw the glow of a fire through the window from me ship, and I knew there's trouble here. Doc left a few weeks ago and ain't s'posed to return fer another few weeks. He left me here ta watch his house.

But my question is, how'd ya get in? There ain't a ship. I'd've seen it. The nearest land is hundreds a miles 'way, so I know ya didn't swim here." The gruff man cracks his bulbous knuckles and compresses his thick gloves anxiously as if they are waiting to pound on us or wring our necks.

Lan and I look to each other for ideas, but our faces remain blank with worry.

> *There is no way this coarse man is going to believe that we time-traveled here to the now-flooded cellar. And I have no way to prove to him that I am related to the man he calls Doc.*
> *Let's see, offer him money?*
> *That's a stupid idea, I don't have any.*
> *The journals! They might prove to him that Doc is my Great Granddad!*
> *But can I afford to show them to this stranger?*

A warm wave of assurance washes over me as if telling me this is the solution.

"I have his journals. He gave them to me." I blurt to the man reluctantly.

"His journals?" The inflection in his voice indicates that he is intrigued, and his tense, broad shoulders relax ever-so-slightly.

"Show me." One wiry eyebrow creeps up his forehead.

Lan's worried expression questions my idea.

I stand slowly and reach up to the mantle above the fireplace where I laid Great Granddad's journals open to dry out after being submerged in water inside my backpack.

Gingerly, I show the man a few waterlogged pages of the journals while watching his face shift expressions like a mime.

Squinting his eyes as he searches my face again, he expresses,

"Where'd ya get these? These belong to Dr. Gardener."

"I told you; he gave them to me." I defend.

"Well, I guess the only way ta find out if yer tellin' the truth is to ask Doc himself.

You two are comin' with me. I hope ya know how to sail."

"Wait, sail? Then you will take us to see Great Granddad?"

"Ya gonna need somethin' waterproof for those journals. We're givin' 'em back to Doc. I don't know how ya got yer grubby hands on 'em, but I'm returnin' 'em to their rightful owner. There are secrets in there ya shouldn't know about."

"Trust me, I know," I mutter under my breath toward Lan.

"Let's be goin' then. I don't know how much longer these waves are gonna stay away from the house." He adds, looking out the window into the darkness churning about.

"May we get our packs and find something to put the journals in, please, first, sir?"

"Don't call me sir. It's Cap'n. And ya got one minute 'fore I leave ya two here to get swallowed alive by them waves. I'll snuff out the fire while I wait. Ya got one minute!"

Lan and I scurry to get the backpack and satchel, which are full of food and supplies. I then run to the kitchen and rummage through the drawers and cupboards, searching for anything that might keep the journals dry, once they dry out that is. Hoping to find some Ziploc bags or something of the sort, I give up and grab a Tupperware container that looks like it is just the right size to protect both journals.

I guess this will work.

"Let's go, Sharkbait!" The man's voice bellows from the entryway.

I dart back to where Lan and The Captain are waiting impatiently in the dark by the front door. Lan hands me Great Granddad's journals, and I carefully place them into the plastic container and seal the lid, letting out the extra bit of air through the last corner before it suctions closed with a satisfying *pffft*. The Captain swipes the protected journals in their container right out of my fingertips.

"I'll be holdin' on ta these!" He hisses as he shoves them into a pocket on the inside of his ragged, long black raincoat. Disappearing into the obscure night through the front door and into the angry waves, he hollers back,

85

"Are ya chum comin'?"

Lan and I look at each other and shrug.

"I don't think we have any other options. And he says he is taking us to Great Granddad. He is the only one that can help us now."

The inky ocean waves roar just feet away from the front porch. Not too far off, we watch as the outline of The Captain climbs into a tethered rowboat, knee-deep in dark, frothy water.

"Here, let's put these on and attempt to stay dry." I propose to Lan, slipping one of Great Granddad's raincoats around her shoulders and placing a pair of his galoshes at her feet. Luckily for us, there are two sets of each near the door. I help myself to the other raincoat and rain boots just in time to hear The Captain yelling something else in our direction, but his words are gulped down by the stormy winds and darkness. We step out onto the covered porch as a sideways blowing sheet of rain stings our faces. I turn to secure the elaborate lock on the large, twisted metal handle on the front door, praying that the water nearing the bottom porch step stays away from this house. I place the skeleton keyring into the front pocket of my backpack and swing it onto my back.

I grasp Lan's hand, but her frozen stance and intense gaze scream into the night. Her reluctance is mutual. The last thing I want to do right now is head into more freezing water.

"It's okay. I'll keep you safe." I force her golden eyes to look at mine.

Her feet are full of trust and move in rhythm with mine. They trudge down the porch steps and disappear into the muddy waters attacking them.

As we approach the small metal boat bobbing up and down, The Captain digs one of the oars into the mud below to help keep the boat steady as I help Lan step inside. As soon as her rubber boots step onto the bottom of the boat, she loses traction and slips onto the seat opposite where The Captain is seated. I throw my leg over the side of the bouncing edge and slip in beside her. The Captain throws the second oar at me, nearly knocking me back out of the boat. Fumbling to get control of the oar, and my balance, I look up at the irritated, scrunched face of The Captain.

"Start rowing, this ain't a free ride."

My hands quiver around the shaft of the oar both from fear and the frigid rain and sea spray splashing them. I plunge the wide end of the oar into the fuming water and stroke it back with all my might. A few strokes later, I can't tell if I'm soaked with rain or sweat. My shoulders and upper arms burn as I fight the waves and do my best to help propel our little boat forward. I can barely make out the metal nose of the boat as I watch it point up toward the ominous night sky, only lit periodically by a violent flash of lightning, and then dive straight back down as if heading into the depths of the bottom of the ocean; straight up and straight down, over and over.

"I thought you asked if we knew how to sail." I finally pant into the cold night air. I watch the warm breath of my words swirl and smack The Captain in the face at the same moment I regret saying it.

He grumbles something inaudible as he points the oar up into the air, forcing my attention to the light of a large ship dipping through the waves ahead like a mirage.

Is that a pirate ship?

I try to paddle faster as I watch the various sails whip in the wild wind and come to life in the strobe light flashes of the storm. From this distance, the ropes and riggings strewn from mast to mast resemble a massive web of a giant, vicious wooden spider. The front of the ship is carved into the bust of a woman with her long locks of hair twisting into the flailing heads of fearsome serpents.

Is that supposed to be Medusa?

However, as intimidating as the large ship appears, it is an oasis of hope compared to this pathetic hunk of rusted metal being tossed about like a toy in an endless ocean of fury. As we approach the two-masted, serpent-headed ship, I watch Lan bite her lip in desperation. The Captain and I do our best to steer the reluctant puny boat toward the significant vessel. Scraping against the ship like fingernails on a chalkboard, The Captain reaches out and grabs the dangling rope ladder and tosses it to me.

"Try to keep her steady while I hook up the hoist." The Captain yells.

I hug the soaked ladder as I wrap my legs around the metal bench of the rowboat and squeeze my thighs in an attempt to steady the violent rocking. Bruises form instantly as my feeble attempt does nothing to hold the little boat in place, and I feel the disappointment beaming down on me from The Captain's fuming stare. I watch as he fights to force the thick roped knots around the dancing metal-pronged hooks on both ends of the rowboat.

"Got her secured, no thanks to you. Now get up that ladder." His demand sounds like one coming from a livid pirate.

Without hesitation, Lan leaps onto the rope ladder and begins climbing urgently. My sore and weak biceps pulse to keep the ladder from twisting around as she climbs. Snatching the end of the ladder out of my hands, The Captain barks,

"Now, you. Go!"

Climbing an unsteady rope ladder while trying to keep it balanced is easier said than done. I don't want The Captain to have to keep me from twirling around, nor do I want to have to climb up the backside of the ladder. Every climb is shaky and unsteady, but I finally throw my hands over the top of the large ship as Lan helps me over the edge. I flop onto the deck like a clumsy fish, bringing Lan down with me.

"Well, at least this ship feels a bit safer than being tossed about in that little boat." My words don't lighten the mood as Lan's wobbly legs try to stand. A strong pair of arms cradle her body and help her to her feet.

"Careful, Miss." A handsome young face smiles at Lan from under the hood of a faded grey raincoat.

"Thank you." Lan's coy smile flashes back at him. She allows him to continue caressing her body as he helps her over to sit on a wooden crate nearby.

I can feel every pulse of my blood instantly pump flames of rage and jealousy through my veins, unlike anything I have ever experienced before.

Another large man runs to the side of the ship to help The Captain up over the railing and onto the deck.

"Cap'n, I don't understand why you didn't just send Fin out there to fetch 'em."

"Ya know I'm bound by my oath to Doc to keep his secrets and protect the…" The Captain's eyes shift in my direction with suspicion as he fails to complete his sentence.

"Now, Sharkbait, hoist that rowboat." The Captain points his thick finger to a set of large ropes wrapped around a metal cleat.

"But Cap'n, I don't think his wimpy arms can't hoist that up on his own."

The Captain scoffs with laughter and hisses, "But it will be entertainin' to watch 'im try."

The two men disappear toward the other end of the ship as their bouts of laughter shoot like blades behind them.

I want to prove them wrong. I want to show Lan that I am not weak. I take off the backpack and satchel and set them onto the deck as I dive for the dense, soaked ropes leading up over the edge of the ship. I begin to pant in preparation. Gripping the thick rope with all my might, my fingernails dig into my white palms. I brace my feet attached to my squatted legs to the inside wall of the ship. Gritting my teeth, I let out a boisterous grunt as I force my legs to stand against the ship's wall and strain to pull the weight of the attached rowboat. The rope doesn't budge, but my hands rip like wet tissue paper, leaving a trail of crimson soaking into each braided strand. My rubber boots slip up towards the lip of the boat, sending my rear end crashing against the side of the ship.

Lan and the attractive fellow's distant mumbles and flirtatious giggles fuel the fire raging in my body. Refusing to give up, I wrap the

89

ends of the rope around my waist, then my forearms, and dig my heels back into the side of the ship. As if having a seizure, my body shakes violently, but I am unable to thrust my legs into a standing position. All I have done is tie myself into an unyielding, crouched position. Allowing every tense, straining muscle to relax, I succumb to defeat with great trepidation. I try to swallow down the angry lump forming in my throat.

Don't you dare cry, Dameon!

My demand echoes in my head aimlessly. Despite the welling of emotions, no tears can form; there is nothing but a reservoir of ice in my tear ducts. There is no expulsion of feelings. They are just left to fester within me as my own storm of emotions brews more violently than the stormy weather howling from every direction around me.

Chapter 10

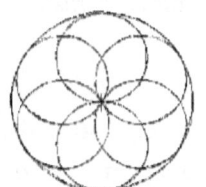

Knots in My Stomach

The pummeling rain and rocking ship make it difficult to get my feet underneath me to stand. A hand reaches down in front of me to help me up. It's him, that guy who was flirting with Lan, while I was made a fool of and left to raise the rowboat on my own. Instead of taking his outstretched hand, I crawl on my shredded hands and knees over to the side of the ship and pull myself to an unsteady standing position. Out of the corner of my eye, I see the young man shake his head at Lan as if to say he tried to help me. I huff an exhale as I wrap my torn hands around the rope, readying myself to pull again.

"You are never going to pull it up on your own like that. It is knotted off and not attached to the pulleys. Here, you take the ends of the rope and wrap it around the capstan." He slips the two knotted ends of the rope off the metal cleat and attaches them to a large wooden horizontal wheel connected to what looks like a giant spool, erecting out from the deck of the ship. Once the ropes are secured on the wheel, he begins pushing the spokes of the wheel and walking it around in a tight circle. I decide to jump in and help him wind the ropes around the spool. The moment he lets go of the wheel for a split second to wipe the rain from his hands, I instantly begin sliding backward in a reverse motion around the spool. With a little laugh, he grabs the wheel again and helps me to push it in the right direction. I can feel Lan just staring at this guy. I can't tell if that is drool or rain dripping down her chin.

He isn't even that good-looking, unless you like the chiseled face, blonde-haired, blue-eyed, surfer, model look. Bleck!

As the lightning flashes, the guy shines a perfect smile in Lan's direction, and I watch as she swoons, or maybe it is just the rocking of the ship. He secures the rope and ties it back onto the metal cleat.

"There we go, all done." He resounds as he slaps my back with great gusto, knocking me back down to my knees. He turns his flawless smile to me, and I feel the bile rise up from my stomach as the acid scorches the back of my throat. It is a good thing I haven't eaten anything in a while, or I would have given him an unwelcome gift all over his rain boots. Instantly noticing the sway of the ship, my head bobs from side to side involuntarily.

"You're looking a bit green. Are you gonna be ok? I've got some medicine below that will help with that. And you, Miss, are soaked to the bone." I watch as he puts his arm around Lan's uncontrollably shaking shoulders.

"Come on, I'll take you below deck to get you dried up."

He leads Lan over to a hatch in the deck floor and swings it open. I can tell it must be heavy, but he makes it look like it weighs nothing. He holds Lan's hands and helps her climb down into the hatch and onto the descending ladder. I stand, struggling to keep my balance, and I cling to the wheel that helped us hoist the rowboat.

"Come on!" he shouts to me over the loud gusts of wind.

My sodden clothes and pointless rain jacket weigh me down to the slippery floorboards. I look over to the edge of the ship to watch a monstrous incoming swell towering toward us. My grip on the wheel tightens as my white knuckles sting from the pelting, freezing rain. There is nothing I can do but watch, frozen, as the wave barrels over the top of us, nearly flipping us horizontally. Gargling through the water and desperately trying to find air, I observe in astonishment as the massive ship launches into the sky like an offering to the Gods as an after-effect of the tsunamic wave. In the sudden lurch upward, my feet slip out from under me, and I slide along the soaked deck like a

92

waterslide. The outstretched hand of the guy near the open hatch grasps me and snaps me down onto the ladder.

"Woohoo, that one was a doozy! I thought it had you there for a second." His laughter is muffled in my waterlogged ears as I snatch my swimming backpack and satchel before they float away. Holding them in one arm, I fumble to escape down the hatch with my other arm. I don't find the situation the least bit comical. The loud thunder above is muted mid-rumble as he closes the hatch and follows me down the ladder. The water from his boots drips down my face. Lan and I are shivering puddles of fear as we take in the living quarters below deck, grateful for the respite from the raging storm.

I watch as the same guy darts to a nearby closet and pulls out two grungy but dry towels and hands them to us. He steps back toward a narrow hallway of doors.

"This one is the head, the one across is the shower. This one is my bunk room. Lan, you can have the bunk room across from mine. Kid, you are welcome to bunk with me, or I can show you the other empty bunk room toward the aft, near The Captain's quarters, but you aren't allowed in The Captain's quarters.

Did he just call me kid? He is only a few years older than me. I'm not a kid!
And I definitely don't want to bunk with him.

"I guess I will take the empty bunk near the… *aft*." I finally respond after weighing my options.

"What's behind that door?" Lan asks, pointing to the door at the end of the hall.

"That's the first mate's, Oscar's, room. Ooof, don't tell him I told you his name is Oscar. He goes by Oz. He seems big and scary, but he isn't so bad if you just stay out of his way."

Noticing the puddle forming around us on the floor, he jumps over to the cupboard where he got the towels and pulls out two pairs of pants and shirts.

"We have some of the old sailor slops here you can put on. At least they are dry and will give you a chance to hang up your clothes for a while to dry them out."

I have no idea what a slop is.
Wait, isn't that something pigs eat?

I run my finger over the dusty canvas pants and yellowing linen shirt, not really knowing where I should go to change because I wasn't paying close attention to his brief verbal tour other than the bunk rooms.

"Thank you," Lan blinks the water dripping down from her hair out of her eyes as she turns into the door that he stated leads to the *head*, which now I see means the toilet.

Not wanting to stay behind, dripping all over this guy, I scurry to lock myself into the tiny shower room. I instantly relieve the weight from my screaming bicep as I hang my saturated backpack and satchel onto a heavy metal hook on the wall. My shoulders reluctantly raise to their normal position as I attempt to rotate and twist out their stiffness. I notice a small cabinet that closes tightly, so I decide to put the dry clothes and towel in there while I turn on the shower. The sound of the rattling pipes behind the wall nearly causes me to jerk the knob back to the off position, but then the showerhead spits out water. The lukewarm water would normally cause me to refuse a shower at home, but it is balmy in comparison to the icy rain and waves I was just bombarded with up on the top deck, so I decide to rinse off quickly. I twist the knob to turn off the water and dry off with great haste. Stepping into the cropped pants feels like stepping into an old scratchy potato sack, and that is about what they look like once they are on, too. The discolored shirt isn't much softer, and it drapes over my thin upper body, but at least it is dry. I wipe the pathetic peeling mirror with my damp towel, wiping the water into streaks instead of drying it off. However, it is enough to see waves of my reflection sneering back at me. My straggly hair flops down into my hazel eyes. I do my best to comb it to the side with my pruney fingers. I take in my mediocre face, and I exhale deeply as I realize why Lan would look at him that way instead of me. Wrapping my drenched clothes up in the towel and unhooking the packs and rain jacket from the hook, I open the small, rounded door and step back out into the tight hallway, which seems even more constricting than before. The guy just gawks at me and then eyes my wad of wet clothes and dripping bags.

"I'll show you to your bunk." He trudges ahead of me through the hall, his shoulders nearly touching both sides at once. Placing a hand on one wall and my full-armed elbow on the other to steady myself, I do my best to follow him as I watch the floor dance in front of me. Unbothered by the swaying ground, he leads me into a dining area, never even flinching or needing to hold on to anything. I clamber my way around the table and row of chairs, using each one for balance, afraid to let go for fear of flying or falling. Once we reach a set of cupboards and lockers, he points to a door that is identical to the ones in the previous hallway.

"There you go. It's been empty for years and has a funky smell, so no telling the shape it's in."

I open the oval door, flip on the light, and watch as roaches scurry and disappear into the cracks. I step into the bunk room carefully, holding onto the door frame. The room is no bigger than a closet, but there is a set of bunks, one on top of the other, and a small cupboard compartment on the wall. On the opposite wall, there are two hooks, so I drag myself over to them and hang the backpack and satchel on one and my dripping clothes and towel on the other.

"I'll go check on Lan." Turning around, he disappears back down the way we came.

They have obviously already introduced themselves to each other and are on a first-name basis.

I slam the small door closed and plop onto the bottom bunk, smacking the back of my head on the frame of the top bunk. Rubbing the base of my throbbing head, I duck it down carefully to lie on the bed, if you can call it that. It reminds me of the board-like cot from my holding cell in the Elementerprise facility. I would almost welcome that cell over this room; at least the air could flow through the bars in there. Here, it is claustrophobic and hard to breathe. The stagnant air trapped inside is dense and leaves the taste of mold, rotting wood, and mothballs unpleasantly on my tongue as I try to squeeze the thick air into my lungs. I strain to focus my eyes on my backpack, swaying back and forth, scraping against the wall. My insides slosh from side to side in a similar manner. Focusing on breathing in the foul air, does little to settle my bubbling stomach or my frayed nerves.

The sound of muted giggles beats against my door, further constricting my lungs. Unable to handle it any longer, I duck my head to stand. The sway of the ship nearly knocks me back down, but I steady myself by holding on to the walls, waiting for the spinning to stop. Although, it never ends. I swing open the door to the shrinking room in hopes that at least a little more air might help. Panting heavily, ready to vomit, I swallow the waves of saliva and stagger out of the room. I slide into a dining chair on the opposite side of the table where Lan and the other guy are sitting much too close together, in my opinion.

"You alright, mate? You look green.

Here, have some of Doc's Ocean Potion."

"It tastes nasty, but it really helps," Lan adds, watching him pour a cupful of green goopy liquid into a medicine cup and hand it to me.

I squint my eyes closed and hold my breath at the fear of seeing or smelling anything gross right now, or I might lose it. I chug it down in one gulp and then let my mouth hang open in hopes of not tasting it, but the bitter barrage of flavors attacks my mouth. Black licorice, citrus, ginger, and a flood of bitter herbs linger through each panting breath.

"Here, eat this. It helps to get the awful taste out of your mouth." Lan cringes as she hands me a dry biscuit that resembles more of a large, thick cracker.

I instantly take a nibble and allow it to soak up any lingering remnant flavors as I swallow hard.

96

"Have some water to wash it down." I hadn't even noticed the guy get up to get me a mug of water. I take a sip and attempt to swallow.

"The Captain calls me Fin. We haven't properly introduced ourselves." He thrusts a strong hand toward me and waits with a smile for me to shake it.

Ugghh, why do you have to be so annoyingly friendly? I really want to just hate you.

"I'm Dameon," I retort, wrapping my arms around my gurgling belly, which I feel is a really good excuse to not have to shake his hand. I watch Lan's eyes roll in disagreement with my childish, unpolite behavior.

He quickly retracts his outstretched hand and picks up the ropes on the table. Then he slides onto the bench close to Lan in one suave motion.

"I'm teaching Lan how to tie different knots. I am sure The Captain is going to expect you guys to help out on the ship in the morning. It might be a good idea for you to learn them. There are only three basic knots you really need to know: the bowline, the clove hitch, and the cleat hitch."

"This is the bowline," Lan exudes with confidence as she twists the rope around itself into a series of loops. She pulls the ends, and all her work unravels back into a single line of rope.

"Well, I'm working on learning it." She lets out an embarrassed giggle.

"Here, you almost had it." Fin reaches over and slowly shows her how to tie the knot again, but Lan is staring at his toned muscles escaping from his too-tight, short-sleeved t-shirt and not the rope at all. The Ocean Potion threatens to make a reappearance, but I take a sip of water and gulp it back down. Fin passes me a small piece of rope and begins explaining each step of the knot to both of us. I do my best to follow each step carefully, but my fumbling hands struggle to keep up.

97

"I did it!" Lan's excitement bubbles over.

"Great. Now, you two keep practicing. I better get back up there and relieve The Captain and Oz at the helm so they can get some sleep."

"Thank you," Lan's smile shoots at Fin. Then, she kicks my shin under the table.

"Ouch, umm, thanks," I add, but it only crosses my lips because Lan's toe jab provoked it.

"You're welcome." He smiles and nods as he climbs up the ladder with ease to the hatch. I am sure his muscles don't actually tighten that much on the climb. He must be flexing them for Lan's enjoyment.

"Ah-hem," I clear my throat, watching Lan's eyes shoot back to me, full of guilt.

"What is wrong with you?" She blurts as soon as he is out of sight.

"What is wrong with me? What about you? Giggling and flirting about."

"Oh, now I get it. You're jealous. He was just being nice and helping us out, and you have been nothing but rude to him in return. Crawling away from him when he was trying to help you up there, refusing to shake his hand."

Her accusations cut deep into my heart, but I can't disagree with her.

"I'm sorry. I don't know what has gotten into me. I'm still trying to process everything.

We almost drowned, my Great Granddad wasn't there, and then the scary captain, and this serpent pirate ship. I'm not sure who we can trust." The words blurt out of my mouth as if they will make my terrible behavior more acceptable.

"It is a lot to take in." Lan's face softens in the glow of the lantern on the wall.

She grabs another biscuit and allows her teeth to crunch through each hard, flaky layer.

"I think I am going to go try and get some sleep," she forces her over-stuffed mouth to stay closed through a yawn, so as not to reveal her half-chewed biscuit. Swallowing, she steals another biscuit and slips it into the pocket of the oversized, potato sack pants, cinched around her small waist.

"Good night." She looks at me and gives a little snicker as she shakes her head, clearly laughing at my display of jealousy this evening.

"Good night." My eyes look down at the floor in shame as I listen to her shuffle down the slender hall and close the door to her bunk room.

I wish that my bunk room, instead of Fin's, was across from hers.

"Be sure to lock your door!" I shout after Lan.
"Already locked," she shouts back through the thin door.
"I'm just at the other end of the ship if you need anything," I holler toward her door again.
"Got it, thanks. Good night," she yells back.

I fumble back to the little bunk room in the opposite direction. I hesitate to close the door, remembering what the room felt like with it shut, so I decide to keep it open. I drop back down on the bottom bunk, careful to duck my head down this time. Sitting here, listening to the creak of the ship and watching as my only belongings sway along the wall, I realize that I am far from home. The thoughts of Jaxson sitting in the hospital bed attached to machines with Mom and possibly Dad at his side make my heart ache.

I wish I had Great Granddad's journals to read right now to keep my mind off being on this ship.

The door to my bunkroom slams from frame to wall, over and over, until it is more than I can handle. I roll off the hard mattress and jump up to slam the door shut while flipping off the light all in one motion. Carefully laying back down on the stone-like bed, I relax my muscles and allow the ship to rock me from side to side; there is no sense fighting the rocking. I strain my ears to drown out the ship's groaning and faint thunder and focus on any noises at the other end of the ship. I refuse to let my heavy eyelids close. I want to make sure Lan is safe.

I hear the wall next to me creak. It must be adjoining a set of stairs or a ladder. The sound of two voices accompanies the shifting weight. The walls inside the ship must not be very thick because I can hear the conversation quite clearly.

"A'ight, Cap'n. Ya told me there is a reason ya let those two drowned rats on board, and ya made me wait until we got below deck and away from Fin to tell me what that was."

"The boy claims to be Doc's Great Grandson. He had two of his journals. If what he says is true, I couldn't leave 'em there to drown. And I can't let these journals get into the wrong hands. If Doc is so protective of his other journals, I'm sure he'd want these ones, too. So, I'm takin' 'em, and the two kids, back to Doc. He can decide what to do with 'em. And don't say a word of this to Fin." The harsh last words of The Captain feel like heavy concrete.

Why wouldn't The Captain want Fin to know about the journals? Doesn't he trust him? The Captain does seem like he is on Great Granddad's side.

My thoughts slosh back and forth in my brain with the swaying of the ship.

Who can I trust?
And how can I get those journals back?

Chapter 11

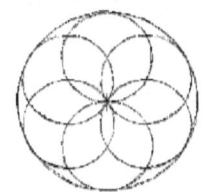

Captain Hurley

*T*he pins and needles in my feet pierce me into groggy wakefulness. My fatigued toes grip the warped floorboards to hold me into place on the hard bunk in their feeble attempt to keep me from rocking back and forth. I attempt to relax my feet and legs, that I didn't even know were tightened all night, but they are solidified into their right-angled position.

> *Why did I sleep sideways on the bed with my feet hanging down?*

I strain my throbbing back and force each vertebra to stack, one on top of the other; arching forward so I don't knock my pounding head on the bunk above me this time. I have never had a drink of alcohol in my life, but I can only imagine this is what it feels like to have a vicious hangover. The moment my head flops forward above my feet, the urge to vomit bubbles up in my stomach like an angry volcano.

> *I think I need more of that Ocean Potion.*

Every tight muscle in my legs screams and feels like they are tearing as I push myself to stand. As if trying to walk while on a roller coaster, my wavering arms scramble to steady my wobbles. Like stepping on shards of glass, my feet revolt into balls of unwilling participants, but I force myself to hobble toward the door of my bunkroom. My fingers fumble around the knob and shakily twist it open. While using my arms to guide me to the table, the sight of the potion inside a slide-proof container on the table sings to me as if it is the holy grail. Snatching the bottle, I do my best to balance while I use both hands to twist off the lid, and I take a desperate swig straight from the bottle. The nauseating flavors burst through my mouth, forcing my face to contort with disparagement. My body instantly begins to sweat, and my breathing intensifies as saliva puddles on the back of my tongue, preparing me for a revisit of the potion.

Air! I need fresh air, now!

Swallowing hard and holding my breath, I dart for the ladder. I scurry as fast as my tight legs will climb, and I force open the overhead hatch. Like a rocket, I shoot out onto the deck of the ship and gulp down the salty air with my head between my legs. Unable to stand for long, I allow myself to drop onto my backside and focus on my breathing and keeping down the potion. Finally, once the wave of queasiness subsides, I allow my scrunched eyes to slit open and take in the encompassing fog swallowing me. Through its viscosity, the obscured dawn smolders beneath the ashen clouds out the back of the ship. Hues of ginger and salmon paint are horizontally drizzled through layers of a grey blurry soot. The sky slowly begins to wake. A distant voice fights its way through the thick air.

"Sleep okay?" The unfortunate, perfect face of Fin wavers into view as his voice corkscrews right through my hammering headache.

Attempting to soften my folded brow, I draw in a long, icy breath through my teeth. Lan's sweet voice telling me to be polite echoes through my head. I force the edges of my mouth upward and nod, causing the world around me to dance dizzyingly.

"Looks like you might need some more Ocean Potion," his annoyingly perfect teeth glimmer through the blanket of greyness.

"I just took some… thanks," I add through my grimace.

As my boiling blood begins to calm, the frigid air bites at me ferociously. I rub my upper arms by reflex as if I can rub out the bitter cold aching my bones.

"You're gonna want a coat. There are some old ones in the closet at the bottom of the ladder."

"I'm fine," my lie chatters through my teeth.

"Alright, suit yourself." I feel his eyes roll through the haze as he bends down to pick up some nearby rope and tosses it to me.

"Practice those knots I showed you last night. I will need your help with the sails as soon as the sun burns off the fog. Looks like we are finally going to get some decent sailing weather today. It's about time." His mutters dwindle in the soupy twilight.

Crawling in the direction of the side of the ship, I decide to pull myself up onto my feet. Swaying with the motion of the ship, my head and body lean from side to side. The waves of thick fog merge with the silver water attacking the sides of the ship. The frothy white caps, like ancient curly hair, are the only things that stand out clearly as I look down into the ocean below. The abundance of grey waters surrounding me floods my mind with the overwhelming task of needing to keep water in the future.

The world needs water to survive in Lan's time. How can I make sure they have some of this water? I know Great Granddad mentioned in his journals that at this time, the Earth's core is cooling and slowing down at a more rapid rate. How can one person warm the core of the Earth back to the correct temperature to sustain a functioning ecosystem and keep the water from eventually evaporating? During this time, there is too much water. It is so difficult to fathom that in the future water will be scarce.

Racking my brain for ideas, I watch as the ocean becomes clearer as the leaden sky forms glints of yellow and reflects the swirls of light. There have only been a handful of times I recall watching the sunrise. Even through the dense clouds and fog, the first light of morning is breathtaking. I try to paint the mural of muted colors constantly changing before my eyes into my memory instead of focusing on the world's impending doom. I welcome the minute warmth on my face from the sun as it fights through the acrimonious frostiness of the biting humid air.

"A'ight Fin, let's take advantage of the perfect wind and get the sails a-blowin'." The unexpected voice of The Captain nearly makes me fall headfirst into the waves.

Gripping onto the side of the ship with white knuckles, I turn my head around to see The Captain emerging through the weakening fog. I watch as Fin unlashes the furthest mast's sail ties. Pulling both ropes, he unties the mainsail. I do recall a little nautical vocabulary, not even sure where I learned it from. Then, as if on a springboard, he jumps into the air, grabs both halyard ropes simultaneously, and allows the weight of his body to bring them down, over and over. I watch as beads of sweat pour down his face, despite the freezing weather. Jumping back and forth from side-to-side, setting both sets of ropes, he looks in my direction, obviously wondering if I am going to help him. I look back to the ocean, trying to pretend I didn't see him looking my way. It is clear to me now how his muscles are so ripped. As the massive sail reaches the top of the mast, he figure-eights one rope at a time, leaning his weight back, setting the sail to perfection. He approaches the foremast as he shouts toward me through profuse panting.

"Come on mate, help me out with the staysail while I fix the jib."

Feeling as though I don't have a choice, I wobble over to him and the ropes, clueless as to what he just said, and unsure of what to do with the mass of ropes in front of me. Watching intently as he checks the ropes, he shows me how to pull down the rope, hand over hand. I take over and pull down the rope as I watch the sail hoist up into a triangle, grateful that this sail doesn't seem to be nearly as heavy as the mainsail. Once it hits the top of the mast, I hesitate and wait for

Fin, because I don't know how to tie it off properly. He finishes working on what he called the jib and jumps back to form two figure eights around the cleat and pulls the rope back through itself to hold it in place.

"We're ready to set sail, Captain." He shouts back toward the helm where the front windows are open wide, revealing The Captain steering the wheel of the ship.

"Fin, you can go get some shuteye. Oz should be up any minute. We're gonna try ta stay ahead of the next storm. With the wind at our backs, and if all goes well, we should be hittin' landfall later tonight."

"Aye, Captain," Fin responds as he heads for the hatch to go below deck.

"Come on up, Sharkbait. I'll show ya how to sail her." The Captain hollers in my direction through the open window.

I scan the deck of the ship, trying to see how to get into what I believe is called the weather helm.

"Port side," The Captain huffs as he points to the left side of the ship. I am glad he points because I couldn't remember if port means the left side or the right side.

Shuffling over to where he is pointing, I see the outline of a small wooden door in a wall of wooden framed windows. Pulling up on the rusted lever, the door swings open, revealing a small set of steep rotting steps. Clutching the metal railing on both sides, I pull myself shakily onto the first step, feeling the step bow beneath me. As the ship sways to the other side, the little door slams shut behind me as I climb the last stair.

"First time on a ship, aye?" The Captain chuckles at my lack of balance as I hold tightly to the wall and scramble to make my way to his side.

"Yes, sir."

"Cap'n!"

"Captain," I correct myself.

"Ain't she a beaut?

Pieced her tagether meself.

Yer in luck today. We're ahead of the next storm. Hopefully, we can use the wind o' the next one to sail us all th'way to shore."

Noticing the violent sway and bouncing of the ship, I struggle to think how it could be worse than this.

"Hold her steady a minute," The Captain gestures for me to take the giant wheel.

I feel the blood drain from my face, and my eyes must have given away my fear because The Captain grabs my quivering hand and places it on the wheel for me as my nerves begin to frazzle.

Wait, what? I don't want to be in charge of this massive ship. What if I flip us over, or make us sink?

As if responding to my worried thoughts, The Captain calmly states,

"Don't worry, just try ta keep her headin' 'way from the risin' sun."

I glance over my shoulder to see the glow of the sun faintly visible through the wall of grey clouds behind us. Gripping the wood of the wheel with both hands, I feel my palms get clammy as The Captain lets go and walks to look out the back windows. In a panic, I check the grey ocean merging with the grey sky ahead of the ship. I turn back again to peek over my shoulder. I watch as The Captain gazes through a wooden sextant, moving it slightly in a back-and-forth motion and checking the measurements. He then peels back his long-sleeved jacket and checks his watch on his hairy wrist. As he points his long, thick finger at a place on the map sitting on the ledge below the back window, he rotates his arm ever so slightly. The glimpse of a tattoo on the underside of his wrist, just below the band of his watch, flashes in my direction. I instantly recognize the symbol engraved upon his leathery, freckled skin. It is the symbol of the perfect ecosystem, exactly as it is depicted in Great Granddad's journal. It is the Seed of Life symbol with the two embedded triangles, one pointing upward and the other downward.

The Captain's tattoo is exactly like the one on the underside of Great Granddad's wrist. I hadn't thought much about it before, but I recall seeing it the first time I met him when he set the tray of tea down, and then again when he handed me his other journal in the observatory right before he…

Suddenly, the door screeches open, and the man I learned last night is named Oz, stomps his way up the few steep steps. His heavily bearded face turns toward The Captain and then toward me. With an audible grunt, he plods his heavy boots over next to mine as he towers over me. I notice the dark tattoos creeping up his neck, out of his hooded jacket, and extending down from the hems of the sleeves, which are too short for his long, trunk-like arms. His dark eyes shoot like lasers down at me and squint with anger. Without saying a word, he reaches his colossal hand and peels my fingers off the wheel. Then, he gives me a shove out of his way, like I weigh nothing. Fumbling awkwardly, I do my best to steady myself against the wall of windows opposite the door.

I let out my breath I didn't know I was holding in, and scuffle my feet closer to The Captain to further myself from Oz. I watch intently as The Captain continues to study the map, which I notice resembles the one on the wall back in Great Granddad's study at the estate. The one where the world is covered in water. The small cabin fills with the grumbles of Oz and the mumbles under The Captain's breath all mixed together with the creaking of the ship.

"So, where are we heading anyway?" I finally gather up the courage to ask The Captain.

"We have one quick stop to make if we have time 'fore the storm, and then we're headin' ta Appalachia," he responds without looking up at me.

"Like the Appalachian Mountains?" My eyebrows shoot up to my forehead.

"Haven't heard anyone call it that in a long time, but ya. Appalachian Mountains/Island, it's all the same place."

The Appalachian Mountains are now an island?

"And we are going to meet up with my Great Granddad there?"
"Doc? Well, that's the plan. I sent 'im a Morse code message ta let him know we're comin', but he hasn't responded yet. Are ya really his Great Grandson?" He finally looks up from the map and into my eyes.
"Yes, si…ummm, Captain," I quickly correct myself so as not to offend him, but I feel Oz's eyes burn into me with my near mistake. He clearly doesn't approve of me.

I secretly wish I could check out The Captain's message for myself. Ever since I learned Morse code at summer camp a few years ago, I have enjoyed decoding messages. It is cool that is how The Captain and Great Granddad converse. But it might be the only way to communicate since I know he stated there were EMPs that destroyed all other means of communication.

"Speaking of my Great Granddad, may I please have the journals back to study them? There is something that I really need to figure out. It is VERY important."
"That is up to Doc. He can choose to give 'em to ya if he wants. My job is to keep 'em safe, and that is what I intend ta do."
I watch Oz's whiskered snarl curl upward into a smirk; clearly, he is not on my side. Something about Oz makes me uneasy.

The prolonged silence grows thicker with each sway of the ship, and it becomes harder to breathe. The urge for fresh air is unbearable and the walls of the small cabin feel like they are closing in tighter with each tilt.

"If you'll excuse me." I bow, ducking my way back down the narrow steps, and I burst out through the small door onto the deck.

The fresh salty air stings my nose, but I welcome it with a large inhale. I stagger up to the front of the ship and watch as the bust of the serpent-haired woman leans her way forward through the low-lying clouds of fog, reaching to envelop us in its grasp. It's hard to imagine that there is land anywhere out there. All I can see, for what seems like forever, is shades of a grey sky bleeding into waves of grey waters. I squeeze my eyes closed to drown out the unfamiliar, dull, muted world, and I lean forward slightly. The spritz of the cold water on my face is piercing, yet refreshing. The sound of the waves lapping against the ship becomes methodically melodious. I inflate my lungs beyond their capacity and allow the wind to wash over me, and I indulge in the simulation of flying. I can't help but allow a smile to spread across my numbing face.

"You look like you're enjoying yourself." Lan's voice carries on the lashing wind, nearly startling me overboard. My hands grip the edge of the ship with greater intensity as I force my head to spin in her direction.

"Lan, you scared me." I attempt to steady my suddenly racing heart.

"I brought you some grits. I think that is what Fin called them."

I can't tell if my stomach is abruptly churning out of hunger, the mentioning of Fin, or the protest of being tossed about on the waves. However, I decide to take the bowl from Lan's hands.

"Thank you." I grin, watching her auburn hair blow behind her as the wind forces her oversized coat and sailing clothes to press against the outline of her body.

I totter over to an overturned crate and sit down, sliding to the furthest edge, making sure there is room for Lan to sit beside me. Delight fills my heart when she does.

"Don't you want some?" I ask Lan, realizing she only brought one bowl containing a single small scoop of white glop.

"I ate with Fin before he went to bed." She shies away ever so slightly, but her sideways glance speaks volumes after mentioning his name with guilt.

"Oh," my cold tone is icier than the frigid wind piercing my cheeks.

I force a spoonful of the lumpy goo into my mouth.

109

I've eaten grits many times, and normally, I like them. But this thick, sticky substance, whatever it is, is NOT grits. With a scrunched face, I stir the gloop around a bit, noticing the disturbing brown specs.

"Ohhhh, Fin says you're lucky if you get weevils, they add protein." She expresses the information in total seriousness. She has no clue how disgusting that is.

I swallow hard, repeatedly, forcing the food down.

"It really does help your stomach to have food in it. You will feel better once you've eaten a bit." She adds, noticing that I am suddenly not feeling well.

I look around for a safe place to set my bowl without it flinging across the deck.

"You don't want it?" Lan stares at the bowl with hungry eyes.

"No, please. Help yourself," handing her the bowl.

Just watching her spoon the gluey sludge into her mouth makes me want to...

I dash over to the edge of the ship just in time for the bite of grits I had to make its reappearance. Instantly, the ostentatious laughter of The Captain and Oz makes my skin prickle and burn from the inside.

"Ha ha ha, livin' up to me name!" The pretentious voice of The Captain, roaring with amusement, floods the air.

To make me even more livid, the stifled giggles of Lan accompany their merriment. I plop back down next to Lan, wiping my mouth, and I allow my fuming glare to bore into her.

"I'm sorry. You have to admit that is a little funny." Her hand jumps to her mouth to hold in another snigger.

"Me getting sick is funny?" I ask, touchier than a septic boil ready to explode.

"The Captain's name is Hurley," she bites her lips to contain the chuckle.

"Fin told me what hurl means."

The comical irony of his name extinguishes the fire in my veins a tad. The more I think about it, the less angry I become. Besides, I can't look at Lan's innocent face and be too upset.

"I guess that is a little funny," I allow a sliver of a smile to form on one side of my cheek.

"How about we go get you some water," she suggests with a smile taking over her face.

I nod and grasp her outstretched hand. We help each other stand and amble like drunken sailors over to the hatch.

Chapter 12

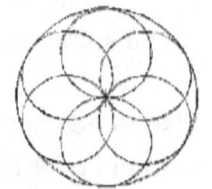

Saved by the Bell

Tottering down the ladder into the main hull, I blink my eyes that feel like they are dried out and on their way to becoming shriveled-up raisins. Blinking out the sting and grit, I crash into one of the wooden chairs at the table as the legs screech along the floor.

"Shhhhhh!" Lan hisses around her finger touching her lips, "Fin is sleeping."

Of course, she cares more about me waking Fin than she does about my throbbing, stubbed toe.

"Here, drink some water," Lan suggests as she hands me a sloshing mug as I plop down onto the bench along the backside of the table.

"He's not so bad you know. You don't have to make that face every time I mention him."

"Who, Fin? I don't make a face."

Lan's eyebrows dart up to the top of her forehead, and her lips purse tightly together.

*Wow, that is the same face Mom makes when she knows
she is right.
Maybe Lan is right. I don't know why I hate Fin so
much.
Perhaps it is the way Lan looks at him.*

"What kind of a name is Fin anyway? Is that his last name, and
is his first name Huckleberry?" My question turns into an
amused chuckle.

Lan's eyebrows jump again, but this time, they include a crease
of confusion just above her perfect little nose.

*Clearly, she has no idea who Huckleberry Finn is, and
once again, she doesn't understand my joke or
reference to literature.*

I sip my water and wallow in the deafening silence, sloshing
back and forth inside the ship.

"We need to come up with a plan to get the journals back.
They are essential for helping us navigate our way here and
figuring out how to retain some of this water for your time."

"We could just ask for them back and explain that we need
them," Lan's innocence beams.

"I already tried that. The Captain said that he will let Great
Granddad decide if he wants to give them to us."

"Well, at least it sounds like we are heading to wherever your
Great Granddad is." Her face is full of hope.

She slides in to sit on the bench next to me. The sway of the ship causes her to slip against my side. Laying her head on my shoulder, she picks up a rope lying on the table. She manipulates it with ease and ties it into a perfect knot.

"Wow, you are getting good at that."

"I've been practicing. Here, I'll show you how to do it. They really are simple once you get the hang of them. These knots aren't much different than the ones Neo uses for climbing."

I can see the longing in Lan's eyes as they glaze over.

Her fingers robotically show me how to maneuver the rope in different ways, but her mind is clearly in the future, thinking about her "family".

"I promise I will get you home to them." I place my hand on hers to ease the trembling.

"I just hope they are okay. I really want to see them again."

"I am sure they are just fine. Come on, let's go look for the journals. I am sure they are in The Captain's cabin, somewhere."

"We can't just go in there and steal them. The Captain will toss us overboard." Lan's head jumps up off my shoulder, ending our idyllic position.

"I didn't say we are going to steal them; just borrow them and look through them while Fin is sleeping, and The Captain and Oz are up sailing the ship."

Shimmying my way out of the bench and table opening, I grasp Lan's hand, and we wobble our way over to The Captain's Quarters sign hanging above an ornately carved wooden door. My eyes swirl and follow each delicately engraved whirl of ocean waves connecting to an angry woman with fearsome six-headed serpents attached to her. The etched door is a true masterpiece of stunning artwork.

"I don't think we should go rummaging around in there." Lan's voice trembles.

"It doesn't seem right."

Ignoring her hesitation, I reach out to twist the rusted, brass metal knob, but it doesn't twist.

"It's locked," I state, running my finger over the skeleton keyhole.

"I could get it open for you, but it depends on what you are looking for."

Fin's voice reverberates off the impressively carved door and causes us to spin around with startlement.

I heard The Captain specifically tell Oz last night not to tell Fin about the journals. I don't understand why he would want to keep them a secret from Fin, but I feel there must be a good reason.

"We were just admiring the beautiful craftsmanship on this door." The lie blurts out of my mouth without hesitation.

Fin's gaze burrows intently into mine.

I think he sees right through my lie.

The piercing sound of a bell echoes through the hull. Fin's eyes dart to the ladder, which leads to the hatch.

"Come on, The Captain needs our help."

Chapter 13

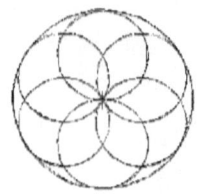

Impending Doom

E merging from the hatch, The Captain's hollering voice instantly barking orders is befuddling. Oz has already lowered all the sails and is heading back to join the shouting captain at the helm.

> "A shoal of squid off the starboard and a shiver of sharks off the port!
> Quick, roll out the harpoon gun!"

My eyes instantly jump to take in the horror of huge shark fins circling just ahead on one side of the ship and massive squid tentacle protuberances on the other. And we are drifting straight ahead toward a smoking, volcanic island.

> "You mean start rolling my death saves now!
> Why are we sailing toward the smoking volcanic island surrounded by sharks and squid?"

"Would you rather go back toward that?" Fin's outstretched arm points toward the ominous dark churning clouds encroaching behind us like a gargantuan demon monster coming to swallow us whole.

> "Seriously, who angered The Dungeon Master?"

"The who?" Fin's face turns red as he strains to lug out a heavy wooden block on wheels that holds a wicked-looking harpoon gun from a closet at the base of the weather helm.

Clearly, he doesn't play Dungeons and Dragons. But if he did, he would see the humor in this dire situation of impending doom in every direction.

"Come on, mate. Give me a hand!"

Lan and I rush over to help Fin surf the deck of the ship while we struggle to get the harpoon gun to the bow. There is a spot along the rail where the base of the gun fits into an interlocking frame. Fin locks the heavy metal chain on both sides to fix the weapon into place. He dashes back to the closet to yank out a large crate. Lan and I scurry over to help him skid it toward the harpoon gun. Fin pulls off the top of the crate and begins attaching the harpoon to the cannon-like weapon. This is unlike anything I have seen before. It appears that the spear is attached to a cannonball at the end of the rod.

"It that a cannonball on the end?" I ask.

"It is a PETN grenade," Fin responds as a look of satisfaction washes over his face.

He aims the harpoon toward the circling sharks.

"Fin! Ya know we shoot up the middle to scare 'em off, not directly at the creatures!
We aren't barbarians!"

"Captain likes me to just scare them off. We could be eating good for months and make loads of money selling all that meat." Fin mumbles as he shoots the harpoon gun straight ahead instead of where the weapon was originally aimed at the beasts. The blast rattles the ship and nearly knocks us off our feet. I stumble to refocus as I watch the swarming waters ahead on both sides of the ship part down the middle, followed by a rippling blast, a large air bubble, and then a small explosion. Water spritzes back into our faces. A puddle of blood expands out from the center of the detonation.

"We got one! I'll get the net. Looks like we will be eating good tonight after all!"

"All ya did was create bait fer more creatures ta come back after the shock waves settle.
Let's hope we've scared some of 'em off long enough for me ta get ta the island.
Fin, attach the charged DD to the dinghy. I don't have much time 'fore the storm reaches us." The Captain announces in our direction as he approaches from the helm.
"Oz, get her as close as ya can to the island, drop anchor, and bring her about. Be ready to sail out if the storm approaches 'fore I get back." The Captain yells up to Oz, who is at the wheel in the weather helm.

"But Cap'n!" Oz shouts back. "Ya sure ya don't want me to go instead?"

"Ya know I'm the only one that can get into the vault, and yer the one that can sail her out of this storm. This is how it has to be."

"Aye," Oz digs around in his pocket, fishes out a gold coin, and tosses it to The Captain through the open helm window.

"Fair winds, Cap'n," Oz shouts as The Captain catches the old, gold coin with moistening eyes.

"I'm not takin' yer lucky coin!"

But Oz just shimmies the window closed on the helm and stares straight ahead of the ship, ignoring The Captain.

"Following seas, mate," The Captain calls back to Oz, kisses the coin, and slips it into his pocket.

The gravity of the dire situation lingers heavily in the darkening salty air.

I turn and watch as Fin climbs down to adhere a small device to the rowboat attached to the ship's side. Upon his return to the ship's deck, he states,

"The dinghy is all set, Captain. Would you like me to assist you to the island?" Fin's hope puffs up inside his chest like a balloon filled with helium. His eyes have been wide since The Captain mentioned a vault.

"Absolutely not! This is my business." The Captain claims as he fixes a handgun onto one side of his belt and a flare gun onto the other side.

"I'll send a flare if I need a rescue. I'm leavin' the dinghy attached ta the long rope so you can help pull me back in faster, so look for me signal. If the storm hits hard 'fore I come back, then cut the rope and set sail without me." The Captain retorts as he scrambles over the ship's edge.

Fin nods with disapproval as he lowers The Captain down into the water.

The livid sharks and squid begin flocking to the area of crimson waters where the detonation occurred as The Captain rows toward their frenzy with gusto.

"How is he going to get through them?" Lan's voice quivers with worry.

Fin throws his arm around her shaking shoulders and states with a smile, "Just wait, the DD will force them away, hopefully." The last bit he mumbles quietly.

119

"What exactly is a DD?" I ask, glaring at Lan since she didn't shudder away from Fin's arm.

"The Deterrent Device sends out sonar and low voltage electricity. The sea creatures hate it, and they usually swim away."

"Usually?" Lan asks as her forehead creases.

"Well, I've only heard about it. I've never actually seen it used. So, I'm assuming it will work. Although, those are the biggest sharks and squid I have ever seen, so let's hope it is powerful enough."

Oz screeches the window back open and hollers,

"Ya landlubbers get ready to drop anchor!"

Fin rolls his eyes and slinks his arm down off Lan's shoulders. He darts aside and grabs a brass telescope from his pocket and hands it to me.

"Watch for The Captain. If he looks like he is in trouble, or if he shoots the flare, pull him back in with the capstan the way I showed you."

Gulping hard, I nod as I grasp the telescope with shaking hands. I am not sure I want to watch the fate of The Captain up close through the lens of the telescope.

"They are swimming away from him." Lan's feet bounce joyously.

I don't have to look through the telescope to witness the fins and tentacles disappearing and creating ripples away from The Captain's little rowboat.

More confident that I can now handle the non-gruesome scene ahead, I stretch out the telescope, close my exposed eye, and use my remaining eye to peer down the long shaft just in time to see an enormous shark jaw readying to clamp down on the side of The Captain's boat.

"SHARK!" I yell with all my might, hoping that The Captain hears my warning.

Fumbling, I look again through the eyepiece to watch as The Captain uses one of his oars to bash the imposing shark's nose. The shark snaps his sharp teeth closed rapidly and barely misses the side of the rowboat. My heartbeat quickens as I watch the shark circle back around to what seems like another go at the intruder. However, instead of attacking The Captain, I watch the shark gobble up the bloody remains of a monstrous squid twice the size of The Captain's boat.

"I see a lot of blood in the water. That isn't The Captain, is it?" Lan buries her head into my shoulder, unable to watch.

"No, it is whatever was left of that massive squid, more like a Kraken. It looks like The Captain is going to make it to the island." I relay in a reassuring voice. "He's almost there. Now, let's just hope that the volcano doesn't erupt."

I pan up to take in the massive mountain resembling outstretched wings. The top looks like the profile of a bird's head with emerging plumes of smoke and ash.

A deep roaring rumble quakes the floorboards of the ship. I am not entirely sure if that was thunder or the angry volcano, but a sudden wave rocks our ship and unsteadies our stance. I quickly gaze back through the telescope to watch as The Captain's little boat bobbles over the large incoming waves and is forced toward the island at a greater speed.

"The anchor is down, and we are set. Did The Captain make it to the island?" Fin rushes back to our side.

"He's almost there," I respond as Fin snatches the telescope from my hand and takes a gander for himself.

"What is he going after anyway? It must be really important if it is worth risking his own life."

"I don't know for sure, but I have an idea of what it might be."

"Treasure? Gold?" I ask, intrigued.

"More like liquid gold." He mumbles as he stares straight ahead with dire intensity and longing.

Lan looks at me and mouths,

"What is liquid gold?"

I just shrug my shoulders. The only thing that I have ever heard being referred to as liquid gold is honey, and I am pretty sure that isn't something he is going after and would keep in a vault on a remote volcanic island.

"The Captain made it to the island and is dragging the boat out of the water.
He is making his way across the beach toward the base of the mountain."
"He isn't going to climb that volcano, is he? He will never make it before the storm hits." Lan's cries echo as the shadow of the sky darkens. Thunder rolls again and vibrates through our souls. We all turn back toward the storm and watch as the rolling ebony clouds flash like a strobe light with lightning.
"We better try to get this ship turned around 'fore it's too late!" Oz's voice is barely audible through the thunder's booming.

"We have to wait as long as we can. We can't leave behind The Captain," Fin shouts back toward Oz. "Or his precious cargo."

Does Fin actually care about The Captain, or just whatever it is that he is fetching?

"Come on, Captain, hurry up." Fin rambles toward the ocean, which is beginning to froth with rage once again as a result of the incoming storm. Fin's fingers wring nervously around the tube of the telescope. "He made it to a cave."

"I'm not so sure going into a cave inside a volcano is a good idea," I warn.

"What is this island anyway?"

"I don't know. It isn't on any of the maps I have ever seen."
Fin blurts as he shakes his head, desperately trying to figure out our location.

He keeps looking at the sun, or the faint light glowing behind the darkened clouds, and then tries measuring, using his fingers to the distance of the horizon in different directions. He walks around aimlessly calculating and muttering various numbers, longitudes and latitudes, and other mumbo-jumbo.

A blinding flash of lightning simultaneously makes its appearance at the exact moment a ship-shattering clap of thunder rumbles us off our feet. Lan and I crawl toward each other and cower together as we watch the darkness swallow the back end of the ship. An incomprehensible curtain of rain inches its way closer and closer. I can feel the spritz of its contents every time a gust of wind rocks the ship. I squeeze Lan tighter and try to steady the uncontrollable rocking of the ship. The howling wind, like ice picks, freezes and screams against our eardrums. The entirety of the storm's full force attacks with rage. There is nothing we can do but flop about on the deck and try to hold onto fixed objects whenever possible. I wrap my arms and legs around the mainmast and sacrifice my death grip for a brief moment to try and catch a barreling Lan as she whizzes past me.

"Hold on! Wrap your arms and legs around the mast like this." I allow Lan to wrap herself around the mast, and then I wrap myself around her as a means of attempting to protect her from the ferocious winds and rocking of the ship. Just when I think the storm can't get any worse, the wall of water attacks us. There was some rain being blown about before, but it was nothing compared to the deluge flooding the deck of the boat now. Between the floodgate waters spewing from the clouds and the massive waves crashing up over the sides of the boat, I can no longer tell from which direction the water is coming.

"No more lallygagging! Let's get her turned around and ready to sail!" Oz's screams are barely audible over the wailing storm.

"The Captain clearly felt that whatever he was after was worth risking his life. We need to wait for him! You and I both owe him our lives, and you know he would never abandon us!" I watch a battle of emotions contort Fin's face as sideways rain pelts against his grief-stricken cheeks.

"I'm not abandonin' The Captain! I'm obeyin' his orders!"

There might be quite a distance between us and Oz in the weather helm, but we can feel the sincere desperation in his voice. Fin wouldn't dare argue with the prevalent respect Oz emits for The Captain. There is a palpable connection between the two older men.

I watch as the blackened sky fills with veins of electricity as if each branch is alive and joins forces to combine and create one giant bolt of lightning. It strikes the main mast with a forceful explosion, much like the blast of light from the time machine. We are all thrown to the deck with great dynamism. The air is pilfered from my lungs, and I am forced to fight the weight of ten elephants to reinflate them. Pain pierces every inch of my body. My hands instantly begin rummaging to make sure every section of anatomy is accounted for after the blast. Squinting the ferocious rain out of my burning eyes, they frantically search for Lan. I sigh with relief, and I am barely able to refrain from laughing as I take in Lan's disheveled appearance and her hair reaching out in all directions in response to the wild static electricity lingering in the air around us. The aching in my body from the initial blow calms and I notice a strange tickle all over my limbs as each strand of hair vibrates and stands guard at the unwelcome current. As soon as I am able, I crawl over the rocking floorboards to Lan's side.

"Are you okay?" My shouts compete with the rumbling thunder.

"I think so." Her words spit out the rain.

I wrap my quaking arms around her quivering body as my eyes follow her searching gaze. They stop their hunt as soon as she sees Fin checking the remains of the splintered mast. My ringing ears try to understand his mumbling. Between the howls of the wind and the deafening thunder, I can barely make out a few words,

"…complete loss! … no use…"

"Get that storm jib up, now! We are turnin' her 'round and getting out of here while we still can." Oz's loud voice booms over the storm's chaos.

"But we need to try and fix the crank on the motor if we want to have any hope of bringing in the anchor and The Captain fast enough."

"NOW!" Oz creates a thunder of his own.

Fin's comment about The Captain forces Lan to escape my embrace and dive for the nearby rolling telescope.

"Sharkbait, start cranking that by hand to bring up the anchor. The motor is shot."

Fin quickly shows me how to crank the wheel around to wind up the rope.

He makes it look so easy.

As soon as I take over, I can instantly feel the weight of the anchor tug back toward the ocean floor. The veins in my arms pulse as I crank with all my might.

"Can't we just fix the motor?" I ask Fin through gritted teeth.

"We don't have time for that, and trust me I have tried."

"Do you have any tools?" I ask as the muscles in my arms feel like they are about to burst through my puckering skin.

Fin dashes over to that same storage closet where he got the crate and parts for the harpoon cannon, grabs a rusty metal box, and slides it my way across the flooded deck of the ship. It pushes a small wave of water to rush over my already-soaked feet and clanks painfully against the side of my foot. In a normal situation, I would have dropped what I was doing and cradled my throbbing foot. Instead, I am forced to gulp down my pain, along with the deluge of water dumping from the sky, and crank with every bit of emotion screaming to explode.

"Fin! The storm jib!"

"Have fun kid. Why don't you fix that one, too, while you're at it?" His long, spindly finger combats the rain and points toward the other nearby capstan and motor clearly attached to The Captain's little rowboat. His laughter of sarcasm feeds my boiling blood as he lunges over to the front mast and immediately springs into the air to raise the storm sail with ease. The moment the sail is raised, the ship changes directions, nearly causing my wet, slippery hands to release the crank. But I am determined to raise the anchor. Lan stumbles over to help me crank when it suddenly stops and refuses to budge any further.

"I think you got it." Her smile flashes brighter than the lightning. "Here, let me tie that off for you." Her hands grasp on top of mine, and a surge of electricity jolts through my body again. I don't want to argue with her, since I know that she is much better with the knots than I am. I can't help but notice how calm and fluidly her fingers tie the large knot around the cleat holding it into place, or how beautiful she is, even with her drenched hair clinging to her wind-scorched cheeks.

"Do you really think you can fix that motor to help bring in The Captain?"

She must have noticed me gawking at her because she seems desperate to find a reason to make me stop.

"What?" I ask, dumbfounded and caught off-guard.

"The motor to help reel in The Captain? Can you fix it?"

Realizing I am wasting precious time, I grab the metal toolbox to see what tools I have to work with. However, it is rusted shut, and I can't get it open. I bash it with my fist, but the only thing that accomplishes is throbbing pain through my hand.

A bone-shattering clap of thunder roars, startling my grip on the wet, heavy box. The moment it crashes to the deck, it bursts open, spilling all its contents into the puddles, growing with each passing second.

"Well, that's one way to get it open." Lan giggles as she fishes through the puddles to help me gather the tools.

Seriously, again? Why do my tools and things always become scattered all over?

I think back to the parts sprinkling the tiled floor on the last day of school and the first time I met Lan as she tossed my satchel on the ground in the tunnels.

Feeling my cheeks burn and ripen, and not from the assailing rain, I drop down to gather the tools back into the box.

"Any sign of The Captain yet?" I attempt to reflect my all too familiar humiliation as I hand Lan the telescope I discover among the dispersed, swimming tools.

Snatching it out of my hand eagerly, she squints through the eyepiece, searching for any sign of The Captain toward the island, now positioned to our rear.

"I don't see him." The worry in her voice motivates my task.

I need to get this motor working if we are going to have any chance at pulling in The Captain fast enough.

Fishing a flathead screwdriver out of the toolbox, I allow the familiar grooves of the acrylic handle to soothe my concerns. My brain zooms in on the motor before me, and the chaotic storm fades away. I use the tip of the screwdriver to pop off the cover to the crank's motor. Relief washes over me, and a smile spreads across my face. The wrinkles on my forehead soften as I am greeted by a familiar friend.

Finally, something I am good at. This is my element.

The thunder shakes around me, but I don't even notice it or the water flooding into my focused eyes. Nothing else exists except me and this machine.

I may not know how to save The Captain or the world, but I know how to fix this motor.

Just replace this with the part that came off here…
Take this off and clean off the rust so it can rotate…
Tighten these bolts…
If only I had some WD40 this would be perfect.

"He's coming! The Captain is coming back!" Lan's exuberance startles my concentration, and the direness of the situation comes flooding back – in a literal wave.

An enormous surge of water cascades over the side of the ship, nearly tipping us over.

Stumbling to secure my footing, I stand ready to crank the mended motor as Lan relays the play-by-play of The Captain's progress.

"He's carrying something, but I can't tell what it is. He's being chased by… something ferocious with big teeth! Get ready to pull him in!" Lan shouts at me as she looks in my direction. I give her a thumbs-up to signal the motor is fixed, and I am ready.

"Pull! Pull!" He's in his boat. Oh!" Lan cringes and nearly drops the telescope.

"Get him in now, or that thing is going to eat him!"

I crank the engine over and over and pray that it starts working.

I watch as Lan impatiently grabs the rope attached to The Captain's boat and begins pulling it back in on her own, without the help of the motor.

With a sputter, the engine begins rumbling and turning the wheel, rapidly winding in the rope attached to what I hope is still The Captain.

As the rope quickly glides through Lan's hands, she fumbles the telescope back up to her eye.

I wade through the water on the deck to her side, trying to catch a glimpse of The Captain for myself.

"You did it!" She exclaims, planting a kiss on my cheek. I feel my cheeks flush once again and not from the battering wind and rain.

"Wait, you actually got that thing working?" Fin interrupts our *moment*.

"We've all tried everything to fix it numerous times."

"He's a genius." Lan's golden eyes bat at me.

"Well, let's hope it keeps working because there isn't much left of the dinghy and The Captain has company." He relays after snagging the telescope from Lan's fingers and taking a closer look for himself.

"And it looks like he got what he was after." A devilish smirk creeps across his face.

"Woohoo, we got him!" Fin whoops toward Oz in the weather helm.

I watch Oz through the veins of the cracked glass as he jolts his head around and pumps his fist triumphantly.

"Can't you shoot that big thing into the water again to get those creatures away from the Captain?" Lan asks Fin as her eyes fill with fear.

"I can't risk harming the cargo… or The Captain," he responds.

"You make sure that engine keeps reeling him in. I'm going to climb down to help get them back up here to safety."

Get what back up here? The Captain, or whatever he is holding?

I watch as Fin leaps over the edge of the ship and monkeys his way down the rope ladder.

130

"Why is Fin so concerned about whatever The Captain just retrieved? He seems to care more about it than The Captain. Did you notice that as soon as he saw The Captain had it, he has had hungry eyes and sudden motivation?"

Lan's eyebrows narrow toward her nose. I can see she wants to disagree with my suspicion, but she, too, has noticed Fin's sudden curious interest.

I run to the edge of the ship and peer down to where Fin is struggling to retrieve an odd metal box from The Captain's exhausted grasp. With the box secured safely under Fin's arm, he then struggles to help The Captain onto the rope ladder and out of the swarming waters. Fin's face is beaming, and it is clear it isn't because of The Captain's rescue.

There is something important in that box, and I am going to find out what it is!

Chapter 14

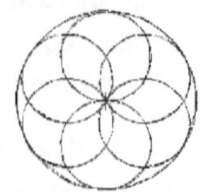

Out of the Storm

The Captain sloshes over the edge of the ship like a waterlogged ragdoll.

"Give... me... that...box." Huffs and puffs The Captain as pure exhaustion narrows his eyes to slits.

Fin, clearly trying to get the box open quickly to sneak a peek, asks, "What is in here that is so important? Is it the..."

"Give it here!" The Captain's sudden boisterous surge makes us all step back as he snatches the metal box from Fin. The Captain cradles it in his arms and strokes every detail with his drenched gloved finger.

"It's impossible for you to open it even if you tried." The Captain wheezes.

The box is clearly some sort of metal puzzle box covered with gears, mechanisms, and endless symbolic etchings. It doesn't even look like there is a seam where it can open. My heart yearns to attempt what The Captain says is impossible.

Fin, go take the wheel and tell Oz to meet me in my cabin. Follow the faint glow of the sun until we reach Port Richmond.

Fin is reluctant to follow orders but knows that he can't argue with The Captain.

"Aye, Captain," Fin's eyes stay fixed on the metal box as long as they can, then roll in displeasure as his boots clomp loudly all the way to the weather helm.

"I take it you are the one that got that motor working to pull me in?"

I nod with a proud smile.

"Perhaps you are Doc's great-grandson after all.

Thank you."

"Anytime, Captain."

"Welp, you two can cut the dinghy loose. It's no good to us anymore. Nothin' but a few boards left. Then ya can bail some of this water 'n swab this deck once we get ahead of this storm."

And The Captain is back to himself. He seemed quite grateful and generous for a split second there until the gruffness took over.

Lan and I help him to his feet. Pulling his arm up is like squeezing a giant sponge. He sloshes to the staircase under the weather helm. I hold the door open for him as he staggers his way down the creaking steps.

Lan and I wobble back over to the edge of the ship and gaze down at the destroyed remains of the rowboat, bobbing violently in wild waves.

"I can't believe he made it back alive." Lan expresses with a slight head shake in disbelief.

"Did you see that box? What do you think is in it? The symbols that were on it. They are the same ones from Great Granddad's journals and the fireplace. I know that is his box."

"Don't even think about stealing that from The Captain. He would dump us overboard, and I don't exactly want to meet those… swimming creatures up close. Did you see those teeth?" Her face grimaces, and she snarls her teeth with fierce mimicry.

"They are sharks and giant squid," I inform as I grab a saw from the rusted toolbox.

"They are what my nightmares will consist of for the rest of my life." Lan corrects.

I saw the rope as far down as I can reach without falling overboard, trying to save as much of our rope as possible. Lan and I work to wrap the remaining rope around the wheel of the crank.

"That was pretty amazing that you were able to fix the motor in time. Do you think you can fix the one for the anchor for them, too?"

"Oh, ya. Good idea. It looks like it is the same type of motor."

As I pop off the cover of the engine, I realize I am correct. It is a larger replica of the one I just fixed.

"Yep, no problem."

"Where did you learn how to fix things?" Lan questions as she squats down next to me to get a better look at the machine and what I am doing to fix it.

"You know, I am not really sure. I have been taking things apart and putting them back together for as long as I can remember. My Mom learned pretty quickly that she couldn't buy me any basic toy that required batteries because I would have it taken apart and figured out before she could tell me no. When most little kids asked for scooters or video games, I begged for little motors and parts to build my own robots and inventions."

"You are brilliant, just like your Great Granddad."

"I wouldn't go that far. He invented things that change the world. I just make junk."

"It's not junk to me." Lan's warm eyes brighten with a hint of glow from the sunlight trying to push its way through the blanket of grey clouds.

I force myself to focus on my task of the engine in front of me, grateful that the rain has slowed down a bit so I can better see what I am doing.

"There, that should do it." I express, wiping my greasy hands on my soaked pants.

"Stellar!" Lan grins.

"Hey, come hold the wheel steady while I fix the Foresail. It will give us a little more speed to try and stay ahead of the weather." I hear Fin shout through the window of the weather helm.

"You want to come help me steer the ship?" I ask Lan.

"Uh, sure. Do you think this is a good idea?"

"Come on," I grab Lan's hand and pull her toward the little door that leads up the steep stairs.

"How much longer until we reach land?" I instantly ask Fin as soon as we enter the helm.

"If my calculations are correct, we should be there in a couple of hours if I can get the Foresail right. Just hold her steady and head for the sun and we just might make it before nightfall."

I wrap both my hands around the large wheel as Fin darts down to the front mast. Obviously, the mainmast is no longer useful after getting struck by lightning.

"So where are we going?" Lan asks as confusion paints wrinkles on her forehead as she attempts to make sense of the maps piled on the tabletop.

"Appalachia. At least that is what The Captain called it. It used to be a mountain range in my time, but I guess now it is more of an island. I remember reading in my Great Granddad's journal how he stated that at this time only certain elevations are above water. That would mean that most major cities all over the world are all gone. Seoul, Beijing, London, Berlin, Washington DC, New York… all washed away."

The realization of the peril of the world poisons my senses.

How can they all be gone? Did the people have time to escape and move to higher ground? Who is in power now? I know that I read about a World War taking place, but where? What are we going to find if or when we do get to land?

I watch as Lan's eyes search the maps, attempting to find the whereabouts of any of the aforementioned cities. She can sense my concern.

"I'm sure it will all be fine. We will find my Great Granddad and he can explain everything. Then, together, we can figure out how to help the Earth heal and keep some of this water."

She knows as well as I do that I can't promise any of that.

As Fin raises a larger sail, I feel the wind instantly propel us forward with great haste. I look over my shoulder and watch as the darkened, angry sky pushes further behind us. Ahead, the skies are still grey, but much more friendly than that monster we are fleeing.

Chapter 15

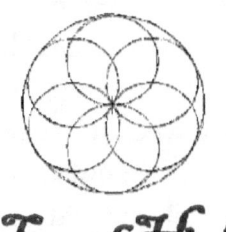

Land Ho!

"*L*and ho!" Fin shouts as his feet jaunt into the air with excitement.

Lan and I must have dozed off huddled together in the weather helm after Fin came back up to take over at the wheel. We jump to our feet to see for ourselves as our stiff salty sailing clothes crackle in protest.

Sure enough, in the distance, I can see where the sun is lowering toward what looks like a thin strip of land on the horizon.

"I've never been so excited to see land in all my life." Lan's feeling of desperation to get off this ship is mutual.

"I can't agree more."

"How are we going to get from the ship to the land? We don't have that little boat anymore. We don't have to swim, do we?" Lan gulps.

"I'll try to get us as close as possible. But it gets shallow pretty quickly. Maybe we'll get lucky, and we can flag someone down to come to fetch us. But that is going to cost a pretty penny." Fin answers. "The Captain is pretty respected around here, so I imagine someone owes him a favor or two."

"Right ya are," The Captain retorts as he hobbles his way up the stairs.

"I've already sent a message to Soarin. He'll take the three of ya to land on his boat.

Then, Fin, you may escort these two to the train station. I have made arrangements for the three of ya to take the train to White

Sulphur Springs. Then, you may take 'em to the woods just outside the West Gate of The Greenbrier, or E-Springs I s'pose they call it now. That's where Dr. Gardener will meet ya. I'll make this journey worth yer time Fin, if ya meet us back at Port Richmond in one week. If ya aren't back in time, we'll be leavin' without ya. That should hopefully give us enough time ta get our mainmast replaced and get her ready ta sail again."

"Aye, Cap'n. And the box? Will you need me to take that to Dr. Gardener as well?"

"You won't be touchin' that box, ya hear?" The intensity in The Captain's eyes bore into Fin's disappointed face.

"Aye, Captain." Those are the words that exit his lips, but I don't believe he means them.

"Now, go get changed and get yer things together. Ya look like a coupl'a drowned rats."

"Aye, Captain," I respond, taking Lan by the hand and leading her out of the helm.

Walking along the deck of the ship is much easier now with the calmer waters. Fin follows us to the hatch and holds it open for us to climb down the ladder.

"Lan, you are welcome to shower first if you would like."

"That would be wonderful, thank you." I watch as Lan enters her cabin and grabs her clothes (well, I suppose they were really Great Granddad's clothes) hanging on the hook, and shakes the crustiness out of them. She smiles at both of us, watching her as she locks herself into the little room with the shower.

"I guess you can go next." Fin offers to me in a rough voice.

"Thanks… for agreeing to take us to meet my Great Granddad."

"Don't really have much of a choice, now do I?" He bumps past my shoulder, stomps into his cabin, and slams the door shut behind him.

> *Okay then. He is clearly not thrilled about having to escort us.*

Can I trust him to take us to Great Granddad?
I'm not sure if it is the sloshing inside my stomach,
hunger, or my gut intuition, but something doesn't feel
right about this plan.

Lan's gentle hums in the shower calm my nerves, and I lean against the mellow rocking wall in the hallway and listen with a smile growing on my face. The rattle of the pipes, indicating that she turned off the shower, causes me to jump off the wall and dart down the hall to my own cabin. I don't want her to know I was just standing there listening to her humming.

I grab my backpack and satchel off the hook on the wall and check inside them to make sure all the tools, supplies, and food are still accounted for because I'm not sure if I can trust the crew on this ship. Once satisfied, I set them on my bunk. Then, I grab Great Granddad's clothes that I had on when we first got on the ship from off the hook. Like Lan, I give them a snapping wave to help work out the stiffness. Little sparkles of salt crystals jump off the clothes in all directions. I drape them, and the towel I used from my first shower, over my arm and head back down the hall.

Lan opens the door just as I approach it.

"Oh, hey." Lan's fingers on her left hand are struggling to comb through knots and tangles in her dripping waves of hair.

"I wish I had a brush. That wind was brutal."

Before I have a chance to respond, Fin opens his bunk room door, hands Lan a comb, and slams his door shut again.

"Ummm, thank you," Lan says to the already closed door in her face.

She points to his door and gives me the look of *what's wrong with him?*

I shrug my shoulders and shake my head in response.

I side-step into the shower room and close the door gently as Lan does the same to her bunk room door.

After a quick shower, I struggle to pull on my clothes since I am trying to hurry, and I haven't dried myself off completely. I grab the rain and saltwater-drenched slops wadded up on the floor and scurry out the door. Hanging the wet sailing clothes and towel up onto the hook in my bunk room, I hear The Captain's voice near my door.

"Sharkbait, I need to see ya in me quarters. Bring yer bag with ya."

Okay. Am I in trouble? Is he throwing me overboard here and making me swim to shore?

I can't control the trembles as my hand grabs my backpack from the bed. I follow the exhausted staggers of The Captain. I watch as he pulls a set of skeleton keys out of his pocket and carefully unlocks the small brass knob of the picturesque carved door. With the key in the keyhole, The Captain swivels the carved head of one of the sea creatures, revealing a wooden button. Pressing it with his gloved finger, I instantly hear clicking, metal grinding, and levers releasing. The Captain's eyebrows dance on his forehead.

"Pretty neat door, aye? Yer Great Granddad designed it and rigged the various locking mechanisms inside it fer me."

The Captain steps into his cabin and points to a page tacked to the wall depicting Great Granddad's design of the immaculate door drawn out on a piece of paper. It looks like it was straight from one of his journals.

The Captain's door

"Oz Carved the image of Scylla for me on the front of the door and worked with your Great Granddad to make the locks work with the art. They're both incredible men."

I am in awe of the brilliant door, but I still feel my nerves crawling under my skin. I am unsure why The Captain needs to speak with me privately in his quarters.

"Come on in and close the door behind ya."

I gulp hard and follow his orders but stay plastered against the backside of the door as far away from The Captain as I can get.

"Have ya ever seen one of these?" The Captain refers to an odd machine with dials and gauges sitting on the built-in desk.

"No, Captain." I squeak.

"Quite a fascinating machine. After Russia's devastating EMP bombs, which fried all our computer systems, I didn't think I'd be able to communicate while out here on me ship ever again until yer Great Granddad rigged this machine fer me. It's called a TARF – a Translational Acoustic RF communicator. It picks up sonar underwater waves and vibrations and puts 'em into binary code, and then it translates the message here." He points to a small screen that has words written in a series of lines and dashes, much like on the screen of a calculator.

Morse Code!
What I wouldn't give right now to take that machine apart and see how it works!

"Anyway, I received a message from your Great Granddad. He said I need ta give ya a Print Chip."

Please, not another chip.

I reach my hand up to feel the small sliver in the back of my neck where I received a chip at the Elementerprise facility in Lan's time.

"There are only a few people in the world with a special coded Print Chip. We are an elite group of people workin' together ta save the world. We're a secret troupe called The Society of Sustainability, The SOSs. There are so many secrets ya wouldn't understand, places only members of the SOS have seen, and dangerous tasks that must be completed ta secure the survival of our planet and the human race. Apparently, ya are who ya say ya are, and yer Great Granddad believes yer special enough ta join our society. Personally, Sharkbait, I think yer too young and naïve to understand what's at stake here. But The Great Doctor Gardener disagrees with me, and he is in charge, so I will respect the task he has given me.
I'll need yer finger."

Hold up, is he taking my entire finger?
Like chopping the whole thing off?

My heart begins to pump wildly as I watch The Captain peel off his drenched gloves. The small tattoo of the fully-functioning ecosystem flashes from the inside of his wrist.

"I have a Printed Chip on me fingertip as well, but ya can't see it. No one knows it's there. But I must always keep it protected. It serves as a key ta enter top-secret places. The Print Chip embeds itself into yer unique fingerprint. It has electronic DNA codes that mix on a molecular level with yer DNA. As far as I know, you're the eighth person currently living, to receive this Print Chip.

Aye, The EIGHTH! Wait, do ya understand the magnitude of this moment? The number eight signifies resurrection, regeneration, and eternity in numerology, astrology, and in The Bible. The Aeonic prophesies have foretold of the eighth member of our society. You're the eighth member. Since the beginning of time, there has never been an eighth living member. Yer the higher being that is said to save us all, who will give us a new beginnin'. Yer The Final Aeon!

143

The Final Aeon? I remember learning about Aeons in History. Does this mean that we are entering the final Eon in time – like we are doomed beyond that, or that I am an Aeon - a 'spiritual being' that will save the final Eon?

Why are people always putting pressure on me to save the world?

Maybe I am just the final person to be named Eon.

Yeah, let's just go with that one. It seems like a lot less pressure.

The Captain grabs my finger and places it in a small device, much like a finger Oximeter they use at the doctor's office to check your pulse and oxygen. I feel a warm sensation and pulsing along the pad of my fingertip, followed by multiple pinpricks all at once. A green light beeps its completion, but the burning sensation spreads down my finger and through my palm, followed by an uncontrollable fire surging in my wrist. I want to scream out in protest, but I remain brave in front of The Captain, watching the process with great anticipation. I cradle my scorching hand in the palm of my other hand and watch as a small red-hot tattoo burns its way into my skin above the pulsing tree of veins on my wrist. The burn marks are identical to the fully-functioning ecosystem symbol on The Captain's wrist, and the one on my Great Granddad's wrist, except mine continues to extend into a deepened outline of two sideways circles, creating a prominent infinity symbol over-laying the ecosystem symbol.

The Captain gasps.

"I guess it is official then, ya truly are The Final Aeon sent ta save the world. Our Great Prophet 'n leader."

The Captain slowly and painfully drops to his knees to a kneeling position and bows his head in respect to me - a gadget-tinkering nerd, essentially a nobody according to everyone back at my school.

"Wait, what? Trust me, I am not a prophet or a leader, The Last Aeon, or anyone important. Get up." I grab The Captain's arms and help him grunt up to his feet.

"I assure ya; this is a significant moment in time. There should've been a great ceremony in yer honor, a feast, or celebration. I hope ya can forgive me for this meager location and pathetic bestowal of yer new role. If I had known who ya were, I would have prepared something more elaborate and waited for the opportune time for the sacred revelation. But we don't have time for that now. Yer Great Granddad simply told me to give you a Print Chip and have ya take him this box as soon as possible."

I watch as The Captain shuffles quickly to pick up the metal box he retrieved from the island and hands it to me gingerly as if it is made of eggshells.

"Whatever ya do, ya must not let this fall into the wrong hands. Ya may only give it to yer Great Granddad, or keep it safe at all costs. Do ya understand? Those are the ONLY two options."

"What is in it?" I ask, trying to understand the complexity of the locked box protecting its contents.

"Honestly, I don't know. I have been protecting it fer years in the secret vault of the cave on Thunderbird Island, and now I've been instructed to give it to ya to deliver to yer Great Granddad. All I know is it's vital ta the world's survival."

I slip the metal box carefully into my backpack. The box doesn't weigh too much physically, especially because it is made out of some type of lightweight metal, but the mental weight that it bears is far heavier.

The Captain opens a drawer in his desk, and he pulls out the plastic container protecting Great Granddad's two journals. He then proceeds to hand them to me.

"I suppose these do belong to ya." The Captain states.

I slip them into my backpack as well, and I am barely able to squeeze the buckle closed.

145

Below where the journals once sat in the drawer is a small pile of black leather gloves. He hands me a pair.

"Sorry, they may be a bit big, but ya need to keep that tattoo covered. No one must know of it. Yer life, and our future, depend on its concealment. No one, not even that las, may know about it, or what it stands for. Promise me!"

"Aye, Captain." I nod, slipping my newly Print Chipped finger into the finger hole of the leather gloves and securing the bottom of the large glove over my still-tingling tattoo to hide it away.

I don't want Lan to see it anyway. It's odd that two minutes ago, my skin was clean, and now it is marked, forever. What would Lan think about me having a tattoo? Would she think less of me? Oh no! What will Mom and Dad say?
That is if I can get back to Mom and Dad.

"Make sure ya get some coats for you and the las out of the coat closet. It's freez'n out there. Feel free to take some biscuits or anything else ya want ta take, too.
Don't talk to anyone on your journey. Don't state where yer goin' or anythin' 'bout headin' ta Greenbrier – I guess the youngins call it E-Springs now since Elementerprise took it over, or your mission of deliverin' the box to yer Great Granddad. Don't let anyone know 'bout that box! Nothin', ya hear? Don't trust anyone! If ya run into trouble, ya can use this map to know of a safe place ta run. Follow the river northwest." The Captain hands me a worn piece of folded leather. "But ya won't be needin' it, I hope. Just keep yer head down, sneak off the train at White Sulphur Springs Station, and Fin will show ya how to sneak down to the West Gate at Greenbrier – E-Springs. That is where yer Great Granddad will be waitin' fer ya. He'll give ya instructions from there. Got it?"

"Yes, Captain," I respond, tucking the folded piece of leather into the front pouch of my backpack.

"Take this." The Captain says, handing me a Glock 19 from his drawer. The cold metal in my hand sends shivers of memories down my arm. It takes me back to holding the laser gun and firing it at the Elementerprise facility, and in the tunnels with the Cole bugs.

I force the gun into the front of my overflowing backpack.

"Now hurry up, Soarin is probably already waitin' to take ya to land."

"Thank you, Captain." I force a worried smile.

"Yer part of the SOS now. Thank ya fer yer willingness to help the cause, and savin' the world." I watch as a tear of honor forms in the corner of his eye, like he is witnessing history, as he bows his head in my direction.

Unsure of what to do, I bow my head in return. Suddenly noticing every creak of the ship, and the waves lapping against us, the room seems to shrink in size, and I feel it is lacking in oxygen. I turn and fumble the brass knob, bursting out of The Captain's quarters. I rush over to the dining table area. Lan is sitting at the table, impatiently tying knots, or at least pretending to be tying.

"What was all that about? You've been in there forever."

"Oh, I just... The Captain told me about ... our mission."

> *Ughhhh, I am so bad at lying. How am I supposed to keep all this from Lan?*

Lan's golden eyes squint with suspicion as she stares at my new pair of black leather gloves.

> *Great, she already knows I'm not telling her the whole truth.*

"Come on. Soarin is most likely waiting on us." Fin interrupts. His voice is full of fury.

"The Captain said we could use some coats."

"Yah, alright." He tromps over to the coat closet near my bunk room, grabs two coats off their hangers, and tosses them to me and Lan. He then proceeds to put one around his own shoulders.

"Alright, let's go."

"He said we could take some biscuits, too," I add.

Fin rolls his eyes, grabs a package of biscuits from a kitchen cupboard, and chucks them at me. I fumble to catch them, but I realize that I can't possibly fit them into my bulging backpack without disclosing to either of them that I am hiding the metal box, the journals, and a gun inside my backpack as well.

"Ready now?" Fin asks with a mocking tone.

I hold up one finger and run down the hallway to get my satchel. I stuff the package of biscuits inside. I dart back to grab Lan by the hand and help her scoot out from the booth bench behind the table.

"Now, let's go find my Great Granddad."

We scurry up the ladder and climb through the hatch to the deck. The salty air whips strongly against us. The sun has recently set, leaving a faint glow of light remaining in the darkening sky.

"Wow!" Lan's face beams. "Look at that!"

I lift my head and take in the breathtaking colors dancing over the water and land like ethereal clouds of animated smoke.

"How is that happening? Is it magic?" Lan gasps.

"Auroras?" I question. "But how are they here? Where are we?"

I want to pull out the map The Captain just gave me, but I don't want to risk Fin seeing the metal puzzle box. I think back to the map from Great Granddad's journal and from the wall of his study and try to recall what I read.

I know that Great Granddad wrote that the poles are shifting, and the continental plates are drifting as well. Which I suppose would allow for auroras to form closer to wherever our current location may be.

"It's the most beautiful thing I have ever seen." Lan expresses with amazement.

"Come on, Soarin is here. Climb down into his boat so we can

get ashore quickly." Fin ushers us over to the rope ladder draped over the edge of the ship.

Once situated on the little benches of the bobbing boat, Fin and the man they call Soarin paddle us toward the approaching line of docked boats. I pull Lan in close to keep her warm. Our billowing breath swirls harmoniously into the bright greens and vibrant teals, blushed with hues of rosy pink and dazzling purple. What lies ahead, I'm not sure, but with Lan by my side, the journals and puzzle box secured in my backpack, and the multi-hued rainbow of light dancing around us, it bathes us in colorful hope for this one perfect moment.

Chapter 16

The Howling

oarin never says a word. He just stares at my face as if trying to figure out why The Captain asked him to come and fetch us and take us ashore. His eyes, half squinting, bore into my soul. I try to focus on the colorful dancing light show instead of his interrogating glare.

"How far is the train station once we get to land?" My words break the obstinate silence.

"Just a couple of miles. But we will have to run for our lives if we want to get on that train before The Howling."

"What is The Howling?" Lan asks. Her voice quivers with fear.

"The Howling begins when the sun sets, and the hungry animals begin their hunt. That is why the curfew exists. It is for the safety of the people. Is the land you came from not swarming with animals?" Fin's eyes narrow with curiosity. "Don't you have The Howling and a curfew where you are from?"

Lan's head shakes slowly from side to side as her eyes widen with horror. Her fingernails dig into my arm even though they are pulled into the sleeves of the oversized wool sailor's coat.

"The government told us all lands are overpopulated with animals since the invasion of water. The animals all had to move to higher ground as the water grew, causing them to condense and over-populate the much smaller land areas. I'm not sure how they seem to withstand the radiation poisoning better than humans, but they do." Fin's teeth chatter. "It's like it makes them stronger as we grow weaker."

"Where are you two from?" Soarin drills us with great suspicion.

Lan and I look at each other and search to find a reasonable explanation for where we come from.

"Far from here." I finally divulge. It isn't a lie.

"And it isn't crawling with animals?" Fin questions with a suspicious stare.

Lan shakes her head again, thankfully.

"Diseases?" Soarin asks.

"We have deadly diseases," I reply, trying to not sound like we are from a completely different time.

Soarin and Fin slide as far away from us as they can possibly get in a tiny boat.

"I mean, we don't personally have deadly diseases, but there are diseases where we come from."

A blast of arctic wind carries a flurry of flakes that dust Lan's hair. However, they seem to linger and not melt as they gently fall onto her wind-kissed cheeks. I reach my hand up to gingerly brush off the flakes, trapping one between my gloved fingers. Upon rubbing my thumb and fingers together, I watch as the flakes turn to an ashy powder, leaving a pale, grey film behind. These are not flakes of laced ice as I expected.

"Is this ash?" I ask.

"Let me guess, your land isn't plagued with fires and volcanoes either? Remind me to follow you home when you go." Fin suggests.

Soarin's glowering glare compounds in my direction.

Luckily, our little boat bumps against the side of a worn, makeshift dock. There are two other boats tethered to the same nailed-together row of boards. Fin leaps out of the boat, and Soarin tosses him a line. I watch as Fin pulls us tightly against the dock and secures the rope to a cleat. He offers his hand to Lan and helps her step up onto the dipping, floating wood.

"Thank you for the ride." Lan smiles back at Soarin.

"My pleasure, Ma'am.

Here are your train tickets.

Now, let's hope we can all make it to our destinations before it is too late."

Putting the tickets into my coat pocket, I nearly tumble into the water trying to step safely onto the dock, with no help from Fin. Trying to balance with a heavy backpack on my back and my satchel around my chest is not easy.

Once Fin steps from the dock onto the land he takes off running toward a row of worn shops. I have no choice but to scramble as quickly as my frozen legs will pump to try to keep up with him. Lan begins to follow behind Fin's sprint. I take her by the hand and try to help pull her along. Or perhaps she is the one pulling me along. Either way, the bitterness of the evening air burns the back of my throat and the inside of my nose. I'm not sure how long I can keep running at this pace, and my body screams at me to stop and rest. However, I do my best to make my strides match Lan's as I struggle to keep up with Fin.

> *Man, I wish I was in better shape right now.*
> *Perhaps I need to take up running.*
> *What am I thinking? Why would anyone in their right mind run like this unless their life depended on it?*

Gasping for air, I feel as though I am back in Lan's time, struggling to breathe through an inadequate oxygen mask. My thoughts wander to Jaxson, and I use him as motivation to keep running.

> *I need to keep running.*
> *I need to get to Great Granddad and find out how I can help Jaxson and the world.*

We run along the edge of a line of trees to what I can only imagine is the edge of a forest. With my head jostling up and down with each gait, I try to look deeper between the rows of trees at my side.

Are there tons of animals in there watching us run, waiting to pounce and eat us?

As if in response to my thoughts, a not-so-distant howl pierces the freezing night air and strikes adrenaline in my body. Lan's grip on my gloved hand tightens as we both have a sudden motivation to sprint faster. My heart beats wildly.

Why do we have to be running so close to the woods?

Fin looks over his shoulder in our direction and shouts, "Come on, hurry up!"

Another howl, this time closer, vibrates against my burning bones and muscles.

Then, there is an entire chorus of lamentations. I'm sure I could throw a rock and hit the animals creating the horrific wails just inside the barrier of trees. Fin screeches to a halt, causing a cloud of frozen snow to rise around him. Lan and I nearly barrel into him, but he raises both arms and stops our skidding feet.

"Shhhhh. We're too late. They already found us."

Our eyes scan the dark woods to the side of us, and I hear the faint snap of a twig. Lan jerks closer to my body, trembling with dread. I try to hold my breath, but it pumps heavily from running in uncontrollable puffs of white smoke against the darkening night. The faint glow of lights from the sailing town is the only solace of light we have. All our heads jump simultaneously toward the direction of movement in a bramble of bushes just in front of us. We watch helplessly as a creature's eyes catch the light and stare in our direction as it stalks slowly closer, one paw at a time. Our only options are to run back in the direction we just came, or to turn and flee into the woods – and those previous deafening howls tell me that is not the option we want to choose. The path in front of us is now blocked by the creeping eyes getting closer and closer.

"Why aren't we running back to the docks?" I pant.

"It's too late," Fin states, clearly trying to weigh our options for survival.

"It's just one beautiful little animal," Lan states as if she yearns to go toward the nearing creature and pet it. With each one of its torturing, stalking steps, my eyes slowly adjust to make out the outline of a large, white fox. About ten feet in front of us, it stops, sits, and stares. It tilts its head to the side to watch us.

"There is never just one animal. They are smarter than that. They all hunt together.

Now is our only chance. Run toward it and keep on running."

Is he serious? Run toward the large fox with glowing yellow eyes?

The fox's peaceful, innocent gawking instantly transforms. Its mouth opens wide, like a beartrap, and the most awful screeching pierces our ears and curdles our blood. Fin takes off toward the horrendous screams, and he kicks his foot toward the creature. Like halting nails on a chalkboard, the fox's alarming cries cease momentarily, then turn to guttural growls, and it snaps at Fin's leg. Fin rolls along the ground as the fox narrowly misses him. Lan and I don't hesitate to run toward Fin and the fox, snatch up Fin, and continue running. With his feet securely underneath him, Fin sprints ahead of us as we watch the line of trees to our side grow with swarms of gleaming eyes. A cacophony of howls, like a blasting soundwave of terror, nearly disrupts our swiftly moving legs. There is nothing we can do now but run. It won't be long before we are devoured by ravenous beasts. I refuse to die without at least trying my best to escape. Fin sweeps close to a tree and snatches a hanging branch. He begins swinging barbarically at any creature that comes near. I follow his lead and grab the largest branch I can carry while continuing my struggling speed. Lan realizes she needs a branch for protection as

154

well. However, as she reaches out to grab a nearby branch, a monstrous wolf pounces from the darkness. His razor teeth clamp down on the flesh of Lan's hand. Her screams mimic the deafening howl of the fox as her arm is jolted out of her shoulder's socket. She is whipped violently across the frozen ground and thrust toward a group of hungry-eyed wolves awaiting their treat. Fin, like a possessed madman, hollers and darts toward Lan and the salivating pack. Without hesitation, I grab out the Glock The Captain gave me from the front of the backpack and shoot the wolf closest to Lan. The echo of the shot causes all the animals to freeze, but only momentarily. Fin uses the opportunity to bash his stick into as many animals as possible. Lan, despite the obvious pain, gets to her feet and begins running with great force. Fin and I follow while fighting off the pursuing wolves and foxes. His constant swinging and my random shooting are enough to help us keep the monsters at a safe distance. With new adrenaline, we run, faster than I ever thought possible. When the hot breath or snarling growl of a creature gets too close, I turn and shoot. Most of the animals have given up the chase or moved on to different prey, but one large wolf remains in pursuit. Much faster than we could ever run, its powerful legs sprint around us and stop in front of us, teeth reflecting the light of the moon. I raise the gun and shoot at the beast, but an empty click resounds instead of firing. Luckily for us, Fin is angry and fierce with this branch, and as I join in with my stick, the wolf realizes it is outnumbered and finally backs down. However, as we pick up running, I can hear the pads of its paws thumping behind us, hopeful that one of us falls behind.

"The train station is just up ahead. We're almost there. Lan, how are you holding up?"

"I'm okay," Lan reassures us, but she is forced to hold her left arm in place with her right hand as she runs. She is clearly dizzy from the shock of the attack and the loss of blood as her pale face reflects the distant light.

"You can make it." I encourage, trying to help support her as she runs.

The dim light of the station shines like a beacon ahead. With each step, the glow increases in brightness and size. A new hope quickens the closer we get. The train whistle blows, forcing Fin to sprint ahead.

"Wait! Wait for us!" Fin shouts, waving his arms around to get the attention of the conductor. But the silhouette of the man in the front of the train just keeps looking forward. Puffs of white smoke chuff from the chimney as a long whistle rattles my worried nerves.

"Wait!" Fin shouts as he approaches the passenger door and begins pounding on it with his fists.

"Please let us on the train! We have tickets!"

As Lan and I approach the train, the passenger door opens, and a man leans out.

"You say you have tickets?"

"Yes, sir. Right here." I reach into my coat pocket, pull out three tickets, and hand them to the man.

"We don't have a medic onboard. She can't get on and drip blood all over the train."

I take off my coat and wrap it around Lan. I tie the sleeves around her middle to help secure her dislocated shoulder and contain the blood pulsing from her hand. Lan's knees buckle from under her, and she collapses into my arms. Fin jumps into action and helps me lift her up before she falls to the ground.

"Please, we need to get her on the train. They are expecting us at The Greenbrier."

"The Greenbrier, you say? The Greenbrier no longer exists. It is now E-Springs. Everyone knows that." The man inspects our tickets, annoyance building in his voice.

"I suspect you have bands to prove your place in society if you're heading to E-Springs?"

"Yes, sir, right here." Fin momentarily lets go of holding Lan with one of his hands to dig in his pocket. He pulls out a metal wristband, and the man on the train uses a small gadget to receive the radio frequency of the RFID microchip in the band.

The man's eyes squint with skepticism about the legitimacy of Fin's band, but the creases in his brow soften when he looks at Lan's helpless state.

"Alright, get on. Quickly. But don't make a mess of the train."

"Yes, sir. Thank you." I gush with humility as we cradle Lan in our arms and follow the man onto the train. We waddle back to a set of two benched seats facing each other.

"You may sit here. We will be at E-Springs in about four hours. We allow the passengers to stay and sleep on the train until the sun rises, but I expect there to be no blood on the seats when you leave." He stomps up the aisle, and we are left to bask in the warmth and safety of the train.

Chapter 17

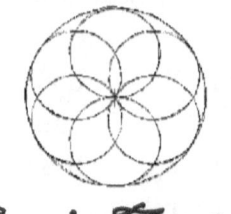

Lan's Ability

We gently place Lan onto the bench as the train begins to chug forward.

"What can we do for her? Do you know how to reset a dislocated shoulder?" I ask Fin.

"What do I look like, a medic? I would have some ideas of what to do for her if she had radiation poisoning, cancer, or The Fever, but this, I don't know."

"Need some help, dearies?" The sweet voice of a woman interrupts our helplessness.

"I'm a military hospital nurse. Trust me, I've seen it all, and it looks like this young lady is mendable. I saw you two hobbling in with her all passed out and bloody, so I grabbed my medical bag and followed you over here."

Before Fin nor I can respond, the light-haired, middle-aged woman seats herself next to Lan, and begins loosening the sleeves of my coat tied around her body.

"I'm pretty sure her shoulder is dislocated, and the wolf got her hand."

"How long has she been out?"

"She passed out just before we got on the train."

"How long has it been since the attack, and why didn't you get her medical attention sooner?"

"It just happened on the way to the train." Guilt plaguing my voice. "We didn't exactly have time to take her to a medical facility while being chased by animals. We nearly missed the train."

"Are you injured, too, Lad?

You must have hit your head pretty hard and are very confused yourself. I will take a look at you next, young man, just take it easy and lie back."

"No, ma'am, my head is fine." I feel my head with my hands just to make sure I don't feel any blood trickling or bumps forming. "I'm perfectly fine," I add.

"Well, then, maybe you are suffering from hypothermia. It is freezing out there. Anyway, something has got you confused. There is no way these wounds just happened today.

Look at how they are healing. New skin has already formed, and well... would you look at that? I've never seen anything like this."

The woman reaches into her bag and pulls out her eyeglass case, which squeaks upon her opening it. She whips out her glasses and places them on the bridge of her nose. Leaning in to get a closer look at what is left of Lan's hand, she responds hesitantly.

"Huh.

Very intriguing indeed."

She reaches back into her bag, brings out a pair of tweezers, and pokes around the end of the nubs of Lan's hand where her pinky and ring finger used to be before the wolf got them.

"Well, I've never...

It appears this young lady is regrowing the two fingers that were taken from her hand."

"Regrowing? What do you mean? That's not possible." Fin states, leaning in closer to see for himself.

I am better off not getting too close. I know gruesome sights make me queasy. Just the sight and smell of Lan's blood-stained shirt is enough to make me want to vomit.

"Yes, you see here, that is new bone. Not bone where flesh has been torn, but new calcification. And you can see here all around it where new tendons and ligaments have smoothed and extended as well. How can this be? I must be dreaming.

159

Here, let me take a look at her shoulder. It is dislocated, you say?"

The woman eagerly fetches a small pair of scissors from her bag and cuts away Lan's sleeve. I can't help but watch the woman reveal Lan's yellow and green-tinted shoulder. There is an obvious dip in Lan's skin where the upper part of her arm does not appear to be connected to her shoulder? The discomforting thought makes me turn and look out into the quickly passing blackness outside the window as I try to take deep breaths of cleansing air.

"Are you sure this happened today? Absolutely positive?"

"Yes, Ma'am," Fin replies with great fascination. He is clearly not disgusted by the thought of Lan's arm pulled out of its socket as he stares down with his mouth hanging open.

"This bruising all around the dislocation looks like it has been healing for at least a week or two. It should be red and swollen after the dislocation, maybe a little bruising just starting. I would imagine this would be completely black and blue in a day or two from the hemoglobin.

But it shouldn't be green and yellow for a good five days at a minimum. How is this possible? I suppose I should put the bone back into place."

I try to ignore the actions of the woman rotating Lan's arm until I hear the most disgusting bone-popping sound. Instant heat flushes through my face, and saliva puddles on the back of my tongue.

"There we go.

Would you look at that?"

My curiosity overpowers my nausea, and I force myself to look at Lan's shoulder, where the woman gawks with captivation. I watch as Lan's shoulder blushes, much like her cheeks often do. As the blood flushes the area, the pink hues wash into the yellows and greens and cause them to fade until they no longer tint her skin a putrid hue. Other than being a little flushed, her shoulder looks completely normal again within a minute or two.

"Who is this girl?" The woman stares at me with pure wonderment, demanding answers.

"You must be a really great nurse. You have fixed her right up." I giggle nervously, trying to avoid answering her questions.

Honestly, I have no idea how Lan's body is healing itself. I can't explain what we are witnessing. Maybe it has something to do with her being from the future. Are all people made up differently in the future? Does the human body evolve to heal itself? If that is the case, then how did Great Granddad die, or why didn't Neo's hand heal itself when he cut it at the Elementerprise facility, or why didn't Einstein's back heal this fast after being thrown back by the giant man at the carnival wreckage site?

"Now I know we are witnessing a miracle. I am certain her missing fingers have grown since I last looked at them." The woman's face drains of color, and she looks like she might pass out any moment herself as she scrutinizes the slightly longer fingers on Lan's hand.

"I think I need a drink." The woman states as she rubs her head in disbelief at what she is witnessing. She fans her face with her fingers.

"Here, why don't you go back to your seat, and I will see about getting you a drink? My treat, for helping our friend." Fin offers.

"Yes, I think that is a great idea. Thank you, lad."

As the woman stands and turns to walk away, Fin reaches up to her medical bag and snatches a vial hanging out of the outside pocket.

"Be right back." Fin raises his eyebrows as an evil scheme washes over his face.

What did he just steal from her bag, and what is he planning on doing with it?

161

Lan begins to stir. Her eyes flutter open.

"Did we make it?" Her weak voice asks.

"We are on the train.

Are you okay?

How are you feeling?

You passed out.

A nurse helped to pop your shoulder back in place, and your hand...

Well, your hand is healing nicely.

How is it healing so quickly?

Does it hurt?"

"Surprisingly, it's not too bad. My shoulder doesn't hurt at all anymore, and my hand just aches a bit." She looks down at her fingers, which are slowly growing new cells.

"I watched that thing bite my fingers clear off. How do I have half of them back?"

Lan reaches up and feels the new growth on her fingers to see if it is real or just a groggy mirage.

"That is what we were trying to figure out. Do all humans regenerate like this in the future?"

"Regenerate. That isn't possible. No one can regenerate. I mean we regrow skin cells and whatnot, but not bone and entire fingers, right?" Lan's eyes look up at me, full of confusion.

"So, you are saying this isn't normal for you either?" My head is reeling. Maybe I did bump it unknowingly somewhere along our journey.

"Are you saying *this* is normal for anyone?" Lan asks, holding up her hand with two of her fingers, slowly regrowing new bone and tissue. There isn't enough growth at a time to physically see it growing. But it is definitely a noticeable change from ten minutes ago. It's like when you get cut, and you don't actually notice a scab forming, or that it is healing, but the next day you realize it is better than yesterday. This is just like that, only at a much faster rate.

"You know. I never really thought that it was odd before, but I don't ever remember any severe injuries as a kid. I would scrape my knee, or whatever, but it was always better by the next day. I don't remember ever being sick. Most kids in my time die young from diseases, exposure, and hunger, but I don't remember ever even having a fever or anything. There was one time as a kid when everyone at the Elementerprise facility got sick with a terrible virus, and many people died. Everyone got it. Everyone except for me. I just thought I was lucky. I recall Elementerprise being curious, and they took vials of my blood to test it against the virus. You don't think something is wrong with me, do you?

There must be some logical explanation for why my fingers are growing back, right?" Her frantic questions erupt from her mouth like a spewing volcano.

"I'm sure we can find some information about this in my Great Granddad's journals. We just need to be careful pulling them out here. I don't want Fin, or anyone else, to know that we have them, okay."

"What, you think Fin is going to try to steal them from you or something?"

"Yes, actually, I do."

"You need to trust him. He is our only other friend in this world."

Fin swaggers back and slides onto the bench next to us. My hand, which was stashed in my bag, freezes, and I refrain from pulling out one of the journals in his presence. I just shake my head with a gentle, *no*, toward Lan.

"Well, we don't have to worry about that lady remembering anything about Lan or her *special ability*."

"What did you do to her? Please tell me you didn't kill her. I can't live with myself if you killed her."

"I didn't kill her. I just got her a drink, just like she asked me to do. I may have added a few drops of her Benzodiazepine to it to help her sleep, and a few more to help her forget about

163

everything she saw Lan miraculously do. This will all just be a weird dream to her when she wakes up, and she'll most likely think she just had too much to drink."

"Thanks, good thinking," Lan smiles at Fin and gestures to me with a, *see he's our friend*, motion.

"How did you know what that medication would do? How do you know you didn't give her an amount that could kill her?"

"Whoa, you're welcome. What's with the third-degree questioning?

If you must know, I watched the nurses and doctors do what they could for my Mom before she died from cancer, and my Dad from radiation poisoning. And they have been trying for years to help my little sister not meet that same fate. So ya, I've seen a few things and know a few things when it comes to helping sick patients." Fin's spouts cause the air around our booth in the train to sink heavily. Lan and I aren't sure how to respond or what we can say to apologize to make him feel better.

"I also know that you being able to regrow your fingers isn't normal, and we need to keep this a secret unless we want to lose you forever. If anyone finds out about what Lan can do, they will take her and put her in a lab for testing. I'm sure companies would pay billions to figure out her secret, especially if they could replicate the ability." Fin's voice becomes distant, and he stares out the dark train window as the frost in each of its corners grows ominously toward the center of the pane like a virus of ice.

"Thank you," Lan whispers to Fin as she wraps her uninjured hand around Fin's and squeezes a grateful squinch.

We all gently rock back and forth with the motion of the train and allow the warm air blowing from the vents at our feet to cradle us into a trance. But I can't get over the hungry way Fin stares at Lan like she is his ticket to a million bucks.

Chapter 18

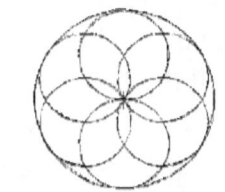

Hiding Secrets

"White Sulphur Springs Station. The end of the line." Shouts a voice from a hidden speaker.

"Come on, we're here," I say, gently shaking Lan and Fin awake.

Fixing my backpack and satchel onto my body I take Lan by her unwounded arm and help to pull her to her feet. We all look down at Lan's injured hand and notice that her pinky is almost the correct length, and her ring finger just needs the top segment.

"Here, you can wear my glove on that hand. Just to make sure no one notices or asks questions about it changing. In fact, just wear both gloves. It's cold out there." I smile and peel the gloves off my hands to give to her. As I slide the last glove off my hand, she instantly notices my new tattoo peeking out from under the sleeve of my shirt.

"Dameon, what is that? Where did it come from?"

Cautiously yanking my sleeve down over the symbol nervously, I spit out a, "shhhhh," as my eyes dart around to make sure no one else saw my mark. But I feel as Fin catches a glimpse of the top edge of my tattoo, and his eyes jump up rapidly and burn into mine.

"You?" His eyes narrow. Blood fills his cheeks, and his hands ball into fists.

"Why you? What makes you so special?"

"It's the end of the line. Everyone out." A train attendant has made his way to us and ushers us out of our booth.

"Okay, thank you. I don't suppose we can use the restroom before exiting so we can clean up a bit?" I ask the man, referring to Lan's stained clothing.

"Sure, it's at the end of the car.

Looks like you had a rough night, Miss.

Are you alright?" He asks, gesturing to her blood-stained shirt. Lan nods.

"I might be able to find you a clean shirt." The young man gives an over-exaggerated wink at Lan and motions toward the direction of the restroom as if he is luring a young child with candy.

"That would be wonderful, thank you." Lan smiles back at him naively.

"Thanks," I add. Trying to make sure he realizes that she is here with two other guys who are willing to fight for her protection.

He watches as we scurry toward the restroom, and then he disappears in the opposite direction.

"Looks like he wants to help you out." Fin's wink mimics that of the young man.

Lan punches Fin with her good hand. "Knock it off, he was just being kind."

She pushes past Fin, goes into the restroom, and slams the door with great annoyance behind her.

I can't help but snort a chuckle once Lan is behind the closed door. For once, I wasn't the one who said something stupid to Lan.

Fin sees my laugh and smiles back. "Girls," he states as a half-smile creeps up one side of his face.

I watch as Fin's smile dissolves as he looks down toward my tattoo again. His lips part to say something about it, but my head instantly jolts toward the sound of running feet coming in our direction. It is the same young train attendant, and he is carrying a freshly pressed button-down shirt dangling from one hand and a clean coat dangling in the other.

"Where is the beautiful young lady?" He asks, trying to hold in his breath as if to show us he isn't winded after his jog down the aisle.

Fin and I point to the closed bathroom door.

Then, I hold out my hand to take the shirt and coat from the young man.

"I would like to give them to her myself if you don't mind." A suave smolder paints his smug face.

Fin, obviously disgusted by the man, swipes the shirt and coat from his hands.

"We'll make sure she gets them. Your services are no longer required."

Through fuming, pursed lips, the attendant squawks,

"The train will be leaving in seven minutes, and you better not be on it." He stomps away, shaking the train under his clomping.

"He needs to get a life outside this train," Fin replies. I nod in agreement.

Knocking quietly on the bathroom door, I inform Lan we have a clean shirt for her.

The sound of the lock clicks, and the door opens a crack. Her perfect arm squirms through the opening and grasps wildly through the air, trying to feel for the shirt. Fin treats it like a game and keeps taunting her with it. He lets it brush against her fingertips and then swings it away with laughter. I shake my head at his immature game, rescue the shirt from Fin's hand, and place it in Lan's open fingers. She whips the shirt back in through the crack and closes the door vehemently.

"You are no fun." Fin pouts.

A man exits from the second restroom door. Fin throws the gifted coat at me.

"You better find a way to hide that tattoo. You seem to have more of a reason for people to be after you than Lan does."

He escapes behind the bathroom door with a slam. Lan comes out, tucking the new shirt into her pants, trying to make the oversized shirt look more presentable on her small frame. I hand her the coat, and she instantly lifts it up to her nose and inhales a big whiff.

"It smells so good." She smiles in a dreamy state.

My eyes roll all the way inside the bathroom, and I close the door behind me. I sniff my hands and realize she is right. The young man must have doused the shirt and coat in cologne before bringing them to her.

As I scrub my hands in the sink, my eyes stay fixed on my tattoo that keeps peeking at me from under the edge of my shirt sleeve.

Why did Fin say that people will be after me because of this tattoo?
How does he even know what it is?

Attempting to scrub away the ink as if it is poison, its permanence laughs back at me. All I have done is cause the skin around the tattoo to become red and irritated.

What have I done?
Why did The Captain brand me?

His bizarre words echo through my head.

"I guess it is official then. You truly are The Final Aeon sent to save the world. Our Great Prophet and leader."
The Final Aeon sent to save the world?
Prophet and Leader?
I didn't ask for any of this.
I just want to be a normal kid, with normal worries.
Like, am I going to be able to make it through next school year without anyone noticing me?
What if I don't want to save the world?

I notice Lan's bloody shirt and my coat wadded up in the trash can. I grab them both out and tear a strip of fabric from an area of her shirt that isn't covered in blood. I wrap it around my wrist to cover the tattoo, and I weave it up and around my palm and through the opening between my thumb and pointer finger to guarantee it will not slip down and reveal my unwanted mark. I tie the two ends together in a knot where they meet back over my wrist.

There.
Now, no one will know about it.
Except, Lan and Fin already know.
I know I can trust Lan, but I don't like the way Fin looked at it. It is like he knows of its significance. Can I trust him to keep it a secret? Or Lan's ability a secret? He seemed pretty sinister when he stated that companies would pay billions of dollars to learn of her secret, and what about mine?

Fin's fist pounds on the bathroom door.

"Come on, we gotta go! The train is getting ready to pull out."

I toss the remains of Lan's bloody shredded shirt back into the waste can and swing my slightly stained coat around my shoulders. Glancing at my disheveled reflection in the mirror, I wipe some water on my face and run my fingers through my straggly hair.

Man, I need a haircut.
But I guess I have more important things to take care of first. Like, go find Great Granddad.

Chapter 19

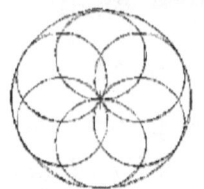

A Saving Squirrel

*W*e step off the train and allow the glow of the frozen white land around us to spill onto our faces. The air is frigid and bites at our squinting cheeks. Tightening our coats up around our necks, we begin walking with our backs to the rising sun, following our long shadows as our guides.

"E-Springs is just down this road. But we need to stay in the trees and go down around the main gates to the end of the grounds. They will never let us in through the main gate. Well, maybe if they find out who you two are they would let you in, but not me. Besides, The Captain said your Great Granddad is going to meet us in the woods near the West entrance."

Fin begins walking through the trees at a quicker pace. Our boots crunch against the crusty snow beneath their treads. Lan and I struggle to keep up without an occasional jogging step. Through the towering, vertical, crystal-covered trunks, I can see razor-sharp tendrils circling along the top of a white-bricked fence, protecting the largest, fanciest building I have ever laid my eyes on. The structure's white glow reflects the morning light, and it is difficult to make out the edges of the massive building against the frozen hillside. The well-manicured trees and landscaping on the grounds surrounding the grand building look tiny in comparison to its grandeur. Four colossal columns mark the center pinnacle of the impressive building, with hundreds of perfectly lined rows of windows reaching out and reflecting the sun like glitter on both sides. Lan and I stop in our tracks to attempt to take in the impressive view.

"Wow!" Lan gapes.

"That is the most beautiful building I have ever seen. Do people live in there?"

"Yes, The Elite.

During World War III, Elementerprise bought The Greenbrier and made it into their headquarters when the waters began rising and flooding their original location. They started offering safe and luxurious living quarters to billionaires and those of importance to our country. When America was under attack, and more bombs were falling every day, people were begging and paying loads of money to come and stay here in the shelter of their underground bunkers. Now, it is its own thriving community where people like me and my family only dream of living. They have the world's top doctors and medical facilities, filtered air free from radiation, and banquets of food. They have been able to repair the damaged wings and now it sits as gloriously as it was in the past. Reminding the rest of the world that we will never be able to afford their luxury unless we offer our lives to them."

The sound of a barking dog in the distance causes every muscle in Fin's body to solidify.

"Quick, hide! Get behind a tree and don't even breathe! The guards and their dogs are out on their rounds early this morning."

Fin leaps behind a tree, puffs up his chest, and I watch as the white air rushing from his mouth seems to cease all at once. Lan and I both jump behind our own nearby trees and do our best to steady our breath and inhale and exhale as little as possible, without passing out. Afraid to look around the protection of the tree to see if anyone is near, I clear my thoughts and do my best to quiet my brain. My ears focus in on every sound around me. I can hear the distant crunching of boots in the snow accompanied by four trotting paws. I strain to listen closely to try and figure out their distance. A similar set of sounds begin to close in from the other direction. There must be two guards, both with dogs on leashes, coming from opposite directions, and they are both about to meet up near our hiding place. If we run for it now, they will surely see us. I hold my breath and pretend I don't exist. Perhaps if I believe it enough, I can disappear, and the dogs won't pick up on our scent. I squeeze my eyes closed and pray.

> *Please, don't let them find us. I have no idea what will happen to us if they do, but I really don't want to find out.*
> *Please!*

The alarming bark of one of the dogs echoes nearby through the trees. The sound of their desperate panting gets closer and closer.

"What is it, boy? Did you find something?" A man's voice interrupts the silence as he tromps behind the dog, clawing through the snow to escape the leash in our direction.

"Alright, go find it." As if in slow motion, I hear the leash drop and scrape against the top layer of the crusty snow.

I turn my head to watch Lan's face gasp in horror as she, too, realizes the released dog is coming to disclose our location, eat us, or who knows what. My head whips to see Fin's reaction and perhaps give guidance on what we should do. I watch as he snatches a small furry creature clinging to his tree and chucks it like a grenade toward the gate. Both dogs bark uncontrollably and dart to what I now see is, or was, a squirrel being torn in two between the ferocious and distracted dogs.

"Dumb dogs. It looks like they just found another squirrel. Let's get back to our posts and get some hot coffee. It's freezing out here. Come on, Duke. Here, boy."

The man slaps the side of his leg, and I hear one of the dogs scamper back to his side. The other man lets out a whistle, and the second dog obediently joins him, licking his bloody mouth.

"See ya this afternoon for lunch."

"Later."

My heart thumps against my chest as the crunch of the footsteps fades in both directions. Rigid, still too afraid to move, I wait until Fin moves from behind his tree.

"That was close." His words finally whisper in a cloud of relief.

"Thank goodness for that squirrel, or that probably would have been us getting eaten." He chuckles.

"So, where is my Great Grandad? He isn't going to get attacked by one of those huge dogs, is he?" My questions swirl aimlessly as a cloud of frozen condensation.

"I've decided I don't like animals," Lan responds, rubbing her hands together and feeling her growing fingers under the leather of the gloves.

"We still need to head in that direction toward the West gate. Then, we will wait as deeply in the woods as we can, away from the guards and their dogs. The Captain said your Great Granddad should meet us there. Let's just hope we don't have to wait too long." Fin's voice shutters in the morning's frosty air.

He begins stomping through the snow. Luckily for us, the top layer is mostly ice, and our boots only sink down about an inch or so.

"It might be a good idea to grab that pine needle branch and sweep our prints behind us to help hide our tracks." Fin gestures for me to pick up the nearby branch.

Nodding, I jump over and attempt to pick up the branch. My hands instantly burn and freeze to it. It is no different than picking up an icicle frozen in place. I brace my feet in the snow and tug, using my body weight to help free it. The sound of snapping twigs erupts, and I fall back into the snow with its sudden release. Fin and Lan just snigger. I retaliate by throwing a clump of ice and snow in their direction. Lan giggles and throws a chunk of ice back at me. This would be the perfect location and opportunity for an epic, movie-quality snowball fight; however, Fin spoils the moment by putting his finger to his blue lips and rattling off a, "shhhhh," like a buzzkill librarian.

"I'd rather not alert the dogs." He whispers and points back in the direction of the massive building.

I suppose he is right.

I stand up, brush the snow off my backside, and pick up the freed portion of the branch. The majority of the needles remain frozen in place on the ground, forming the perfect fossil imprint.

Wishing I had the gloves I gave to Lan, I shrink my arms as much as I can and try to stretch the sleeves of my coat to reach down far enough to offer a bit of protection against my sharp, freezing grasp around the branch. I begin dragging the branch behind us like a broom, sweeping away our footprints as we trudge on, trying to step lightly and quietly.

After a bit of walking, Fin points his red finger back toward the immaculate building.

"That is the West gate. So, I say, we find a safe place to hide and wait for your Great Granddad."

He heads back further into the trees, and Lan and I follow. We discover a drift of snow that has piled up against a large tree, making a half-circle of protection.

"I don't suppose you have a blanket or anything in your backpack, do you?" Fin asks.

"We could put it down and huddle together here to try and keep warm."

"Ummm, I think I do," I reply, digging around carefully in my backpack, so as not to expose any of its contents, trying to feel for the scratchy, burlap blanket from the tunnels. I do my best to hide the journals and the metal box with my hunching body as I tug the blanket out of the opening. I shake it out and fold it on itself to try and give us two thin layers between us and the snowy ground. Laying it down in the center of the natural snow barrier, I smooth it out with my hands. Lan plops down in the center, and Fin and I sit next to her on both sides. We all sit as close as possible, hoping that together, we can muster a bit of body heat.

"I don't suppose a fire would be a good idea?" I ask, wishing it is a possibility, but knowing it isn't.

"Not unless you want to be discovered," Fin replies bluntly.

"Can we at least eat a little of the food we brought?" Lan bats her eyelashes in a pleading manner in my direction.

"Now that, I can go for," Fin responds.

I grab the biscuits we took from the ship since I figure those probably need to be eaten first, and I hand one to Fin and Lan.

"This is all you have in there? I've been eating these for the last few months." Fin's disappointed face scrunches in protest.

"We have other food, but I don't know how long we need it to last, and these were on top," I state.

"I'll take yours if you don't want it," Lan suggests. But a ravenous Fin takes a bite of the hard biscuit and crunches it with angst.

"Why does your Great Granddad want us to meet him here?" Fin questions.

"Is he in there with those hoity-toities?"

"I don't know."

"Well, does your family have a lot of money?"

"I'm not really sure."

"What do you mean you aren't sure? Either you have lots of money or you don't.

Have you ever met your Great Granddad? Did your family ever have a nice house?"

"I have met my Great Granddad once; it was just in a different... place."

"Like wherever you are from?

Where are you from?"

"It's complicated."

"Complicated how? Who are you two? I think I deserve some answers."

"Lan and I are from two different... places."

"Like across the great oceans?"

175

"Something like that."

"I live with three men who raised me underground in the tunnels." Lan smiles, speaking honestly, but the explanation sounds a little crazy. I search Fin's face for a reaction, but it remains stoic. Perhaps that is an acceptable answer.

"I guess you could say my family, or what is left of them, lives underground, too, in a bunker." Fin relates.

So, I am the "odd-one" here that wasn't raised underground? Do I tell Fin my family just inherited a mansion, and now we own two houses, above ground? Or will that just make him resent me even more?

I decide to not divulge any information about my living conditions.

"Then why were you on that ship with The Captain and Oz?" Lan asks, saving me from having to tell Fin anything.

"When my Mom and my Dad died, my little sister and I sold our little family bunker and went to live with my Mom's sister, our aunt. We used the money to buy the vaccine for my little sister, but she was already very sick and needed other medicine. I joined the army as soon as I could. Most kids join because the military promises you the vaccine, food, and a small stipend, which I was able to give to my aunt and sister. But the war was… horrible." Fin pauses and stares blankly, his face contorts as if he is in pain. If his eyebrows scrunch together any tighter, they will fold on top of each other.

"As soon as my troop came back to Appalachia, I ran away and vowed I would never return to Elementerprise's army. I feared that if they ever caught me, they would torture and kill me, and probably hunt down the little family I had left and imprison them, too. So, I ran until I got to the coast, and then I started swimming as far as I could swim, understanding that I probably wouldn't make it very far in the frigid waters. But that is when The Captain and Oz found me scrambling to stay afloat, and I have been on three voyages with them since. We go out on the water for a few months at a time for different jobs. When we get back to Port Richmond, The Captain pays me my wages and lets me travel back to visit my aunt and sister to give them the money we make. But my sister is still really sick. At least, I think she still is. It has been nearly four months since I last saw her."

"Then go to her. You don't have to wait here with us." Lan exclaims.

"I need to finish this job. The Captain hasn't paid me yet, and I won't get paid until I get you two to your Great Granddad and I get back to The Captain. Only then will he pay me." I see moisture build in the wells of Fin's worried eyes.

As if being pummeled with a ton of bricks, it hits me. Fin is just like me. He is just doing whatever he can to help save his little sister. Just like I am doing whatever I can to help save Jaxson.

"We will do what we can to make sure you get back, get paid, and get to your sister." I feel empathetic tears burn my own eyes.

It is a good thing it is so cold, or I am afraid the tears would have trickled down my cheek if they weren't frozen.

"My Great Granddad will know how to help your sister. That is why we are searching for him now. He is a great doctor. We need him to help us save my little brother."

"I knew it. He is the one that made the vaccine that has saved so many people, and The Secret Serum that you have in your box, right?"

"Wait, how do you know that I have the box, or what is inside it?"

"I'm not an idiot. I know it's in there. And I saw those symbols. I have also spent many nights listening to The Captain and his "secret" conversations. I'm not as clueless as everyone assumes. My father knew a lot. He used to work for Elementerprise to get medicine, and I often ran errands for him as a boy. So, I take it your Great Granddad is working for them, too?"

"NO!" I shout, louder than I probably should have.

"Are you sure? From what my father said, your Great Granddad discovered the vaccine which lessens the effects of radiation poisoning and The Fever. Elementerprise is the one that funded and mass-produced it. He has helped save millions of people world-wide."

"Sounds like your Great Granddad to me." Lan smiles.

"Well, have you opened the box yet? Is there truly a life-saving serum in there?" Fin's eyebrows raise.

I suppose there is no point in hiding it if he already knows I have it. I fish it out of the top of my bag and turn it over in my hands gently. I trace my numb fingers over each intricately detailed swirl and shape, all connected into one giant masterpiece. There doesn't seem to be a keyhole for a key. No number pad to type in a code. It is like a giant metal puzzle, and I have no clue how to open it. I try to push on certain symbols and attempt to slide anything in any direction, but nothing seems to budge.

"Don't you know how to open it?" Fin asks.

"No, do you?"

Fin gestures for me to hand him the box, but I am still unsure how I feel about trusting him. Not wanting to look like a selfish child, I reluctantly pass it over to him. An unsettling pit begins to grow in my stomach as I watch him fondle the box and attempt to open it. As soon as Lan reaches out her hands for a turn to inspect it, I instantly begin to feel better once the box is passed to her. She studies the box, searching for any sign of a crack where it might open.

"Are you sure it even is a box with something inside?" She asks, with her eyes squinting at every odd, raised piece of metal.

"This has to be it. It matches the description exactly. I knew that was what it was the first time I saw it in The Captain's hands when he retrieved it from the island." Fin exudes with excitement.

"I hear it makes humans invincible to all diseases, radiation, poison… It makes you like a super-human."

"Is there anything in the journals about the box?" The words fling from Lan's mouth like daggers of betrayal.

"Journals? What journals?"

"Lan!" Everything inside me coils like a defensive snake.

"Oops, sorry."

"Your Great Granddad's journals? Do they tell you how to make the medicine?

Can you help my sister? Can I see them?"

"NO!" I snap, taking both Lan and Fin by surprise with my harshness.

"They are full of **secret** information. No one is to touch them or look at them. Understand?" The frigid air around me is nothing compared to the coldness I am feeling within. I stand up, snatch the metal box out of Lan's hand, and stuff it back into my backpack. With my backpack and satchel snug around my body, I stomp off in the opposite direction of the large white building and traipse deeper into the woods. I don't know where I am heading, I just need to be alone for a bit.

How could Lan do that? What was she thinking? She just blurted out and told Fin that I have my Great Granddad's journals with me. It was bad enough with him knowing about the box and what might be inside, but him knowing about Great Granddad's secrets is too much. How am I going to keep them safe? Who is to say he isn't going to steal them the first chance he gets and sell them to the highest bidder? I can't even imagine what would happen to the world if all Great Granddad's secrets get out.

Wait, that is exactly what happens, isn't it? Maybe this situation is the demise of the world and the future as we know it. I must keep these journals and this box out of the wrong hands. But how?

Do I just go off on my own and leave Lan and Fin behind?

Would I even survive out here on my own?

Chapter 20

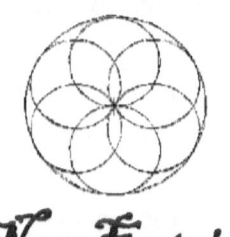

New Entries

"Dameon?" Lan's voice whispers through the trees.

I stop in my tracks and contemplate whether or not I should hide from her.

"Dameon, wait." Lan jogs up behind me. My feet want to run, but my heart wants to stay.

"I'm sorry. I wasn't thinking. I realize I shouldn't have said anything about the journals with Fin around. Can you please forgive me?" Her moist eyes plead for forgiveness.

"Ya, whatever," I respond as I keep on walking, but Lan keeps following.

"I really do think we can trust Fin. He is just like you, you know. He is in the same situation with his little sister as you are with Jaxson."

"I know. That is the problem." I stop and turn to stare at Lan. "I would do anything for Jaxson, especially if someone I knew had information that would help him. I'm worried Fin will do the same. I don't know if I can trust him. I can't let him get Great Granddad's journals, no matter how important the cause is. They contain secrets he can't know about – that no one can know about. That is the problem with the world right now already. They know too much. The world becomes too power-hungry with the little bits of information they did steal from my Great Granddad. Imagine if they have all of it. There wouldn't be a future. You wouldn't be... Well, I don't know what would happen to you or Einstein, Erb, or Neo. I don't know how all that works. I don't know how any of this works. All I do know is that I need to keep the box and the journals safe and in my possession."

"I know, and again, I'm so sorry for mentioning them. I will do everything I can to help you keep them safe. I know how important they are.

Is there truly a life-saving serum in that box?" She asks with her eyes widening.

"I have no idea what is in the box or if it even opens.

But maybe we can look through the journals to see if we can find something about it."

As I suggest that to Lan, her face lights up and she stands a little taller.

"You don't hate me then?"

"I could never hate you." My grin matches Lan's. And that is the truth.

We both sit on a nearby fallen log as close as we can get to each other without being in each other's laps, hoping for a bit of warmth. And I would be lying if I said I don't enjoy being close to Lan without anyone else around. I drop my backpack onto the tops of my feet and dig around inside to find one of Great Granddad's journals, and hold it out for Lan to take.

Lan reaches to grab it with her injured, gloved hand.

"How are your fingers doing?" I ask, looking at the full glove.

Lan peels the glove off her hand and we both look down at it in awe. Although her last two fingers look thinner than the others, they are completely formed and are the perfect length. The nail beds are starting to form on both fingers as well.

"They feel just fine." A shocked Lan states as she opens and closes her hand, testing their perfect functionality.

"Amazing." I gawk. "They are almost completely back to normal."

"I don't understand. How is this possible?"

"I don't know. Here, you check out this journal and search for anything about your special ability, the box, the serum, or anything helpful, and I will check this one." I suggest, handing Lan the journal and fetching the other one for myself. "I don't remember ever seeing anything in them about regeneration, or the box, or the serum. But then again, I feel like there are new things in here I haven't seen before every time I open them." I add.

"Wait, that's it. I am pretty sure new entries appear as Great Granddad enters them because I know this journal entry wasn't here the last time we looked at this journal before we came here." With pure shock, I run my finger across the words on a new page of scratched ink. "Look, the last entry we read was dated May 12, 2079." I prove, flipping back to the page we read while back in Great Granddad's study, which told of this time and place. "This new entry is dated May 14, 2079. That would have been yesterday, I believe, and it wasn't here before."

"What does it say?" Lan questions, looking closer at the page as if it is magic.

I whisper the new entry to Lan.

May 14, 2079

They are holding me hostage in the E-Springs –
Greenbrier facility. There is no way they are going to let
me go until I produce the ATHP (Ambystoma
Tardigradas Homosapien Provectus) Serum. They have
somehow found out about it and its ability to change and
progress our DNA to create what they are calling "Super
Humans". The unique DNA of the Axolotl (Ambystoma)
allows the human cells to regenerate and regrow organs
and body parts.

I stop reading and look at Lan. Our synchronized gaze moves
downward to look at Lan's regenerating fingers with sudden
realization, that it appears Lan has somehow received this serum. Lan
looks back at me, and her perplexed expression begs to comprehend.
I continue reading, thirsty to understand more:

The Tardigrade DNA allows humans to withstand
radiation and extreme temperatures. These, when mixed
with the Advanced Human DNA and the healing waters of
the White Sulphur Spring, make this serum highly sought
after.

No one, not Elementerprise, not China, not Russia, NO ONE, can get their hands on this serum! They don't understand the long-term effects. It CHANGES the human DNA, and it eventually takes over until there is hardly anything human left about them. There are only a few successful ways of killing these creatures. If they die a "normal" death, they aren't truly dead, they just lie dormant, with their bodies changing and evolving until they reawaken.

Lan's breathing suddenly quickens.
"Does this mean I have had the serum?
Is this my fate?
Am I going to become one of those *creatures*?"
Her fear falls over us like a thick fog.
I grasp her hand and squeeze all the love and support I can transfer.
"Don't worry, we don't know anything for certain. You could just have a really cool special ability to regrow fingers." I try to muster a façade of a smile. Lan tries to bob a slight nod, and so I continue reading.

I only recently made this discovery. There is only one version of the serum that has proven to be successful with little to no negative effects, at least that I have witnessed thus far. I have been working on it secretly for hundreds of years, and the only vials of this serum are well hidden and protected by The SOS deep in the volcanic vault.

But for now, I fear it, and the secrets of the ATHP Serum, are at risk of exposure, and I am unsure if I will be able to escape this prison and meet my party to ensure their safety. The new leader of that secret society is now responsible for its concealment. Only then can he truly save the world.

I run my fingers over the drawn design at the bottom of the journal entry. It is the same symbol of the fully-functioning ecosystem overlayed with the Seed of Life symbol both The Captain and my Great Granddad bear on their wrists, signifying their membership in the SOS. And drawn here, in the center of that symbol, is a new addition of the infinity symbol – what I have learned is my unique symbol. This beautiful swirl of ink is the same symbol as the freshly created mark on the underside of my wrist. My tattoo suddenly feels warm below the torn shreds of fabric I wrapped around it on the train. Its zeal radiates down my arm and floods my body with a new sense of pride and responsibility.

I close my eyes and attempt to allow the fervor to wash away my doubts, but like poison, my skepticism extinguishes the torridness, and my head pounds with waves of confusion.

"Why me?" I beg Great Granddad for more of an explanation.

"You? You are the new leader of the secret society he talks about in the entry?" Lan questions.

For a moment, I almost forgot Lan was by my side. I swallow hard, take a cleansing breath, and carefully untie the tattered ends of the fabric covering my wrist. As I unwrap its protection, I reveal the same imprinted symbol from the open page in the journal.

The lines between Lan's eyebrows crumple together above her nose. Her mouth drops open as she watches my tattoo radiate a pulsing red glow in reaction to the symbol on the page.

"How? When did you get this? Did The Captain do this to you? And how does your Great Granddad know about it? What does it mean?" Her fingers feel like shards of ice as she traces the now blackened, but still pulsing, lines of the symbol on my wrist.

"The Captain and my Great Granddad are part of some secret society, and when you become one of their members, you are marked with this symbol. Only my mark has the infinity symbol in the center, which is different than the others. The Captain said that it means I am their leader, the predicted prophet, or something like that. He said that I am The Final Aeon sent to save and protect the world.

But, why me?

I don't even know how to help save Jaxson.

Or keep water on our planet for your time.

And now I am supposed to keep this serum from getting out, too?

It's too much.

I don't think I can do this."

I try breathing in the frosty air, but it stops like a glacier wedged in my throat. Unsure if it is because of the bitter chill, or the overwhelming emotions of panic plaguing me, but I can't seem to fill my retching lungs.

"Dameon?

Are you okay?

Your nose. It's bleeding.

Dameon?" Lan's worried, quivering voice becomes an echo, distancing itself from me with each pulse of my blood pumping through my ears.

I feel the trickling blood drip over my top lip as the engine of anxiety revs inside me and hammers my head like an anvil. Every small insignificant breath I squeeze in comes rushing back out over my cracked lips in a fit of dry coughs. I wheeze in tiny bits of air, but it isn't enough. A heaviness as thick as mud sludges over my thoughts. The trees dance around me, and my head slams into the ice and snow as blackness consumes me.

Chapter 21

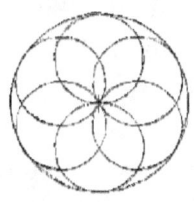

The Fever

*I*t's interesting what my mind hears when I'm in a dreamlike state between consciousness. Even the quietest of places grows to a cacophony of sounds as my hippocampus struggles to form pictures of the discombobulation. An overbearing hum vibrates against the brain and befuddles all thoughts.

A car engine, or some type of generator perhaps?

My eardrums focus on the scratching, which is so intense I can feel it on my brain like a back-and-forth motion of insanity.

Scrubbing?
No, it's more like sketching on paper.
The in and out breaths of someone else sleeping.
The sound of metal scraping against metal in a constant swirling motion in the distance.

The sounds become less abrasive and more soothing as my body allows the sense of smell to accompany the sounds.

Wax, not from a candle, but more like elementary school... crayons.
Burning metal meshed with meat cooking.

"That's amazing. Can you teach me to draw like that?" Lan's voice soothes my aching ears like sweet, warm honey.

I force my eyes to squint open. I stare up at the fuzzy outline of Lan's chin. The silhouette of her face blurs into view. I try to say her name, but my mouth and body are paralyzed and unable to respond to my will. I become aware of my parched tongue as it scrapes against the roof of my mouth like sandpaper. It suddenly feels uncomfortably too large to fit inside the arch of my teeth. Lan's face tilts down to look at mine.

"Dameon, you're awake!" She strokes my face with a cool, wet cloth, which feels scratchy, yet soothing.

"You scared me. You were shaking uncontrollably. I wasn't sure you would wake up." Her face comes closer to mine, and I can feel her warm breath slowly evaporate the moisture from the cloth on my face.

"He's awake!" Lan states, clearly talking to someone else in the room or living space.

The area around us is dimly lit by two electric lamp sconces buzzing on the walls. One is near me, Lan, and a frail little girl all huddled together on a bed of blankets and a foam mattress, and the other one is standing in a pathetic cooking area.

"Where are we?" I finally manage to squeak.

"Fin brought us to his aunt's bunker after you passed out."

My eyes struggle to stay open, but I force them to look around at the small bunker. It is no more than maybe ten feet by ten feet. There is a set of bunk beds on one end with ratty blankets hanging off the sides. The foam mattress bed we are lying on sits on the floor adjacent to the bunks along the wall, with my feet stretched out below the bottom bunk. The wall above us is plastered with drawings and colored pictures of everything the mind could imagine, but mostly of a little princess in castles and beautiful, lush lands. There is a heavily locked door directly across from us, which I can assume is the only way in and out of the bunker. There are open shelves next to the door along the wall. They are scattered with supplies, buckets, and some ancient-looking, rusting cans of food. At the other end of the room sit a few cabinets, a sink, and a one-burner stove. A woman with stringy, greying hair falling out of a twisted bun stops stirring whatever is in the pan on the burner and looks over her shoulder at me. She brings over a metal mug and hands it to Lan.

"Glad you're awake, deary.

Try to drink as much as you can. It will help with the fever." She commands.

I try to lift my arms, but they are too weak, and I can barely grip the warm mug. Lan takes the mug for me, helps me lift my head, and tilts the rim slightly to my parched lips. I sip, sputter, and cough the water as it reaches my burning throat, and unfortunately, some of it sprays Lan's face.

"Sorry."

"It's ok, keep trying."

I try to push my way up a bit to more of a sitting position and rest on my shaky elbows just long enough to take a sip of water. I pant but force it down.

"Thank you," I wheeze, lying back down, unable to hold myself up any longer.

"Where is Fin?" I ask, realizing he would be hard to miss in this small bunker.

"You mean Maddox? He is out trying to find you the vaccine." The woman states.

My face must have contorted at the name Maddox because Lan mouths the words,

"Fin's real name is Maddox."

"Vaccine, for what?" I ask, trying to move past his real name.

"You have radiation sickness and The Fever, deary. Surely, this isn't your first time with either? There is no way you have made it this long without getting them without the vaccine."

"No, Ma'am. I have not had either"

"Where are you from? Another planet?" She giggles, amused by her own joke.

"Or, have you just been down in a shelter for your entire life, and this is your first time up to the surface? I've heard a few

191

stories like that. I can't imagine staying underground that long. I need to go outside occasionally, or I would lose my mind if I were down here all the time. That happened to my friend's husband, you know. They were all underground for too long, and James lost it, plugged up the exhaust pipes to the bunker, and the couple and their two kids fell asleep and never woke up. Not a terrible way to go, I suppose."

The little girl with her back against the wall sitting on the other side of Lan immediately stops drawing on her pad of paper and looks up at Lan with wide, concerned eyes as the bunker fills with an unsettling silence in reaction to the woman's story.

"Dameon, this is Sophie. Fin's - Maddox's, little sister."

"Nice to meet you, Sophie," I look up at the dirty-blonde-haired girl with hazel eyes set deeply above two darkened circles. She smiles a weak grin.

"Nice to meet you, too." She nods like a little princess with the best curtsy she can muster from a seated position.

"So, are you the talented artist?" I ask, gesturing to the wall of art hanging above her head. Her pale cheeks blush slightly, and she nods proudly.

"You must like princesses. Wait, are you a real princess?" I ask with a slight wink.

She chortles bashfully, but her giggle turns into a barking cough, which rattles her small body. She hacks until she is blue in the face and gasping for air. The ragged woman grabs a spoon and a bottle of honey and runs to Sophie's side. She pounds on Sophie's back and tries to spoon a bit of honey into her mouth whenever the gasping girl stops coughing long enough to get a bit of air. Sophie struggles to swallow the honey, and after a few minutes, her cough subsides to one that is a bit more manageable.

"You can't be getting her all worked up now. I ran out of her medicine weeks ago. We're just lucky I was able to trade for one last bottle of honey to help with her cough. Here, I'll get you all some soup. The warm broth might help you both feel better." She shuffles over to the pan on the burner. She takes three metal mugs and dips each one into the pan and scoops out a bit of soup into each mug. She clinks a spoon into each mug and balances the three mugs over to us.

"Luckily, Maddox got a rabbit for our stew before he went out."

Sophie carefully grabs a mug and sips the soup. The edges of her lips turn upward. I do my best to push my way back up to my elbows and slide my body up against the wall behind me to help hold me up. I wait for a moment for the room to stop spinning before I force my trembling arms up to reach for a mug.

"Do you need help?" Lan asks.

"No, I think I got it, thanks," I reply, bringing my knees up so I can rest the mug on them as I catch my breath.

Lan takes a sip of the rabbit soup.

"MMMMMM, thank you. This is delicious."

"It's just a bit of rabbit and salt in water. What I wouldn't do to get a can or two of vegetables or an onion." Her voice trails off in a trance.

I take a sip of the broth, and it stings the back of my throat like liquid fire. I fight the urge to cough and take another sip to help satiate the urge. I get a little piece of meat with my broth, and although it is quite tough and chewy, it tastes a bit like flavorless chicken.

I nearly jump and spill my mug of soup as a series of knocks pound on the door. The rhythm of knocks is clearly a deliberate pattern, and Sophie instantly squirms with delight.

"Maddox is back," she squeals.

She begins to get up, but the woman shakes her finger and gives her the look of, *don't you dare get up.* Sophie slumps back over with a sigh but anticipates her brother coming through the door. The woman unlocks a series of locks bolting the door closed. With the final click of the last lock, she opens the door a sliver and peeks through to double-check that it is Maddox. Once she sees him, she opens the door wide for him to stumble in and embraces him the second he does.

"I'm so glad you're back. I was starting to get worried." She huffs as she secures each lock back into position.

He slides off his coat and gloves and places them on a shelf near the door.

"Maddy!!" Sophie shouts with her mug-less arm reaching up for a hug.

"Soph-bug!" He squats down to give her an embrace and ruffles her matted hair.

Lan smiles at the exchange of affection.

"Good to see you awake. You feeling any better?" He asks, looking at me.

"Umm, I guess a bit, thanks to your aunt's soup, Maddy." I try not to snigger at saying his nickname that Sophie used for him.

"It's still Fin to you! No one calls me Maddy but my family, got it?" The tone of his voice would frighten even the bravest man.

I nod as he clears his throat and regains his composure. His voice turns softer once again.

"I'm sorry. I couldn't get you the vaccine. Everyone is out. I was prepared to work all week to get it, but there isn't even a vaccine to work for." He states with great disappointment. He leans in closer and whispers in my ear.

"Look, you have two choices if you want to live. One – go to E-Springs, they will give you the vaccine, but who knows what they will ask for in return. Or two - use the serum from the box on yourself." He sits back but continues to stare into my face, waiting for me to respond.

The thought of either option makes me nauseous.

The woman brings Fin a mug of soup.

"Thanks, Aunt Hellen."

"It's good to have you home, Maddy."

"It's good to be home."

Home.

That word jabs at my heart. The ache in my soul intensifies, and there is nothing I want more than to go home right now. I look at the way Fin looks at Sophie, and I yearn to see Jaxson. I want to check on him and see how he is doing.

Has he improved?
Is he still in a coma?
But I can't expose him to this fever!

Sophie's coughs interrupt my self-loathing. They intensify to the point where she can no longer hold her mug of soup without sloshing it all over. Lan grabs the mug from her and holds both mugs in one hand while patting Sophie's back with her other.

"She sounds worse. Isn't there anything we can give her?" Fin questions his aunt.

"I wish there was. You can give her some more honey, but that only helps for a short while because I've had to thin it down."

The pain of her response looks worse than my longing for Jaxson.

If only I had some medicine for her.
Wait, I brought a few inhalers and Epilanthdopram
injections in my backpack!

I set the mug of soup on the ground and muster up enough energy to lug my nearby backpack to where I can get to the front pocket. Fishing around through the contents, my hand feels the cool metal and plastic container of an inhaler, and I pull it out.

"Here, have her breathe in a puff of this. It should help." I hand it over to Fin.

"Where did you get an inhaler?" Aunt Hellen asks.

"I haven't seen one of these since I was a kid."

She kneels down next to Fin and snatches it from his hands, then pushes him out of the way. She quickly gives it a shake, pops off the cap, and places it between Sophie's sputtering purple lips. She gives the inhaler a pump and tells Sophie to breathe it in.

"Try to suck it in and hold it for as long as you can." Aunt Hellen instructs.

Sophie follows directions, sucks in the medicine, but is only able to hold it in momentarily before coughing it back out.

"Let's try it one more time," Aunt Hellen says.

Sophie sucks in another puff and is able to hold it in slightly longer this time. Then, she takes a few breaths before a small cough escapes. We all watch and breathe along with her, noticing that her coughing fit is calming down.

The inhaler is working!

"Thank you." Aunt Hellen replies as a teardrop expels from the corner of her eye and drips down her face like a game of Plinko over her skin spots and wrinkles.

Sophie gives me an exhausted smile and lays her head down on her pillow. She curls her fatigued body into a ball on her side.

"Let's let her get some much-needed rest now." Aunt Hellen whispers.

My head falls back against the wall, and my eyes close with relief.

"Looks like you need some rest, too." She states as she picks my mug up from the ground and shuffles her feet to the sink.

Fin chugs down his soup and offers to take the other two mugs from Lan.

Lan smiles and tries to move as little as possible since most of Sophie's frail body is curled up against her like a cat. Lan strokes the fever-drenched curls from Sophie's forehead.

My own head pounds with fever, and I, too, just want to sleep. I allow my aching body to slowly slump down onto the foam mattress. Lan wiggles her body down, carefully sandwiching her way between me and Sophie. I feel my body temperature change from the Sahara Desert to the frozen tundra. I know that I am also sick, dangerously sick. I no longer have the ability to open my eyes, no matter how much I want to.

"There are two injections of Epilanthdopram and one more inhaler in the front pocket of my backpack." I struggle to whisper to Lan before incoherence sets in.

"I just want you to know, just in case Sophie needs them. Or if I need them, or whatever." I sputter.

"You are going to be fine." Lan's whispers are like the antidote to my worries.

"You have to be." She adds.

"The world is counting on you." She whispers in my ear and kisses my burning cheek.

Chapter 22

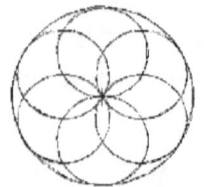

The Effects of Radiation

My consciousness throbs awake like an open wound oozing into the darkness. My nightmares still strangle the edges of my thoughts. My neck is so stiff I can't swallow, and the fact that my mouth is drier than a desert doesn't help. Trying to move sends shards of glass slicing through my body. My fatigued arms don't have enough strength to push me up to sit. It takes me a moment for my befuddled mind to recall where I am. I force my shaking hand to slide over the outline of a nearby body, rising and falling with each sleeping breath.

Lan.

The edges of my mouth conquer the fatigue to quiver a smile.

The darkness surrounding me weighs me down like tar, and the stale, stagnant air from being underground is too thick to breathe as my lips scrape apart.

Water.
I need water.

I recall seeing a small door slightly ajar in the corner of the bunker, which must lead to the bathroom. My body loses energy more rapidly with each slight attempted movement, but eventually, I make it to my hands and knees with my chest panting and head bobbing. I force my way to a staggered stance. Pain wreaks havoc on my stomach, and I hunch back over. Feeling my way through the darkness with my hands, they finally reach the small handle of the door. The throbbing pain in my head is so overbearing I barely notice as I stub my toes on the lip of the bathroom door frame, which sticks up out of the floor. The muscles in my quads wretch as they tug my foot up and over the lip, stepping into the bathroom. I plop down onto the toilet and quietly pull the door closed, panting, as if I just ran a mile. As the door clicks closed, a small, dim fluorescent light flickers on. My eyes scream closed, and the ache in my head revolts. With a few labored flutters, my eyes finally squint open enough to take in some light. Gratitude floods my wheezing mind as I take in the compactness of the bathroom. I am able to remain seated on the commode while my hands fight against gravity to stretch upward to the small sink within my arm's length. My unsteady fingers grip weakly around the peeling plastic knob of the sink. My other hand flops to grab a small plastic cup at the back of the sink. As a small trickle of water flows from the faucet, I place the cup under its glory and allow it to stream into the cup. Unable to hold my arms up much longer, I twist the squeaking knob to turn off the flow. Wrapping my trembling hands around the cup, it takes the rest of my energy to get the sloshing water up to my peeling lips. I sip and allow the water to puddle on my tongue, soaking it like a dry sponge. The metallic taste of the cool liquid churns my queasy stomach, but I fight the urge to spit it out and force it to the back of my throat. Swallowing is painful and difficult, but I allow my constricting muscles to take over and force the water down. I cough but choke down another sip savagely. My arms flop down on top of my thighs as I allow a bit of rejected water to drip its way from my chin onto my arm. I watch as it finds the path of least resistance around an open wound of flesh. It's as if my skin is beginning to reject the radiation poisoning inflicting my body. I unfurl my brow slightly and allow my eyes to open enough to look upward at my grim reflection in the small peeling mirror attached to the front of a medicine cabinet. My sunken eyes are barely being held up by dark half-moons. The track of dried blood crusting from my nostrils stands out against my otherwise ashy, pale skin. It's difficult to tell if I even have lips since the color of their flakes is no different than the white-grey muddling around them.

I look worse than Jaxson did in Lan's time.
Is this how it ends?
Alone in a little bunker bathroom in a distant time?

Even my thoughts are too tiring. I wheeze a breath into my lungs through a few shallow spouts. I need to cough, but I don't have enough energy. I allow my head to fall against the wall next to me. I wish I could go back and lie down next to Lan, but I don't even have the will to fight my eyelids to stay open. The hum of the generator and the buzzing light soon dissipate to silence.

"Dameon, are you okay in there?"

Lan's whispers penetrate my painful existence; at least, I think I still exist. I try to answer her, but the words stay trapped like a prisoner inside my mind. My voice doesn't even vibrate, and my head seems to be cemented to the wall like heavy bricks. The click of the bathroom door echoes pain through every cell. I want more than anything to open my eyes and take in Lan's face, but they refuse to cooperate. Millions of pins and needles shoot through my hands as Lan grasps them and pats them.

"Dameon! Dameon, open your eyes!"

I allow a small sliver of light to fester in, but it is too painful, and my eyelids squeeze closed again.

"Fin!

Help!

Please!"

Lan's voice pounds against my skull like a wrecking ball, but that pain is nothing compared to the jarring flood of agony exploding vehemently as my body is whipped through the bathroom door and placed onto the cold floor. The discomfort and muffled words come in waves. There are moments when they are too much to bear and others when I can't tell if they are miles away, perhaps being thrust upon someone else entirely. Then, like the fang of a fiery serpent piercing my skin, I am injected with boiling lava in my thigh. As if awakening every fiber as the fire rushes through my veins, I am suddenly aware of the scorching pain engulfing my body. A release of anguish emerges from my lips in the form of a scream as my eyes snap open.

"Ah, there you are. I thought we lost you there for a second."

Fin's witty voice covers up his hidden concern.

"Dameon!" Lan's arms wrap around my chest and squeeze out a painful cough.

I notice the injector pen still gripped in her fingers.

Epilanthdopram, she just injected me with
Epilanthdopram.
We are down one injection.

"We have to go, now! We need to get him to the doctors at E-Springs if he is going to have any chance of getting the vaccine to survive. They won't give him the vaccine if
he is too far gone, or if they don't think they can save him."

"But I thought you said that you can't go back there?" Lan's voice is full of apprehension.

"We are leaving, NOW!" Fin's voice demands.

"Go ask Tim down the road to borrow his sled and dogs; he owes me a favor."

"We don't have time for that, and the guards will hear us coming and will have their own dogs attacking us before we even get there." Fin's words jab back at Hellen.

He puts on his coat and zips it up to his chin. He then adjusts the hood up over his ears.

"Let's go!" He shouts, shoving his hands into his gloves.

I push my way up to stand, my shaking legs can barely hold my weight. Lan helps me wobble over to the door to put a coat on.

"At least put him on the sled." Hellen's voice quivers.

"I will. I'll make sure he gets there." Fin announces as he exits the door.

Hellen drapes us with blankets and gloves and shoos us out behind Fin.

"What about the backpack and satchel?" I ask Lan.

"Do you want to hand all your things over to Elementerprise?" Hellen asks, overhearing my question.

"I can't just leave them here." I gasp with desperation.

"I promise to keep them safe for you." Hellen steps in front of my stagger.

A sense of sincerity beams from her gaze.

"Come on, Dameon. We have to get you to E-Springs."

"But, Lan... you know I can't leave... ALL my things behind."

"Sophie will guard them with her life, right Sophie?" Lan asks.

"You have my word." Sophie places one hand over her heart and the other in the air with a promising vow. "Cross my heart, hope to die, stick a thousand needles in my eye."

"Alright. Thank you, Princess Sophie." I let a weak wink flutter in her direction. "I know I can trust you."

"Bye," Sophie's melancholy voice wafts after us as her little chin begins to quiver.

"Bye, Sophie. We'll try to be back as soon as possible." Lan replies.

"Draw me a picture," I add.

Sophie's little nod and forced smile paint their way into my mind.

"Thank you," Lan hugs Hellen.

"Alright now, get going. Take care." Hellen squeezes my hand as the wrinkles around her eyes squeeze tighter.

Lan helps me out the door, and I hear the various locks click behind us. I wave my quivering hands in front of me to feel for the rungs of a ladder. Lan helps me to steady my body and force my wobbling legs to push up off the ground. The glow of daylight is only a few feet above my head. Fin's long arm reaches down to help pull me up out of the hole. I don't even have to climb before I am lifted into the biting cold wind and plopped onto a worn sled. Fin runs back around and helps Lan climb out of the hole. He then closes the hatch door and covers it with snow and branches. You would never know there is a bunker below us housing a woman, a little girl, and my most prized possessions.

Please keep them safe.

The adrenaline from the injection must be wearing off. I wish that I could stand and walk to E-Springs myself, but I am forced to gulp down my pride and allow Fin and Lan to pull me instead. Fatigue plagues me once again as I watch the bare branches above me sway like dancing skeletons against a murky grey sky. The mesmerizing flakes of snow and ash flutter and frolic in the wind. The swishing sound of the sled below me as I am dragged across the top of the icy snow hypnotizes me into a trance.

Chapter 23

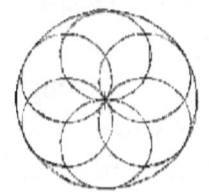

E-Springs

The sound of barking wolves as they attack me from all sides resonates in my ears. My eyelids crack open under the thin layer of ice, which has frozen my eyelashes together.

Not wolves.
Dogs.
Guard dogs.

"I can't go with you. This is as far as I can go. I'm sorry." Fin's words churn through the wind.

"You aren't going with me either." I form the raspy words in Lan's direction.

"I will go by myself. I won't allow either of you to risk coming with me." I sputter, forcing my spinning head up to a sitting position.

"He does need to walk to the gate if he wants the chance of them letting him in." One of Fin's eyebrows rises above the other as he helps me to my feet.

"I'm not going to just let him go in there by himself." Lan's voice is full of disgust.

The barking of the dog behind the gate grows in intensity.

"What is it this time?" Shouts the voice of the guard approaching the yelping dog.

Fin looks up and locks eyes with the guard up ahead. The color instantly drains from Fin's face as the chest of his coat begins to rise and fall rapidly.

"I'm sorry. I have to go." Fin mutters as he turns and runs back through the trees, dragging the empty sled behind him.

My knees begin to buckle, but Lan is right here to keep me steady. We watch for a moment as Fin disappears into a blur in the distance like a ghost. The barking dog whips my focus back toward the gate ahead.

"Hey, you two need to get out of here!" The guard shouts in our direction.

"Please, my friend needs your help." Lan hollers back as she tugs me in his direction.

"Don't think for one second that I am going to let you in here. Go on, get lost, or I will allow the dog to make you leave." With that command, the massive German Shepherd's bark turns into a

hungry snarl.

"Please, he needs the vaccine," Lan begs.

"Yes, him and hundreds of other rats that aren't worth our time. Go on!"

"You must help him. His Great Granddad is in there." With Lan's plea, we near the gate.

The dog's eyes bulge in hopes we will be his next meal. I can feel his thoughts devouring me. I just focus on staying erect and shake the need to pass out from enervation.

"If his Great Granddad finds out you are refusing us entry, your life will be on the line."

A distant howl stiffens Lan's stance and fires our urgency.

"Now!" Lan's voice explodes like a grenade, small yet fierce. It escapes her lips with such conviction that even the dog sits submissively, his haunches planting into the snow.

"I'll need to scan your bracelet chip, Ma'am." The guard squeaks.

"I don't have my bracelet with me." Lan lies. "You will just have to trust us."

"You may scan mine. My chip is in my neck." I allow my heavy head to fall forward.

"In your neck, sir? But only the highest elite have chips implanted in their neck."

As my head flops, the ground appears to keep getting closer. The white snow distorts below me as Lan catches my stagger. The guard unlocks the gate and helps to steady me as soon as it swings open.

I feel his gaze on the back of my neck as his muscular arm assists me forward through the black iron. His other arm slams the gate closed, and it locks into place with a boisterous clank. After we make it about halfway to the tunnel barrier door, which seems to be hiding under a mound of frozen earth, the guard lets out a sharp whistle. The dog, who had been obediently waiting for the command, instantly tromps through the snow to our side as if this is all a game. His sizable tail wags jovially, and steam releases off his pink tongue with each pant.

"Corporal, what is the meaning of this? These rats aren't approved for admittance." A deep voice huffs.

"Sergeant." The guard stands as straight as possible with me slumped against him, and he uses his other arm to salute the man standing at the large metal door ahead.

"This one claims to be a relative of an elite inside, and he requires medical attention, sir."

"Then he needs to enter through the front gate like all the other guests."

"I'm afraid there is no time for that, sir. He needs help, now."

"Please!" Lan uses her beautiful, golden eyes to plead with the higher-ranking soldier.

The man at the door puffs up his chest and lets out a long sigh in the form of a circling cloud of crystalizing breath.

"Alright, but be quick.

Private Gnash, cover the Corporal's gate until he returns."

"Yes, sir." The younger soldier at his side half shields one eye in a perfected angular salute.

He darts off toward the gate, and the gargantuan dog follows him, playfully prancing in the snow. The Sergeant turns to the large metal, vault-like door. He types in a code on a keypad and allows his eyes to be scanned by a red beam of light. A piercing beep sounds, followed by a reverberating latch unlocking. He then places his gloved hands on a large metal wheel and twists it open like on a bank vault. Although the massive door appears extremely heavy, he is able to swing it open with ease. The lights inside the corridor zap on in sequence one after the other and appear to extend into an endless tunnel.

"Thank you." Lan smiles. The man's face blushes, and not because of the fierce cold biting his cheeks.

"You're welcome, Ma'am." A hint of a smile glints in his eyes for a split second.

The guard half drags me into the corridor as the Sergeant slams the vault door closed behind us. The clunking lock echoes ahead as it secures into place at our backs. I do my best to convince my feet to keep trudging in time with the pounding boots of the guard at my one side and Lan's feet at my other. But my head bobs and dips beyond my control. The infinite tunnel of lights flickers, at least, I think that is the light flickering. Perhaps it is my mind or my vision. The faint sound of a wobbling wheel shrills in the distance and grows in volume until it finally reaches us.

"Place him on here, Corporal." The sound of a woman's voice fills my head. My feet are swept out from under me as I am placed on a gurney and wheeled briskly ahead. The face of a dark angel pops into my blurring vision.

"Hang on, baby. We're almost there." Her sweet Southern drawl is like warm sweet tea in my ears. I may not be able to see her smile under the mask covering her nose and mouth, but her dark eyes are sincere and squint in the corners. Her latex-gloved hands slide an oxygen mask over my nose and mouth, and I am flooded with the scent of new plastic and a hint of honeysuckle. I no longer feel my body or pain. I force my eyes to stay open and watch as the lights clinging to the cave-like ceiling whiz above me in a slow-motion, strobe-light pattern. I squint as the ceiling changes as we go through a series of doors. Each room is filled with a different commotion of sounds. The narrow walls of the next room are tiled in small blue squares. An aroma of bleach and soap seep their way into my mask.

The squeaking wheels stop suddenly.

"Judgin' by your healthy appearance, I'm assumin' you have had the vaccine already?" The woman asks Lan.

"Ummmm, yes?" Lan's response sounds more like a question than a statement.

"Well, then, just to be safe, you can head to that room. Once inside, take off all your contaminated clothes and put them in the hazardous waste bin on the wall. Then, proceed to the door on the other side of that room. Through that door is a shower room. Wash your hair and body thoroughly in the streams of hot water with the soap and shampoo provided. Don't be startled; the water will be coming from all directions, and it feels like it is burning you, sweet pea, but it isn't hot enough to actually burn you. But it will help wash off all the contaminants and radiation. After being out in that cold, it ought to feel real nice. There are clean towels and scrubs by the exit door to put on. We'll meet you on the other side once I get your friend here decontaminated as well.

Do you have any questions?"

Lan shakes her head with confusion, clearly trying to understand the situation.

"Come on, young man, let's get you cleaned up, too."

She continues to push my gurney into the next small room, where she helps me shed my clothes. My body instantly starts to convulse into shivers and contracts into a fetal position, making our task more difficult. I watch the blue-tiled walls close in around me.

"Hurry now, let's get you into the hot water." She states calmly, helping me into a shower chair with wheels. She pushes me forward as the water forcefully sprays from all directions. I can't

209

distinguish the temperature of the water because every droplet feels like acid. The steam billowing around me tells me it must be hot. She grabs a body scrub brush off the wall and begins to scrub. I see someone moving near the gurney we left behind. Another woman comes to change the sheets on the bed. I squeeze my eyes closed and focus on breathing through the pain. Every scrub of the brush feels like she is peeling off my skin. I look down at the water puddling around my feet and it is tinged with crimson. My head begins to spin, and the urge to vomit overcomes me. I relieve my nausea and vomit all over the blue-tiled floor. It's full of red blood, and it swirls down the drain. If I had the hydration or the energy, I probably would be crying or screaming out in pain. But there is nothing left in me, nothing I can do but close my eyes and wait for this torture to all be over.

"Poor thang. How have you gone this long out there without the vaccine? You truly are a miracle, sugar.

There now, all done." The scorching water stops. She pats me dry with a scratchy towel and attempts to help me stand to get back on the fresh gurney, but my weak legs won't cooperate.

"Nancy, a little help here?" The woman asks.

The woman who changed the bedding on the gurney appears at my other side, and together, the two women lift my slippery body back onto the crisp, clean gurney. The pain zinging from head to toe sends another surge to vomit, but I do my best to swallow it down. I don't want to risk having to go through the agony of another shower. The women cover my shivering body with a thin gown and then layers of warm, white blankets, and I allow my eyes to close as they place the oxygen mask back on my face.

"I got him from here, thanks, doll." The woman states to Nancy.

I am wheeled into the next room, where Lan, dressed in papery scrubs, swishes to my side.

"Are you okay?" Her tear-filled eyes search mine.

Unable to speak, I just give an affirmative blink.

Heading into the next room, I am flooded with the aroma of bleach mixed with iodine this time. Flopping my head to the side, I can see rows of patients in beds, some sitting, some lying, some don't appear to be moving at all. Finally, the squeaking of the wheels stops again, and a curtain is drawn, following the track of a "U" shape around me. Then, the real commotion begins. A doctor appears from behind the mint-green striped curtain, and he begins asking hundreds of questions. The sweet voice of the woman who helped to wheel me here tries to answer as many questions as she can.

"Patient's name?" The doctor asks, as the nurse rolls my head to the side and scans the chip in my neck, the chip that was placed in me at the Elementerprise facility in Lan's time.

"Unknown, the guard said he came in through the West gate and claims that he has a Great Granddaddy that is high-up here, or somethin', ain't that right, darlin'?'"

"Interesting, his chip isn't registered in our system, and it is unlike anything I have ever

seen." The doctor sounds perplexed as he examines my neck further.

"What is your name, boy?" He asks, his words muffling in his medical mask, as he stares down at my face.

I try to answer, but I am unable to form the words.

"Dameon, his name is Dameon Gardener." Lan's anxious voice pipes in.

"You really shouldn't be here, miss. Put on a mask and have a seat over there." The nurse gestures to a box of disposable masks and a metal chair in the corner. "I will take you to a room once he is stabilized."

Lan takes a step toward the chair and moves out of the way of the scrambling nurse and doctor, but she doesn't sit. Her eyes are glued to me, flooding with worry.

"I assume he has not had the vaccine?" The doctor asks.

"No, sir," Lan answers again.

"I thought she told you to put on a mask, young lady." The doctor jabs.

Lan snatches a mask from the box and places it over her nose and mouth with a huff of annoyance.

The doctor nods at the nurse as she grabs a needle full of a clear liquid and gently presses it into my exposed upper arm. I don't even feel the prick of the needle. My body is numb. I watch as a tear leaks out of Lan's eye and spills down her perfect cheekbone. It disappears under the upper edge of the blue-filtered mask. I try to smile at her under the oxygen mask, but the muscles in my face don't respond. I simply focus on opening my eyes each time they blink closed. It is the one thing I can do to communicate to Lan that I am still okay. Maybe opening my eyes is for my sake. I am afraid to let them close. I'm worried they may not open again. The nurse starts an IV in my arm, but again, I feel nothing. The words of the doctor echo in my head as he barks orders, telling the nurse all the fancy medication names to inject into my IV. But I drown out their drudging voices, the beeping of the machines, the chaos of sounds all around me, and I try to focus on Lan's face as my eyes blur shut and eventually refuse to open.

Chapter 24

On the Mend

M y eyes flutter open. I am tucked into one of the beds in a line of many, all full of patients. I push my way up to a sitting position and fluff my pillows behind me to help keep me propped in that position. Grogginess fogs my brain, and I notice an IV bag full of fluids being pumped into my arm.

They must have me on some heavy medication.
I can barely focus on anything.

"Good mornin', sunshine." The familiar face of the nurse inches toward me.

"How are you feelin' today?"

"Ummmm, pretty good, actually," I respond, noticing that the pounding headache and excruciating pain in my body have subsided.

"Just a bit dizzy," I complain, as the machines around me leave a blurred trail behind them as I look between them.

"Oh, that's just the pain meds. I can turn it down if you are feelin' better." She responds cheerfully as she reaches to twist a plastic dial connected to my IV tube, closing off the drip.

"Thank you." I smile as gratitude floods my heart.

The fact that I can speak and smile, and my body responds when I tell it to do things, fills me with elation. Who knew that those little things I took for granted would be so important to me? I suck in a deep cleansing breath, full of life. I let it wash over me, and I become fully aware as it pumps through every cell in my body.

I am alive!

I notice patches of scabs where I recall gaping wounds splotching my arms when I was in the shower.

"How long have I been here?" I ask, referring to my healing lesions.

"You have been out for a couple of days. You gave us all a scare there for a while. But I'm thrilled to see you are awake and doing well." The woman opens a tub of opaque goo and smears some on my scabs with a cotton swab.

"There you go. You should be as good as new in no time."

"Thank you… Ma'am."

"Oh honey, you can call me Nurse Felicia." Her dark chocolate eyes sparkle with kindness.

I smile back, but it shifts into a hacking cough.

"I'm afraid you might be stuck with that cough, though. Some children outgrow it, but at your age, it's probably here for good. Our lungs get to a point where they don't heal as well as they did when we were younger, and the damage to your lungs is quite extensive. I'll just keep prayin' they improve. My prayers have worked on you so far. You're a down-right miracle, praise Jesus." Her gloved dark hands press together in a prayer formation.

"May I get up now? I need to go find my Great Granddad." My antsy words flitter about.

"Shhhhhh, now, darlin'. Lan, that pretty girl you came in with has been workin' on that. You stay here in bed, and I'll find her and let her know you are awake."

Felicia leans down to whisper close to my face, "And I would keep who your Great Granddaddy is a secret 'round here. There are many people who would be wantin' to get their hands on you if they find out who you are. But don't you worry, your secret is safe with me." She relays with a wink.

214

"Now, lemme go find your friend and have her bring you some breakfast to fill that skin-and-bone belly of yours before it jumps up and bites your liver." She gently pats my stomach and chortles.

"May I get up to use the restroom, please?" I ask as she turns to leave.

"Sure, Hun. It's the door right over there." The permanent creases next to her eyes web together in a tighter weave as they squint into a smile. She points to an open door not far away.

"Let me just get you unhooked." Her gentle gloved hands move like clockwork to unscrew the tube attached to the IV in my arm. Then, she proceeds to pull out various tubes from all sorts of unpleasant places, where I don't think they should have been, to begin with.

"Oh, I should probably warn you. Don't be alarmed if it's blue when you go."

My face scrunches together at her warning, and she decides to give me an explanation.

"It's the medication. It is helping to rid your body of the radiation." She adds.

"Ummmm, okay. Thanks." I struggle to drag my legs over the side of the bed. They drop like heavy weights to the floor. With quivering arms, I push myself up to a standing position, and Felicia steadies my wobbles.

"There ya go, easy does it." She states.

"You want me to help you?" She asks.

I wait a moment for the room to stop spinning, and I take one taxing step.

"No, thank you. I think I got it," I respond. There is no way I need someone to help me go to the bathroom. Even if Felicia is by far the sweetest person ever.

"Alright, darlin'. Just push the red button in there if you need help."

"Thanks," I utter, shuffling my socked feet with gripper bottoms along the reflective white, tiled floor. A draft of cool air blows at my backside, and my arms instantly swing back to secure the opening and close it tightly. My cheeks flush, and my eyes scour the room of patients behind me to make sure none of them caught a glimpse of my vulnerability. I quickly flip on the light, close the bathroom door behind me, and lock the door. I plop down onto the toilet seat and pant heavily. I only walked a few feet, but I feel like I just ran a marathon.

Felicia wasn't kidding.
It looks like I ate Smurfs!

I flush down the swirl of blue and sturdy myself at the sink. As I scrub my hands, I look up at my reflection in the mirror. I barely recognize the face staring back at me. My wild hair resembles a brown mane that flares out in all directions. My sunken, yellow eyes look back at me and make me think of Jaxson. The pillow creases on my face make me look wrinkled. I suddenly look older, like my Dad or even Great Granddad. I splash water on my face and let the warmth wash away my sickly appearance. But it is just water, after all, not a miracle potion. The water does help to tame my hair slightly, however. I soak the spazzing, greasy strands and comb them down with my fingernails.

At least that looks a little better.

I cup a handful of water and sip it refreshingly into my parched mouth. I swish it around my teeth and instantly taste the metallic flavor of dried blood. I spit out the tinted water and continue flushing my mouth until it is no longer pink.

I definitely need to ask Felicia if I can get a toothbrush.

I suddenly feel self-conscious about talking to Lan with my horrendous breath.

Lan! I need to hurry back to bed. Felicia said she would be sending for her.

I shake off the water from my hands, not even taking the time to put them under the air dryer. I open the bathroom door and rush, as quickly as my feeble legs can move, back into my bed. I tuck the blankets around my body tightly, making sure that there is no way Lan, or anyone, can see anything I don't want them to see. I pant and cough and try to catch my heavy breath. I see that Felicia, or someone, has brought me a cup with a plastic straw, and it is full of ice water. I reach my shaky hands over and sip down some water, and it helps to calm my coughing fit.

As I look up, I see a beautiful girl in a black and white maid outfit gliding toward me with a tray of food. Not just any beautiful girl, Lan. My heart flutters in my chest like a bunch of moths searching for light, and that light is Lan. Her auburn hair is swept upward. A few stray hairs have escaped her loose bun. And her eyes, her vibrant golden eyes, are filled with euphoric embers.

"Dameon, you're awake!" She squirms, nearly dropping the tray of food, as she leans down to wrap her other arm around me in an embrace.

"Lan, what are you wearing?" I refrain from letting the laughter welling up inside me escape.

"If I want to stay here, I have to work and earn my keep." She sighs, brushing a few crumbs from her uniform.

"But it isn't so bad. I mostly deliver food to rooms and take their dirty dishes back to the kitchen. You wouldn't believe how much food people waste."

She leans down close to my ear, and her over-boiling secret explodes out of her mouth.

"I might sneak some of the untouched food left on the plates. I never knew there were so many delicious things to eat!" Lan's face glows with excitement as she giggles with embarrassment. I can no longer hold in my pent-up giddiness, and I laugh along with her. At least until it turns into an uncontrollable cough. She sets the tray of food down on my lap and hands me the sloshing cup of orange juice from the tray she just brought.

"Thank you." I stumble over my words, unable to look away from her splendor.

The moment swells with tongue-tied silence.

"Here, try the waffles and syrup." Lan finally spouts, shoving a bite of food in my mouth with a fork.

The buttery syrup oozes its way down my chin, and I watch as Lan practically drools at the sight.

"It's SO good, isn't it?" She licks her lips as if helping me taste them as she sits on the edge of my bed.

"De-wish-us." I attempt to say as my dry mouth attempts to produce enough saliva to chew and swallow the barrage of fluffy waffles. "You want some?" I push the plate toward Lan.

"No, you need to eat them to get your strength back."

"I can't possibly eat all this myself." I banter coyly.

"Okay, if you insist." She jumps at the opportunity, seizes one of the sections of waffle, and dips it into the plastic container of maple syrup. Bringing her face over the tray, so as not to waste a single drop of syrup. Her eyes roll to the back of her head as she devours it.

I could honestly watch her eat all day. I love how much she enjoys food. I can't imagine growing up without ever tasting anything other than those putrid food ration bars.

I shake my focus from watching her eat. I don't want to come across as creepy.

"So, have you found my Great Granddad yet? Is he still here?" Licking her fingers, Lan replies, "I have asked around. There is one young man named Eli who works in sanitation, garbage detail, they call it. He has seen some things that sound promising." Her eyes shift around the room as she leans in close to my face.

"He is sent down below the basement to collect trash. No one else in service even seems to know there is anything beyond the basement. He says that down there is where they do top-secret things. He says there are a lot of hazardous and biological waste materials he is told to dispose of discretely from down there in a secret incinerator. Lots of test tubes and sciency stuff, too. He even said that there is an old scientist down there that isn't allowed to leave. That must be him. Eli is going to take me down there tonight after most of the guests have gone to bed. The only problem I have is that if any guests from the floors that I am in charge of ring for food, I have to deliver it, no matter what time it is. I think I might be able to ask Scarlett to cover for me, but I'm afraid she is too nosy and asks too many questions."

"Come and get me before you go. I must go down there with you."

"No, Dameon, there are too many stairs for you. We will have to take the servant stairs all the way down there. We can't take the elevator. The elevator operator would never let us
get on the elevator. I know, I've tried. It's just for guests. Even when I have heavy trays full of food, I'm not allowed on them."

"Ahem…" The doctor who helped me when I arrived here, clears his throat.

Lan jumps up off the side of my bed and straightens her shoulders back tightly like a soldier.

"Off you go, miss. My patient needs his rest, and you have work to do."

"Yes, sir." Lan nods her head in polite obedience. She turns to leave the hospital wing but looks back over her shoulder and mouths the words, "I'll come back later," in my direction. I give a little nod to her in return, and then finish it with a look of *you better come back for me*.

"Dameon, it is nice to see that you are awake."

I nod.

"How are you feeling today?"

"Pretty good," I respond.

He checks the readings on the machines.

"It looks like you are doing well, all things considered. But let's keep you full of fluids for now and continue monitoring you." He reattaches the line to my IV and places the electrical pads back onto my chest. The machine next to me begins beeping with each rapid beat of my heart.

"Your heart is racing a bit.

Is it because of that girl?" He asks in a joking manner, placing an ice-cold stethoscope onto my chest, nearly causing me to jump out of my skin. Luckily, as he moves it to different locations on my body to listen, it grows warmer with each touch.

He then places an oxygen meter onto my pointer finger. It is the same finger that The Captain placed a similar-looking device which pricked my finger with hundreds of little needles, injecting me with whatever substance spread up my hand and imprinted me with the ink for the tattoo on the underside of my wrist. The doctor and I notice my freshly wrapped bandaged wrist simultaneously.

Has he seen my tattoo?
Or was it Felicia, or another nurse, who wrapped my
wrist for me?

The doctor grasps my wrapped hand in his and flips it over. He takes his other hand and attempts to peel back the bandage to see what is hiding underneath. I flinch my hand back away from him and hold it protectively. The oxygen meter is tugged from my finger and flings off the side of my bed. The doctor's bushy eyebrows, like dark furry caterpillars, crawl downward toward his scrunched nose in disapproval.

"Did you do something to yourself that you are ashamed of?
It's okay.
We are all living in difficult times."
"NO!
I didn't…
It's not…"
The rate of beeping on the machine increases dramatically.

"Okay. Alright, calm down." The doctor places his hands on me gently and looks around the hospital room to make sure no one else saw my spout of sudden rage.

"Would you like me to get your oxygen levels from a finger on your other hand then, please?"

I take a few deep breaths and steady my heart rate. Then, I slide my unbandaged hand toward the doctor. He fetches the dangling meter and places it on the pointer finger.

"Dameon, I was told you claim to have a Great Grandfather here. Is that correct?"

I am unsure whether or not I should divulge any information. Felicia told me to not say anything to anyone about my Great Granddad. So, I just sit, silently watching the little red numbers fluctuate on the oxygen meter, and ignore the doctor's question.

The doctor leans in closer to me and his eyes burn into mine.

"Is Doctor Dean Gardener your Great Grandfather?" His question appears to be a loaded gun, ready to pull the trigger depending on my answer.

My beeping heart rate spikes again, and suddenly I feel like I can't suck in enough oxygen. A cough forms in the back of my throat, and I let it escape, over and over, directly into the doctor's masked face.

"Oh, doctor. How is our patient doin'?" Felicia extinguishes the thick tension lingering in the air. The doctor stands up straight, and he regains a professional composure.

"I believe he could use some oxygen." He states matter-of-factly.

"I will be back to check on you soon." His words cut like a threat.

I watch the doctor walk forcefully out of my curtained section, tearing his mask from his face and wiping it violently with a disinfectant wipe.

"He seems a little intense, but don't let him get to ya. I've found that most doctors thrive on intimidation." Felicia whispers.

"Here, let's put the mask back on for a while, okay." She states, placing the plastic mask over my nose as she turns on the oxygen.

"Now, what was he so worked up about?" She asks.

"He was asking me about my Great Granddad."

"You didn't tell him anything, did you?"

"No, why?

What do you know?

Why do I need to keep my Great Granddad a secret?" I suck the fresh air in.

"Look, Darlin', I've been a nurse here a long time. I enjoy working here in the medical wing and helping patients. But I have seen a lot of things and heard a lot of things. Most people don't even notice me in the room while they are discussing things, and I plan to keep it that way. I have also been asked to take care of some odd patients over the years. Ones that Elementerprise won't let out into the world. They are prisoners kept below, like lab rats. Scary creatures, if you ask me. I refuse to go near them or have anything to do with them, even when the bigwigs say my job and livelihood depend on it. Between you and me, I think they are afraid to get rid of me and let me out into the world. I know too much. And they are right. They know that I'll keep quiet and do my job if I know what's good for me. And so that's what I do. I keep my head down and do what the good Lord intended me to do. I keep helpin' people."

"So, what does that have to do with my Great Granddad?"

"I heard them say that your Great Granddaddy is the one that made those creatures the way they are. And that he is the one who has figured out how to save them and everyone from the radiation and poisons of the world." Her dark eyes intensify and grow larger.

"I have reasons to believe that he is also being kept against his will deep below with those creatures."

I throw the blankets off the lower half of my body, rip off the oxygen mask, and attempt to stand to go after him.

"No, you must stay here in this bed." Felicia holds me down.

We both notice another nurse assisting a nearby patient looking over at us to watch my sudden outburst.

"Must be the fever making you so hot, Darlin'. But you gotta stay in bed and keep covered if you want to feel better." She covers my actions and talks loud enough to appease the investigating looks from the other nurse.

Felicia then proceeds to tuck the blankets around me extra tight while smiling in the other nurse's direction and gives a slight giggle as a secret language between nurses, mocking the stupidity of patients. The other nurse giggles back and gives a little shake of her head, communicating that she understands all too well that patients can be difficult. The other nurse turns back to her business.

"Please, you must stay here. Everyone is watchin' you like a hawk." She whispers without moving her lips as if she is a ventriloquist.

I hate to comply, but I feel I have no choice.

"I overheard the doctors saying that you have The Serum in your possession. Is that true?

They have searched through your clothes and things. Trust me when I say they have searched everywhere. They have even scanned every inch of your body, inside and out, but haven't found anything."

"No, I don't have it." I think about the metal box tucked into my backpack at Fin's bunker.

Fin! He better not touch it!

"I have to go. I need to leave The Greenbrier as soon as I can." Panic pulses through my veins.

"Shhhhhh, everyone will get upset if you call this place The Greenbrier. It's called E-Springs now, ever since Elementerprise took it over. I'm afraid you need at least

223

another day or two before you will be strong enough to go anywhere. You just stay here and keep out of trouble. I will do what I can to keep the doctor and everyone else off your back. Then, I will see what I can do to help you leave.
Deal?"

I nod with disbelief that Felicia is being so kind to me.

"Why are you helping me?"

"You can trust me. I come from a long line of witch-doctors." The edges of her smile grow beyond the mask on her face.

"Don't worry, most witch-doctors use the earth to help heal and keep the devilish spirits away, not to harm people like everyone believes."

She places her medical gloved hand gingerly over my bandaged wrist and leans in closer.

"And I've seen that symbol before. I know what it stands for. I know how you are.

As long as I live and breathe, I will help to keep you safe." Her eyes close respectfully, and she bows her head gently.

I scan the medical wing around us to make sure no one is witnessing her odd display.

"You are the one that bandaged my wrist?"

"Yes, sir. And I plan to make sure no one else sees it, don't you worry." She removes the oxygen meter from my other finger and places it back on the machine.

"How about you get some rest now, sugar? Just keep quiet and get some sleep. I'll be back on shift tonight." She pats my arm and walks away, her thick, souled shoes squeaking with every stride. Her ebony skin stands out beautifully next to her white scrubs as she disappears.

Looking around the room, I suddenly feel like all eyes are on me, watching my every move. There is one middle-aged man a few beds away that doesn't even appear to be sick. His healthy eyes scrutinize my every breath.

Are all these people actual patients, or are some
planted in here just to spy on me?

The other nurse keeps looking over her shoulder every few minutes to watch my actions. I gaze up at the black orbs hanging in the corners of the room. I also notice a little blinking red light on the heart-rate monitor, one that clearly has nothing to do with the beating of my heart.

There are cameras everywhere.
I am being watched.

I sink down under my blankets, trying to dematerialize. I squeeze my eyes closed, wanting to escape the scopophobia infecting my brain.

Chapter 25

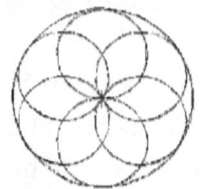

The Interrogation

I spend most of the day dozing; trying to sleep as much as I can, because the hours I am awake seem to ache by drudgingly. The watchful eyes of others scald my nerves. Someone other than Lan brings my lunch, and my dinner.

> *Lan, where are you?*
> *Are they watching her, too?*
> *Maybe they have her locked up and she can't come to see me.*
> *Staying in this bed is driving me crazy.*
> *I want to go look for Great Granddad.*
> *I NEED to go look for Lan!*

My eyes skitter around the room, desperate for any information. I pick at the sides of my fingernails anxiously. My apprehensive foot twitches repeatedly under my blanket. Despite rolling from side to side in the little bed, my hips ache from lying so long, and my tailbone feels like it has attached itself to the hard mattress. I've been waiting for Felicia to return, but I haven't seen her either.

"Excuse me, Ma'am?" I ask a younger nurse who entered the wing a few minutes ago.

"Yes, are you okay, sir?" She asks, instantly checking me over.

"Yes, I'm fine. I was just wondering if I might use the restroom and maybe go for a walk? You know, get out of bed for a few minutes? My hips are killing me."

Amusement washes over her.

"Ahhh, I see. You have hit the stir-crazy stage. Don't worry, that's perfectly normal."

"I need to get out of bed for a bit if that's possible."

"You are in luck," she mentions after reading my file on the chart.

"Looks like you get to go for an appointment with Dr. Steinberger shortly."

"Dr. Steinberger?" I ask.

I recall reading the name tag of the doctor who has been treating me, and his name is Dr. Conrad, so I know this Dr. Steinberger is a different doctor than the one taking care of me.

"Yes, you'll like him. He is a psychologist. He has a bowl of candy on his desk." She adds, raising her eyebrows with enticement.

Seriously, does she think I'm eight? No amount of candy is going to make me want to go and chit-chat with a psychologist. Besides, he has probably been instructed to get me to tell him everything I know about Great Granddad and The Serum.

"No thanks, I think I would rather stay in bed." I roll my eyes.

"Sorry, it's not optional.

Oh, look, here comes Shelly to get you now. Let's get you into a wheelchair."

"If I have to go, may I at least walk there without the wheelchair?" I know that I need to walk to get stronger and build up my stamina so that I can work my way up to get down to Great Granddad.

"Sure," Shelly replies before the nurse can answer, over-hearing my request. Shelly is clearly not a nurse. She is wearing a fitted grey blazer with red pinstripes and a tight black pencil skirt. My guess is that she is the psychologist's secretary, personal assistant, or something like that.

"But it's proper protocol for patients who have been bedridden to be transported via wheelchair as a safety precaution." The nurse's eyes squint at Shelly.

"If the kid wants to walk. Let him walk." Shelly responds bluntly.

"Here, how about I push the wheelchair along with us, that way if you get tired, you can sit. Does that work?" Her question is for me and not directed to the nurse.

I like this lady already. She treats me like a person and like my opinion matters.

"Sounds good to me," I reply.

"Fine, just let me get him unhooked." The nurse huffs with frustration as she detaches my IV and electrode pads.

I tear the constricting blankets off my legs and swing them over the edge of the bed. I instantly feel the breeze on my backside, and I fumble with embarrassment.

"Would you be more comfortable in a pair of pants?" Shelly asks.

"Yes, PLEASE!"

"Can't you at least get him a pair of those scrubs or something to put on?" Shelly asks the nurse.

I can see the nurse clench her jaw below her mask. She stomps her way over to some drawers along the wall, pulls one open, and snatches out a pair of pants. She clomps her feet back to us and whips the pants in a downward motion, helping them to uncrease from their papery, starched, square folds.

"This is all we have for patients. I hope they are to your liking." She adds with a mocking tone.

"Thank you," I say, pulling the thin, scratchy material up over my legs and tying the drawstring at the top.

"Is that better?

Good, let's go."

"Hold up, he at least needs to wear a medical mask. We don't need his weakened immune system catching someone else's germs." The nurse forces a mask over my mouth and nose and flicks the white strings around my ears.

"Fine." Shelly pushes the empty wheelchair ahead, and I do my best to keep up with her.

As we make it to the door, I gasp for air from under the blue mask, but I refuse to sit in the chair. I know that the nurse is watching, and I won't give her the satisfaction of proving she was right about my needing to be pushed in the wheelchair.

"You alright?" Shelly whispers so that only I can hear.

I nod with a covered façade of a smile because I am too winded to speak.

She punches a code into the keypad with her fancy, long, red fingernails and looks over her shoulder at the nurse with gloating pride.

She swings the door and holds it open for me. My pants swish through the doorway and into the adjoining hall. Shelly joins me at my side, pushing the empty wheelchair.

"You sure you don't want to sit now?" She asks with sincere concern, letting her guard down as soon as the door clicks closed behind us.

"No, I really do want to try walking, but I might hold on if that's okay?" I pant, leaning a bit of my weight onto the wheelchair.

"Absolutely," She tears off the medical mask she was clearly forced to wear.

"I hate these things. They are required when entering the hospital wing, but they just mess up my lipstick." Her painted red lips smile to reveal perfect, white teeth, like in an orthodontia ad.

"I appreciate you holding it together back there for my sake. Those nurses always think they are better than me. I'm not ashamed of my job. I enjoy working for Dr. Steinberger. And the best part is, I don't have to wear those unbecoming, drab nurse scrubs."

Her red high heels clack against the tiled floor, sending a resounding echo ahead of us. Her perfect blonde wavy curls bounce elegantly with each step. I can imagine her walking the red carpet, or a runway, not escorting my pathetic, dragging self down this long, dim corridor.

"Here we are." She stops and taps in another code next to a door.

The sign above the door reads **Dr. Steinberger**.

She holds the door open wide for me and tells me to take a seat, gesturing to the wheelchair or the row of chairs along the wall of the small office.

I choose to plop down into the wheelchair, not because it is my selected choice but because it is the closest option, and I feel my legs might give out on me if I take another step.

Shelly walks around to the other side of her desk. I know it is hers because the nameplate sitting on the well-organized desk states, **Ms. Shelly White.**

The cool air blows a shiver down my neck as goosebumps pucker instantly all over my body. I wrap my arms around myself and attempt to keep my teeth from chattering.

Shelly picks up an old phone receiver from her desk and speaks into it,

"Dr. Steinberger, I have Dameon here to see you." Her voice is stereotypical of every secretary from every movie.

"Bring him in." A booming voice responds in surround sound. It echoes both from the other end of the phone as well as through the door across the small room.

"Dr. Steinberger will see you now." Shelly relays, as if I didn't just hear his response for myself. She pushes my chair through the door and turns me to face the grey-haired man sitting behind a large, cherry-wood desk.

"Ahhh, Dameon. I'm glad to hear you are up and about. Thank you for coming to see me. Would you like to have a seat on my couch or perhaps one of the armchairs?"

230

"I'm fine right here, thank you," I respond, not wanting to move, unable to move.

"Can I get you anything to make you more comfortable? Water, perhaps?" He asks.

"Yes, please," I shiver.

"How about a warm blanket, too?" Shelly adds.

I nod my stiff neck.

"This office is a safe place.

A place of honesty and mutual respect." Dr. Steinberger begins his spiel.

His words sound so rehearsed and hollow.

"I am going to ask you some honest questions, and I expect you to give honest answers.

Does that sound alright with you?" He asks for my agreement, but I don't really think I have the option of turning him down.

Luckily for me, Shelly comes back into the office. She places a cup of water on a side table and wheels me closer to it so I can reach it easily. She then wraps a blanket around my shoulders. It has clearly come from a warmer, and I instantly feel my cold, rigid muscles relax with its hug. She drapes both sides down and around my legs, resting on the footrests of the wheelchair.

"There you go." Her flawless teeth gleam as she rubs my arm.

"Thank you, Shelly." Dr. Steinberger states with a smoldering smile that seems as fake as cubic zirconia.

Shelly nods and closes the door gently behind her as she exits. I am left in the claustrophobic office alone with the psychologist.

I wish that I could be anywhere right now other than here.

"Do you feel comfortable with me taking notes about our conversation? It will solely be for my benefit. Nothing we discuss here will leave these four walls."

*So much for **honesty** and **mutual respect**, huh?*
I can see right through your lies.
I already know you have been asked to question me.
I just wonder how long after I leave this office will you
run off to whomever you report to at Elementerprise
with the details.

"Not much of a talker, I see. That's okay. How about I ask you to confirm what I already know about you? All you need to do is nod in affirmation or shake your head no. Deal?"

I just stare at the glass of water on the stand and watch as a drop of condensation streaks down the outside of the glass like a teardrop. Dr. Steinberger stands from his chair and paces closer to me. He stops and sits against the front side of his desk, his notepad and pen ready in his hands.

"Your name is Dameon Gardener, correct?" I humor him with a slight nod.

"You came to the West gate here at E-Springs seeking medical attention?" I nod again.

"You have an ID chip implanted into your neck, signifying you are someone of importance?" I pause, thinking about whether or not I should nod.

I listen as the hands of the clock painstakingly tick...tick.....tick.

"Dameon, I need you to either confirm or deny that you have an ID chip implanted in your neck." His voice sounds more brash as he restates his words.

I roll my eyes to the ground and nod. I refuse to look up at the man, staring at me through his wire-rimmed glasses clinging to the tip of his nose. I can feel his silent intensity attacking the top of my slumped head.

"Do you have any relatives currently staying at E-Springs?"

Staying here, or being held prisoner here?

I shrug my shoulders. Again, I can't honestly confirm that my relative is "staying" here. I have not seen Great Granddad with my own eyes.

"Are you sure you don't know? Or are you testing the waters here?" His voice is abrasive.

I wonder how long he will last until he loses his cool.

"You arrived here with a girl, Lan. Is that correct?"

I don't know how much longer I can keep this up.
I am not going to involve Lan in this conversation.
I need to keep her safe.

"Ah, you stopped bouncing your leg when I said her name.
You care about Lan, don't you?" He sets the notebook and pen on his desk to step closer to me. He sits in the nearest armchair, intently invading my personal space bubble.
"You would do anything to keep Lan safe, wouldn't you?"

Can he read my thoughts?

He remains at the edge of the armchair but leans forward, placing his elbows on his knees as he rests his chin on his clasped hands. He stares me down, waiting for my move, like in a game of Chess where he just claimed *checkmate.*

Don't blurt out! Just breathe. If I explode, he knows
that he can use Lan as leverage. If I stay silent, he
knows that I am hiding something. No matter how I
react, he's got me right where he wants me.

233

I just shrug my shoulders again and do my best to act uninterested despite my screaming emotions pulsing through every fiber of my body.

"Are you trying to show me that you don't care about Lan?"

What is the correct answer here?

I stare at the floor. Beads of sweat accumulate on my forehead, but I refuse to respond to Dr. Steinberger's question.

"Then you won't mind if we interrogate her?
Or torture her until she talks?"

His question slithers around me like a snake and he just glowers at me like a creepy statue with an evil grimace plastered on his smug face.

Guilt and dread rise up from my stomach, and the acid burns the back of my throat.

"Don't touch her." My words escape my lips before I have a chance to swallow them back down.

"Ah, so you can speak again. Look at the progress we are making." He claps his hands triumphantly as if his evilness construed a brilliant breakthrough.

"So, I am guessing you are a bit more willing to answer my questions now that you know what is at stake here?"

I am touchier than a septic boil. If he breathes on me the wrong way, I will explode.

"Who is Dean Gardener to you?"

My heart thumps against my aching ribcage like a beast raging to escape. The anger firing within me constricts my words from forming, and I can do nothing but huff air forcefully through my tingling lips.

"Do I need to have Shelly fetch Lan for me?" These words are my last straw.

"Dean Gardener is my Great Granddad." I spout with desperation, hating myself for giving in to him.

"Good boy. And what do you know about The ATHP Serum?" His face inches closer to mine. His rancid breath poisons my thoughts.

"I'm sure you know more about it than I do." I over-articulate my words, freely allowing my spit to attack his much too close face.

"Where is it?" He doesn't falter or move an inch.

"I don't know." I allow my sincerity to laser into his mind. My eyes don't flinch in the slightest bit.

> *That's the truth. For all I know, Fin has taken the serum and sold it to the highest bidder, or perhaps he has already used it on Sophie. I truly can't be sure. I honestly don't know.*

"Does it work?
I need to know if it works!"

"How would I know?"

"If you care at all about that girl, you will tell me everything you know about that serum!" His words rattle the walls as his bony fingers dig into my upper arms and shake me back and forth. I can feel my brain clattering in my skull.

The sound of something crashing to the floor outside the door in Shelly's office jolts us both back into reality. Dr. Steinberger regains his composer, removes his grip from my arms, and takes a deep breath as he sits back in the chair. His tightly pursed lips loosen with each one of his cleansing, over-exaggerated, breaths.

"I am going to give you some time to think about this conversation. I don't care how, but you better find out about that serum and be ready to tell me about it during our next conversation, or I'm bringing in the girl. Do you understand?"

I just stare down at the tiles on the floor as he leans in to whisper in my ear.

"And we have the world's top military interrogator here who is willing to do **whatever** it takes until she gives us the information we need if you are unwilling to cooperate."

An unswallowable lump forms in my throat and blocks air from entering or escaping.

Dr. Steinberger calmly stands, grabs the handles of the wheelchair, and wheels me to the door. He nonchalantly opens the door and wheels me through the frame with a satisfied sneer.

"We are all done here for today, Shelly. Please return him to his hospital bed. This young man has made a lot of progress already. I believe we have come to an understanding. Isn't that right, Dameon?" He smiles at me and pats my back as if I have just won a baseball game and learned a great life lesson.

Shelly smiles an awkward smile as her hands take control of my wheelchair. She wheels me toward the door to the hallway, and Dr. Steinberger opens the door for us like a gentleman.

"I can't wait until our next meeting." His deceitful words sound cheerful, but the threat is eminently crystal in my mind.

Chapter 26

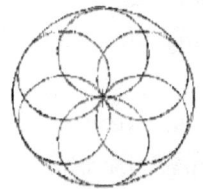

Venturing Down

The young nurse from before helps me get settled back into my bed and hooks me up to the monitors again. She pats the sweat from my brow with a cloth and places a thermometer into my mouth under my tongue. It feels like forever before a beep squeals its completion.

"101.4. Looks like you still have a fever." She fetches two white pills, and places them into a small dispensing cup and hands it to me. "Here take these," she states, handing me my cup of water to wash them down.

I follow directions and gulp them down since they might help the headache piercing my skull.

> *It is probably my fuming rage making my blood boil though, not the fever.*

The nurse tucks me into bed and turns to move on to the next patient.

"Ummm, when does Nurse Felicia come back on shift?" I ask.
"Why, do you have something against me being your nurse?"
"No, you're fine. I mean, I just…"
"In about an hour." She huffs as she walks away. "Everyone always prefers Felicia."

I painstakingly watch as the nurse makes her rounds and checks on each of the patients in a clockwise direction, including the man who seems to be watching me and all the other patients as if it is his job.

The minutes labor by slower than cold tar going uphill in a snowstorm. My eyes constantly stretch back to the time posted on the heart-rate monitor, and I swear, I can count more than sixty seconds before the numbers change.

"I want my mom." A little voice from across the room whimpers. I watch as the nurse sits on the edge of the bed of the young boy and talks to him with a calming voice. I can't make out the words that she is saying to him, but they seem to remedy his troubled heart and lull him back to sleep.

> *I wonder if Jaxson is awake yet.*
> *I hope he is awake.*
> *I would do anything to see him right now.*

Agony slowly impales my heart with a red-hot fire poker. My chest begins to heave with waves of longing. My eyes scorch and blur, but I bury my head into the pillow and curl up into a ball under the blankets.

> *I refuse to show them I am weak.*

I bite my lip and focus on steady breaths while trying to think about anything other than Jax, Mom, or Dad. I try to think about the joy of tinkering with my gadgets, but my nostrils flare with a burning twinge because I can't do that right now, either.

> *Lan.*
> *Think about Lan.*

I try to think of the way her laugh sounds. The way it is infectious and makes me feel her simplistic joy with every giggle and snort.

> *Has Lan already gone down to find Great Granddad without me?*
> *Or is Dr. Steinberger holding her for questioning?*
> *He better not do anything to her!*

I squeeze my eyes shut and wrap my weak arms around my fetal-positioned body, trying to steady my uncontrollable shaking and hyperventilating breaths.

The reflexes of my body explode outward, and I fumble to free my head from the safety of the blanket when I feel a hand touch my arm. I am ready to attack the assailant, but the deep, calming eyes of Nurse Felicia stare back at me.

"Shhhh, it's okay, Dameon. It's just me."

My racing heartbeat begins to calm as the melodious pitch of her voice pacifies my nerves like a lullaby.

"Lan wishes for you to meet her at the servant's stairwell. I promised her I would inform you. But I don't think this is a wise plan, Dameon. You aren't strong enough to go on such a galivant, and it is dangerous. I don't think you understand what Elementerprise is capable of. What they would do to you, or to her, if they find out you have been snooping around. They don't care about you. You are dispensable. All they care about is that darn serum. Once they get it from you, well… Please, just tell me that you will stay in this bed and won't get yourself into any trouble." The creases between her brows deepen.

"I need to find my Great Granddad.

I need answers.

I need guidance."

I slide my legs out from under the blanket, and I dangle them over the edge of the bed. Sitting up suddenly causes a rush of blood to drain from my face. The room spins around me.

"Tomorrow, perhaps. Give your body one more day before you take on the stairs. Trust me, you don't want them to find you passed out in the stairwell. How will you run away and escape from the guards if you need to? Dameon, you aren't strong enough."

Those words, "you aren't strong enough," pulse through my veins like motivational fire. There is nothing I hate more than when someone tells me I can't do something. It drives me to prove that I can, and I will.

"I'm going." I place my tingling feet onto the cold hard floor and muster a wobbly stand.

With a disapproving sigh, Felicia surveys the room and whispers, "Suit yourself, but I warned you that this isn't a good idea. Don't come crying back to me when your plan fails, young man. They have eyes everywhere. You will get caught. But, if you want a fighting chance, you will need my help to get out of here. Just sit back in bed and drink this for a moment while I distract Nancy with an errand." She pours an orange liquid into a cup and hands it to me, gesturing for me to drink it. The burst of orange flavor explodes on my tongue, and the cool, refreshing liquid slides down my tickling throat. I avoid the urge to cough, and I chug the rest in one swig. The sweet flavor is replaced with a salty aftertaste. It's not horrible, but not exactly enjoyable either. It reminds me of Gatorade, but much sweeter and saltier.

"Good, that may help raise your electrolytes, blood sugar, and blood pressure a bit. Here, why don't you just take the bottle with you." She whispers, replacing the small cup in my hand with the plastic bottle of the orange drink. I'm not thrilled about the thought of drinking it, but I am willing to if it means that it helps me have the strength to find Great Granddad.

"Thanks," I reply.

"Now, just sit tight while I go talk to Nancy. I will signal for you when it is clear for you to go. Once you exit this room, go down the hall and take your first right. Hurry down that corridor all the way to the end. There, you will see a door that leads to the stairwell. That is where Lan said she will be waiting for you. I would suggest hurrying through the hallways since they are under surveillance. I don't believe the servant stairs are monitored, so you should be safe once you get there. Be safe, and hurry back. I'm not sure how long I can say you are in the restroom before Nancy gets suspicious." Felicia whispers to me as she unhooks my tubes from the machines. She then turns and I watch as she looks up to the ceiling and utters a prayer under her breath as she walks toward Nancy. I am unable to hear what she says to her, but I can tell Nancy isn't happy about being sent on an errand. She grunts and rolls her eyes as she steps hastily out of the room. Once she exits, Felicia scurries to the door to catch it before it clinks closed. She opens it a crack and watches as Nancy stomps down the hallway. As soon as the coast is clear, Felicia motions for me to come. I slump off my bed and scurry my socked feet along the tiled floor to meet her at her side. She swings the door open far enough for me to slip through. I give her a smile of appreciation and spurt,

"Thank you!"

"Just hurry back.

Godspeed, child." She adds, but I am already pumping my wobbly legs down the hall and am nearing the first turn to the right before she finishes. I raise my heavy hand to support my flailing body and nearly tumble as I round the corner. Unsure if it is my nerves or my weak heart, but the hall sways, and I feel like I am back on the ship in wild waves. I take a moment for the floor to steady before I step forward. But, as soon as it stops wavering, I force my legs to keep moving despite their Jello-like unsteadiness. The sound of my thumping heart pounds in my head and echoes with my scurrying feet. The only other sound is the sloshing liquid in the plastic bottle gripped in my sweaty hand. I watch as the walls dance around me, and I do my best to blink them into a more stable bounce. My lungs scream for air and cough and wheeze with every constricting breath.

I wish I had one of those inhalers right now.
Keep going, Dameon.
You can make it.

A stairwell image depicted on the sign next to a closed metal door ahead of me bounces into view like a beacon of hope. But the sudden sound of footsteps behind me rattles that optimism as adrenaline jolts through my body. My neck stiffens, and I am too afraid to turn around to see who, or if, someone has seen me. I push off my unsteady legs and lunge for the metal shaft knob to the stairwell. My trembling hand scrambles to open the door. I practically fall into the opening as I pull the door toward me and quickly close it behind me. My shaking legs give out from under me, and my back slides down the cool metal door. My heavy head drops on top of my knees, and I pant, struggling to suck in adequate air. My weary thoughts wade through a thick fog, unable to even think of the words to pray in hopes of being undetected. My tongue feels numb and thick in my mouth. I try to lift the bottle of orange drink, but my arm stays limp by my side, not having enough energy to even twitch. My eyes struggle to stay open and blink wildly, but the stairwell landing continues to pixelate as a tunnel of black grows around me like a monstrous blob. My vision fades to black. My whole body begins to tingle as if my blood is suddenly released from every pore. Unable to contract my muscles any longer, I feel my scrunched legs lose control, and I slump to the corner.

My eyes flash open.

How long was I out?

I suddenly become aware of my body again. I wiggle my toes and pull my legs up underneath me. I force myself up to a sitting

242

position, noticing my abs and core feel exhausted as they struggle to hold me up. My eyes fall to the bottle of orange drink lying horizontally at my side. I wrap my fingers around the bottle and retract it to my lap. My other hand wavers and shakes, trying to unscrew the cap. I am finally able to open it, and it takes both my hands working together to force it up to my prickling lips. The liquid fills my mouth, and I swish it through my teeth, attempting to moisten every dry crack before I swallow. It isn't cold, but the wet orange libation is euphoric. I continue to sip, swish, swallow, and breathe until my arms can't hold the bottle up any longer.

> *Where is Lan?*
> *I thought Felicia said Lan was going to meet me at the stairs.*
> *What if I went the wrong way?*
> *Could this be the wrong set of stairs?*

I flop one of my hands up to my eyes and do my best to rub the blurriness away. I strain my eyes to focus on the sign on the wall.

2B
Floor 2
Stair B

> *It looks like I am on floor 2, and I need to get to the basement.*
> *Should I wait here for Lan?*
> *Or has she already gone down without me, thinking I wasn't coming?*

I chug the rest of the orange drink and take a few cleansing breaths, mustering up the strength to attempt to stand. I set the empty bottle on the ground and use the corner walls to shimmy my way up to a standing position. I am grateful for the support of the walls, but they do nothing for the swimming sensation in my head. I breathe a few times as the world seems to settle. I lean my way along the wall and switch my balance to the other foot as I reach for the handrail of the descending stairs. One last deep breath in, and I allow my quivering foot to drop to the first step down.

> *I have no choice. I need to get to the basement and hopefully find Lan and Great Granddad.*

Although I'm a bit shaky, I make it safely to the next landing as I read the sign showing 1B. Without hesitating I continue down the next flight of stairs. My thighs and calves ache, but I continue down the stairs. My lungs burn as if on fire as my foot reaches the final landing. There are no more stairs to go down. I recall Lan saying that her friend goes below the basement to collect trash, and that is where she thinks Great Granddad is being kept.

> *How do I get down below the basement?*
> *The stairs stop here.*
> *There must be another set of stairs somewhere on this basement floor.*

There is just the metal door that exits the stairwell. I wrap my fingers around the handle, force it down, and pull the door slowly toward me. Once it is open a crack, I do my best to peek into the basement. My ears strain to hear, to ensure there are no voices. The last thing I want is to run into someone, anyone other than Lan. I slowly pull the door open and gaze into the glow of the dim overhead lights. I instantly notice long, dark, thick pipes that stretch along the damp concrete walls. Not far ahead, there is a door with a sign that says ELECTRICAL ROOM – Danger, high voltage. Beyond that, there is a sign next to a door that says, SUPPLY ROOM. The instant barrage of voices in the distance causes my muscles to tighten. Simultaneously, the sound of footsteps in the stairwell above me parade on my thoughts of escaping back up the stairs. The heavy boots above me are slow, yet steady, as they gain in volume. Peeking out the door, I weigh my options. The voices in the distance sound like two low-toned muffles. If I wait much longer to decide, the person coming down the stairs is sure to find me. I carefully slip through the open stairwell door and into the open hallway of the basement. The voices are coming closer, and there is nowhere to hide. I lurch my body toward the nearest door of the electrical room, praying that I don't find anyone in there. Luckily, the doorknob opens freely, and it isn't locked. I slide my body into the room and close the door quietly. There is a small space to the side of the door where the wall protrudes back into the hallway. It is just the right amount of space to step into and hide. Although there are no overhead lights turned on in the electrical room, there is a rainbow of glowing and blinking lights flashing from various directions. I can see the room extends back quite a long way, and it is filled with what appears to be large electrical boxes that extend from the floor to the ceiling. Pipes and wires snake around the large machines and completely cover the concrete walls. The hum of the various generators *buzz*. The smell of melting electrical wires is concerning, but that is the least of my worries. The person who created the footsteps in the stairwell and the two other voices have intermingled just outside the electrical room door.

"Have you seen a patient wandering around down here?" A booming voice asks, followed by the sound of shuffling feet and banging pipes.

"Nope, it's just us down here." Replies one of the voices that were approaching.

"You sure they came down here? Not sure why anyone would want to come down here." Retorts the other voice.

I feel a tickle on the top of my foot, and I wiggle my toes to ease the urge to move out of fear the men outside the door will hear me. But, as I wiggle my toes, I notice the tickling moves closer toward my shin. Shifting my eyes downward, I see a large, brown rodent sniffing my leg. Its long whiskers titillate the hairs on my shin. Before I have time to think about any repercussions, I kick my leg out of my hiding place. The alarmed rat squeals and spreads its flailing body as it flies through the air and clunks into a metal door of one of the large electrical boxes, right in the center of the Elementerprise Symbol.

Bullseye.

The smile on my face quickly dissolves as the man from the stairwell also hears the *clank*.

"What was that? Is someone in there?" I hear his hand rattle the knob and open the door.

I suck in my breath and hold it in, afraid my thumping heart might give me away.

All three men poke their heads into the electrical room, just feet away from my hiding spot. Body odor and the stench of cigarette smoke waft into my nose without me even inhaling.

The stunned rat scurries to escape further commotion and skitters under the large pipes running along the bottom of the wall.

"It's just the rats."

"Maybe it will end up like the one last week that chewed on the wires and ended up a fried critter. It smelled like burned chicken down here for days." He chuckles, forcing his rancid breath in my direction.

I watch as the larger man surveys the room, stepping in to look behind the machines and pipes. My lungs burn and scream for me to suck in a refreshing gasp, but I'm afraid that will give me away. Instead, I squeeze my eyes closed and do my best to let in the slightest, slow, steady stream of air. I let it out just as carefully, afraid to release too much air at once.

"Speaking of fried critters, did you hear what is happening in the West? They had a surge of warmer air, which caused the snow to turn to rain."

"What does rain have to do with fried critters?"

"It wasn't normal rain. It was acid rain. It is killing everything it touches. The water supplies have all turned sour, too. They said the only people surviving are the ones in bunkers that have a previous supply of water."

"Is that what is killing everyone out there? I heard it was a new deadly virus?"

"I heard the new virus is coming from and spreading through the water. The docs here were saying that it is a bioweapon from China, or is it Russia, or the Middle East? I can't keep track of our enemies these days."

"All I know is it is in our best interest to keep our heads down and do what we need to do to stay employed here with Elementerprise. They are the only ones that can keep us safe now. I'm not going out into that world."

"You got that right."

"Come on, let's get back to work. There's nothin' here but rats doing their best to survive like the rest of us."

I watch as the three men file out of the room and close the door behind them. I suck in a big breath of air and push it out forcefully. It feels good to breathe normally again. I lean my head against the outside wall and listen as three sets of feet pound up the stairs. I strain my ears and wait to move until I can no longer hear them. I wait a few minutes longer just to make sure I am alone.

Acid rain and viruses spreading through the water?
Maybe I am too late.
Perhaps my plan to save the world's water supply is already foiled.

My eyes tinge with fire as I exhale anger through my nose boisterously.

I can't think about that right now. I need to find Lan and Great Granddad before I worry about the poisoned water in the world.

Chapter 27

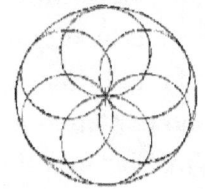

The Injection

J spring my body away from the cement wall and out of my hiding place. I walk over to the door and open it a crack. Before exiting, I pause and listen, making sure that no more workers are waiting for me outside the room. The only sound is the constant hum of the power generators, random zapping electrical currents, and an occasional scamper of little rodent feet.

Gulping down a hard lump of anxiety, I step my trembling foot out into the light spilling onto the floor from the long bars of overhead lighting in the corridor. I place my unsteady hand on the thick piping along the wall and begin to follow it. My fingers follow the pipe as their form of guidance for my wobbly steps. Finally, the corridor comes to an intersection. Suddenly, feeling like I am back in the tunnels of the future, I am unsure which direction will lead me to Lan and Great Granddad. I squint my eyes down the hallway to the right, and I can see what looks like a few rooms with metal doors; the view to the left is similar. However, the corridor straight ahead looks much longer and appears to lead on forever. The overhead fluorescent lights flicker, and I focus on the seemingly never-ending rows of glowing bars blurring together into a dim tunnel. The hallways to the left and right don't seem to go very far, and I don't see anything that looks like stairs or an elevator, just plain, grey, metal doors.

I suppose I need to keep venturing forward.

An unsystematic, cold breeze blows against me, causing the muscles around every one of my hair follicles to contract simultaneously. It is accompanied by an intense wave of nausea. Surveying the corridor around me, I do not see any vents or air ducts of any kind. There is no logical explanation for the sudden anomalous shutter of cold air other than my gut intuition telling me to go back up to the safety of the hospital bed. But I force my feet to keep walking and inching their way forward through the labyrinth of shadowy concrete and pipes. I begin to think I can't walk any further when I see the corridor come to an end. However, instead of the mundane concrete and pipes that have filled the previous passage, there is a metal gate, ornately twisting and guarding a metal-caged elevator.

> *Yes! This is it. This must be how I get down to where they are holding Great Granddad.*

I have an instant burst of adrenaline that propels me toward the web of metal. My fingers crawl over every inch, trying to discover a way to get the locked gate open. But the metal doesn't budge. Sweat builds on my temples as I attempt to force the metal elevator door, but my quick breaths of unsuccess follow.

> *How am I supposed to get this thing open?*

I pound my fist against the steel out of frustration, but it only results in throbbing knuckles. I allow my eyes to do the searching this time.

> *There must be a keyhole, card reader, or some way to make this open.*

My eyes fall on a small metal plate that appears to be screwed on top of what was once a lock. I attempt to use my flimsy fingernails to loosen one of the screws, but clearly, this idea is not going to work.

How is anyone supposed to unlock it if the lock is covered over?
Unless this metal plate is some sort of card reader.

I lean my head down to get a closer look at the plate as a blinding red light scans my eye. My eyelids slam closed in retaliation, and my fingers fly up to rub the burning sensation out of my retina. Blinking wildly, my blurred vision finally clears to see the glow of a fingerprint symbol appear on the metal plate. Swallowing hard, I raise my shaking pointer finger, place it on the glowing symbol, and squeeze my eyes closed. I hear a loud clank as the elevator gate door scissors open like an accordion retracting. The metal screeching against metal is deafening as if each hinged piece is screaming out in agony. As the metal gate reaches the point where it can't open any wider, I wait for the echoing shrieks to make their final wave through the emptiness before stepping inside. Terror races through me as I step into the metal-caged contraption. My heart rate and panting breath quicken. My leg nearly buckles beneath me as I transfer my weight, stepping onto the textured metal platform that serves as the elevator's floor. As soon as I place my other foot beneath me, the metal gated door snaps closed behind me.

I lurch around to face the door, my blood pumping impudently in my ears like racing drumbeats. My sweating palms reach up to grasp the metal to see if it will open and free me from the sudden feeling of claustrophobia, but the gate doesn't budge. Instead, my white knuckles wrap around the twisted openings as I feel the floor beneath me begin to drop. I watch as the lit corridor from which I came shrinks in size until the crack of light closes completely. The one small zapping light above my head is dim and flickers with the descending movement. I can feel the concrete walls surrounding the elevator shaft slowly flowing upward. I bite my lip as my eyes shift from corner to corner of the box, scouring for buttons to press. I have a sudden need to push a button, to feel like I am in control of where I am going. But there are no buttons; there is no control. I am at the mercy of the moving metal, and I hang on tightly as if it is my hope, praying it is dragging me down to Lan and Great Granddad.

The cage stops abruptly, and the metal surrounding me rattles. Similarly, every one of my nerves rattle against my bones. I steady my body after the jolting halt, ready to exit the elevator, but the metal of the cage door doesn't even squeak. Again, I do my best to try and force the door open, but it doesn't respond to my weak force. I search for a similar metal plate to press my finger against, but there isn't one on the inside. I try to touch the backside of the metal plate that read my fingerprint to open the door the first time, but nothing happens, regardless of where I place my finger on it. I lean my face toward it in hopes that it needs to scan my eye again first, but it doesn't work. I continue to move my head around the door of the gate, trying to catch a beam of light. Realizing I must look like a bobbing, weaving bird performing an odd mating ritual dance. I stop and freeze. Clearly, there is not a retinal scanner waiting to approve my exit. I kick the door and begin to pace back and forth along the metal floor. I count out each one of my four steps in one direction, pivot, four steps in the other direction, pivot, and repeat.

Think, Dameon. How would one get an elevator cage door to open?
There are no buttons.
There are no scanners.
Maybe it is voice-activated with a password like at the Elementerprise facility in the future?

I scurry my feet closer to the door and speak to it as if it is alive.
"Open.
Door open.
Elevator open.
Open sesame?
Please open?
OPEN NOW!"

Vexation floods my body as I shake the metal door. I can feel my boiling blood pulse through the veins on my neck.

The low guttural cackle from the shadows outside the elevator makes my skin crawl unexpectedly. I stand like a statue. Someone is watching me, laughing at me.

"Who is there?

Please, help me get out of here."

"Why? Watching you squirm in that cage is very entertaining." The voice uttering these words hits a chord of familiarity in my brain.

No, it couldn't be. How could he be down here?

"Fin?

What are you doing down here?" I ask as he steps into the dim light of the elevator. His face is the same but with a new glow of betrayal.

"Why are you wearing that uniform?" My brain is storming with questions.

"You look like you could use some Ocean Potion, kid." His words hiss.

"You said you were never coming back here."

"I also told Elementerprise I would deliver you, and I did. Thanks, you were worth a hefty sum. You made it pretty easy, too. I didn't even have to drug or drag you here. Well, I did drag you here, but that was because the radiation and the fever did all the dirty work for me. It all worked out."

"But I saw you. You look terrified. You ran off."

"I guess you can add acting to my repertoire." Half of his face raises in a devious smile. "I ran back to the bunker for the box with the serum, then came back, and told them at the front gate that you were here."

You liar!
How could I have trusted you?

253

"You gave them the box?" My fingernails dig into my palms as I pound on the gate, wishing it was his face. I can't control my ferocious breathing, and it forces spit from my mouth with each burst.

"Trust me. I tried to keep the serum and use it on my little sister, but I could never figure out how to open that stupid box. My plan was to have you open it for me, but obviously, you are worthless."

"So, you just gave it to them? How could you? You have no idea what you have done." My head begins to pound with rage.

I wrap my fingers around my forehead and try to squeeze out the plaguing pain or hold my brain inside my skull to keep it from exploding.

"That was the livelihood of the future, and you just gave it over to the people that have been causing all this destruction."

"You truly are confused, aren't you? You are just like your Great Grandfather, you know that? Totally selfish."

"Selfish?"

"Yes, selfish. You both know about the serum that can save the world, and yet you want to keep it for yourselves.

Elementerprise wants to replicate it and give it out to everyone in order to save as many lives as possible." His eyes squint at me as if I am the villain.

Maybe Fin is right.
Maybe the world does need this serum.
Perhaps me helping them mass produce this serum is how I save the world. But then, why didn't my Great Granddad just give them the serum in the first place? Why would he go through all the trouble of protecting it on that island? And his journal entry said to keep it safe.
None of this makes any sense.

"So, now what? Are you going to turn me in to Elementerprise?" Defeat overtakes me.

"I was told to take you to your Great Granddad."

"You are taking me to him? Then why am I still in this cage? How do I open the door?"

"You can't. It must be authorized from the outside." He states, leaning down toward the metal plate.

I watch as the red beam of light scans over his pale blue eye. He then stands and presses his finger against the sheet of metal. The spring in the door releases, and the gate squeezes open. My lungs inflate as if they were gasping for air, which I know is ridiculous because I was only in a metal cage with plenty of ventilation and oxygen. But it was as if my brain felt trapped in a tiny box.

"How did the elevator open for me in the basement?"

"Trust me, while you were in the hospital wing, they scanned every inch of your body and have it all on file. And we were expecting you. You honestly thought you got through the hallways without being seen? You were like a drunken sloth up there."

Embarrassment flushes my cheeks. Fin grabs my arms, twists them behind my back, and pushes me to walk forward. I want to struggle free from his grasp, but even the slightest movement in a sideways motion makes my shoulders feel like they will tear from their sockets.

"I wanted to come to get you when you passed out in the stairwell, but they told me to wait down here for you. They knew you would come. And for some reason, they didn't want any of the other workers to know about you. They thought me dragging you down here would have made too much of a scene. Like I couldn't have been discreet. Whatever."

I take a few painful trods. The swishing of my papery pants and his well-starched fatigues echo against the damp earthen walls surrounding us.

"Did you ever even go to war? Or was that all a lie, too?"

"Yes, everything I told you was true. I just left out the part where they caught me the first time I came back after being at sea. I have secretly been doing jobs for them at the same time I have been doing jobs for The Captain. Elementerprise thought it was a great idea for me to keep up my charade and get more information from The Captain."

"Does The Captain know who you really are? That you are working for *them*?"

He lets out a chuckle.

"That old fool has no clue. To him, I'm just a runaway who needed help escaping. I did what I had to do to earn his trust, and I always came back when he told me to. But none of that matters now. Elementerprise has The Serum, and now they know all about the vault in the *secret island*."

"You told them about the island? How could you? This is bigger than just the serum!"

"I know. That is why I told them. It is my leverage for them to keep me. Only I can take them there. I am valuable to them, and I can use that information to get whatever I want, even medicine and the best treatment for Sophie."

"Or I could tell them where it is," I spout.

"Really? What are the coordinates?"

I want to tell him, but I have no idea. All I know is that it is somewhere in an eastern direction off the shores here.

"I knew you didn't know. See, only I can take them there. Well, and probably your Great Grandfather, but that stubborn old kook won't tell them anything. Trust me, they have done everything to get him to talk. That is why they are bringing you in, so that hopefully, he will cooperate with them regarding The Serum. I suppose there is always The Captain, but he seems more loyal and stubborn than an old dog."

Fin's insults about Great Granddad and The Captain are like a hot match igniting flames of hatred. I would do anything to know karate or jujitsu right now to take Fin down. But unfortunately, I have only ever done those types of things on video games, and even then, Jaxson always beats me.

"Here we are." Fin allows his eye to get scanned and places his finger on the glowing sheet of metal. The metal door in front of us slides open, and Fin shoves me inside, letting my restrained arms go loose. I straighten my back and stretch my shoulder blades, making them scrape together behind me. I then roll my shoulders forward, and the motion is like freedom. After I have stretched out the pain, I look around the odd room. It is a dimly lit laboratory. My weary eyes instantly fall on Great Granddad. He looks like he is maybe in his fifties or sixties, much younger than when I saw him in Lan's time. His hair is a wavy mess of grey with streaks of brown. The creases on his forehead deepen as his unmistakable striking blue eyes peer into my soul, trying to communicate their desperation. A small shake of his head and guttural sigh in my direction convey that he wishes I wasn't here. I want to run to him and wrap my arms around him, but Fin's grip on the back of my neck squeezes tighter, sending pain shooting down my body, all the way to my toes.

Groans and growls from the moving shadows of caged creatures lining the back wall catch my attention. Some of the creatures being held back by the rusting bars are enraged and appear to be famished beasts willing to do whatever it takes to eat us. There are definitely some human-like forms, but many also have animalistic qualities to them. I squint my eyes to look at them more closely. One of the creatures has strange feathery tentacles forming a collared mane around his head. Like sensors, they react to the wave of changes in the air around them, squirming and alive. Another creature sits with his obesity, rolling into mounds of blubber like a giant can of biscuits bursting at the seams. His squishy forehead and plumping cheeks rest on a tubular nose. I feel my own face scrunch together as I realize he has an extra set of stubby arms protruding from his portly belly, and at the end of the nubs, there are curling claws of fingernails scratching at the air.

He must have received an extra dose of Tardigrade DNA.

As I peer into some of the other cages, I see that the creatures are much more human but have perfectly sculpted muscles as if they live in a gym and only drink raw eggs, protein powder, and steroids. Their round orb, fish-like eyes are like black ebony and stare at us with hatred as they pull against the thick chains attaching them to their cages. One of the muscular creatures has slits for nostrils, like an axolotl, or a snake, instead of a human nose.

Hmmm, looks like Lord Voldemort has been working out.

Lan jumps against the bars of her cage at the end of the row. Her arms flail outstretched in my direction.

"Dameon," she whimpers.

"Lan!" I attempt to run over to her, but Fin snatches my shoulders and holds me in place.

"Not so fast." He grumbles.

"Let her go!" I shout.

"It appears we need to study her further." A man in a white lab coat, stitched with the Elementerprise symbol, hisses as he snatches Lan's wrist through the bars and strokes her newly regrown fingers.

"She is exactly what we have been hoping for. Proof that this evolved serum works."

"She doesn't belong in a cage. Let her out!" My nostrils flare. "Doesn't she?"

I watch as a tear falls down Lan's cheek, and her lips purse together tightly.

"I will let her out of the cage if you open that box for us." His balding head gleams as he tilts his head with anticipation toward the metal puzzle box on the table in front of Great Granddad.

Great Granddad's gaze toward me intensifies as he shakes his head ever-so-slightly, telling me that under no circumstances should I open this box for them. His message is clear, but as I whip my eyes back to Lan, how can I not do as they ask?

"I can't." Defeat plagues my existence.

"Can't? Or won't?" The man near Lan questions, slowly walking over to me as he folds his hands behind his back.

"I don't know how to open it. I've tried everything." My words are truthful. I can't open it, no matter how much I want to.

Great Granddad releases a pent-up gust of breath with relief.

The sinister man grasps my face with his dark-spotted hand. Anger pulses through me as he squeezes my cheeks and studies my face.

"I believe you are telling the truth." The man utters so close to my face that his spittle festers on my chin.

"Therefore, you are only of use to me if your Great Granddad cares for you at all."

His glare moves from me to Great Granddad. He roughly removes his hand from my face and deliberately points his finger to the ground. Fin kicks the back of my legs abruptly. My knees jolt forward and smash to the ground with a thud, and my body sinks to the cold concrete.

"Are you willing to save your Great Grandson?"

My eyes plead in Great Granddad's direction.

"I barely know this young man." Great Granddad blinks the heartache out of his eyes and refuses to look at me.

"You won't mind watching me kill him then, in front of you?"

"Great Granddad!" My voice explodes with every human emotion at once.

Lan's cries flood the laboratory and prick at every fiber of my body.

I watch as my Great Granddad swallows hard.

"He is but one life. I must think of the livelihood of the entire world."

My heart crawls up into my throat and explodes in a volatile spew of seething fury.

"I thought you said I was the livelihood of the world. You're a liar. Tell them, tell them the truth. You have the ability to save me! Just open the box!"

"Ahhh, you care about the livelihood of the world, do you?

Perfect, bring me the injector." The man's words form a pit in the bottom of my stomach, and they swell inside me like a cancer.

Injector?
Injector for what?

My body flails against Fin's grasp. However, two more men, like gorilla torpedoes, attack me from the shadows and secure me in place. I am unable to move.

I watch as a great battle ensues on Great Granddad's face. I can tell he is weighing his options. I am assuming the way I am being held in place that I am the one about to receive whatever the *injection* is. My entire body is paralyzed with fear as my heart hammers against my chest. A man with a worried expression carries a plastic tray lined with foam in his trembling hands. It cradles an injector pen, similar to the one used for Epilanthdopram.

"You must inject it into his chest, near the heart." The man in the lab coat instructs, pulling down my loosely tied gown draped over my shoulders, all while carefully watching Great Granddad's reaction to each of his slightest movements.

I squirm and attempt to fight against the three strong men holding me still, but my weak body is no match for their brute strength.

"You claim that you do not care for this young man, but do you care about the demise of the rest of the world? Once we release this virus, there is only one thing that can stop it, and you know what that is: The Serum inside that box. Just open the box for us, and you can avoid releasing this deadly plague on the world!

What's it going to be?

Death for everyone?

Or life?"

The question lingers in the air like a thick, dark fog.

"Great Granddad, PLEASE!" I shout, tears pouring from my desperate eyes.

I feel my chest rise and fall rapidly, and my fingernails dig into my sweating palms.

Great Granddad puffs up his chest and turns to look at the wall in the opposite direction. Who knew the slight movement of a head, a deferred glance, could be so powerful, sealing the demise of me, and the rest of the world, all at once?

"So be it."

The man in the white coat nods his head in affirmation to the sweating man with the injector.

Squeezing my eyes closed and clenching my teeth; I ready myself for the incoming stab to my exposed chest.

"Nooooo!" Lan screams.

Thump!

As if being struck with lightning, a jab of pain explodes in my chest.

I instantly turn to rubber as the three men release their hold on my infected body. I slump to the ground, overcome with unconsciousness.

Chapter 28

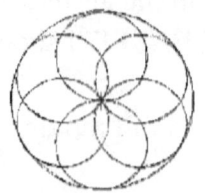

The Great Escape

My eyes snap open.

Hyperventilating in panic, my eyes strain to focus on everything surrounding me: the dim laboratory, Great Granddad now seated and working at the table, and the row of creatures in cages along the back wall. I can see it all through the bars of a cage of my own. I feel a warm squeeze on my hand. I turn my head to look over and see Lan's soft hand reaching through the bars to caress mine. Her body is leaning against the bars of her cage as close to me as she can possibly be, despite the barrier. I look up into her beautiful face, filled with worry. But the fake smile she forces is a relief that at least I am not going to die alone.

Wait, am I dying?

I slide my other hand up to my chest and touch the spot where I remember being stabbed with the injection. I wince as a wave of pain surges through my pectoral muscle upon touching it. I take in a deep breath and feel a twinge of discomfort in my chest as my lungs inflate.

It was real.
It wasn't just a nightmare.

I take a brief mental check of my overall status. After a few satisfying breaths, I realize I feel just about the same as I did before I was injected. I still feel a bit shaky from the fever and illness I had, but so far, no noticeable new symptoms other than the tender injection site. I push myself up into a sitting position and crisscross my legs beneath me, just to make sure I am capable of sitting upright.

"Are you okay?" Lan's eyes search over my body as if she, too, is making sure I'm alright.

"I feel okay. What about you?

I'm so sorry I got you into this mess." I squeeze the soft skin of her hand.

"There is nowhere else I would rather be." Her smile is sincere this time, and it makes me melt into a puddle.

"Okay, so let's figure out how to get out of here," I whisper, realizing there is still a guard in the room with a very large and impressive gun.

"I'm not sure how much time I have before…well,
I'm not really sure what is going to happen."
"I heard the man say to your Great Granddad that you have about twenty-four hours before the capsule dissolves. Once it dissolves, the virus has roughly a twenty-four to forty-eight-hour incubation period. After which, you will be contagious for three to four days before you even start seeing any symptoms. You and the other people who become infected won't even know you are sick as it quickly spreads until it is too late."
"So, I'm assuming the life expectancy isn't good?"
"The important thing is you have time before you infect others." Great Granddad chimes in. Lan and I hadn't realized we were talking loud enough for him to hear our conversation. Simultaneously, our heads flick in his direction.
"Hey! No talking to the prisoners!" The man guarding the room states, aiming his massive gun at Great Granddad's head.

Great Granddad's hands fly up to his sides in surrender, but his eyes burrow into mine. I sense his regret. I know he did what he had to do. But what I don't understand is why.

"You have a job to do." The guard nudges Great Granddad's arm with his gun.

"Yes, sir." His blue eyes fall to the liquid in the eyedropper before him.

"Unless you are ready to open that box?"

Great Granddad doesn't respond to him. He painstakingly drips one drop of the amber liquid into a petri dish instead.

"You two spread apart. No touching!" The barrel of his gun turns to point in our direction.

I feel my eyes roll as Lan and I slide just out of each other's reach. The man-creature next to me flexes his bulging muscles and lets out a boisterous grunt. I am afraid to move any closer to him.

Ok, we obviously need to get out of these cages and out of E-Springs as soon as possible. But, even if we can get out, where will we go? I don't want to go anywhere where I might infect people. I can't go home. I can't go back to Jaxson, or Mom and Dad.

The heaviness of my dire situation weighs down on me like a pile of boulders, making it hard for me to breathe.

If I go away on my own, far away from anyone else to die, will this virus die with me? Is Lan immune to this virus because she seems to have had The Serum, or would I be putting her life in danger, too, if we are together?

The obnoxious tinkling of glass against glass makes me cringe.

But then, my brain begins to hear patterns in the tapping and sliding. I raise my head and focus on Great Granddad. He is staring at me, his eyes constantly checking to make sure that the guard in the room is not suspicious of his deliberate clanking. At times, he taps the tip of the eyedropper onto the surface of the petri dish, and other times he slides the tip across it.

Tap tap tap... pause.
Slide tap slide tap... pause

Are those sounds representing dots and dashes?
Yes! Great Granddad is using Morse code!
Tap slide... That is the letter A.
Tap slide slide tap... P.
Tap... E?
Ape? Yes, the creature next to me resembles an ape.
But why would Great Granddad say ape?

I allow my face to rise into creases of confusion along my forehead.

Great Granddad glances at the guard, who is still bobbing his head methodically – clearly jamming out to a song in his head, or does he have earbuds in? Great Granddad slides his hand across the wooden table and sweeps an imaginary speck onto the floor. He then stares at me as if to say, "Ok, I'm starting over. You ready?" I nod, questionably, hoping I am understanding this as a form of communication and not that I am just starting to lose my mind. I strain my eyes to try and watch his movements to make sure that what I am seeing and hearing harmonize.

E...
S...
C...
A...
P...
E...
Escape!

I nod furiously, making sure Great Granddad knows I got the first word: escape. I then shrug my shoulders to relay that I don't understand how I am supposed to escape. My eyes scan the area around me, trying to find anything that may be of use. I see a small pile of bones just behind my cage. They must have belonged to a rodent – probably eaten by the last creature caged in here, and the small bones were tossed out of the bars. I reach my hand back and grab a few of the promising small bones while moving my body as little as possible. The last thing I want to do is draw the guard's attention to what I am doing. I feel Lan's eyes watching my every move. She clearly knows that I am up to something. I give her a little half-smile and a wink. She smiles in return. I nonchalantly show Great Granddad the bones in my hand, and he nods in approval. If there is one thing I am good at, it is tinkering with small tools. And picking locks just happens to be something I have practiced many times in my bedroom. True, I am usually using my lock-picking toolset, but I hope these bones will be strong enough. I find a few long, skinny ones and one that may just be jagged enough to use as a rake.

Great Granddad sweeps his hand across the table again, signaling he is beginning another word. I nod.

ILL...MAKE...SMOKE
HOLD... BREATH
RUN...
USE...MAP
FIND...NIBI...IKWE

Nibi ikwe? Did I catch that last part correctly?
What is a nibi ikwe?

I decide to ask Great Granddad about the last part of the message.

I use my fingernail to tap and slide along the concrete floor the same way he did with the eyedropper to tap out the letters nibi...ikwe. I then shrug my shoulders to let him know that I don't understand.

"Hey, cut that out. What are you two doing?" The guard questions my odd behavior.

I instantly yawn and stretch as if that was what I was doing all along.

I watch as Great Granddad nods.

Why is he nodding?

Yes, what?
What is nibi ikwe?

Great Granddad begins tapping and sliding the eyedropper once again. I focus in, hoping for an explanation.

READY...

I repeat his original instructions in my head over and over to make sure I remember each detail.

I'll make smoke.
Hold breath.
Run.
Use map.
Find nibi ikwe.

I nod as an uneasy feeling builds in my stomach. I mouth the words, "Hold your breath, ready?" toward Lan and wait for her to nod. I nod again to Great Granddad to let him know we are ready.

Before I have a second to think, Great Granddad grabs two vials of liquid from his table and tosses them near the guard's boots. They both crash together on the cement and instantly create a smokey haze billowing up around the guard. Lan and I look at each other and suck in as much air as we can before the thick cloud has a chance to make it over to us. I jump up and use two of the small rodent bones to pick the lock on my cage. I struggle for a moment, but then I hear the click of the mechanism releasing. I sidestep to the lock on Lan's cage.

CRASH!

More glass bottles explode on the ground, causing me to startle and drop one of the bones. I drop to my hands and knees and begin frantically feeling around for the bone.

The guard's hollers suddenly stop as I hear his heavy body collapse to the ground. The animalistic grunts, howls, and shouts coming from the cages erupt next to me. I hear as a few of them slump to the ground. One of them makes guttural gagging noises as my hand feels the long, skinny bone brush against my fingertips. Grasping it desperately, I pick it up and begin to pick the lock on Lan's cage. The various plumes of smoke have wafted over to us, making it difficult to see what I am doing. I am forced to rely on the familiar feeling of using the long, skinny bottom bone to apply the pressure against the lock, and the jagged-ended bone as my rake – jiggling it until I feel each pin of the lock move into the proper placement. As soon as the clink of the lock opens, Lan bursts through the cage toward me.

"Come on! Run!" Great Granddad shouts to us from the exit door as he swings it open.

As soon as we rush through the door, we all take as many steps as we can before our lungs are screaming for air. Gasping and coughing, we breathe in the safe, fresh air of the corridor as we continue running. I notice that Great Granddad has the metal box in his hands. My head pounds and I struggle to keep up with Lan, but she holds my hand and helps to pull me toward the elevator.

"How will we get out of the elevator?" I ask, barely able to form words as I desperately suck in air.

"You can't. They made me design it to require two people, one always on the outside, so I couldn't try to use it on my own without them knowing. You won't be able to take the elevator, or you will be trapped, and they will know you are inside it as soon as you are scanned. But I happen to know about the security ladder." Great Granddad spouts between breaths. "What ladder?" Lan asks.

"Do you still have those bones?" Great Granddad asks.

I nod, nearly causing me to fall. We follow Great Granddad's lead as he shows us which twists and turns to take in the maze of dark, pipe-lined corridors.

"It's here, behind this door. Can you get it open?" Great Granddad asks.

Jiggling the handle, I lean down to see what type of lock I am dealing with.

I nod, doing my best to steady my shaking hands and catch my breath. I feel as though I could use another one of those orange drinks Felicia gave me. Attempting to swallow the dry, burning sensation in my throat, I strain to lift both arms to the lock. The lock is simple, and I have it open in no time.

"Hurry, climb!" Great Granddad's voice echoes in the ladder shaft above us.

Lan begins to climb first. As soon as her feet are just above my head, I grab onto the first rung and climb up behind her. Every muscle in my body begins to quiver, struggling to keep up with the demands of climbing. My arms burn as they pull up the weight of my body. My calves, hamstrings, and even my glutes scream for me to stop.

"I've reached the end of the ladder. Do I just go through the door up here? Where does it lead?" Lan's climbing hesitates.

"Go through the door and head to the right." His voice reverberates past me to Lan.

She reaches up to the door and opens it a sliver, peaking through the crack.

"Okay, come on." She whispers down.

Her hand reaches back toward me and gently grabs onto my bicep, helping me up off the ladder. We both help Great Granddad up since he was forced to climb with just one hand. This resulted in him using the elbow of his other arm since his hand was cradled around the metal box. As soon as all three of us are up, we begin running. It takes everything I have to keep pumping my legs.

> *Will all this running make the virus capsule inside me dissolve faster?*
> *Has it already dissolved, and I am already a virus breeding ground?*
> *I'm not sure how long I was out after I was injected.*

"How are we getting out of here? There are guards at every door." Lan asks.

"Not at the service exit where the dumpsters are." Great

Granddad huffs.

Lan nods and continues to guide me down the hallway. But she stops as she approaches two large swinging doors.

"I hear voices in the kitchen."

Great Granddad and I freeze.

"Let me go in first and see who is in there. I will act as though I am just getting a late-night snack for some guests."

"Ohhh, a late-night snack sounds great." I joke.

Lan puts her finger to her lips with a "shhhhh." She brushes her hands over her uniform, but it does nothing to help the filthy, wrinkly mess.

"Lan!" a young man's voice shrieks as the kitchen doors swing behind her.

"Eli," she responds.

The voices are barely audible, so Great Granddad and I lean in to listen closely through the doors.

"Is anyone else in here?" Lan asks as the sound of scampering feet follows her.

"Just me, and Reggie washin' pans in the back." The voice of Felicia states quietly.

"Did you find who you were looking for?" She asks.

"Yes, they're right here." Lan's voice approaches as her hands push through the doors and grab onto my arms. She pulls me into the kitchen. Great Granddad follows us.

"You're looking good. Do you need a snack?" Felicia asks.

"Yes, please!"

"I'll do anything for my patients." She winks, handing me a flakey biscuit from a plate. "You need more of the electrolyte drink?"

I want to shake my head in refusal, wishing that I could have something, anything, else to drink, but she has already grabbed one out of a large industrial-sized fridge and handed it to me.

"You must be his Great Granddad." She states, handing him a biscuit and offering him an orange drink, too. He sets the metal box down on the massive butcher block counter briefly to take the food and drink.

"Yes, Ma'am, thank you." He nods.

"My pleasure." She smiles back, gawking at the carvings on the box.

"I'm assuming you are on your way out?" She asks as if she understands our urgency to leave.

"You're leaving us?" Eli, a gawky teen with frizzy dark curls, asks.

"I'm sorry, we have to go," Lan responds.

"Shhhh, someone is coming." The sound of two sets of footsteps can be heard echoing outside the kitchen doors. "Hide!" Felicia whispers.

Out of instinct, I shove the rest of the biscuit into my mouth. I snatch the metal box in one hand and chug down the drink with my other.

"Quick, in here," Eli suggests, gesturing to a large rolling garbage bin.

Lan and I jump in as Eli struggles to hold it steady. I wave for Great Granddad to join us, but there is clearly not enough room for him. He shakes his head and ducks around the corner into the walk-in pantry room. The smell of decaying food invades us as Eli tosses a few bags of trash on top of Lan and me to make our hiding place more inconspicuous. At the same moment, I can hear the kitchen doors swing open, and the two sets of boots parade onto the tiled floor.

"Good evening, boys. Is there something I can get for you?" Felicia asks as if this is just her normal nightly routine. "I'm just grabbing some biscuits and drinks for a few hungry patients. Would you care for some?"

"No, thank you, Ma'am." A deep voice replies.

"Have you seen anyone else come in here?" The other voice asks.

"No, sir. It's just me, Reggie washin' the pans, and Eli taking the trash out.

Go on son. I told you to take that out and get to bed, now. Go on!"

Eli struggles to push his extra heavy trash bin toward the back of the kitchen.

"Yes, Ma'am," he grunts.

"'Bout time you got that trash out, boy." A booming voice, which must belong to the person they call Reggie, states. It is followed by pans clanking and water splashing.

I hear the rattle and struggle with a door, and then icy air bleeds down between the cracks of the plastic bags on top of us. The vibration of the wheels over unlevel gravel causes my entire backside to tingle.

"Hurry up, kid, it's cold out here tonight." A distant voice calls from further outside.

"Yes, sir," Eli responds.

Lan's hand finds my arm, and she squeezes it tightly. Her nails dig in deeper as we hit a large bump.

We stop moving suddenly, followed by an ear-piercing screech, which is worse than a screaming banshee. A cringing shutter shivers through my body as heavy metal scrapes against metal. With a lurch, we are pushed another short distance.

"Okay, we are at the dumpster. Do I just throw you guys in, or what?" Eli's muffled whispers navigate their way down to our curled-up bodies.

"Can anyone see us?" Lan asks.

"There is just one guard out there, but his back is to us now."

"Okay, toss the bags in, and we will sneak out behind the dumpster."

"Okay." He grabs one of the garbage bags and removes it, revealing Lan.

"You aren't going out in the woods tonight, are you?" He asks through quivering puffs of breath.

"We can't exactly stay here undetected for long. They will be looking for us." Lan's whispers are full of fear.

"Then make sure you at least cover yourselves in mud. That helps mask your smell from the beasts. And reapply often. It is your only hope of making it out there during The Howling."

"Thank you, Eli. I will never forget you."

"What about Great Granddad?" I ask, popping my head out from under the other bag.

"I promise I will help him escape, but you have to go now, hurry!" Eli grunts as he tosses the heavy bag into the dumpster with a *thunk*.

During the commotion of flying trash bags, Lan and I ungracefully flop over the edge of the unstable garbage cart and dash around to the back of the dumpster. Our warm breath puffs white clouds against the frigid night air. I wish I had a coat or even a real shirt. The bitter air feels like hundreds of small knives tearing at my open back. The thin medical gown and papery pants do nothing to protect from the cold. My body begins to shutter, and my teeth chatter.

"Come on, let's run for that fence while the guard is opening the door for Eli," Lan suggests.

I nod, suck in a breath of air, which instantly freezes the back of my throat, and I grip the metal box with trembling fingers. Together, we stand, look over our shoulders to make sure the guard is still preoccupied, and run.

Chapter 29

The Ice Pack

The top of the fence is crowned with sharp, barbed wire. I take off my hospital gown, fold it over a few times, and throw it up onto the sharp rolls of metal. It is an unsuccessful attempt to cover the relentless talons. Lan takes off the canvas apron from around her waist and throws it on top of my gown.

"Yea, that will probably be more helpful," I state, realizing the thin hospital gown wasn't going to give us much protection from the razor-sharp shards of metal. And then I realize that I am standing shirtless in front of Lan, my ribs poking out much further than they used to, as the biting wind gnaws at my open flesh.

> *I am not sure that was a great idea.*
> *I wonder if I die of frostbite, will the virus freeze with me?*

With shaking, scrawny arms, I give Lan a boost and help her climb up the slick fence. Once she gets to the top, she carefully swings her leg up and over the draped barbed wire and secures her leg on the other side of the fence. Like a trained spy, she widely swings her other leg up and over the top, never even touching the apron. I follow her lead and begin to climb the fence. She made it look so easy. But the flimsy metal is not secure, and it buckles and weighs down in certain spots, making it difficult to get my feet into a crevice sturdy enough to hold my weight without falling. Not to mention, I am climbing the best I can while holding the metal box under one arm. Once I get to the top,

Lan's hands are reaching up, ready to take the box. I drop it to her carefully before I ready myself to maneuver over the vaguely covered sharp wire. With the first swing of my leg up over the top, my paper-thin pants catch a sharp barb and slice it open. My eyes widen with the tearing sound, hoping that I am still covered. I don't hear laughing from Lan, so I continue, hoping that I am not stuck in the grasp of the fence. I swing my other leg up and over while trying to balance my shaking arms, one hand on this side of the fence just below the barbs and one hand on the other side of the fence just below the barbs. My arms fight to hold me steady so I don't slice my chin, hovering from side to side, narrowly avoiding painful cuts. It takes every twinging muscle to shift my weight to the leg on the outside of the fence as I swing my other leg up over the top. I look up to where the guard is standing, and I watch as he begins to turn around in our direction. Either out of fear or unbalance, my hand releases from the top of the fence. I fall with a painful thud next to Lan. I collapse to the ground as the shattering pain in my socked feet escalates up through my legs. The slight hill on the other side of the fence makes gravity feel stronger, and I roll down a short distance in summersaults. Lan scurries to my side.

"Are you okay?" She whispers, ducking out of view of the guard, who hopefully doesn't notice my cloud of kicked-up dirt and snow.

"Yep," I groan. "Just trying to get covered in mud as Eli told us to do," I muster a pained smile as I wipe my snowy hands all over Lan's arms. She lets out a quiet giggle and chucks a frozen clump of ice at my shoulder.

"So, what's the plan now?" She asks.

I run my hand over the frozen ground beneath me.

"Well, I'm afraid we won't be able to cover ourselves in mud. This ground is completely frozen under this snow." My numb hand tries to rub off the stinging pain on what is left of my thin pants, which seem to be dissolving in the snow.

"We can try getting some mud down there closer to that stream." I point to where a sliver of the moon makes a reflection of a scythe on frozen black glass.

Lan nods as we half slide, half run, down the hill toward the dark snake-like river, frozen in place. The sound of the guard dogs barking behind us echoes in the night, followed by distant howls in response to their alarm. The resonances fire our motivation to get down the hill even faster before we are discovered from either deadly fate. Unable to move our legs as quickly as our bodies are propelling us, we slide the rest of the way down the hill on our backsides. I dig my thinly protected feet into the snowy bank just before we crash onto the inky ice. The crusty snow slices through my socks and into my heels like knives. I wrap my shivering arms around Lan and help her stop before she crashes into the frozen river. In the dark night, it is difficult to tell if the shards of ice and snow have cut through my feet and calves or if it is just the fierce cold attacking them. The force of our bodies on the bank causes the ice covering the river to crack. The chilling echo sounds like glass breaking. I slam the back of my heel into the ice, hoping my frozen bones don't shatter along with it. I plunge my hand down into the glacial water, scrape my hand against the side of the bank, and bring up a handful of polar, black mud. A moment of realizing that spreading freezing mud all over our already shivering bodies may not be the brightest idea is splintered the moment I see silhouettes of hairy beasts breaking the crest of the hill on the opposite side of the frozen river. The largest creature lets out a gut-wrenching howl. Lan's eyes grow in the moonlight as she snags the clump of bitter mud and begins wiping it on her body. I dip my hand back into the water, unable to tell if it is freezing cold, or scalding hot, as numbing pins and needles grow up my arm. Rubbing the gunk all over my chest, the thoughts of the buried capsule just below scream against the sludge. I grit my teeth and smear as if my life depends on it, which it does. I want to scream out to fight against the biting cold I am smearing all over my body, but I don't want to draw attention to us. I am still not sure if the beasts on top of the hill know of our presence. Lan dips her hand into the dark water, causing another chunk of ice to break loose from the bank. It splashes into the river. The heads of the large wolves all snap in our direction at once.

Lan and I become statues, afraid to even breathe. She carefully retracts her hand out of the water and wraps it in her uniform to help cuddle out the cold. We silently lean onto each other and huddle together, fearing to make any sudden movements. The moment the leader of the pack begins sprinting down the hill toward us, the other beasts are instantly at his tail. We have been spotted. There is nothing for us to do. We won't be able to outrun them. They are much too fast. I look down at the water rushing below the thick layer of ice, but Lan's look of death tells me she would rather be eaten alive than drowned in icy waters. I begin praying that the fifteen feet of ice between us and the other side of the river, now swarming with wolves, will create a life-saving barrier. The puffs of the leader's warm breath shoot into the dark night like a steam engine. The moonlight glints on his snarling fangs. I look into his eyes, which are like two deep caves set atop his growling snout. Panic closes around us like a shield. Lan's crouched body shakes violently against mine. The beast lifts his thick paw and places it gently onto the ice, his gaze never leaving us. The rest of his pack waits impatiently behind him, ready to attack at any moment. Once the leader's paw is secure on the ice, it picks up its other front paw and gingerly places it on the ice. Although the beast appears bulky and heavy, the ice seems to be holding beneath its hefty weight. His sides expand and retract with each of his breaths.

If those wolves get across this river, we are dead.

The beating of my heart pounds ferociously in my chest. My eyes urgently shift from side to side, trying to catch a glimpse of an idea. The beast's eyes stay fixed on us as he moves one of his hind legs onto the ice. Out of desperation, I grab a large piece of ice that broke free in our initial crash. My fingers burn as they wrap around its sharp edges. Adrenaline pumps through my veins, and I hurl the heavy chunk of ice at the stalking wolf. Lan grabs hold of me before I fall into the water, as it takes all my body weight to throw the heavy chunk. The block of ice crashes at the feet of the giant wolf, smashing into the sheet of ice below him. Like a windshield, shattering veins

277

grow in all directions from the blow. His gaze jumps from us to the cracking ice under his paws. Without hesitation, I pick up another chunk of ice. It may not be as large as the first, but I hope that it is large enough to finish the job. Chucking it with all my might at the wolf, he retracts back just in time before it hits him. It lands with an earth-shattering crack, breaks through the ice, and is swallowed into the river. The large beast is unable to turn around in time. The wolf was able to dodge the incoming chunk of ice, but its hind legs slip from the bank into the frigid waters, now rushing freely below him. With a boisterous yelp, a nearby wolf snaps its teeth into the neck of its leader to help pull him up onto the bank, but he is not quick enough. Both beasts are swept into the white, frothy currents, their bodies breaking through more shards of ice in their struggle. The wolves left on the bank begin frantically barking at the two in danger. One attempts to get close enough to help them, but quickly backs off as more ice breaks away into the rushing water. The two wolves scrambling in the river use each other as stepping-stones, aimlessly struggling to get on top of the ice. However, in the fight to survive, they both end up slipping under the cover of ice left uncracked a short distance downstream. The pack of wolves remaining on the bank bite and bark at the ice, unable to get to the two shadows drifting below the now thick, dark cover of ice. The pack, unwilling to give up their rescue, continues along the bank helplessly. Lan and I watch in shock as their barks and yelps echo into the distance as the river bends out of view.

My stiff body is unable to move once the coast is clear. I realize that I no longer feel cold. Sudden exhaustion plagues me, and it would be so easy to let my eyes close and fall asleep cuddling next to Lan. I shove those poisonous thoughts out of my mind.

"We need to get moving, now, or we are going to freeze to death sitting here," I state as the pain and feeling explode through my veins again as I force myself to stand.

I help Lan up next to me and peel her frozen fingers off the metal box she has been clutching onto. I help her to retract her hands into her long sleeves, hoping that will help to warm them.

"How far away is Fin's bunker?" I ask. "Do you think you can get us there?"

"It is less than an hour's walk." She looks around, getting her directions straight.

"We need to get around to the other side of E-Springs, and then I think I can get us going in the right direction. But do you think it is safe to go there?"

"It beats freezing or being eaten out here. I need my bags and the map. And a shirt and some actual, untorn pants would be nice." I chatter, unsure if I can make it that far in these conditions with only mud and thin paper protecting me.

"Okay, we will have to go this way." She states.

"Come on, let's hurry."

I firmly hug the metal box against my body with one arm and hold Lan's hand with the other. Trying to run feels like forcing stiff rubber bands to stretch to their breaking point. It wouldn't surprise me if my legs snap and shatter.

Just keep running.
We must keep running.

Lan's head turns to look over her shoulder as she realizes we need to get back up the hill so we can head around the outside of the large building.

Oh, please, not up the hill. I am struggling already, and we have only been running on flat ground.

I suck in as much cold air as I can before coughing, and I follow her lead up the hill. I wish my thighs were still frozen or numb because now they burn like lava. I keep my eyes focused on the line of skeleton trees bouncing at the top of the hill as my goal. I find that setting smaller, more manageable goals is extremely helpful. If I think about the daunting task of running all the way to the bunker, I am not going to make it. Near the top of the hill, running is out of the

279

question. Each step feels heavier and more difficult than the last, which I suppose they are because the slipper socks on my feet are now clumps of snow and ice. At least they no longer feel cold or pain. Those sensations stopped back down by the river. As the hill finally levels out, I am forced to drop my head down between my knees and catch my breath for a moment. The cacophony of howls, hoots, and crepuscular cries in the night is enough to make my skin crawl.

"We don't have time to wait." Lan spouts between puffs of breath, looking at my heaving chest.

Realizing she is right, I remember that my clock is ticking. Like breathing swords, I suck in as much air as I can and force my feet to keep moving past the bone-deep fatigue. I set my gaze on the dark branches ahead. But I can't shake the feeling of impending death. Even the dead branches hang like dried-out veins, and the trees in the distance resemble dead lungs. They are constant reminders that, much like me, the Earth is slowly dying. I am unsure if there is a thick fog falling over the trees, blurring them out, or if that is just a haze forming over my eyes. I watch as the woods are blanketed with a diaphanous, gauzy fabric. I keep running like a machine, but I am no longer sure if I am still awake or drowning in the *hazy phase*. The *hazy phase* is what I call that groggy time when I am in between the world of wakefulness and the land of slumber.

"We've got to be getting close, but all the trees look the same, so I'm not positive.

It's hard to know if this is it." Lan's voice spurts with weariness and uncertainty as she steps into a small clearing of trees. The moonlight through the fog and clouds shines momentarily, causing her auburn hair to glow like an angel's halo on top of her head.

She drops down onto her hands and knees and starts sifting through the few inches of snow and ash like a desperate puppy in search of its favorite bone.

"I think this is the right spot. Start helping me dig. More snow and ash have fallen since we were here last, so I think the hatch is covered." She gasps with exhaustion between each frantic dig.

Between the two of us, we are able to search quite a bit of ground in a short amount of time.

What if we are in the wrong clearing of trees?
It all looks the same to me.
Maybe if I wasn't half-zoned when I saw it last, I would
be able to tell if we are even in the correct vicinity of...

"The bunker! I found it!" Lan lets out a triumphant whoop, and a not-so-far-off howl in reply makes her instantly smack her hand over her mouth, realizing we aren't out of the woods yet – literally.

I scuffle over to where she is crouched and holding back her excitement. Relief washes over both of us like a warm blanket. We work together to force the frozen metal wheel in a twisting motion until the hatch lock releases with an echoing clang. We brace our stance and tug the hatch open.

SNAP! A nearby twig breaks. Lan and I freeze momentarily, our eyes scanning the darkness from where the sound emerged. A large snowy owl dive-bombs in our direction. Its beak is like an enormous dart heading directly for my face. I duck just in time, but its raptor-like talons snag a clump of my hair.

"Ouch, go, go, go!" I shout to Lan, dropping the box and pushing her down the ladder inside the hatch as I watch the owl circle back around toward us. The black pupils inside its large yellow eyes hone in on me. As soon as Lan's head is down, I jump anxiously into the hole and slam the hatch closed above my head. The sound of the owl's claws raking across the top of the metal is like fingernails on a chalkboard. With a twitching coil, my shoulders jump up to my ears as my head jerks to the side. I rub my head and allow my fingers to survey the damage of owl-yanked hair as soon as my feet touch the dirt ground.

He didn't get too much hair.
It will grow back.
My hair is the least of my worries.

Chapter 30

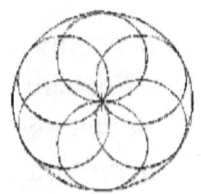

Painful Goodbyes

*I*n the dense darkness, Lan knocks on the metal door to the bunker.

Four distinct even knocks,

a two-beat pause,

two knocks,

a two-beat pause,

one knock,

and three quick taps with a fingernail; right hand, left hand, right hand.

We wait for a moment in the deafening silence.

She repeats the pattern again.

Nothing.

I hear her hand lower to the handle and she pulls it with a rattle, but it is locked.

With less patience, she repeats the secret knock again.

I am so grateful that she remembers the knock code. As soon as she did it the first time, it came back to me, but I never would have been able to recreate it without having heard it again.

Tap, tap, tap, her fingers stab out the last three beats with great intensity.

Locks clicking on the other side of the door are like music to my ears, and I am finally able to let out the breath I didn't know I was harboring.

As the door swings open, an innocent voice sings, "Maddy!"

Fin's Aunt Hellen's shocked face scrunches together with confusion.

"Hi, we just came back to get my things." I smile awkwardly.

"I hope it's alright that we're here."

"Yay, you came back!" Sophie squeals.

"What are you... get in here. You're filthy and practically naked. Are you crazy running around out there like that? Come in, come in." She yanks both of us inside. Then, she sticks her head back out into the hatch and looks up the ladder to see that it is closed.

"Where is Maddy?" She asks, eyeing the metal box in my hands.

"That is the box Maddy came back here to get from your things, and he was ranting and grumbling angrily when he couldn't get it open. He said you had asked for it. What is it? Where is Maddy?"

Lan and I look at each other, not exactly sure how we should respond.

"Is he coming back, too?" Sophie asks, clapping her hands with glee.

"Ummm..." I look down at the floor, racking my brain for the correct answer.

Does Hellen know that Fin is at E-Springs? I recall her saying that she thought he never wanted to return to them. Does she know the truth about him working with Elementerprise?

"Oh, no. No! Don't tell me something has happened to him."

Her hands shoot up to her mouth, and her eyes narrow with dread as her forehead folds inward.

"No... I mean, not that I know of," I spout, doing my best to avoid any unnecessary emotional upheavals.

"He's not with us," Lan states simply.

I nod in agreement for more reasons than just the physically obvious.

"Oh, good." Hellen lets out a sigh of relief. "He is probably already back on that blasted ship. At least he seems happy sailing with those two crazy men, and it helps buy medicine for Sophie, so I guess I can't complain about his choice." Hellen pushes us over to the bed and wraps us in blankets as she continues babbling.

"Although I must admit, it is stressful thinking about him bobbing around on the stormy ocean. But I suppose it is better than him being carted off to fight in the wars. Or working for Elementerprise - they just want to control the entire world and will do anything to gain power, and I mean anything. No good can come from them. Except it looks like they helped you recover. I mean, you were able to make it back here at least."

Then, she clicks her tongue and shakes her head in disbelief as she gets on her hands and knees and takes off my worn socks, caked with ice melting into puddles on her floor.

"They couldn't even give you some warm clothes and proper shoes before they sent you away? These feet!" Her gasping, grimacing face speaks volumes. "You'll be lucky if your feet don't fall off. Frostbite for sure. Hopefully, it is just superficial, but only time will tell. Let's get them warmed up. I will boil some water so you can soak them." She scurries over to the cramped kitchen area, puts some water from a large jug into a pot, and places it on the electric burner.

I lift my right foot and place my ankle on top of my knee. Tilting the bottom of my foot up to where I can see the damage, I am greeted with an angry, crimson, blistered sole.

Lan gasps.

I touch the bottom of my foot with my finger, but I don't feel anything. It looks like I have walked across hot coals, and my feet are scorched.

"Does it hurt?" Lan's eyes glisten with concern.

"No, actually. I can't feel anything." I reassure her with a worried shrug.

285

Although, I don't think that is a good sign.

"Are your feet really going to fall off?" Sophie's pale face fluctuates to an even lighter shade of white. She looks like a ghost.

"We won't let that happen, will we, Sophie?" Lan leans closer to Sophie and whispers to her as if I can't hear her next words. "Even if we have to sew them on real tight." She winks.

Sophie lets out a nervous giggle, which is followed by a cough.

"There won't be any feet falling off on my watch," Hellen states, placing a large bucket filled with a little water in front of my feet. "Start off with this warm little bit, and I will keep bringing you more. Put your feet in, and we'll warm them up slowly. And here are some rags so you can wipe off all that mud, too."

"Thank you," I say, flopping my heavy feet into the water. I can feel that the water is about room temperature on the tops of my feet, but the bottoms of my feet can't even tell if they have touched the bottom of the bucket.

"It's the least I can do for you after you gave Sophie that inhaler. It has helped her tremendously."

"Oh ya, I drew this one for you." Sophie's bashful chin tucks to her chest as she pulls out a colorful drawing from under her pillow and leans over to hand it to me. Her eyes peer up through her blonde eyelashes.

I take it from her shaking hand and look down at the picture as a smile grows across my face. Pride bubbles up from my frozen toes. It is a glorious picture of me with a superhero cape billowing behind me, one hand on my hip confidently, and my other hand raised into the air, grasping a beaming inhaler as if it is a magical relic.

"Awe," Lan stifles a giggle. "Look, you have a cape."

"Thanks, Sophie. It is my all-time favorite picture!" I try to stand to give her a hug, but my feet, which are trapped in a metal bucket, prevent it, and I nearly fall.

She giggles, stands, and crawls onto the bed next to me, wrapping her arms around me in a hug. But, instead of feeling warm and squishy inside, a choking pain suffocates me. Tears burn in my eyes. For a moment, I am unsure if it is just a memory of Jaxson hugging me, or if it is really him, I am feeling nuzzled against my side. Tears singe my eyes, my nose burns, and a fiery lump forms in my throat, strangling my breath. I force myself to pat Sophie's bony arm gently once I shake the thought of Jaxson from my wavering mind. I don't want her to think I am not grateful for her sweet gesture. But I have the sudden urge to get out of here. I can't breathe.

Suddenly, a warm tingling sensation swirls around my ankles. As if in a trance, I turn my gaze down to see Hellen pouring more water into the bucket around my feet.

I place my other hand on my chest, feeling my heart rate racing uncontrollably, and again, I can't swallow. The edges of everything in my vision suddenly blur.

Oh no, has the capsule dissolved?
Am I contagious now?

Panic floods through my veins, drowning out all sanity.

I look into Hellen's eyes and watch as they shrivel in her sockets like raisins. Her skin begins to wrinkle, and blood squeezes out from her pores. Her crimson hands clasp her heaving chest, gasping for air.

No! It's starting.
I have infected Hellen!
She is dying.

"Dameon, I can't breathe!" Sophie wheezes. I turn to watch her bulging, pleading eyes as she coughs a blood-spraying hack. As if her muscles are dissolving under her instantly yellowing skin, she turns into a sickly skeleton at my side.

"No!" I shout, panting and sloshing water all over the floor.

"I'm sorry, is it too hot?" Hellen asks. She looks normal and healthy again – nothing like the morbid bleeding corpse she was moments ago.

I rub my eyes, unsure if what I am seeing now is real or if the horrifying state I witnessed a few seconds ago was real. In pure desperation, I whip my head to look at Sophie. She looks okay, too, other than her big eyes questioning my bizarre outburst.

> *I'm losing it!*
> *Or hallucinating,*
> *or sick with anxiety…*

"Dameon, are you okay?" Lan asks, looking deep into my eyes, searching for an explanation for my sudden, odd behavior.

"Yea. Sorry," I add, looking at Hellen.

"I just… we really need to get going," I spout with desperation to Lan.

"You aren't going anywhere on these feet," Hellen demands, forcing my feet back into the bucket of warm water and then wiping the rest of the mud from my chest.

"I truly appreciate your help. But it isn't safe for me to be here. We need to go, now!" I pant to Lan. She nods gently, understanding my urgency.

"He's right; we really do need to get going." Lan agrees, looking at my panting chest. I gaze down at the exposed golf ball-sized bruise where I was stabbed with the injector pen.

"But your feet, you can't possibly go back out in the cold like this. Please, just stay for the night. You know it isn't safe out there after dark," she pleads.

"I'm afraid we don't have a choice. It's a matter of life and death," I whisper.

"Then, at least sit here a moment longer, and let me get you some warm clothes and a few things to help you survive. I can't send you out there with nothing."

"Thank you, we would appreciate that," Lan states.

"But you just got here," Sophie's little voice whimpers.

"I wish we could stay; I really do. But we can't." Looking into

288

her puddling eyes breaks my heart all over again. Her little round chin quivers, sending shards straight through my emotions.

"I'm sorry, I'm running out of clothes and coats to give out. These might be big on you, but they will hopefully keep you warm."

"But Auntie, that's your coat," Sophie says when she sees the worn coat Aunt Hellen handed to Lan.

"Hush, child, I can find or make another one."

Lan pushes the coat back toward Hellen, shaking her head. "I can't take your coat."

"I insist. The only way I will allow you two to leave here is if you are bundled with everything I can give you."

Lan wraps her arms around Hellen's neck, "thank you!"

"Don't thank me unless you make it through the night out there," she mumbles under her breath.

Lan takes the bundle of clothes into the little bathroom in the corner of the bunker and closes the door gently.

"I really don't think it is a good idea for you to go. It isn't safe out there during The Howling hours. Can't I talk you into staying at least until morning?"

There is nothing that I would like to do more than agree with her. But my pounding heart beats like a ticking time bomb.

"If we stay, you will both die." The painful words whisper over my lips.

"But what about your girlfriend? Don't you care about her safety?" Helen whispers back, barely audible.

"She's not my... I will do everything to keep her safe." But even I am not sure if my words are possible.

How can I make sure Lan stays safe?
What if I do die?
What will happen to her then?
She doesn't have anyone here in this time.
All of her "family" is in the future.

"You know what, you are right. I need to go to keep you all safe. And Lan would be better off here. Can I leave her here with you? Will you promise to make sure she stays safe?"

"Why don't you both stay here, please!" Helen's eyes beg with great intensity.

"Yes, please stay with us!" Sophie chimes in.

"I can't!" I grab the pile of clothes and boots from Helen, and slosh to the other side of the room to grab my backpack and satchel. I shove the metal box inside the bag for safekeeping and swing it up onto my bare shoulder.

"I can't thank you enough for helping us out, but I have to go to keep you safe. Please, keep Lan here and keep her safe."

With those words, I unlock the multiple locks on the metal door, swing it open, and head into the darkness, alone.

The silence of the small metal area at the base of the hatch clouds my senses. I struggle to slip off what is left of the papery scrub pants and slip on the much thicker canvas pants Helen just gave to me. They must be Fin's or perhaps his dad's. Luckily, my hands find a leather belt in the pile of clothes, and I feed it through the loops around the top of the pants quickly and cinch it up tight around my waist, which I notice is most likely much smaller than it was when I left home. I feel a flannel shirt with buttons, and I struggle in the darkness to get it on the right way. I am unsure if I found the correct buttonhole for each button. Next, I find a pair of wool socks. I hate the scratchy feeling of wool against my fingers, and it makes me cringe. I get the same icky feeling in my teeth, like when you accidentally bite down on aluminum foil. But I don't have time to be picky. I am filled with gratitude as I fumble the rough, thick wool over my numb feet. I force them into the boots, which are still a few sizes too large for my swollen feet. I feel a twinge of pain as I tighten the laces as tight as I can pull them.

I hear sudden mumbles echoing against the metal tomb around me. I can make out what must be Lan's muffled voice, and it doesn't sound happy. Helen's voice pleads in return.

Uh oh, Lan knows I am trying to leave without her.
I need to hurry if I want to keep her safe.

I force my arms into the sleeves of the coat and feel the ground around me, making sure I am not leaving any articles of clothing behind. When my hands don't find anything else, I swing my backpack onto my back and slide my head through the strap of my satchel, securing it around my chest – my chest, which happens to be encapsulating a deadly virus.

I climb the ladder with haste and use all my arm strength to open the hatch above my head and swing it open. I climb through, checking to make sure there aren't any lurking creatures nearby. Before I can close the hatch, I hear Lan open the door from the bunker below.

"Dameon! Dameon, wait!" She shouts.

Without hesitating, I slam the hatch door closed and take off running. I have no clue if I am running in the right direction. I'm not even sure where I need to be going. All I know is that I need to make sure Lan doesn't find me or follow me. I can't risk infecting her or anyone. And so, I run. I run into the night, weaving around the towers of bare trees and pumping my legs as if my life, and everyone else's lives, depend on it.

Chapter 31

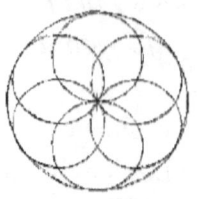

The Box

*D*ameon! Wait for me!" Lan's voice chases behind me. The pace of her crunching strides is much faster than mine. She is closing in. The columns of bare trees provide nowhere to hide, and so I stop the charade; I won't be able to outrun her.

> *Who am I kidding?*
> *She is way faster than I am.*

My feet stop and I lean my hands against the frozen trunk of a tree, bracing myself as I pant thick puffs of breaths into the cold night air.

"Go back!" I gasp and cough.

"I'm coming with you."

"Go!" My shout is much harsher than I meant for it to be, and I try to suck it back in. But much like the struggle I am having to suck in any air, I can't. Unfortunately, words don't come with gift receipts, and they can't be taken back.

"What is wrong with you?

What were you thinking?

That I would just stay there with them? For what, forever?

That I would just let you go by yourself?"

She makes it sound like it was such a stupid idea.

"I'm not safe to be around. We don't know for sure if you can't get infected with whatever I have, or am going to have, or whatever."

"Well then, at least we will die together."

Her eyes peer into mine. She grabs my hands from off the tree and squeezes the numbness out of them. Suddenly, I don't feel cold, I don't feel exhausted, I don't feel anything except my heart rhythm beating in time with hers. And for the first time since getting injected, I don't worry about dying. I am just happy to be alive and living this moment with Lan. My face, as if drawn in by a compelling magnetic force, uncontrollably inches toward hers. My eyes close, soaking in every sensation zinging through my body as my lips brush up against her velvet lips.

Hoot hoot!

Reality slams back down on us, forcing us to jump apart as the piercing shrills of the owl attack us like daggers.

Stupid owl!
You are the bane of my existence!

Out of reaction to the nuisance, I reach down, grab a handful of crusty snow, and chuck it as hard as I can at the interrupting owl.

Lan stifles a giggle as I watch a sideways smile creep across her face. She grabs my hand and leans back in to finish the kiss. But now, all I can think about is infecting her and making her shrivel and decay in agony as I saw in the vision of Helen and Sophie haunting my thoughts.

"I'm sorry." I pull away. "I can't live, or die, with myself if I get you sick.

Please, go back down to Helen and Sophie before it's too late."

"And what if it already is too late?

What if I am already infected?

I can't go back down there, and you know it.

I guess you're stuck with me now."

The boisterous noises of nature swell around us and can't be ignored.

"If we have any chance of surviving, Helen told me there is a hunting hut or blind - I think that is what she called it, about five minutes west from here. She said there is still a draft that blows through it, but it should keep the chill out and will give us some shelter for the night."

"I do need some time to look at the map The Captain gave me, and I need to get the box open as soon as possible," I add.

Looking up at the blur of light shining from the moon between the layers of fog, clouds, and snowing ash, I see where the glowing orb hovers now in the sky compared to where it was, and in which direction it has been moving.

"Come on, west is this direction," I state, intertwining my fingers in hers. The feeling of her hand nestled inside of mine fills me with a sense of security.

Together, we take off running, the backpack on my back jumping up and down with each jaunt. The frigid wind bites at my face the faster we run, but the wailing creatures around us fuel our pace. Our eyes scan the never-ending sea of tree trunks and hills, looking for the shelter. After running for a few minutes, I begin counting in my head to sixty, so I know when a minute has gone by.

> *If Helen said the hut was about five minutes from their bunker, does that mean five minutes of running or walking? She would probably be walking, so that means we should be getting close. And did she mean we need to go directly west of their bunker? If so, we may need to go back north in that direction since I ran a short distance south after leaving there.*

I pull Lan north toward the direction of the bunker.

"We should be getting close. I would imagine it will blend in and be difficult to see, especially in the dark." I whisper, trying to make sure my voice is not audible to howling creatures surrounding us in every direction.

I squint to see a small knoll covered in sticks and skeletons of shrubbery.

*That would be the only likely spot, considering
everything else for as far as I can see in every direction
is a sea of vertical tree trunks, which are not wide
enough to hide a hunting blind.*

As if seeing the knoll at the same time, Lan picks up her pace and begins darting toward the mound. The closer we get, we can see that it is covered in sticks and snow as if they were padded around the lump like plaster.

"This has to be it." I flop onto my hands and knees to examine it more closely for an entrance. A puff of snow whirls around my dropped knees like dandelion seeds full of hope and wishes. My hands brush against a piece of tree bark hidden below a layer of ice. I knock against it and a hollow echo resonates behind the wood. A smile forces my frozen lips to creep upward. I dig and scrape frantically to find the outline of the oddly shaped piece of bark. I tug and fight to finagle it open, dragging it against the opening of crusty snow. The scratching sound echoes in the night like fingernails on a chalkboard. At last, the bark door is ajar, creating an opening just large enough for a person to crawl through.

"After you." My hand gestures toward the dark hole like a gentleman.

Lan drops to her hands and knees and crawls her way into the obscure den. I crawl in after her.

The doorway quickly opens up to where we can stand freely. We shove the door closed. I feel along the flap of my backpack and open the pocket to fish out my flashlight. As I flick it on, we are greeted with a small, rounded dome igloo made of wood, mud, and ice.

"Look, there is an oil lamp," Lan discovers, twisting the knob and lighting the room with a flickering glow. I turn off my flashlight to save the batteries for when we may need it.

I jump toward a shotgun, leaning up against the frozen wall. I instantly check the chamber to see if it is loaded. Unfortunately, it is empty. However, not too far away, I see a faded, rusted, metal ammo box. Fumbling to get it open, I see there are three slugs amongst a pile of empty shells inside.

"Well, we have a little protection," I state to Lan, holding up the ammo box.

"That's good. Now let's figure out how to open the box that really matters."

I nod in agreement and pull out the metal puzzle box, turning it over in my frozen hands. I place it in my lap as I briskly rub my hands together, attempting to gain some feeling back in my fingertips. I need to be able to feel if any symbols click or budge when pressed. I force my frozen fingers to try pushing, sliding, pulling, or altering any section of the box to no avail.

"Maybe there are some clues about how to open it in one of the journals," Lan suggests.

"Here, you are welcome to check." I toss her the bag containing the journals. "I have searched every page, but there is nothing about how to open the box in them."

She reaches in and pulls out the latest of Great Granddad's journals and begins flipping through the pages as I continue fiddling with the box. The minutes speed by as if in hyperdrive as dread pulses through my veins with each pump of my heart.

"Here, what about this?" Lan's eyebrows shoot upward as she leans in to get a closer look at the metal box in my hands. "It has some of the same symbols."

I look over at the open page of the journal in her hands.

1st —Explore/inhabit Turtle Island 2nd —Round Lake/ water with stones 3rd —Food grows on water 4th —fight faced man could mean death

5th —False promises 6th —Balance sickness and grief 7th —one path green, one dark and sharp

"That page wasn't there before. I would have remembered it. How are new pages appearing in the journal? Great Granddad must still be adding new entries." I attempt to wrap my brain around the thought of Great Granddad drawing in this same journal right at this same moment.

"But you have the journal. How could he be writing in it at the same time?" Lan's eyes squint with confusion.

"Well, technically, he hasn't given it to me yet, remember? He doesn't give it to me until your time, in the future. So, maybe, since this is the *past,* according to your time, he still has the journal, too."

Lan's face scrunches together.

"You are making my brain hurt." She shakes her head in an attempt to release the discombobulation toiling her mind.

"Well, however it got here, it looks like this page contains the same images that are on the box. It also explains something called *The Seven Fires Prophecy*. It looks like each image depicts a different prophecy."

I notice that situated in one of the corners of the box there is a small flame, and in the center of the flame is a small hole. I push against the flame, and I feel it jiggle ever-so-slightly.

"It looks like it needs a key, but where would I find a key small enough to fit this tiny hole?"

"Didn't you have an entire key ring of keys?"

"Yes."

I begin to search for them in the front pouch of my backpack because I remember placing them in here after I used them last.

"But I'm pretty sure they are all too large for this tiny keyhole. It's almost like it isn't an actual key; it's more like a...
That's it!"

"What? What is it? Did you find the key?"

My hands sift through the backpack, but not for the keyring.

"I'm pretty sure it's in here. I remember putting it in."

My fingers brush over the familiar leather and metal of the wristband I found in Great Granddad's cellar. Clutching it, I pull it out with enthusiasm. I instantly begin to pull the small metal piece used as a key to wind the music box. Sticking the tip of my tongue out between my lips in concentration, I attempt to place the miniscule key into the hole on the metal box. Lan jumps to my side with excitement as both our eyes double in size when we hear a satisfying click of acceptance.

"It fits!" My fingers shake with eagerness as I twist the key to unlock the box. Another triumphant tick echoes through the tiny hut, and I feel the key is now able to slide along a track of etching through the box. As the key slides, I can no longer pull it out, as the two small teeth keep it from pulling free. Instead of removing it, I am able to slide it along a carved labyrinth of track.

"It's a maze," I blurt my realization.

"Move it that way, over to the picture of the first prophecy." Her fingers point to show me the picture of the turtle in the journal. I maneuver the key through a maze and make it to the carving of the turtle on the box. As the key completes the tracing of the outline, I feel another mechanism inside the puzzle unlatch.

"Yes, it's working! Which one comes next?"

Lan then guides me through each intricate carving in the order of The Seven Fires Prophecy. I glide and wiggle the tiny metal rod, tracing each image, glowering at the sound of a locking mechanism releasing as I finish each correctly shaped pathway. As I glide the rod through the seventh prophecy and through its lush pathway, I notice that the box still won't open. It appears that the maze through the puzzle box isn't complete.

"Now, where does the key need to go?" I ask Lan.

"That's it. Those are the seven images it shows in the journal. There isn't anything else."

"There has to be more," I suggest, my desperate eyes scouring the journal page.

I search the box for a possible next step. And then, I see it. The infinity symbol, although easy to miss if you aren't studying every swirling detail on the box, catches my eye.

> That must be it. The Captain said I was the final Aeon, The Eighth Prophecy, and this is my symbol.

I think back to The Captain's words. They echo through my mind as I work the key through the maze to get it to the infinity symbol.

> The number 8 signifies resurrection, regeneration, and eternity in numerology, astrology, and in The Bible. The Aeonic prophesies have foretold of the eighth member of our society. You are the eighth living member. You are the higher being who is said to save us all, who will give us a new beginning. You are The Final Aeon, The Eighth Prophecy!

Click!

The sound of another ball bearing drops inside the box and the key is freed from the maze. I place the key back into the holding strap on the wristband. My fingers then dive back to the metal box and turn white as they attempt to force it open.

"It still won't open," I complain, shaking the box with frustration.

A sudden, overpowering burning sensation pierces my wrist like it is being held to a flame. Tearing the wrapped bandages off my scalding wrist, I grit my teeth in pain. My tattoo glows like a red-hot iron. The burning ember on the infinity symbol pulses, tracing the sideways figure eight. I don't know if the thought enters my mind instinctively or if there is an actual magnetic force compelling the symbol on my wrist to gravitate toward the infinity symbol on the box. The less space there is between the two symbols, the more my wrist aches and longs to connect to the twin, metal symbol. I try pulling my wrist away, just to see if I am imagining all this, but the moment I even attempt to raise my wrist, an instant wave of excruciating pain scorches to my gut and inflicts instant nausea. I give up resisting and allow my wrist to connect with the box. A jolt of euphoria blasts through my body. Every cell, from the tip of my head to the tip of my toes, tingles with satisfaction. I am in a state of pure nirvana. As if the box absorbs the fiery burning from my wrist, I watch as the glowing crimson spreads from the infinity symbol on my wrist like lava, bursting through to every crevice of the carved webbed maze, flowing gloriously around every etched image until the entire box is aglow. Then, a soul-awarding click resounds, and the top portion of the box pops apart, creating a separation. A clear crack in the lid can be opened. I look into Lan's eyes, reflecting the light of the box as if they are glowing suns, as a wide smile takes over her scarlet cheeks.

"You did it!"

Without a moment of hesitation, my trembling fingers gingerly lift the lid of the box open to rest on the revealed hinges. And there, cradled to perfection in a dark grey cloud of foam padding, rest three syringes full of a glowing red liquid.

My chest begins to heave quickening breaths. My heart thumps uncontrollably. Trickles of sweat build on my forehead. I squeeze my dry eyes closed as the barrage of bickering thoughts argues in my brain.

What if I inject myself, and it doesn't work?

What if I end up like those monstrous creatures in the cages at E-Springs?

What if whatever this serum is is worse than whatever they injected me with?

What if they didn't inject me with anything harmful at all, and this was all just a ploy to get me to open the box for them?

My eyelids flap open suddenly as I survey the hut around me, sure to find spying eyes. I'm worried that at any moment, Elementerprise's men will burst through the frozen walls and seize the syringes.

"What are you waiting for? Go on, do it."

"I don't think I can." My shaking voice whispers as I feel the blood drain from my face. My legs and arms suddenly feel numb, and I become like a statue.

"It's just a little needle," Lan rolls her eyes.

"No, it's so much more than that," I sputter. "What if..."

"You don't have time to think about what-ifs. You know you

don't have a choice." Lan cuts me off and snatches one of the syringes from the shaking box in my trembling lap.

She's right. I know I need to do this.

"So, what will it be? Arm? Leg? Butt cheek?"

My eyes snap to her as my chin drops at her last suggestion. Our eyes connect, and then a minuscule amount of pent-up tension bursts from our lips in a chuckle.

"Ummmm, arm, please." I choose the least embarrassing body part.

I take off the coat Hellen gave to me and roll up my sleeve to reveal my rather scrawny upper arm. Suddenly, I wish I had a bit more fat to help cushion the incoming jab. I suck in a deep breath of air, squeeze my eyes closed, and brace myself for the sting. But I am attacked with so much more than just the sting of a needle. It feels more like liquid fire scorching its way through my veins. I begin panting and letting out small puffs of air through pursed lips to help me get through the pain. And then, the real agony begins to wreak havoc. All at once, it feels like every atom in my body is being strangled or ripped to shreds simultaneously. I can no longer keep the screaming in my head silent. As if every part of my body cries out at once, an excruciating holler erupts from my mouth as an intensifying pain boils my insides. My heart beats in triple-time, and my panting quickens. I want more than anything to open my eyes to take one last look at Lan, but my eyes are squeezed too tightly, and the pain is too much to even allow that slight bit of movement.

This is too much.
I'm dying.
I'm not going to make it.

Chapter 32

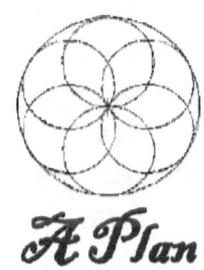

A Plan

"Dameon?
Can you hear me?"

The pain riveting my body begins to lessen with each pulse of my rapid heartbeat. I pry open my eyes. Lan's voice wraps around me like a security blanket.

"Dameon?

Are you okay?"

My eyes find hers and my head drops weakly in a slight nod.

"I'm okay," I finally muster in response to her as well as a reassurance to myself.

I continue to wheeze out puffs of labored breaths as if blowing continuous dandelion wishes. I slowly unclench my fists, pulling my fingernails out of my sweating palms. I release the tension in my shoulders and roll them backward, allowing my neck and spine to readjust to a more comfortable alignment. I suck in a cleansing breath and steady my heart. The all-over pain turns into more of a tingling sensation, and I feel like my body is buzzing. The feeling is reminiscent of when I was super thirsty on a walk home from school over a year ago, and I decided it would be a good idea to try an energy drink that all the kids rave about. The jittery feeling from the abundance of sugar and caffeine made my stomach churn, so I haven't tried another one since. I wish that I had something to eat now, that is what helped me feel better after that drink. I realize that I am feeling hungry. Not just hungry but ravenous.

"I think I need to eat something. You hungry?" I ask Lan, realizing she is now holding the metal box in her hands. I am not sure how she ended up with it. Did I drop it? I don't even know how long I was in a state of pain, or what happened during that time.

"Ummm, I guess. Are you sure you are feeling alright?" Her eyes look over me, making sure I really am okay.

"Yep, I'm actually feeling much better now. Just starving."

I reach into my backpack and pull out the hard sea biscuits we took from the ship, and I pass one to Lan. I bite into one and it practically crumbles to ash in my mouth and on my lips.

"Ya, jus' as har' 'n' stale as 'fore." I struggle to form the words as the biscuit turns my mouth into a desert; some of the sand-like crumbs escape through my lips in the process. I know something is wrong with Lan because she hasn't even taken a bite yet, and she always dives into her food like she has never eaten before.

"What, you're not hungry?" I ask once I can finally gather enough saliva to swallow the dry lump of biscuit.

"I am, I just… a minute ago, you were writhing in pain, and now, you're acting as if nothing even happened."

I don't really know what to say.

"How do you know if it worked? Do you feel any different?" Her eyes deepen into a squint.

"I know I am really hungry," I spout, fishing a can of chili from my backpack.

"I'm glad we brought some food with us from home." The word home escapes my mouth without thinking about it.

> *Home? Do I consider Great Granddad's estate my "home" now? What about our other cookie-cutter house? Are we going back there at the end of the summer if Jaxson is feeling better? That is if I can get back to my time.*

I feel Lan's scrutiny intensify.

"Here, do you want some?" I pull out two spoons, handing one to her. I pop the top off of the can as a little red sauce spurts onto my pants. Without hesitation, my finger instinctively swipes off the rogue slop, and I lick it off with great satisfaction.

Lan looks at me with questioning eyes. I pass the can to her and allow her to dip her spoon into the can first. Her eyes don't leave the goofy grin on my face as she scoops a bitefull onto her spoon. Her eyes finally break away from me and close, followed by, "mmmmmmm," as soon as the chili enters her mouth.

"Sorry, it is so much better when it is warmed up."

"It gets better than this?" Her eyes grow bigger.

Wow, Lan really needs to try more foods if she thinks cold, canned chili is delicious.

I realize I am staring at her, so I quickly dive-bomb my spoon into the can for a little distraction.

"Alright, let's look at the map The Captain gave me and see if we can figure out where we need to go from here. Great Granddad made me repeat the directions: *Use map. Find nibi ikwe.*"

I dig the map out of my backpack and carefully unroll the worn, soft leather. Thankfully, the map has a key showing me what all the symbols mean: mountains, rivers, forests, etc...

"Okay, this is clearly E-Springs, labeled Greenbrier on here." I point to the large structure on the map."

"How do we know which way to go? The map covers a lot of land." Lan's body slumps over the map.

"I don't see anything on here that says nibi ikwe."

"What is a nibi ikwe?" Lan's eyes squint at the map's smaller details.

"That's the problem; I have no clue, and there isn't anything even similar shown on here.

Does the journal tell us what it means?" I ask, assuming Great Granddad wouldn't send me on a wild goose chase.

305

Lan straightens her back and focuses on the journal in her lap as I dig around in my bag to find the other journal to scan. I look through countless pages of ingenious inventions, mathematical equations, scientific elements, and theories. I'm tempted to stop and read about the descriptions of some of the interesting organisms, but I will have to come back to them when I have more time.

"Here are a bunch of other strange words. I think they must be a different language." The pitch of Lan's voice jumps an octave with excitement. She thrusts the open journal toward my face so I can see the explanation of words for myself.

"*Nibi* means life or living, and *ikwe* means water." The discovery bursts from my sputtering lips.

"So, we are looking for life or living water on this map? There are lots of rivers, streams, and lakes on here. How do we know which of them is the living water?" I ask, still searching the map for clues.

"The Springs! It must be the White Sulphur Springs! Eli told me about how they believe that the water from White Sulphur Springs can heal you and give you eternal life. That is why they built the resort at E-Springs."

"Like The Fountain of Youth?" I ask.

Lan's brow folds down toward her perfect little nose as her shoulders shrug. Clearly, she has never heard of The Fountain of Youth.

I close my eyes and breathe in the idea of White Sulphur Springs. A warmth of affirmation spreads over me like warm syrup oozing over a stack of steaming pancakes.

"So, I guess we are heading to White Sulphur Springs."

"It is just an idea. How do we know that is where we are supposed to go?" Lan asks.

"I have a feeling you're right. Great Granddad told me to find *nibi ikwe*, where else could that be except White Sulphur Springs? Besides, I have a feeling I have heard that term before. I can't explain it, but I just get a sense that is where we are supposed to go. But is that spring still at E-Springs? I really don't want to go back there. We just escaped. We may not be that lucky next time."

"Eli said that the spring at E-Springs is fed from the original White Sulphur Springs, located up the mountain from their location. We could try to find the water source that leads into E-Springs. But what are we supposed to do when we get there? Drink the water or something? I don't see how going to a spring is going to help us save the world."

"I guess we'll find out when we get there. If we can't find anything, then we will head back to the train station and find our way back to The Captain. Maybe he will be able to communicate to Great Granddad or the other secret society people, or he may know what we need to do with this serum."

Lan sucks in a breath of hesitation, but she nods her head.

"I guess that sounds like a plan." She states as she forces a wavering smile on her face.

She dips her spoon back into the can of chili and takes a large heaping spoonful. She dips her lips toward the can to meet her overzealous bite, not spilling or wasting a single drop. Her fake smile is replaced with a more sincere one. Our spoons take turns clanking into the can until there is nothing left to scrape out.

"Alright," I say, licking my spoon clean. "I suppose it is time to head out." I begin to put one of the journals into my satchel.

"Wait, we are leaving now?" Lan's question turns into a drawn-out yawn. "I thought maybe we would wait until morning. You know, make sure you aren't infected before going out around people."

How can I argue with that? I don't want to infect anyone. I suppose it isn't a bad idea to wait a few hours just to make sure I don't get sick. And I sure could use some sleep.

"Yes, I guess you are right." The words barely cross my lips when we see the shadow of a large prowling animal through the small slits of the shelter walls. The silhouette of the beast paces back and forth, tracking our scent. Fear freezes our breathing, and we both sit like statues, just watching the shadow and waiting, hoping it will give up and go away. Lan draws her fingers up over her mouth to quiet her breathing. But, in the slight movement, Great Granddad's other journal slides from her lap and hits the dirt ground with a *thud*. A small puff of dirt creates a cloud around the old leather. Instantly, the lurking shadow stops and darts to the section of the wall our backs are leaning up against. Swallowing hard, I hold my breath, too afraid to breathe. But it is too late. The creature knows we are here. Hot breath escapes his nostrils and forces its way through the open slits of the blind, warming the back of our necks. Lan's eyes bulge and scream out in silence. I place my hand on top of hers and hope the little bit of courage I have passes to her. The animal rams its head against the wall at our backs. A stick that was plastered to the wall flings forward from the force, scraping the side of my neck. Lan lets out a helpless yelp as she scurries across the ground to the other side of the shelter. Her movement excites the animal even more, and it lets out a boisterous, snarling growl.

It is a massive bear.

As quietly as I can, I reach my hand up to catch the drop of blood trickling down my neck. At the same moment I discover the scratch on my neck is bleeding, I hear the oversized nearby nostrils sniffing in the coppery smell of my blood. I crawl over to the opposite wall quietly, putting as much space between me and my stalker as possible. I reach out and wrap my shaking fingers around the cold metal of the rifle leaning up against the wall. Lan's eyes watch as I reach down slowly and open the ammo box, pull out a slug, and load it into the weapon. The loud click, click of the loading reverberates off the thin slats of wood, angering the giant bear. His dagger-like claws slash through the mudded sticks and snow where we used to be sitting.

I can now see outside more clearly through the gashes where he sliced through the wall. I watch the beast back up into the darkness. A drawn-out puff of air exhausts through his nose and mouth like a freight train, and then he charges toward the hut.

I run up to the wall and put the tip of the barrel right up through the largest torn open slit in the branches and snow.

BANG!

Before the bear can slam into the wall, which surely wouldn't have held against his cumbersome weight, the sound of the gun shooting toward him startles him and makes his claws dig into the frozen ground beneath him. He skids to a stop, just inches from plowing down the hut. While keeping my eyes fixed on the bear, I reach down and snatch another slug out of the ammo box, tipping it over in the process. The clinking sound of other empty shells hitting the ground and rolling away from my feet confuses the bear. In a *grrrumph*, he shakes off the pain of the bullet that clearly just grazed the side of his round body, and his livid eyes narrow to gaze into the hole at me. The outline of his shadow triples as he stands up onto his hind legs, stretching up tall. Towering over our hut, he lets out a roar that rattles the earthen walls around us. The dirt and metal shells on the ground bounce and shake with the vibration.

"What are you waiting for? Shoot him again!" Lan pants heavily.

I have a clear shot of the beast's chest right in front of me through the wall, but I can't do it. I can't shoot him. Not from close range like this, it's not right. He is just hungry.

The light from our lantern glints off his large, salivating fangs, and I can see the ravenous look in his eyes.

He won't spare us.
If I want to save Lan, I have to…

"Shoot!" Lan shouts.

And the muscles in my finger tighten against the trigger.

The bear drops to the ground as we feel the thunderous waves under our feet. Then, all I hear is the pounding of my rapid heartbeat in my ears.

"Is he…?" Lan shuffles her feet closer to the damaged wall to look out, but she hesitates to get too close.

I lean up to the hole in the wall to watch as the rise and fall of the beast's fur hovers and then deflates in one last exhale.

I pause and wait. Then, I nod toward Lan.

"What now?" Lan asks. "Is it safe to stay here for the rest of the night?"

"Safer than out there, I suppose."

"So, does that mean we can stay?" She asks with a coy smile.

"I guess so," I reply, not wanting to go out during The Howling to encounter more large, hungry beasts.

I pull the scratchy blanket from my backpack and hand it to Lan. She sits in the least drafty corner, pulls her knees up to her chest, and drapes the blanket over her huddled body. She pats the ground next to her and opens a flap of the blanket for me to join her. I drop down and cuddle next to her. Our shivering bodies slowly begin to shutter less frequently. The sound of the wind whistling through the holes and cracks in the walls resembles a lullaby. I relish in the warmth of Lan's body curled into mine.

Chapter 33

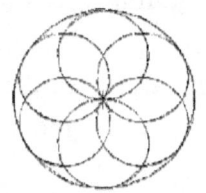

The Hunter

*T*he sound of gnarling teeth and ripping flesh startles me awake. Lan is still breathing deeply in slumber with her head lying on my shoulder and her mouth gaping open. I can't help but smile to myself at her adorable, vulnerable state. I attempt to strain my head forward to catch a glimpse of which animal, or animals, are eating the bear on the outside of the wall, but my neck feels kinked and too stiff to move. I want to rotate it to help loosen it up, but I don't want to wake Lan lying against me. Squinting my eyes into the light growing through the torn gaps in the wall. I focus them to see a pack of wolves fighting over the remains of the half-eaten bear. I am hypnotized and held in a trance. It is one of those situations where I hate to watch the gruesome scene before me, yet I can't look away. It's like when you pass a terrible accident on the highway. My stomach rumbles at the sight of the animals eating as if to ask, "where is my food?" I try to adjust my position to allow some blood flow and feeling to stream back into my legs without moving the top half of my body, which is holding up a peaceful Lan. However, I have persistent pins and needles in my legs that need to be uncrossed and straightened if I want them to regain feeling. As soon as I uncross them, it is like the dam is opened, and the floodgate of feeling spreads the pain down to the tips of my toes. Wiggling my feet ferociously to fight off tingling pain, I accidentally jiggle Lan awake.

Lan's heavy eyelids struggle to flutter open as she reaches up her hand to rub out their hesitation. She lets out a lion-like yawn, stretches her arms out wide, and straightens her back in a series of cracks. However, her body instantly freezes with rigidity the moment she realizes there are hungry animals feasting right outside the thin, scraped-open wall. Everything about Lan becomes frozen, everything that is except her large, golden eyes searching me for guidance.

"Shhh," I slowly bring my fingers to my lips without allowing any noise to leave my mouth.

"Don't make a sound," I mouth the words, but I don't have to worry. I don't even think Lan is so much as breathing.

As silently as possible, I unroll the worn map to double-check the direction we need to go to get to the White Sulphur Springs. I trace my finger along the route of water heading directly northwest. Lan blinks a slight nod of understanding. I quietly roll up the map and slip it back into my backpack, followed by Great Granddad's journal we used as guidance. I secure them with the other book in my satchel. I then run my fingers over the metal carvings of the box. Inhaling deeply, I become very aware of my body, my heart pumping wildly in my chest. I feel great, better than I have felt since I was thrust into this time. A smirk grows on my face as I think about how my diseased body is probably healing itself with each breath I take, thanks to The Serum. I place the box into my backpack and cinch the top, followed by the click of the buckle.

Once everything is secured, I place my hands on the cold ground at my sides, ready to carefully push myself up to stand. Lan's white knuckles shoot to my arm, and she digs her fingernails into my flesh. Her eyes bulge with desperation, and she shakes her head.

"Please! Let's wait!" Her lips mouth the words. Her glossy eyes shift to watch the teeth of the wolves tearing at what is left of the bear.

I want to leave now. The sooner, the better, especially since the animals are obviously distracted. But Lan is probably right. What if one of them does notice us leaving? Would it be worth the risk just to be a few minutes ahead?

And so, we wait. We wait until the last yelp of the wolves indicates there is nothing left to devour. I crawl on my hands and knees over to the break in the wall to see the remnant pink snow, most of which has been lapped up. A distant howl pierces my ears, and the pack darts off in the direction of the cry in the trees.

"I think we are clear," I relay to Lan, pushing myself up to standing.

I reach my hand down to her and help her to her feet.

"Let's go."

"Thank you for waiting. I couldn't go out there with them eating like that." She looks down at her fingers, which were chomped off not long ago. The flesh and bones in her fingers may have healed perfectly now, but clearly, she is still mentally scarred.

"Sure." I can't think of anything else to say.

I rush over and sift through the empty shotgun shells on the frozen ground to find the one remaining slug. I snatch it and load it into the barrel.

"We only have one shot left. But it is better than nothing. Maybe we can find more ammo along the way." I know that possibility is doubtful, but the thought slightly steadies my nerves.

Lan puts on her gloves and tightens her coat up around her neck.

"Ready?"

She nods, but her eyes are full of reluctance.

I slip my hand over hers and squeeze it tightly. Together, we shove our shoulders against the wood, acting as a door. It scratches across the packed ground. The screeching causes the vultures looking for leftover bear to squawk off and fly into the sky. They remain, circling above our heads, ready to strike at any moment like lasers. I look up through the ash and snow falling through the lightening grey sky. It is like looking through a grey fuzzy sweater. However, I can see the faint, hazy glow of the sun rising. I get my bearings and determine the direction we need to head.

313

"According to the map, there should be a river a few miles ahead in this direction. We should be able to follow the northwest fork all the way to The Spring."

We take off running. My blood pulses through my veins. After a few minutes of sprinting, I realize I am not coughing, heaving, and gasping. In fact, I have not even broken a sweat, and oxygen pumps through my body as if I am sleeping.

I feel like I can run like this forever.
This is awesome!

Out of curiosity, I pump my legs faster and faster, and I know I am ten times quicker than I used to be. In the past, I would have dropped dead by now. It is difficult to imagine that just a few days ago, I was in a hospital bed hooked up to machines, barely able to walk down the hallways, and look at me now.

Lan smiles at my speed and picks up her pace to match mine.

"It definitely looks like you are feeling better."

"It looks like whatever was in that serum is working. I feel amazing!"

Lan squeezes my hand, and together we whiz through the blurring trees. The only sound is our thudding feet tromping on top of the crust of snow. Occasionally, one of our steps breaks through the upper layer of frozen snow, and our foot drops down about six inches, nearly causing us to tumble forward. However, we help to steady each other when that happens and continue dashing without skipping a beat. Eventually, the trees begin to thin, and they grow farther apart until they stop altogether. We both screech to a halt as we get to a row of ghostly white mounds the size of vehicles.

"This must be the road that leads to E-Springs. It doesn't look like any of the cars are running anymore. I remember reading about a mass EMP that fried all the cars and anything that ran on computers. It doesn't look like anyone is around. Where is everyone? Isn't this supposed to be a town?" I look around in every direction, as far as my eyes can see through the cloud of grey, but there is nothing to see; no movement of any sort other than the occasional gust blowing a wad of tattered trash, causing it to tumble and dance across the monotony of lumps of white and grey.

"The river forks. Which way do we go?" Lan asks.

"We need to continue following the northwest fork," I reply, pulling her in that direction, away from the inkling of the forgotten civilization. "Wait, let's duck in here first and see if there is anything left that we may need," I suggest, referring to the tomb of a gas station.

I tug on the handle of the front glass door, but it is locked. Not that it really matters; most of the windows are broken out, and it is easy to climb through what someone once attempted to board up.

Just as I had suspected, there is absolutely nothing remaining on the shelves. There are a few bottles and jars that have clearly fallen off the shelves, but even their contents have already been eaten or taken, and there is nothing left but a bit of broken glass on the tiled floor. It is nothing more than a shell of a gas station, and the empty shelves are its bare skeleton bones. Just then, the squeak of a hungry mouse echoes off the stripped walls and scurries from under an empty, half-chewed box of *Oaty Boat* cereal. It darts to a pile of warn cardboard boxes in the corner of the floor.

"Unless you want to eat a mouse, I don't think there is anything left in here."

"Is mouse good?" Lan asks, without an inkling of how odd that sounds.

"Ummm, I was joking. Besides, it was nothing more than bones anyway."

I pull Lan back toward the broken boards on the window and help her climb through without snagging her pants or cutting herself on the broken glass.

I know it is pointless to check in any of the other ramshackle businesses or corner stores in the little town. There has clearly been nothing left here for quite a while.

A sense of loneliness aches in my bones. This world is so depressing and barren. The atmosphere is reminiscent of Lan's time, a time of desperation and minimal survival. Lan is clearly lost in the thought of people at one point having the convenience of buying things at the stores as she stares longingly at the broken, ice-covered sign of the corner store, which appears to have been called "The Quick Stop," but now it looks like it says, "..ick S op." as the mounds of ice and ash cover the missing letters.

Yep, that name is more fitting for what it is now anyway.

Lan and I follow the grey, frozen bank of the river toward the barren trees reaching up toward the sky.

"It shouldn't take us too long to get to The White Sulphur Springs now."

We traipse in silence. Even the sound of our feet seems to get lost and muffled in the thick snow and ash.

I grow tired of looking at grey; grey sky, grey ash, grey snow-covered ground, grey mounds of what may have been bushes or rubble of houses and buildings, nothing but lumps of grey as far as we can see. It feels like we are walking in a black and white photograph of muddled, snowy ruins.

"What do you think Einstein, Erb, and Neo are doing right now? Do you think they are looking for me or trying to figure out the machine to get me back? Or have they given up, forgotten about me, and moved on with their lives?"

Lan's furrowed brow valleys down toward her nose.

I grab her hand. "There is no way anyone could forget you. I'm sure Erb is racking his brain trying to figure out how to work that machine."

"His little round glasses perched on his whisker-spotted, chubby cheeks," she reminisces.

316

"And his lips pursed together tightly around the little tip of his tongue poking through them like a snake when he's concentrating," I add. We both let out a pent-up snigger. It feels good to have a small release of laughter, a small inkling of color in an otherwise grey world.

The sight of steam rising above the ground is a welcomed sight up ahead. The river at our side begins to widen and leads us to the bubbling culprit. The banks around the river are free from snow, and dark mud thickens around the border. We can feel the heat pouring from the sizzling water. Closing our eyes, we soak in the warm humidity circling around us like a sauna. Lan leaps to the edge, pushes up her sleeves, and dunks her hands into the boiling, murky water.

"Ohhh, hot, hot," She mutters, pulling her frozen hands back out of the water. She repeats the process, keeping her hands submerged for longer periods of time with each dip until she can handle holding them under permanently.

"Ahhhh, it feels amazing!" Her eyes roll back into her head. "I wish I could put my whole body in it. It is freezing out here."

"Go ahead," I reply. "No one is going to stop you." I look around and gesture to the empty, bleak world.

"I don't know," she states. "Maybe just my feet." She proceeds to sit down on the edge of the squishy bank and takes off her shoes and her socks. Dipping her toes in, she allows them to adjust to the hot temperature. Then, she slowly puts more and more of her feet into the churning water, allowing them to acclimate to the heat. After they have completely disappeared into the milky grey, she pats the ground next to her as an invitation for me to join her. As if I have springs in my shoes, I jump over next to her and rip off my shoes and socks. Lan and I look down at my feet. Although they are shriveled from moisture, they look perfectly healthy. There are no more blackening blisters, just peeling pink, healthy skin. Lan and I smile, realizing that my body is healing itself, just like Lan's. I don't even take the time to let my feet slowly adjust to the scorching heat. I just plunk them all the way in. It takes everything I have not to scream out in overwhelming pain, but after a minute of wincing and gritting my teeth, the heat feels great on my feet. In fact, I can feel the heat spreading from my feet and growing up my legs, warming me from the bottom up. I agree with Lan; it would feel amazing to jump in and bathe my whole body in the bubbling warmth.

A wooden arrow suddenly whizzes past my arm, stretched out behind me, holding up the weight of my upper body. The sharp arrowhead tip sinks into the bank, separating Lan and me with a *thwap*. We both instantly whip our heads around to look back into the trees in the direction from which it came. However, there is no one there. The trees just sway in the wind. There is no sign of the assailant. Lan and I look back at each other. Another arrow attacks the rifle sitting at my side, forcing it to slide into the boiling water before I can save it.

"What the...?"

At the very next moment, a third arrow whizzes past our faces, hits the tail of the first arrow, and splits it directly down the center. I spring up out of the water with my hands in the air, gesturing my surrender to whoever is attacking us. I can't help but dance my feet back and forth, keeping the bottoms of my feet from freezing to the ground beneath them. Squinting my eyes, I lean my head in to find any sign of a hunter. But again, I can only see a grey cloud of fog swirling around the towers of tree trunks.

"Hello?" I shout toward the trees.

"Is someone there? You can come out. We don't mean you any harm."

Just then, another arrow soars toward Lan's feet, still dangling in the water. She is forced to draw up her legs rapidly from the bubbling liquid.

"I'm guessing they don't want our feet in the water," I whisper through the side of my mouth to Lan. She instantly begins fighting to pull socks over her wet, wrinkly feet. I narrow my gaze to search about twenty feet lower in the trees where this last arrow was released from in the opposite direction. With my hands still raised in the air, I lower my body back toward Lan.

"We will just get our shoes back on and be on our way then." I holler into the mist. I wait a moment before dropping my hands, but I realize no one is responding. I carefully lower my hands and grasp my cold, sweaty socks, unrolling them from their wadded state and whipping them right side out. With my eyes fixed on the trees around us, I place my freezing toes into the sock and wiggle it up around my ankle. I get the other sock and both shoes on in record time.

"Which way should we go?" Lan whispers. "We are clearly being watched."

"I guess we'll go in the opposite direction from where the last arrow came." I shrug.

She nods in agreement. We grab our things and slowly walk backward, toe to heel, afraid to turn our backs to the attacker, just waiting for them to show themselves. However, there is not even a hint of movement from anywhere. Once we meet the line of trees, we about-face and begin walking forward in the same direction, praying our backs aren't pierced with another arrow. We walk in silence for a few minutes, my ears straining to hear the slightest snap of a twig to see if we are being followed. When I don't hear anything, I glance back over my shoulder to search through the fog. But there is no one there. We continue walking, like in an eerie nightmare. I can almost hear the intense, spooky music playing in the background of my mind, slowly building in intensity until…

THWACK!

Another arrow stabs into the tree directly in front of us. Lan and I both stop dead in our tracks.

"Now what? Clearly, we are still being followed," Lan mouths.

"Honestly, I'm not sure what you want us to do. Please, just let us be on our way." I say over my shoulder to the invisible stranger. But there is no reply. I take Lan's hand and pull her back in a different, random direction until… *Thunk!*

"Seriously?!?" I throw my hands up in frustration. "What do you want from us? We don't have anything." I lie, thinking about the precious metal box and Great Granddad's journals of information cradled in my bags.

319

But again, the only sound that meets my ears is the whistling wind.

This time, Lan pulls my hand toward the direction directly down the middle of the two arrow-pierced trees, which nearly missed our heads. Holding our breath, we walk on cautious tiptoes, half waiting for an arrow to stop our trek. After a few minutes of silence, we breathe a little easier but continue moving forward.

After a few miles, I notice the orb glowing through the blanket of clouds in the sky, is now directly above our heads. It must be close to noon. My stomach grumbles, and Lan's belly rumbles in reply.

"Do you think it is safe to stop and eat a snack?" I whisper to Lan. I pause my steps and wait to see if there is a reaction.

Are we still being followed, or am I just being paranoid now? And where are we heading? I don't want to get lost.

Clunk!

An arrow sinks into the frozen ground less than half of an inch from the back heel of my shoe.

"I guess that answers our question." I roll my eyes, and we reluctantly continue walking.

The ground slopes upward, and we continue hiking up the incline. Unsure of where we are being led, we keep walking until another arrow appears in front of our faces, letting us know we need to head in a different direction. There is still no sign of the person leading our journey; it is as if the arrows just fling from out of nowhere, letting us know when we need to change directions. I try to peek over my shoulder immediately after each directing arrow to catch a glimpse of the archer. I can tell Lan is also trying to see who is behind us, but each time we are left baffled.

The deafening silence is finally invaded by the distant sound of muffled, trickling water. The sound increases with each step until, finally, we are staring at a cascading waterfall of ice. The closer we look, we can see the inside layers of the fall are still flowing with water. Every once in a while, a drip of water makes its way outside the outer frozen layer. Unfortunately, the drip doesn't make it too far before freezing to the outside and becoming part of the more permanent frozen structure before us. We just stand here like we, too, are frozen statues.

An arrow clinks into the wall of ice just above our heads. Free-flowing water gushes through the hole just long enough to attempt an escape but soon meets its frozen fate.

"Now what? This is the end of the trail. We can't climb the ice waterfall." I finally say to the oblivion.

The sound of an arrow being let loose echoes to the right of us, and my eyes shift that direction just in time to see the arrow whiz behind the waterfall and disappear.

Lan and I look at each other, our jaws dropping.

"Are we supposed to go behind the wall of ice?" Lan's eyebrows raise.

An arrow of affirmation darts into the ground behind us, propelling us forward.

"I guess so," I say, staring at the arrow, which again nearly missed my foot.

I shuffle my feet toward the edge of the waterfall, where the arrow disappeared. The closer we get, the more I can see that there is just enough space behind the frozen wall for us to slip behind. The first step behind the frozen wall is like stepping into a frozen wonderland. There is just enough sunlight coming through the ice that it appears to be glowing. There is ice on the outside of the rocky mountain cliff to the right of us, completely encompassing us in a tunnel of turquoise. Lan and I stop in awe to take in the mesmerizing tunnel of ice. The few steps we take toward the center of the tunnel are magical. However, the random popping and crackling of ice are a bit unnerving, making me wonder if the glass walls of ice might shatter at any moment. My eyes watch the movement of water still flowing down through the center of the ice.

As soon as the rock splits to form an opening, I look to see what lies on the other side. We are greeted with an open mouth of a well-lit cave. Peering over my shoulder, I realize entering the cave is our only option moving forward.

My thirst for curiosity is overwhelming, and I really don't have a desire to test whether or not the person following us will let us leave. I fill my lungs to capacity and duck my head into the cave.

Chapter 34

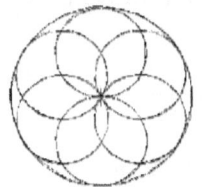

The Eight Fire Prophecies

*W*ith Lan close behind me, we hunch over and make our way through the stone tunnel. The rock roof above us slopes upward until we can stand with ease. We are in a wonderland of orange and brown dripping stacks of endless scoops of ice cream, or at least that is what it looks like. They are formations of stalactites and stalagmites, creating a magnificent world full of castle-like towers in all directions. I could spend hours just luxuriating in the amazing formations of rocks and crystals. After a few more steps, the cave opens to a massive stone room containing a circle of wigwams. In the center sits a fire pit, flooding the open space with warmth. The light reflects off the mounds of surrounding rock towers and bathes this secret community in a rich, marmalade glow. The flickering lights waver to show a bustling tribe of people. As if they all see us standing in the opening of the cave at the same time, their bustle of daily commotion halts as their ginger-glowing faces stare at us in shock. Trust me, the overwhelming feeling is mutual and heavy, like a thick, cinnamon fog.

I see a few of the children, whose game of chase was halted upon our arrival, whisper to one another while pointing at us as if we are an unexpected spectacle. I am half tempted to back out slowly and pretend we were never here; that is, until I look over my shoulder and see the silhouette of a young man thrusting a spear at us and prompting us to continue forward. I instantly notice the bow draped onto his back and a quiver of the all-too-familiar fletching feathers sticking out the top.

So, he is the one that has been following us and leading us here.
But why?

As I turn back to take in the odd tribe before me, I am greeted with a new circle of spears pointing at me and Lan. I nearly jump out of my skin.

Where did they come from? I only looked away for a moment.

My heart pounds in my chest, and my brain reels for inspiration.

"We were just looking for *nibi ikwe*." I try to sound confident, but my nerves are unraveling.

As I mention *nibi ikwe*, I watch all their eyebrows dance as if synchronized swimmers on their foreheads. I am unsure, but I swear their tense, muscular shoulders soften ever so slightly.

"Madja," a stunning woman's voice sings calmly as she exits a wigwam and glides toward us. She is the epitome of grace, beauty, and confidence. Her long, straight, black hair is so shiny it gleams like a full-mooned midnight. It changes color in the firelight to include hues of blues and purples, like iridescent oil.

I look into her warm mocha and ebony-striped eyes with as much respect as I can convey. With a slight bow of my head, I repeat,

"Please, my Great Granddad sent me to find *nibi ikwe*."

Her steady eyes instantly drop to look at the rag wrapped around my wrist sticking out from the sleeve of my coat. She stares deeply into my eyes as she raises her palm to the men who seem eager to turn me into a shishkabob. As she lowers her hand, the men lower their spears in unison. I let out my harboring breath. She gestures with her hand for me and Lan to follow her, and just in case we didn't get the message, the men with spears jab them in our direction, forcing us to follow the woman. She strides with perfect posture as if she is holding up this massive stone room with her head. She guides us through the center of the circle of wigwams to the largest one at the far end, the one from which she emerged. As she approaches the wigwam, another man with a spear holds open an animal skin flap for her to enter the opening.

She must be the leader of the tribe.

The man holding the flap narrows his eyes at me, threatening me. With a grunt of disapproval, he shoves the spear toward me as a reminder that he is ready to attack if I so much as breathe incorrectly. I gulp down a lump of saliva and follow the woman into the wigwam, with Lan practically tripping over my heels. As soon as we cross the threshold, the flap whips closed behind us. Light dances in the shadows along the stick walls.

"Please, sit." The woman's voice is just as warm as the fire in the center of the hut. She gestures to puffs of buckskin on the floor circling the fire.

I try to shake off the shock that this woman speaks English as Lan and I plop gently onto the animal-skin pillows.

"May I see?" The woman asks after sitting next to me, her head nodding toward my wrist. She holds out her hand, waiting for me to give her my wrist.

"I'm sorry, but I need to find *nibi ikwe*," I reply, praying my refusal is well understood and accepted.

Please don't be offended.
Don't call in that big guard outside the door.
And I hope she knows what a nibi ikwe is.

Her intense gaze softens, and her eyes catch the firelight and sparkle with a chuckle.

325

Placing her elegant hand over her heart, she states,
"I am Nibi Ikwe, leader of the Algonquin people."

Nibi Ikwe is a person.
She is Nibi Ikwe!

Bowing my head with foolishness, I apologize,
"Please forgive me. I did not know."
Softer than velvet, her fingers brace under my chin to raise my
head back to her level.
"If you truly are The Great One, you should not bow to
anyone.
I have waited so long for you.
Please, may I?" She asks again, cradling my wrist in her hand
as if it is a delicate flower.
I look at Lan for her opinion, but she just stares at the woman
with wide, curious eyes.
I use my other hand to untie the fraying fabric and reveal my tattoo.
Catching her breath, the woman sighs and bows her head toward me.
When she finally raises her head, her eyes are moist with tears.
"I have waited for this day for hundreds of years.
You have finally come to fulfill the prophecy."

Hold up, hundreds of years? How is that even possible?
This woman doesn't even look like she is pushing forty.

"I am hoping you can provide some guidance. I am not sure
what I am doing here or what I need to do. I don't understand
what prophecy I am supposed to fulfill." The words spew from
my lips like pent-up emotional lava. I stop myself before I show any
more vulnerability or immaturity.

"You don't know of The Great Prophecies?" She asks, shock painting her beautiful face.

I shake my head with shame.

She takes a handful of sparkling dirt from a leather pouch hanging on her belt and tosses the dust into the fire. The flames dance into a rainbow of colors, like paints washing onto an invisible canvas hanging in the air above the burning logs.

"Thousands of years ago, there were seven wise prophets. Each shared their wisdom with our people and guided our ways. The first prophet announced that our nation was to leave our familiar lands and follow the sacred Megis shell of The Midewiwin Lodge to a new meeting ground."

Her words magically orchestrate the colorful dancing flames, causing them to change and portray her story. As she mentions the sacred Megis shell, the flames swirl to depict a glowing cowry shell, bringing her story to life. As the flames morph, she continues.

"The sacred Megis would lead them to the chosen Turtle Island, linked to the purification of the Earth." Like a movie of smoke, the colors whirl to show the turtle-shaped island.

"This sacred place was said to be both at the beginning and the end of this great journey of their life's quest. They were told there will be seven stopping places along the way. They would know the chosen ground had been reached when they came to the land where food grows on the water." Puffs of colorful rice fields promenade before us.

"Our people were warned that if they did not leave and follow these instructions, they would be destroyed." The flames suddenly fizzle into small bursts, abruptly dissipating the vibrant visions.

The woman reaches into her pouch, pinches a bit more of the soil between her fingers, and tosses it into the fire. The flames spring to life once again as she continues her story.

"The second great prophet told our people that the nation will be invaded by a large body of water, and the direction of the Sacred Shell will be lost." The flames wave in hues of turquoise and cerulean and overcome the glowing Megis shell, washing out its glowing magic.

"He told that this will cause our people to diminish in strength. However, a boy will be born to point the way back to our traditional life and wisdom. He will direct our people to the stepping stones of our future." The waves of blues swirl to form stepping stones.

I instantly recognize the images glowing before me now. The turtle, the swirling water with the stepping stones, they are the symbols etched into the metal box. As I traced each line with my key back in the hut in the woods, the images were etched into my memory. And now, it is like those memories are appearing before me in plumes of vivid smoke and flames as they bring the prophecies to life.

"The Third Prophet stated that our people will find that chosen ground in the West, where the food grows on the water, and they must move their families to this land in order to prosper from it." The glowing images show their people floating in birch bark canoes through the flourishing rice fields.

"Next, my people were visited by two prophets who came as one. One of the prophets told of the coming of the light-skinned people. He said if the light-faced people come wearing the face of brotherhood and a handshake, then there will come a time of wonderful changes for good. They will bring new knowledge, and together, we could all form a mighty nation. This new nation will be joined by two more, so that the four will form the mightiest nation of all. However, the other prophet said to beware of the light-skinned race because they wear the face of death. Our people needed to be careful if they came carrying weapons because then they will fool our people and fill our hearts with greed for the riches of the land. He said if they were our brothers, they would need to prove it and need to gain our trust. If when they come, the rivers run with poison and the fish become unfit to eat, you will know they wear the face of death." The smoke of the first prophet brings a jovial sequence, whereas the second prophet's depiction is dark and grim. The waters turn to blood-red poison, speckled with rotting, floating fish. The air around us becomes thick with a rancid, nauseating odor that churns my belly with an urge to vomit.

"The Fifth Prophet said that during this time, there will be a great struggle full of false promises of joy and salvation. But, if our people accept these false promises and abandon our teachings and way of life, it will cause the destruction of our people." I watch as the people follow the ways of a more modern society, only to have the prosperity turn into slithering snakes and a withering land.

"The Sixth Prophet said that during the Sixth Fire, the false promises from the last prophecy will become clear. Those deceived by the false promises will take their children away from the teachings of the elders. This will upset the elders, and they will lose their purpose in life. A new sickness will grow amongst the people, and our balance will be disturbed. The cup of life will nearly become the cup of grief." A disturbing vision of children being sent to schools where they are taught new things, but in turn, their old ways of life diminish as their villages are brutally attacked by soldiers and burnt to the ground. The leaders of the tribes watch as their people become sick and die in agony.

"The Seventh Prophet who came to the people was very different from the other prophets. He was young and had an odd light in his eyes. He said that in the time of the Seventh Fire, a new people would emerge. Our people will retrace their steps back to their elders and ask them to guide them. But the elders will be silent and have nothing to offer them. However, there will be a rebirth of our Nation and a rekindling of old flames. A sacred fire will once again be lit." The fire before us ignites into roaring flames of light.

"But the task of the new people will not be an easy one. The light-skinned race will be given a choice between two roads. If the people choose the wrong road, their destruction will cause much suffering and death to all Earth's people." As she explains the wrong pathway, I see a world, much like the future one I visited in Lan's time, play out before me. The new technology leads the people to greed and wars. The bombing causes the Earth and all its people to burn and die.

"However, the other pathway is less traveled and still green. He states that we will be wise to follow a young leader depicting the sign of everlasting eternity. He will be the one to help guide the world down the right path, the road full of new growth and prosperity. He will help to gather all nations and all people together to light the Eighth and Final Fire, an eternal flame of peace, love, and brotherhood." I am overcome with the vision of flames joining together with outstretched arms circling in peace and love, burning brightly. They circle together, creating a blazing symbol of infinity. Simultaneously, the symbol on my wrist begins to tingle with warmth. As I lift my wrist to look at it, it glows as brilliantly as the flames encircling in front of us.

"Yes, you are the leader we have been waiting for!" She exclaims, a tear of joy glints in the firelight.

Lan beams with respect as she stares at my dumbfounded expression of realization.

As doubt washes over me, it distinguishes the glow on my arm as well as the burning flames in the firepit. My emotion darkens the entire atmosphere surrounding us like a plague.

"How am I supposed to lead the world? I don't know what I need to do."

Lan places her hand on mine. Almost instantly, a tiny ember reignites the fire in the pit.

"You will figure it out. I believe in you." Her words fill my heart with hope.

The woman smiles warmly at Lan.

"But before you can save the people, you must first save Mother Earth. She is dying. These floods won't last. Soon everything will burn."

Lan and I look at each other as we both know the truth behind her statement.

"The heart of Mother Earth is cooling. It is causing her to become unbalanced. Her poles are already beginning to shift, causing the Great Lights to form in unnatural locations. If you do not keep her heart warm and moving, it will eventually stop, making the Earth uninhabitable, and She will die."

"Wait, you want me to heat up Earth's heart? Like, her core?" A snort leaves my nose as I try to hold in my laughter. "This isn't some make-believe Sci-Fi story. I can't just journey to the center of the Earth and heat up the core." I begin to push myself up to stand.

I am not going to stay here and listen to this nonsense. There is no way I was prophesied to save the Earth and all people. And I surely won't be able to affect the Earth's core. This lady is crazy! I think she has been sniffing too much of that magic smoke.

"Sit!" The woman's voice, although not loud, is demanding enough to cause the earth below us to quake, as if she controls it, just like she controls the flames of the fire.

"Do not mock me or Mother Earth." Suddenly, the tattoo on my arm burns with such intensity my legs can no longer stand. I fall back down to my knees.

"The wise prophets have foretold of your coming. You will succeed, but only if you have faith in the guidance of The Great Spirits. They are on your side."

The small pop of a burning log draws all our attention to the fire. From the burst grows a shell, a glowing cowry shell, identical to the one from the smoke vision prophecies. But it is as real as a growing seed.

"It appears The Great Spirits are giving you a gift, The Sacred Megis Shell. It will help to guide you to Thunderbird Island where you may access Mother Earth's Heart. Your Great Grandfather has told me he has left instructions for you there." She reaches over, grasps a metal rod, and rescues the radiating shell from the glowing ashes. Tearing off one of the long leather strands from her braided belt, she ties the shell onto the center of the strand. Gliding over, she crouches behind me and ties the two ends of leather around the back of my neck, directly over my microchip. My hand jumps to the shell, and I lift it off my chest. I'm instantly overwhelmed by its emanating power. A zinging warmth zaps through my fingers and rushes all the way down through my body like a current of wild lightning.

> *Wait, this is actually happening?*
> *My Great Granddad left me instructions on how*
> *to reach the Earth's core, and I am going to use a*
> *magic shell, that just appeared from the ashes, as my*
> *guide?*
> *This is EPIC!*
> *Or perhaps it is all part of the smoke hallucination.*

My cheeks ache from smiling so widely. Giddiness bubbles through me like champagne.

Lan hovers close to my face as she studies the glowing shell tied around my neck. She reaches up and gently touches it with the tip of her finger with caution as if it might scald her. As she makes contact, the glowing instantly ceases.

"Oh no, I think I broke it." Lan scoots back away from it.

"No, it will work for The Leader when the time is right." The woman states.

"Thank you. For teaching me about The Fire Prophecies, and for the shell…" I add.

"The shell was not a gift from me but from the Great Spirits. It belongs to you."

The Earth rumbles. I'm not sure if it is out of anger or in a manner of saying it's time to go, but it quakes violently.

"You must hurry! You are running out of time." The smile on the woman's face has changed to a scowl of worry as she helps us to

332

our feet. She guides us to the door flap. As soon as her hand touches the hide, the flap opens from the outside with the help of the muscular guard's hand.

"I will send you with some food for your journey," the woman states. She turns to the guard and says, "*naajimiijime*". The guard glares at us but clearly follows her orders and heads off to a different wigwam. Moments later, he returns and hands me a bundle with a grunt. The instant aroma of dried meat fills my nose with instant temptation. Lan's eyes grow and she is practically salivating.

"Thank you," I reply to both the guard and the woman as I secure the bundle in my overflowing backpack.

"Thank you, Great Leader," the woman replies, bowing her head to me.

She leads us over to the entrance of the cave.

"May The Great Spirits guide your every step," she states, squaring her shoulders and standing with pride and assurance in her graceful delivery.

How does one respond to that?
Thank you?
You, too?

Instead of selecting the wrong words, I bow my head with gratitude. It just feels like the respectful thing to do.

I turn, grab Lan by the hand, and duck through the mouth of the cave and into the tunnel. The walls of ice glowing brilliantly around us.

Chapter 35

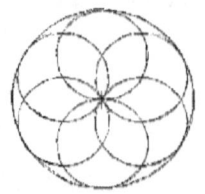

Smells and Tails

The trail from behind the waterfall is slippery, and it is difficult to secure my footing. But I hold strongly onto Lan's hand, and we make it out from behind the waterfall safely.

"Now, where are we supposed to go? Do we need the map?" Her eyebrows knit together.

"We need to get to The Captain," I respond, with excitement pumping through my veins.

"And the fastest way to The Captain will be on that train. We just need to go back the way we came."

"We can't exactly follow our tracks," Lan states the obvious, pointing down at the fresh layer of snow and ash.

"We came down here from that ledge up there, so we need to hike up there first. Then, we need to head East and South. However, directions will be a bit of a challenge. It is harder to see the sun now." I say, tilting my head up to look at the sky.

When we were traveling before, it was a fluffy blanket of grey, and now it is a turbulent swirl of dark fury. I notice the vast amounts of ash thickening the haze as well.

"Come on, let's hurry," I add.

We begin to hike up the hill. Although my legs feel worked, they don't burn or protest like I thought they would. In fact, I don't even seem to be heaving air as my normally out-of-shape lungs would be, either.

Strange.

I must be getting in better shape with all this hiking and walking.
Or is it more than that?
Is it possible that The Serum is making me stronger?

I shake the absurdity from my thoughts as Lan and I make it to the top of the ridge. I suddenly feel unsure of my direction. Slow puffs of my breath swirl into the greyness surrounding us as I clutch the shell hanging against my chest with my free hand. I close my eyes and suck in a clarifying breath through my nose. A foul, rotten egg odor jabs at my nostrils. I can't get the putrid smell out of my mind.

"Do you smell that?" I ask, sniffing the air like a hunting dog.
Lan takes in a big whiff of air.
"You mean the delicious meat smell coming from your backpack?" She asks.
I continue sniffing the air uncontrollably.
"I mean, that meat does smell really good." Her eyes grow bigger, begging for the meat.
I glance at her, and her hinting smacks me in the face.
"Oh, the meat. You want some?" I ask, unsure how she can think of eating anything with the overpowering, nauseating stench attacking us.
"Sure," she blurts, before I even finish asking.
I huff out a laugh and pull the meat out of my backpack. I unwrap the cloth and hand her a long chunk. It looks smoked and dried to perfection. I attempt to inhale its glorious scent, but the rotten air sours the experience.
"You sure you can't smell that? It smells like… sulfur. It's disgusting." I wrinkle my nose, still biting into my own hunk of
meat; I mean, I can't pass up jerky.
"Honestly, I don't smell anything except this delicious meat." Her eyes roll back in her head as she savors a bite, not wanting to swallow.

335

"I think we need to follow the smell." I finally suggest, hoping she doesn't think I sound crazy.

"Why would we want to follow a smell that you say is gross?" One of her eyebrows spikes.

"I just have a gut feeling," I reply without thinking how weird it sounds. The shell in my hand heats up with my words.

"Umm, okay. If you think we should go toward the nasty smell, then we go toward the nasty smell. As long as I can have another piece of meat." She adds with a smile.

"Sure." I hand her a piece of meat, completely satisfied with her enthrallment.

I re-wrap the bundle and secure it in my backpack as I begin sniffing the air.

"Come on, this way." I grab her hand again and pull her in the direction from which the odor is permeating, like the foulest, ancient cheese. I can almost see the pungent smell waves, it is so strong.

But it must be my imagination because that would be impossible, right?
You can't see smells.
How can she not smell this? It's worse than when someone lets off a stink bomb in the boy's bathroom at school.

I can't really explain how I know we need to follow the smell; I just know. It is like the thought was whispered into my mind as soon as I touched the shell.

With every step we take, the smell grows in intensity and rancidness.

"Surely, you can smell it now, right?" I ask Lan.

She sniffs the air and shakes her head. "Nope, nothing."

Please don't tell me this is my superpower!
Of all the superpowers out there,

336

super-smell would probably be the last one I would want.

The air becomes so thick, I can hardly stand it, as I finally see the culprit. The putrid, boiling White Sulfur Springs is now a bubbling bile yellow instead of the soupy grey like before.

"Ugh, I can smell it now." Lan protests. "What happened? It wasn't like this when we were here not long ago." Her nasally voice exclaims as her fingers pinch her nose.

"Oh, now the smell is too strong for you?" I ask, rolling my eyes.

"There must be something leaking into it from below the crust." I crouch down and stick my finger into the bubbling, fetid stew. Pain strikes the tip of my finger like scalding acid. For all I know, it could be scalding acid. I instantly retract my finger and douse it in the snow with a sizzle.

"Youch! That is definitely too hot for a dip." I wince, not wanting to remove my finger from the cooling ice.

"I wouldn't want to get in there like that even if it wasn't hot." Her tongue sticks out of her mouth in disgust.

"Well, at least now that we've found the spring, we can follow the river all the way down to E-Springs and the train station," I say with a forced smile, inspecting the blister forming on my finger.

"Great job. Now, let's get out of here." She states, still plugging her nose.

Her pace is much more rapid than before. She must really want to get away from the smell. Honestly, the smell doesn't even bother me much anymore. I barely even notice it once we are about a half-mile away.

So, how was I able to smell it on top of the ridge when we were miles away from the spring, but now I can't smell it at all?
Odd.

I guess I don't have super-smell after all.

I actually feel somewhat relieved. Thinking back to the latrines at the Elementerprise facility, or the Port-a-potties at summer camp, or the boys' locker room at school, I am so grateful I don't have super-smell.

Colors of purple and pink begin to steam from the horizon behind us. Within fifteen minutes, it turns burnt-orange like the Earth is on fire, but I realize now it is just the sun beginning to set. The shadows of the trees grow like a giant's long, spindly fingers with each step.

"We need to hurry if we want to catch the train tonight," I say, quickening my pace to a run. Lan follows my lead.

"I'm not waiting until tomorrow morning for the next one." She exhales, moving to a sprint.

I am able to not only keep up with her, but I find myself having to slow down every once in a while to make sure I don't get ahead of her. My breath quickens with my pace, but I don't feel out of breath. I feel like I can run like this forever. In fact, I somewhat enjoy the adrenaline of being able to move this swiftly through the trees. I see where the trees open up to the vibrant, sherbet hues glinting off the windows of the magnificent west side of E-Springs. The sound of our running feet pounding through the snow echoes into the darkening night. Like a speeding metronome, I enjoy the sound of my pulsing blood pumping against my eardrums. Suddenly, my steady symphony is interrupted by the sound of dogs barking in the distance. Nearly tumbling through the snow, I halt in my tracks and hold up my hands for Lan to stop running as well. We need to get around the building without anyone spotting us, and dogs barking at our arrival is not going to help us go undetected. The two dogs behind the razor-wire gate spot us even though we have become frozen statues. However, our breath still pumps into the air, announcing our location loud and clear.

"We need to go back to the line of trees and follow it the long way around," Lan whispers between pants.

"It's too late. They know we are here, and they will continue to bark at us for the entire perimeter. I have a better idea. We need to get closer."

"Closer? Are you crazy? Do you want to get caught? Or worse, eaten?"

"Trust me," I whisper, moving quickly toward the pair of yapping dogs. I continue running and simultaneously swing my backpack to the front of my body. I open the flap, my legs still pumping, and pull out the bundle of wrapped meat. I fling my backpack to the back of my body and slide my arm back through the strap. At the sight of what I am about to do, Lan speeds to my side as if her life depends on it.

"Not the meat!" Her whispers stab at me like desperate swords.

But it is too late. I have already torn off a little piece and chucked it as hard as I can. It sails perfectly through one of the openings of the fence. Both dogs dive for the delicious-smelling treat. They snarl at each other and fight over the small morsel. The larger dog gulps it down in one bite. They both follow us along the fence with their tails wagging and salivating tongues hanging out. I can sense the frustration of the other dog and fear it will bark if I don't throw another piece of meat. Lan runs alongside me, knowing that she can't complain about the meat because my plan is working.

"Only small pieces!" Her voice is no longer a whisper.

I don't know which is more entertaining, the dogs begging for the meat or Lan being upset that I am sharing it with the dogs. I attempt to hand her a bite, but she just rolls her eyes, unamused, and keeps running. I laugh to myself as I toss the piece to the dogs.

As we get to the Northeast corner of the fence, the dogs realize they are out of room and can no longer follow us. They both let out a bark of displeasure. I stop running. I tell them to sit while pointing my finger at the ground, the same way I recalled the guard gesturing when he told them to sit. Both their wagging behinds plop into the snow like obedient soldiers. I can't just leave them sitting like this without a treat, so I tear the remaining piece of meat in my hands into two larger chunks and toss them to the dogs. Gnawing happily, they don't even notice Lan and I dart away from the E-Springs grounds toward the train station.

The whistle blow of the train in the distance is like a blow to my heart, nearly strangling my breath.

"Hurry! Faster!" I encourage.

"We aren't going to make it." Lan pants.

"Yes, we will. We have to." I grab her hand and pull her faster toward the sound of puffing steam. The whistle toots again.

We reach the deserted highway. The only way to know that is what it once was is because of the tombstones of white car-shaped blobs permanently frozen in traffic.

However, the frozen statues of cars aren't what's important.

Just ahead, I can see the train chugging out of the station.

Plumes of smoke puff methodically as it inches forward.

"Wait!" I shout toward the train. But there is no one hanging outside the train to hear my plea.

"We don't have a ticket this time." Lan points out between breaths.

"Then I guess they better not find us," I reply. "But we are getting on that train."

We are forced to pick up our pace as the train's chugging speed increases. Now, I begin to feel my muscles tire. Or maybe it is just my mind thinking that I am too exhausted to make it. I shove the hazardous thought out of my mind.

I am not going to wait here through another Howling. The train is right there!

As if a distant wolf hears my thoughts, it howls into the night, forcing my legs to push off and leap for the railing of the caboose. My sweating hands grip the frigid bar, practically freezing on contact, but that only helps me not let go. I pull myself onto the platform, turn around to lean over the bar, and reach my hand out for Lan.

"Come on, you can do it. JUMP!" I shout, desperate for her hand.

She hurdles toward me, and I grab her flailing hands. However, her legs dangle below the train and drag along the icy tracks. I tug her upward with all my strength, and she comes flying into my arms. It would have been a beautiful kissing-fest moment, except her hands instantly drop to her shins and press at her bloody skin showing through her torn pants.

"Oh no, are you okay?" I ask, trying to inspect the damage.

"Obviously, I'll be fine. It just stings right now," she states, pulling the fabric out of her scrapes.

And that is the cool part. She really will be fine. Not only does the human body heal itself over time, but hers will probably be healed by tomorrow.

Does my body heal as fast as hers now, too?

I remember my blistered fingertip from the boiling spring. I know it is a lame injury compared to Lan's bloody scrapes, but it was some pretty nasty, blistered skin. I rub the tip of my finger with my thumb, and it is pain-free and as smooth as butter. I dig my thumbnail into the tip of my finger, expecting pain, but I feel nothing other than the pressure of the nail. It is all healed.

Awesome!

I wiggle my toes in my boot, feeling every pain-free movement. There is no more burning pain, no numbness. I can feel everything, without wincing.

I enjoy the moment as I snuggle Lan close to my side and we watch as the glow from E-Springs gets swallowed by the navy haze of night.

Chapter 36

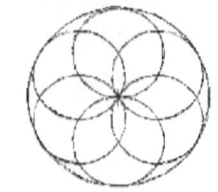

Take Warning

he latch holding the door shut to the caboose car seems to be frozen in place. With a little jostling, I pry it open.

"Come on, let's go in. It's got to be warmer than out here." I claim.

I hold the door open for Lan and allow her to step in first. As soon as I enter, I help the door close quietly behind us. I swing my backpack in front of me and loosen the strap to open it. I feel around inside for a flashlight. Pulling it out, I flick it on quickly. Shining the beam to show the train car contents around us, it is evident that we are in the luggage car. Suitcases, trunks, and duffle bags of all sorts line metal shelves. After a little rearranging, I make Lan and I a little space behind a few bags, just big enough for us to sit behind without being seen if someone were to come into the car for baggage.

"Here you go, our hideaway for the night." I gesture to the now open space.

"Thank you, looks perfect." Her teeth gleam in the beam of the flashlight.

Squeezing into the space is more difficult and awkward than I had anticipated, but we are able to finagle our bodies into a position that seems manageable, not quite comfortable, but manageable. I want to try to put my arm around Lan to keep her warm and soften behind her back, but there is no way I can get my arm back there without a lot of wiggling around. It wouldn't be a very suave move at all. There is clearly no heat in this car, but at least being bundled behind the luggage is cozy and much warmer than the frigid temperature outside.

Lan winces as she tries to move up against me. I can see that her skinned leg is pressing against the metal bar of the shelf. A zipper flashes in front of me, which is connected to the pocket of a piece of luggage. I zip it open easily and shine my flashlight inside. I snatch out a clean-looking cotton shirt. I roll it up and wiggle it into place to act as a cushion between Lan's bloody shin and the metal bar.

"There, is that better?" I ask.

"Much, thanks." She stares into my eyes and plants a kiss on my lips. Suddenly, I don't feel an ounce of cold.

"So, is there any of that meat left? Or did you feed it all to the dogs?" She winks with a flirtatious smirk.

I fumble to jiggle the top of the backpack open enough to tug out the bundle. I unwrap the cloth and pull out the biggest chunk I can freely pull out, and I hand it to Lan. She inhales as a wide smile grows across her face.

"Thanks." She snatches the meat from my hands and savagely bites into it with a tearing sound. "MMMMM, it's so good!"

"Agreed," I state, ripping into my own chunk. The tangy meat is perfectly seasoned, and my tastebuds sing a hallelujah.

As soon as Lan licks the last bit of salt from her fingers, she leans her head onto my shoulder. A few rocking motions from the train car and her breathing deepens to an almost catlike purr.

I should take this opportunity to get some sleep. But my mind is buzzing with worry.

How am I supposed to heat the Earth's core?

I do my best at putting the jerky back into my backpack and struggle to pull out Great Granddad's journal from the satchel at my side without moving my shoulder and disturbing Lan's peaceful state. I squeeze the back end of the flashlight between two pieces of luggage so that it shines on the journal resting on my knees, shoved up against my chest. The familiar crackle of the journal's spine is like a security blanket of comfort to my ears. I skim my eyes over every page of brilliance.

I hope to gain even a fraction of my Great Granddad's knowledge someday.
How does he know so much about everything?

I search for anything discussing Thunderbird Island or the Earth's core. I am already pretty sure that Thunderbird Island must be the island where The Captain stopped and got the metal box. Although the stormy skies made the top of the island difficult to see, I recall a brief moment on the ship when I was able to see through the clouds and fog and thought to myself that the outline of the top of the mountain resembled the head of a bird. It must be where I need to go. If I can get back to The Captain, I am sure he can get me there. Let's just hope he is still at the shore with his ship.

I turn page after brittle page until my heart leaps with excitement. There is a page that depicts how to reach the core of the Earth. It doesn't give an abundance of details, except it shows a page titled The Five Ocean Core Detonation. It depicts a five-point star symbol. There is a sketched map of the world, and at each of the following locations, there is an image of a nuclear bomb: The Puerto Rico Trench in the Atlantic Ocean, The Southern Sandwich Trench in the Southern Ocean, The Java Trench in the Indian Ocean, The Challenger Deep in the Pacific Ocean, and The Molloy Deep in the Arctic Ocean.

My heart suddenly plummets down to my toes.

Hold up! Nuclear bombs? There is no way I am going to drop nuclear bombs into the oceans.

I am flooded with a tsunami of nausea. Suddenly, I am not so sure I am going to like Great Granddad's plan.

Is it safe? Will this help the world or blow it up?

I force my eyes to research further. It appears that the nuclear bombs are already placed since there is a placement depth written next to each bomb drawn on the map. It also shows multiple detonation trigger locations, all with the symbol of the five-pointed star. It states that all locations must activate their trigger for The Five Ocean Core Nuclear Bombs to be detonated. The detonation trigger sites shown on the map are Cheyenne Mountain in Colorado, Mount Weather in Virginia, Pine Gap in Australia, Porton Down in England, and Menwith Hill in England.

How am I supposed to activate all the triggers at the five different locations around the world? I can't possibly get to all of them in time.

I continue reading all the details of the plan, skipping over the scientific jargon that soars over my head. However, I carefully read the last section about all the studies guaranteeing the safety of this detonation project. I read Great Granddad's scratchy handwriting.

We have found that due to the extreme pressure at the core, which is nearly 3.6 million atm., the nuclear explosion will have little to no effect on the surface of the Earth. There will be no extra greenhouse gasses or atmospheric changes (other than what is produced from resulting earthquakes and volcanoes — which are likely to increase as heat is released and plates may shift. However, not to the extent of causing deadly damage to our planet. The final outcome and planet sustainability far outweigh the temporary chaos it may cause.)

So, other than some earthquakes and volcanoes, it sounds like sending nuclear bombs to the core shouldn't be too bad, and I won't blow up the planet.
At least, I hope not!

My thoughts are interrupted by what sounds like distant, muffled gunshots and screaming. I quickly slip the journal back into my satchel, close the flap, and flick off the flashlight.

Is it just my mind playing tricks on me? Or is there deadly commotion occurring in the next train car?

I focus on listening.
CRASH!

Perhaps glass breaking?
Definitely, some bashing and thrashing.

CLUNK!
CHINK!

Things being thrown against metal or the wall of the train?

PWRAP!
Another gunshot is fired, followed by screams and muted yelling, but I can't make out the words.
WHACK!

There is definitely something going on in there. Should I wake Lan?
Please don't let whatever is taking place in that car come in here!

I try to listen beyond the speeding *thump, thump* of my heart, and the *click-clack* of the train, but I can't find any other sounds. I lean my head closer and strain my ears.
WHOMP!
The door to the luggage car flies open and bangs against the shelves of bags.

Lan startles awake, and I instantly throw my hand up to cover her mouth so she doesn't let out a scream.

"Shhhhh," I whisper in her ear; it's more of a movement of air than an actual sound.

Clearly, whoever just barged in here didn't hear me, right?

My chest heaves wildly and I fail at controlling my breath. I squeeze my eyes tightly in hopes that it helps us disappear and keep us hidden. It was just like when I was a child and I had the strange notion that if I closed my eyes and I couldn't see the person looking for me, then they couldn't see me either.

Please don't find us.
Please don't find us.

The person who entered the train car has no audible footsteps, but the sound of bags being pulled from the shelf and getting thrown to the ground makes their location easily known. And they are getting closer.

Lan's body shakes next to mine.

Thinking back to the gun The Captain gave me, I know it is still hiding in my backpack.

I shot at the wolves.
How many rounds are left in here?
Is there still a bullet left?
I can't remember.
Well, if I don't know whether the gun is loaded or not, neither will the assailant.
Ugh... where is it?

Trying to silently dig through my pack and not give us away is nerve-racking. Just a few bags away, I feel a whoosh as one is yanked from the shelf and tossed to the ground. Finally, I wrap my fingers around the cold handle of the gun and pull it out with shaking fingers. I aim it at the suitcase, blocking us from the person on the other side. A small amount of light rocks from side to side, pouring in from the train car ahead of us through both open doorways. It glints off the massive blade of a darkened machete gripped in the person's hand, moist with crimson liquid.

Fresh blood.

The light creeps its way between the cracks of the stowed bags and shines on Lan's pale, trembling face. I gulp as I attempt to steady my hand, clutching the gun with my other hand, as the suitcase in front of me slides out of place, revealing a stone-hard stare from dark, coal-like eyes.

I nearly drop the gun from shock.

It is the face of the young man who was following us in the woods. The one who shot his arrows to help guide us to Nibi Ikwe.

The chiseled cheekbones bow forward upon seeing us, revealing his perfectly parted black hair.

"They try to find you. They killed many." His English, although broken, is clear to understand, as he points back toward the car from where I heard the commotion.

I help Lan wiggle out of our hiding spot. I stand on my half-asleep and tingling legs and step toward the other car. My mouth gapes as I look at the two men in Elementerprise uniforms sprawled out on the carpeted aisle floor, blood puddling around their slit necks. My heart throbs for the few innocent passengers slumped over in their seats, clearly shot.

Lan's quivering hands cover her mouth, her head slightly shaking from side to side.

"They'd killed you." The young man states again. "I forced to kill E-men for you. Keep you safe."

Lan looks the same way I feel. These innocent people were killed by the Elementerprise men looking for us.

Trying not to focus on the guilt poisoning me, I turn and face the young man who saved us.

"How did you get on the train? How did you know they were coming for us?"

"I follow," he replies. "Saw E-men get on train, and you get on train. Watched. They search two cars for you. They kill all. They'd kill you."

They probably wouldn't have killed us, but I'm sure they would have taken us back to E-Springs, and I would have wished they had killed us.

"Thank you." I manage to form the words, unable to swallow, knowing that those men killed two cars of people looking for me and Lan.

"Almost there. Get off before more find you," he commands. "I watch. Keep you safe."

I feel the train beginning to slow down. He's right. We need to get off now if we don't want to get caught.

"Thank you." Lan's eyes look over his face with sincerity.

"Go, now," he replies.

I duck under the strap of my satchel, put the gun back into the backpack, and throw it onto my back. Grabbing Lan's hand, I guide her through the door leading to the back platform. I look over my shoulder at the young man watching us leave.

"Thank you," I nod. He bows in return.

Surfing the unsteady boards below our feet, I wait for the train to slow down a bit more, pausing until I feel we can jump safely without getting hurt.

"One, two, three."

Lan and I leap from the platform, and our bodies crash to the ground. The air is expelled from my lungs, and my ribs squeeze around them like constrictors. I gasp and roll, gasp and roll. After losing the thrusting momentum, I slide to a halt. I instantly push myself up to my hands and knees and look toward Lan to make sure she is okay. I watch as she rolls on the ground like a rag doll rolling down a hill. But, as soon as she stops rolling, I see her sit up, relatively unharmed. I am able to suck in a big breath of relief. Our breath puffs out in heaving clouds as we watch the train continue into the faint lights of the station.

Just ahead lies the tree line that we followed to get to the station the first night we were here. I help Lan to her feet and dust the ice and snow from her back. Her hair looks like tangled lumps of snowy dreadlocks. I don't think I can help her fix that, so I don't even try, and I stifle my laugh.

"Are you alright?" I ask, checking her over. I notice that the gashes on her legs from getting on the train have already closed and are pink with new skin.

She cracks her back and rolls her neck.

"Yep, I think so. How about you?" She asks.

"I'm good. Let's get out of here. I don't want to be around when that bloody train gets to the station."

I straighten the bag on my back and at my side as Lan and I jog along the line of trees, not wanting to get any closer than we need to. The cries of hungry animals echo between the trunks, helping us keep our distance. Unsure of how far we need to run before turning toward the East, I pull out the Megis shell, which had found its way under the collar of my shirt. I tighten my grip around the smooth curves and ridges.

"Please, help to guide me to the ship," I whisper through panted running breaths.

My feet nearly tumble over each other as my focus is drawn to the ethereal glow emanating from the shell. I feel the shell tugging my hand forward as if it is being pulled by a strong magnet. I try to push it toward the line of trees, but I can't fight it to even budge in that direction. The compelling power is too strong. I have found that my feet have become dumbstruck. I can't help but attempt to persuade the shell to move in a different direction. Lan's face reflects the glowing light, her smile inching toward her ears.

"Wow!" She utters. "It's so beautiful!"

"It is showing me which way to go; come on." I beam with pride and bask in its light, my feet propelling in the forceful direction of its guidance.

Unable to peel my eyes away, I feel perfectly content running toward its hypnotizing radiance. I notice my hand grasping the shell begins to swing outward, toward the East, until it is parallel to my shoulder. I turn and run in that direction. Lan's feet traipse in my deep footprints in the snow. I see a few shacks and shambles of dwellings, and beyond them glows the faint hope of morning.

The further we run, the more colors begin to swell into the dark sky. It isn't long before it grows into a glorious canvas of bubblegum, fuchsia, and magenta. Lan and I both stop to gawk at the majestic moment.

"It is the most beautiful thing I have ever seen." Her mouth gaping open as the warm, rosy light turns her eyes into two gemstones of pink topaz.

"Pink sky at night, sailors' delight. Pink sky in the morning, sailors take warning." The words gust past my lips without thinking.

"What?" Lan's left eyebrow climbing.

"It's a saying. It means that although the morning pink sky is beautiful, sailors know it is a warning that terrible storms are coming."

"So, it isn't a good day to be out on the water?" Lan gulps.

"It can't be any worse than last time, right?" I let out a nervous laugh and pull her toward the glowing sun rising in the sky.

Chapter 37

Marina

The closer we get to the coastline, we begin to see a few scrambling people. All of them tend to their own routine and business of preparing fishing nets, mending sails, or carrying crates. However, I can feel their gazes watching us through the corners of their eyes, or under their eyebrows, pretending not to succumb to their curiosity. I secure my shell necklace safely underneath my shirt. I don't want to risk it being seen by any greedy eyes.

"You need fish? I got fish. Nice and fresh." An older woman with sprawling grey hair and blackened teeth hisses. She holds up a clump of decaying scales clinging to a brittle skeleton of bones. One of its eyes has completely rotted away, leaving a crawling divot of greenish-grey goop. The overwhelming stench of fish rot punches me in the gut. I watch as Lan holds in her dry heaving.

"No thanks, we're good," I reply, trying to rush past the rancid odor.

My eyes scan each wrinkled, windburned, and bundled face, searching for Captain Hurley, Oz, or the man who brought us to shore. But all the desperate faces are unfamiliar. Suddenly, the foul, salty air is twinged with a pleasant odor of baked goods and yeast. Lan's eyes grow, and I know she smells it, too. Her feet begin to trail in the direction of the heavenly aroma. It is coming from a hooded, cloaked young woman carrying a basket with unraveling gloved fingers. We watch as she walks toward the old woman peddling her "fresh fish." The hooded woman reaches her hand into her basket and pulls out a biscuit. Although it is quite flat and appears rather heavy, it still smells like heaven compared to the other nasty stenches, thickening the air around here.

"Here you go, Marjory. Shhhhh, don't tell the others." She winks at the old woman, who tries to give her the rotten fish in return, but the movement causes a shlop of gelatinous goo to slink to the ground at her feet.

"No, thank you. This one is my gift to you." She smiles at the old woman.

"Thank you, dear." Her dark, teeth leering.

Then, the old woman turns her spazzing, frizzy hair in our direction. "At least some people still know how to take care of their elders." Her words jab at me and Lan.

"Sorry." I retort, wishing now that I shared a piece of meat or something with the old woman.

"I'll take your biscuits." A man reaches his grubby, frost-bitten fingers toward the kind, young woman's buttoned-up coat. She slaps his salivating face and walks toward the docks as if she regularly needs to stick up for herself, and her biscuits.

"Excuse me, Miss." My words follow after her.

"Don't bother with that one." The denied man grimaces, rubbing his red cheek.

"You won't be getting anything from her."

I take Lan's hand and pull her past the grumbling man.

"Excuse me?" I try again.

"I only sell if you've got money." She replies, but she never turns around to us; she just continues walking.

"I don't want your biscuits. I just want to ask you a few questions."

Her feet stop walking, but she doesn't turn around.

"Everyone wants my biscuits, and I am busy selling them to paying customers," she replies, curiosity growing in her voice.

"I was just wondering if you know a Captain Hurley. We're looking for him."

"Captain Hurley?" Her head slowly turns toward me.

Out of the corner of my eye, I see two large, uniformed soldiers grab two unsuspecting young men, pick them up, look at their faces, and then throw them down to the ground like discarded trash. Lan and I look at each other as the same thought plagues our minds.

They are looking for us.

I grab Lan's arm and pull her down to crouch behind a nearby icy pile of empty crates and barrels.

"Oh, come on. They'll find you here in no time. This way." The biscuit woman gestures for us to follow her.

Like a spy in the shadows, she leads us to what may, at one point, have been an alleyway, but now it is just the bottom remains of shacks covered in snow. She gestures for us to crawl behind a square heap. It looks like a dumpster buried beneath layers of ice and snow.

> *How in the world will we be able to get in there? The top doesn't look like it has been opened in years. I will never be able to lift the hordes of snow piled on top – which I can't even tell where I would need to lift, considering it is now just one cohesive grey and white mound, like granite.*

After her shoving, we shimmy and squeeze through the small space between the back of the dumpster and the shack behind it. The backpack on my back and satchel draped over my body make it difficult for me to fit through the narrow space. The woman pulls aside a piece of icy plywood to reveal an opening hidden in the back of the dumpster where the metal has been cut away. She gestures for us to crawl in.

"Is this a dumpster?" I ask.

"Do you want to hide from those creeps, or not?" Her eyebrows raise.

The sound of the men shouting and shooting is all the motivation I need as I crawl inside the square of raggedly cut, rusted metal. My backpack snags against a sharp edge, and I am wedged into the opening. The young woman unhooks my backpack, and I feel her foot against my behind as she gives me a kicking thrust forward with the bottom of her warn boot. She then crawls in after us and lights a lantern sitting in the corner. Luckily for us, it doesn't seem like any trash has been thrown in here for years. Other than a lingering odor of fish guts, this appears to be someone's sleeping space, complete with hoary brown straw sprinkled along the ground and a worn, ratty blanket in the corner.

"Does someone sleep here?"

"Not anymore." Her longing eyes sink to the worn straw. She picks up a brittle piece, rolls it between her fingers, and watches it crumble to dust.

The uncomfortable silence bears down heavily.

> *So, do I ask her about the person, or do I just let it go and change the subject?*

Lan's head bobs toward me with wide eyes, gesturing for me to say something.

"I'm sorry. Was it someone close to you?" I ask, shrugging my shoulders at Lan.

"My father. He was a fisherman. He would often stay here before or after a voyage if he was too tired to make the trek back home, or if he had a lot of fish to sell. But the waters have become unsafe. Many sailors lately haven't been making it home. My mother says he is still out there somewhere, but… he would have been back by now. He wouldn't have left us. Anyway, it's been almost two years. I like to come here from time to time. It still smells like him. I can close my eyes, and it's almost like he is here." She closes her eyes and inhales deeply, an aching smile hinting across her face.

Lan inhales and wrinkles her nose as her eyes shift warily. However, she quickly paints a façade of condolences as soon as the young woman opens her eyes.

"Anyway, you asked about Captain Hurley?"

"Yes, do you know him?" I lean toward her with interest. "Do you know where we can find him?"

"He's actually the reason I came here today, too. Well, and to sell some of my pathetic biscuits." She raises her basket. "Oh, would you like one?" She opens the top flap of the basket and pulls two biscuits from the bed of cloth inside. Lan and I take them graciously and nibble on their blandness as she continues.

"I am nearly out of yeast, flour, and sugar, and Captain Hurley is the only one who still manages to find the ingredients I need. Who knows where he gets them from, but I don't care, as long as he will sell some to me. We are the only bakers left for miles, and if we can't sell goods, then I don't know what we will do. I have two brothers who are away at war, and we probably won't see a dime until they return, if they return. And my younger brother and two little sisters keep Ma busy, and they are always asking for more food. My father had some kind of deal with Captain Hurley to get ingredients, and now I want to see if he is willing to make a similar deal with me. We need those ingredients. Anyway, that is why I am looking for him. Why are you?" One of her eyebrows raises with her interrogation.

"Ummm, we need him to take us on his next voyage," I reply with honesty.

She hesitates for a moment before letting a sputter of laughter escape. Lan and I look at each other questionably.

"Oh, you're serious?" She asks once her giggling subsides.

"Why, does that seem like an odd request?" I ask.

"He's Crazy, Captain Hurley. He goes on the most dangerous voyages. The ones that no other sailors are looney enough to take on. Some people say he has sold his soul to the devil himself, and that is why he is allowed to sail through the Bermuda Triangle and other dangerous waters. Trust me, you don't want to go with him. I have personally seen young sailors board his ship and never return." She leans in closer to us as if prying ears are listening. "People say he sacrifices them to the sea monsters in return for safe passage."

Now, it is my turn to laugh out loud.

"I'm not joking. Ask anyone out there, and they will tell you the same thing."

"We've been on his ship. We weren't sacrificed to sea monsters. Not saying we didn't see any, or that he isn't a little crazy, but…"

"Wait, you've been on his ship, The Scylla?" She whispers the name as if it will jump out from the shadows and gobble her whole.

"Like the legendary sea monster with six serpent heads? Oh… that makes sense." The image of the serpent heads carved onto each of the two masts, as well as on the ones emerging from the woman on the bowsprit of the ship, flashes through my memories.

"You didn't know the ship's name?" She asks, flabbergasted.

"But you claim to have sailed on her?"

"Honestly, I never asked, and it never came up."

She shakes her head. "Well, I guess you have lived to tell the tale. And you want to get back on? I guess that is saying something about you.

Like you have a death wish, or you are also crazy." She mumbles the last bit under her breath.

"Well, can you help us find him or not?" I ask, getting straight to the point.

"What is in it for me? Can you help get me the ingredients I need?"

"I am happy to ask him for you."

She looks unimpressed. "I can ask him myself."

"I can put in a good word for you?" I allow the words to kindle my smolder.

Lan's eyes flutter with annoyance at my verbal tap dance.

"Alright, fine. I need to find him anyway. But you better not cause me any trouble. I know those guys were looking for you, the way you were trying to hide from them. If I get caught, I have no clue who you two are, got it?"

"Sounds good to me," Lan huffs.

"Why are they looking for you anyway? You AWOL or something, running away from the draft? I'm not judging. I can only hope my brothers can escape and make their way home. I've heard awful stories. You wouldn't believe what their lives are like. But we need the money."

"No, we haven't been drafted or escaped or anything like that. They just... we sort of... have something they want."

"Did you steal it? Are you thieves?" She asks, drawing her basket inward toward her body and wrapping her arms around it protectively.

"No, it is mine." I defend.

"Something valuable?" She asks, eyeing my backpack and satchel.

I feel Lan's bony elbow dig into my side, clearly telling me to watch what I say.

"Are you going to help us find Captain Hurley, or not?" I blurt nervously.

"Alright. I will go and check things out and ensure the soldiers are gone. Don't move until I get back. If I don't return shortly, then I would hope you have the decency to come find and help me escape them."

"Deal," I say, putting my hand out for her to shake, realizing now how lame that is. It's not like we are making an official agreement or anything. Lan's sigh agrees with my afterthought, and I drop my lonely, hovering arm.

"I am Daemon, and this is Lan. What is your name? You know, so if we have to come looking for you, I can ask for you by name."

The young woman slides the board aside, "I'm Marina."

She crawls out of the hole with one arm still clinging to her basket, and slides the board back, leaving me and Lan alone in the dumpster.

"Marina? I suppose that is a fitting name for a fisherman's daughter.

359

Do you believe all that nonsense about The Captain?" I ask.
"I mean, he is pretty strange and eccentric, but I guess you
grew up with guys like that." I throw the joke her way to see if
she is listening.

She slaps my upper arm with the back of her hand.

"Hey, no mocking Einstein, Erb, or Neo. I really miss them."
She adds, her voice dropping suddenly.

"Well, then let's get our job done here, and get you back to
them." I attempt to sound happy about that plan, but the words
are like a hooked gutting knife twisting through my heart. I
know she senses my leeriness.

"I saw something in one of the journals back at your Great
Granddad's place while you were making us those sandwiches,
which sound amazing right now, by the way. I read the page
that warns if you alter the Earth in the past, there is something
called The Grandfather Paradox."

"Yes, I've seen Back to The Future. I know what The
Grandfather Paradox is. It is if you alter something in the past,
it can affect the future. But I'm pretty sure some physicists or
some sciency group of people disproved that theory, I think."

"According to your Great Granddad's journal, it is very real.
He writes about how the death of his wife and his daughter are
his fault because of something he altered when he went to the
past. And how your Dad's parents, your Great-Granddad's son,
and his wife were killed in that accident because of something
else he altered. He warns not to go to the past and alter things
because it does indeed change the future."

"Well, luckily for me, I am in the future now, and my life is
perfectly safe in the past, so I shouldn't be affected by anything
we do."

"But my life is in the future from now. If we save the world
and change its course, then I... or Einstein, or Erb, or Neo...
Will we still exist? Will I ever be born? Can I ever go back?
Will I have a family to go back to?"

The thought of Lan dissolving like Marty McFly takes my breath away. I hadn't thought of that outcome or how what we are about to do may affect her future and her existence.

"I distinctly remember it saying something about going into the past is often *a one-way ticket*."

"I won't ever be able to see them again, will I?" Her chin begins to quiver, and her golden eyes swim in flooding tears.

I don't know how to answer because I don't have the answers. Will Lan disappear if she tries to go back to her time? Will the family she has always known still be there? I honestly don't know.

"I don't know, maybe you are part of a Grand Predestination Paradox, and you will be born no matter what. But right now, I do know that I am so grateful to have you safe and here with me. Can we just focus on that for now? We'll cross that other bridge when we get there, together, okay? Or you can just stay and live with me in my time, once we get back that is. I promise to make sure you are happy." Saying those words out loud fills me with euphoria. My heart dances wildly at the thought of spending the rest of my life with Lan.

"Yeah, I guess that does sound nice. Let's just focus on saving the Earth right now. That is a more important issue anyway."

She smiles away her tears and lays her head on my thumping chest. However, I can't help but sense there seems to be a distance of hurt and longing wedging its way between us.

> *Will I ever be enough for Lan? Can she live her life never knowing what happens to her "family"? Would I be able to handle that if the tables were turned?*

The plywood door slides aside, and Lan huddles closer to me. Marina pokes her head into the dumpster and whispers, "Alright, it's clear. Let's go!"

Chapter 38

Scylla

arina's free arm gestures for us to follow her. Lan and I crawl out like toddlers at her heels. I hold the satchel close against my belly as it nearly scrapes against the ground, making sure I am low enough this time for my backpack to not get caught on the way out.

"A reliable source told me that Captain Hurley is getting his ship ready to sail this morning. If we hurry, we might be able to catch him. We need to watch out, though; you have a pretty hefty price on your heads. Those two men are willing to pay heavily for you. You know, I could feed my family for a long time if I turn you in myself."

"So, why aren't you turning us in?" Lan's question puffs with innocence.

"I have reasons why I don't want to help those guys, so don't give me a reason to not want to help you." Her gaze burrows deep into Lan's soul. Her warm breath twirls through the air like threatening tendrils of smoke. She is like a grenade, and at any moment, she could pull the pin.

Lan gulps and quivers.

"Shhhhh, we need to sneak around there." Marina's finger points around a fishing shack.

"Don't let those guys see us. They will do anything for a quick buck. They are looking for you to turn you in for sure."

Lan and I give a meek nod in understanding and follow Marina into a squatting waddle behind a cart of sailing gear. Feeling like a

Russian dancer, we stay low and shuffle our way around the shack. As soon as we are behind a roofless wall, just tall enough to hide our standing bodies, we push up, relieving the weight from our thighs and knees, and run around the backside. Marina points her finger toward the concentrated cloud of fog. Squinting and trying to rub the haze out of my eyes to no avail, I can barely make out two shadowy figures. The air is clearer closer to the dark sand, and as I turn my eyes downward, I can see the feet of the men scuffling around a rowboat, its backend bobbing as the waves lap against it. It is almost comical how I can see their feet almost fully, but their bodies become more ghostly and dissipate to mere shadows the higher up I look.

"The fog is so thick over the water this morning. They are insane to try and go out now." Marina whispers. "You sure you want to go with them?" Her forehead forming wrinkles.

I drop my chin and begin to run toward the mysterious feet and into the opaque clouds.

I can hear Lan's footsteps on the crunching, frozen sand at my back, followed by another set of feet. The shadowy figures become more humanlike with each step. Captain Hurley's obscured face finally forms once I get within ten feet.

"Captain." I attempt to shout a whisper, not wanting to draw anyone else's attention. I hope now we are nothing more than dark figures through the blanket of fog to any searching enemies.

"Please, we need to come with you. I need your help to get to the island."

"Yes, I know. Giiyosewinini just left here and told me you were comin'. He also let me know that Fin won't be comin'." The wrinkles near The Captain's eyes crease tighter.

"*Giyowini*, what?"

"Nibi Ikwe's hunter, Giiyosewinini," he responds. "Hurry, they are comin'." The Captain helps Lan step into the rowboat. I swing my leg over the dipping side and slide onto the seat next to Lan. The Captain climbs in and signals for Soarin, the same man who rowed us here, to untie the rope tethering us to land.

"Are you coming, too?" Soarin asks Marina. He hunches over,

placing his gloved hands onto the edge of the boat, ready to push us into the water.

"Me? I…" Marina's face contorts with the decision bobbing in front of her.

Gunfire rings out as bullets whiz into our cloudy view.

Marina's heaving chest pulses a few times before she drops her basket of biscuits and swings her leg up over the bouncing edge. Soarin catches her elbow and steadies her, helping her sit on the bench closest to his thighs, pressed against the tip of the boat. Shots rochet off the ground near his feet as he ducks forward and lunges toward the rowboat. We plunge forward into the water. The frigid spray that greets us takes our breath away and stings our faces like a thousand icy pinpricks. I grab one of the oars and begin to paddle fiercely. The Captain does the same on the other side. Soarin pushes off the bottom of the shore with his strong legs, now deep below the water, thrusting us forward once again. His last propelling jump is also his leap into the boat. Like a merman, his body erupts from the water as his arms extend and catch himself on the rim of the boat. Simultaneously, The Captain jumps to the opposite end to help keep us balanced. However, the sudden tipping from end to end rocks the rest of us passengers like ragdolls. I do my best to help steady Lan and Marina as Soarin swings his leg up over the side and rolls into the boat, followed by a wave of icy water.

"Row!" Soarin shouts through the sound of firing guns behind us. I snatch the oar just before it escapes over the edge, and I pump my arms in a rowing motion. Soarin rescues the oar from the other side and begins rowing as well. His movements are much stronger than mine and he is forced to switch sides of the boat every few strokes to keep us going in a forward motion. I feel the new strength in my arms, but I still struggle to keep up with his brute force. I look at the wind whipping Lan's hair like wild flames across her concerned face. She and Marina have their arms around each other for warmth and comfort. The hood that was once covering Marina's hair has now blown back to reveal a head of brown shoulder-length curls. Her chocolate eyes swim with uncertainty. Her young adult face suddenly appears almost child-like and afraid, like she too was forced to be an adult much too young. I glance over my shoulder to see a swirling cloud of mist. I listen for any sounds of pursuit, but I can't hear anything over the lapping waves, just the fierce winds and the repetitive sloshing of the oars dipping in and out of the water.

"They don't appear to be followin' us," the Captain states, attempting to peer through a telescope he pulled from his pocket and extended toward the shore. However, I am sure he can't see more than a few feet ahead through the thick fog. He turns to look in the opposite direction, collapses the telescope back to the size of a pen, and returns it to his pocket. He pulls back the hem of his coat sleeve to gaze down at a compass wrapped around the wrist of his glove, like a watch. He points in a slight diagonal, forward direction.

"She's that way," he spouts.

Soarin and I attempt to steer the rowboat in the direction of his pointing fingertip. I continue to dunk the oar into the silvery waves, glinting with white frothy caps, repeatedly until my body and my mind become numb from the repetitiveness. The sound of a distant bell chimes my thoughts back into existence. We row toward the beckoning bell with hopeful anticipation. Lan and Marina's eyes look longingly toward the glorious dinging as it gains in volume.

As if appearing from behind a magical white gossamer curtain of a great magical stunt, the ship instantly materializes through the fog. I never thought I would be so excited to see a ship. But my heart begins to jitter as each of the serpent heads emerges through the haze. The emotion that overcomes me this time is pure elation, the complete opposite of the fear I felt the last time I beheld its grandeur. And this time, I notice the faded, crackling paint displaying the name *Scylla* on the side of the ship. The letters are so faint that I see now how I missed it in the dark the first time I approached her.

"Scylla." The name hisses into the wind toward the ship. The name is beautiful, but she is a fearsome beast to behold, both in legend and in life.

Marina's jaw drops to her chest as she takes in the ship.

Lan gulps.

Soarin and I steer our teetering boat toward Scylla's dangling ropes. Nearly tipping the rowboat, I reach for one of the ropes and slip the looped end onto the hooks at the tip of our boat. Soarin does the same at the other end. I realize the ropes are just tied around the loops at the top of the railings and not around the wheel at the top. We are going to have to hoist the boat up from down here.

"We pull on three." He shouts to me over the whistling wind and crashing waves.

"One, two, three." We both reach up as far as our arms will go and we hoist the little rowboat so that only its bottom is lapping the waves.

"One, two, three," Soarin shouts again. This time, I jump a little to compensate for Soarin's long arms and height.

"One, two, three." His words echo as our little boat scrapes up the side of the large ship. Muscles I didn't even know existed tighten and flex with each pull. Finally, the knots tied in the hoist ropes slam against the rim of the boat, indicating we have reached the secured height as far as it will go. The rope ladder draped over the edge of the ship dangles in reach. The Captain steadies the ladder and gestures for the girls to climb up first. Marina doesn't budge from her dumbfounded, statuesque, hunched position, so Lan climbs up first. As my eyes follow her body climbing up the ladder, I see Oz's beard lean over the edge as he reaches his hand down to help her up over the lip of the ship. It's hard to see his expression from this distance through the fog, but it is clear that it isn't pleasant. In fact, I am sure that I hear his displeased *grumph* echo down through my ears as Lan's shoes disappear over the edge.

The Captain helps Marina to her wobbly legs and places her hands on the rung of the ladder just above her head. He lifts her up so she can secure her footing, and she begins to climb. Each stretch of her arm is shaky, and the rope ladder quivers below her like a scared puppy tail, but she makes it to Oz's waiting outstretched hand. She vanishes in one quick swoop.

"You next, me boy," the Captain bellows to me. Soarin grabs my rope and ties it off.

Without a moment of hesitation, I jump for the ladder and begin to climb. The Captain's words resound at my feet.

"Ya are coming aboard, right?" The Captain asks toward Soarin.

Despite my curious urge to look down to see his reaction, I turn my face up to the mist of rain and focus on Oz's outstretched hand.

"Ya know ya can't go back there. They'll be waitin' to shoot ya fur sure," the Captain's words disappear into a crashing wave.

I extend my scorching arm to grasp onto Oz's massive forearm. He wraps his long, thick fingers around my forearm, and he lifts me up toward the sky. I feel like a plushie toy being plucked from the claw machine, only to be thrown up unto the deck as if discarded just as quickly. Lan and Marina help me to my feet, and I turn to see Soarin's red face clamber over the edge. A few moments later, The Captain gracefully swings his leg up over the edge and jumps to his feet on the soaked deck. Oz helps to steady The Captain and turns to walk toward the helm. His shoulder thrashes against mine, nearly knocking me off my feet.

"You're like a bad penny." Oz's foul breath mutters toward me as his large boots tromp off. "And, ya brought even more strays with you this time."

"A'ight then, we're all on board safely. So, off to Thunderbird Island?" The Captain's eyes widen with excitement as he straightens his raincoat and hat.

So that's it then? I guess we aren't going to discuss the fact that we were all just chased and shot at? I'm starting to think these dangerous situations are a normal occurrence for them.

"We could use a hand with the sails, Soarin', if yer willin'?"

367

"You can help him out, aye Sharkbait?" The Captain's wrinkles on his right eye collapse into a wink.

"Aye, Captain." I smile back.

"I am going to take Marina down and get her some dry clothes if that is okay," Lan states. Marina's mouth is still agape as she stands there dripping and shivering.

"Aye, welcome aboard, Marina. Yer father was a good sailor, and a dear friend o' mine.

Ya ladies are welcome to anythin' I've got down below." The Captain nods a respectful bow.

"Thank you." Lan's warm smile glows. "I think she is in shock." Lan turns and whispers in my ear. She then wraps her arm around Marina and leads her over to the hatch to take her below deck.

"Weigh anchor! Let's get her turned about 'n headin' southeast." The Captain announces as he swirls his finger in the air, gesturing the turnabout.

Soarin lets out a grumble as he slumps around, pulling ropes and tying them off. He definitely doesn't make it look as easy as Fin did, but Soarin is a bit more of a stout man and a bit older than Fin, too.

"Are you just going to stand there, or are you going to help?" He finally shouts.

"I, ummm, ya. What can I do?" I ask.

"Grab those ropes and hoist the staysail and the foresail as far as you can. I'll help you finish and tie them off. I want it done right," he gripes.

I jump at the ropes and pull, hand over hand, until I can't pull them anymore. Soarin steps in front of me, grabs the rope from my hand, tugs it one more time, and loops it around the cleat in a figure-eight motion. He ties it off with a hitch knot. He does the same with the other rope with ease.

"Luckily for us, you know what you're doing," I state with a half-hearted laugh, seeing if I can lighten the mood. His narrowing eyes and hefty sighs speak volumes. Soarin clearly doesn't want to be sailing with us.

"Is anyone back there going to worry if you don't come home tonight?" I ask, attempting to get to know the gruff young man better.

But my question obviously upsets him, and he stomps off to the back of the ship.

"Okay then, good talk.

I'm just going to go down and check on the girls. Just holler down if you need my help."

I yell toward the back of his shaggy dark hair, clawing at the back of his neck under his knit cap, but my words get lost in the sound of the lashing wind.

I make my way over to the hatch, lug it open, and step down onto the ladder. Closing the hatch above my head, my ears instantly pop and rejoice in the reprieve from the loud, gusting wind and waves pounding against them. As my feet reach the bottom of the ship, I see Lan sitting in the booth on the backside of the table.

"Mind if I join you? How is Marina?" I ask.

"She is taking a shower," Lan responds, sliding over to make room for me.

I take my backpack and satchel off, slunk them onto the table, and slide in next to her with a sigh.

I hear the pipes thump against the wall as Marina turns off the shower. I lay my head down onto my folded arms on the table and close my eyes. Every fiber of my body is exhausted. Lan joins me in laying her head down and we just sit, listening to the waves lap against the outside of the ship as we rock back and forth.

"Do you need some Ocean Potion?" I open my eyes to see Lan's eyes watching me with her question.

I pause, breathe deeply, and realize that I have been on the ship for a while now, and not once have I noticed feeling the least bit seasick.

"No, I actually feel pretty good," I say, the words surprising me.

"I guess that serum is working then." The side of her face that is not laying against her arms creases upward into a smile.

"Yep, I guess so." I sit up and scoot to the edge of the bench. I reach down to untie the boots on my feet. I pry them off and squeeze my feet out of my soggy socks. Wriggling my toes, I notice that other than looking like wrinkled raisins from being wet, they look perfect. There is no inkling of frostbite or peeling skin.

"Well, would you look at that?" I laugh.

Lan sucks in her breath and holds it in over-dramatically. "I'll look, but I am not getting any closer to them. Oooweee." She fans her nose, indicating that they stink. I sniff in and realize she is right.

"Oh, and I'm sure your wet feet smell like roses." I shove her fanning hand away playfully.

She scoots back against the wall so she can maneuver her naked, wriggling feet up toward my nose. They smell like feet but nowhere near as rancid as mine.

"Ewe, gross. Get those stinky things out of my face." I shift my body weight onto her lifted leg, forcing it back down to the bench. I have her legs pinned beneath me as the ship rocks suddenly, knocking my upper body onto hers. I just smile and gloat at her triumphantly as if I won the game of king of the mountain. She leans her head up toward me, causing her lips to meet mine. I feel the edges of her mouth curl into a smirk.

"Hmmm, it turns out it isn't just your feet that smell," referring to my breath. She giggles as if she is now the champion in our little game by denying me a kiss.

"Ahem," Marina clears her throat. "Sorry, am I interrupting something?"

I sit up and let Lan free with great reluctance. She and I share a playful smile.

"Are you feeling any better after your shower?" Lan asks Marina.

"Yes, I'm good. I just can't believe that I am on the famous Captain Hurley's Scylla. Is he just being nice before he feeds us to the sea serpents? Does actually know who I am? Was he really friends with my father? I always wondered how my father came up with the stories about Captain Hurley. I'm starting to wonder if he added the scary embellishments just to make the stories more exciting and to frighten me as a child. Captain Hurley doesn't seem as rough and tough as he made him out to be."

"No, The Captain is just rough on the exterior," I assure her.

"Well, if it is alright with you, I am going to shower next. Or perhaps you should go next." Lan wafts her hand at me again, referencing my foul stench.

"Oh, hush. Go shower." My cheeks flush as I pull her up to her feet and playfully push her toward the hallway leading to the shower.

"You two are adorable." Marina's words break my stare toward Lan.

"She's amazing." I feel my cheeks darken even more.

"I just hope that someday I can find someone that looks at me the way you look at her. But it's not like the world is in a place where I can get out and meet someone, you know?"

"It looked like you had guys crawling all over you when you were selling your biscuits," I say, trying to make her feel better.

"Ewe, gross old men." She nearly gags. "Besides, I need to help out Mama. I don't know what she would do if I ever left. OH NO! What is she going to think when I don't return tonight? How long are we going to be gone? She is going to be beside herself with worry." Tears form in her eyes, and her chest begins to heave in a pant. "I've never not come home. She'll think I'm dead. And the kids…" A tear escapes down her pink cheek, and she is unable to finish her thought.

I don't know how to act with an emotional young lady. So, I fumble to get her a drink of water, place it in front of her, and gently put my hand on her shoulder.

"They will be okay, and you will be back to them before you know it. Imagine how excited they will be to see you." I reassure her with a pat of my hand on her back.

"If they ever see me again." Her words turn into a full-blown sob.

Just then, the hatch opens and Soarin's massive goloshes squeak down the ladder, dripping.

"What did you do to her?" He references Marina's wailing.

"Nothing! I was trying to make her feel better."

He rolls his big dark eyes and waves his manly hands, gesturing for me to move along out of his way once again. I grab my bags off the table and make my way down the hallway, glad to get away from the hysterical emotions spewing from Marina.

I see that Marina and Lan have already placed their shoes in a room with two bunks where Lan slept the last time we were here. I decide to put my things down in the room across the hall where Fin slept. I hang my backpack and satchel on the hook and plop down onto the bottom bunk, being careful not to hit my head on the top bunk. At least I learned that much from our last voyage.

I listen to the sounds of Lan in the shower. She's ringing out her hair while washing it as a sudden rush of water slaps against the shower floor pan. The sound of Soarin's calm, deep voice echoes in the distance.

"It's Marina, isn't it? Do you mind if I sit with you for a moment?"

Her sniffling ensues between his questions.

"You know, I sailed with your father once. It was my first voyage with The Captain. Your father took me under his wing and showed me the ropes, literally." He chuckles at his own lame joke. Marina seems amused as she spews a courteous giggle and momentarily stops sniffling.

"I was about sixteen and he was like a father to me on that expedition. I will never forget the one night up on deck. There wasn't a cloud in the sky. There were stars as far as we could see in all directions. We sat there for hours gazing at the stars as he told me wild stories of his adventures on the seas."

"He was the most wonderful storyteller." I can hear the smile in her voice.

"Did he include sea monsters?" She chortles.

"There were always sea monsters." There is a long pause before his voice continues.

"But the thing I remember the most was getting back to our home port, which was a bit further out on the land than it is now. He had two of his children waiting for him. One was a boy, and the other a girl, a few years younger than me, her brown curls blowing wildly in the wind. She was clasping a basket full of baked goods. The pure joy on their faces once they caught a glimpse of their father was enough to make a teen boy yearn for his own father. I could see that you loved him very much. You know, you gave me one of your fluffy biscuits that day."

"I think I remember that." Marina's voice is quiet and longing, but no longer crying.

"Why don't you ever buy my biscuits now?" She asks. "I always see you sitting in your rowboat, just waiting to bring in sailors or take them out to their boats," she adds.

"Some sailors use your biscuits as payment from time to time, and I accept that payment graciously. But I must admit, your biscuits have gotten flatter and harder over the last few years. They are nothing compared to that first one that melted in my mouth."

"Well, it is harder to get the ingredients I need to make them like that."

"Perhaps I can help you get what you need."

"Really?" Her voice rising in pitch.

"We might be able to work out something. There isn't a sailor that comes into our port without my services. The water is too shallow to bring their large ships in. And you would be amazed at how many don't have a dinghy."

"Sounds like you do pretty well for yourself transporting sailors. Is that why you don't go out on voyages anymore?"

"Why would I go anywhere else? I am needed at the port. And I realized that sailing for days on end, being surrounded by waves, can be very difficult and isolating, but don't you worry. I will be with you on this voyage, so you won't get too lonely. And I'll make sure to get you home safely to your family."

"Thank you. I really appreciate that." Both of their words are filled with enough flirtation to make me want to vomit, even without being seasick.

I have been focusing on their conversation so intently that I didn't hear Lan turn off the shower or come out of the shower room.

"Your turn." Her dripping wet head pokes around the frame of the small, rounded door to my bunk room.

Her thumb points back over her shoulder. "Is Marina okay? I thought I heard her crying again a minute ago."

"Oh, ya, I am pretty sure she is going to be okay now. Soarin is taking care of her." I say with a wink.

"Oh. Ohhhhhh." I watch as the lightbulb goes on in Lan's brain, realizing what I am getting at.

"Awe, that is so cute." She lets out a little squeal followed by a quiet, quick handclap as she turns to take her wet clothes and towel to her room across the hall. I forget how adorable Lan looks in the plain, baggy sailor slops.

"I like your outfit," I say after her.

"Look, you had the bags with my other clothes in it. I'll change into them while you are in the shower."

"Don't bother. I like this look on you."

She rolls her eyes.

I dig in my backpack for my clothes and realize that I had on the paper scrubs or what was left of them when we changed back at Fin's bunker, and I didn't bother to bring the dissolving threads. I do, however, pull out Lan's black and white skirt outfit from E-Springs and toss it to her.

"I liked this look as well, so it's up to you," I say with a smirk.

"Hopefully, these don't take too long to dry," she states, referring to the tangled wad of clothes in her arms.

"I grabbed some slops for you when I got some out for me and Marina. They are in the shower room."

"Thanks," I say after her, but she has already disappeared into her bunk room.

I head into the shower room. I take off my shirt and use it to wipe the already foggy mirror. I am greeted with my reflection through the streaks of water. I can't help but notice my cheekbones seem more defined. My eyes are brighter, not yellow, and are no longer resting on sagging, dark half-moons. My complexion is glowing and flushed, not grey and ashen as it appeared the last time I saw myself in the mirror. I run my fingers over my abs.

Hold up! I have abs?

I look down at my washboard stomach.

It may not be as defined as Fin's or Neo's stomach, but I do Indeed, have an outline of a six-pack, not just scrawny ribs sticking out.

I, Dameon Gardener, Geeky Gadget Boy,
have abs!

I take a moment to delight in the occasion by flexing in the mirror. My arms and my legs are more muscular, too. They aren't as puny as before.

Sweet! I can't wait to see Seth Jergenson's face when
he sees me next school year.
That is if I make it out of here alive.

Chapter 39

Danger Ahead

$\mathcal{T}$he sound of a muffled bell wakes me with a jolt.

I must have laid down on my bunk and fallen asleep after my shower.

I stretch my arms and sit up straight, my back cracks like firecrackers. My brain is still fighting off grogginess as Lan's panicked voice screeches through the open door frame.

"Pirates! Come on, they need our help up there." Her words shock my body into action.

I jump forward off the bottom bunk while slipping my shirt over my torso.

"Pirates, like *argggg*?" I ask, closing one eye and pumping my fist across the front of my chest like I have seen in pirate movies.

"There are two ships we can see guarding the island. I'm not sure we are going to be able to get to it without a fight. The Captain says we don't have enough ammo for that fight to be fair. We are going to need to get creative if we want a chance. And you are really good at that type of thing, so come on. They need you!"

Lan's words about needing to get creative instantly spark an idea. I sidestep back to my backpack and search around for a moment to find the wristband from Great Granddad's basement. Sure enough, the little vials are still full of the elements, and the laser on it should work… that is, unless it got damaged from being waterlogged.

"Hurry up!" She tosses a pair of rubber boots toward me as she darts out of the doorway. My toes dive inside the boots, and I wriggle and fight to pull them up over my now beefier calves while running after her. We climb up the ladder to the deck with great haste. The sound of firing cannons and sloshing water, mixed with yelling voices, swirl around my head dizzyingly. Lan and I jump up into the commotion of thick smoke and spraying water. Soarin and Oz are loading the harpoon gun with a PETN grenade, and Marina is spraying the water cannon at an incoming cannonball. Her spraying directly positioned on the cannonball helps to slow down the cannonball, but it still crashes into the side of the ship. A loud *CLANK* shakes the wooden floorboards beneath our feet. The sound is odd and not what breaking wood should sound like. I run to the edge of the ship and look overboard. Where the beautiful wood used to be, there are now sheets of some type of industrial-strength metal protecting this side of the ship.

"Ha Ha! Thanks to yer Great Granddad lad, The Scylla is protected from their cannonballs." The Captain's boisterous slap on my back nearly knocks me over the railing of the ship. "He created these titanium plates, which are impenetrable by cannonballs. I love his brilliance. Looks like we got 'em bolted in place just in time."

He turns to ask Soarin and Oz, "How many PETN grenades do we have left, boys?"

"Only two after this one, Captain. We need to make them count. Accuracy is going to be crucial," Soarin states. "Do you want us to wait until we are closer?"

"They are still a bit out of range. Hold steady momentarily," he replies.

"Will it do much damage to their ship?" I ask.

"It should do enough to hopefully scare 'em off." The Captain replies.

"Hopefully? So, you aren't sure?" This doesn't sound too reassuring to me.

"What if I added an Einsteinium bomb to the grenade."

"I am not even sure what that is. And where are you going to find Einsteinium in the middle of the ocean?" Soarin questions.

I hold up my wristband and take out the small vial containing Einsteinium.

"Anyone have a tin can?" I ask.

"I'm sure there are some down in the garbage bin below," The Captain suggests.

"I'll go find one," Lan volunteers. "You stay up here and help." She disappears down the hatch.

"We're close enough now, Captain. Do you want us to shoot or wait?" Soarin questions.

"Let's fire one harpoon grenade. I'm hopin' they'll see that we aren't here to play. I don't want to kill 'em all, just run 'em off," The Captain responds.

Marina's eyes reveal shock. She sees that perhaps The Captain isn't as mean and barbaric as she once believed.

"They are getting ready to fire another cannon, Cap'n," Oz shouts as he looks through the telescope. "It is aimed higher this time. At our sails!"

"Soarin, shoot the harpoon, quickly! Marina, be ready with the water cannon and do what ya can to slow down that cannonball. I'm goin' to the wheel to do what I can to steer us away from the shot. Dameon, get that bomb made and attached to the next harpoon."

"Aye, Captain," we all reply in unison.

The Captain scurries to the helm to steer the ship.

Once The Captain is gone, Oz pulls out a long-barreled gun that looks like something a military sniper would use.

"We just got our mast and sails fixed. I'm not letting them get destroyed again."

"Oz, where did you…" The Captain's shouts from the helm window are cut short by the ear-blasting sound of the rifle's shots. I always thought sniper rifles were quiet. The painful ringing in my ears disproves that theory, but I don't have time to react as a cannonball rips the foremast to shreds. I duck and cover as shards of wood and debris whiz near my face. Luckily, the cannonball lands in the water on the other side of the ship. However, there is no way we will be using a foresail, staysail, or jib anytime soon.

"I'm sorry. The sound of that big gun made me jump and drop to the deck. I wasn't able to shoot the cannonball with the water. It's my fault they hit the sail. I'm so sorry." Marina's words turn into sobs as she covers her face with her hands and drops her head into her squatting lap.

"Oz, a little warning next time," shouts Soarin as he rushes to Marina's side.

"I got two of 'em," Oz informs. "But they had already lit the cannon fuse 'for I got 'em."

"I said we're defending our ship, not killing pirates!" Hollers, The Captain.

"We won't have a ship to defend, Cap'n if we don't kill 'em!" Oz argues back, aims his sniper rifle, and shoots off another shot. The smirk on his face reveals he got another one.

"Ya know me rule, Oz! No people-killin' on me ship if we can help it! Ya broke yer oath, mate. Once we start shooting guns at them, they will start shootin' guns back at us. It's the rule of the ships." As if The Captain's words are bullets themselves, Oz's body suddenly jolts, and his face turns white like stone. The rifle slips from his fingers and crashes onto the deck. His hands jump to his unbreathing chest. He brings them down in front of him to see they are covered in blood. Oz has been shot. Marina buries her soaked face in Soarin's chest. Lan has since returned with the can and leaps to Oz's side as he crumples to the deck. Another bullet whizzes past my hair. Without thinking, I dive for the rifle at Oz's feet, swoop up the gun, and instantly focus my right eye through the scope. I can see the burly man on the other ship as clearly as if he were standing right in front of me. He smiles to show his mouth full of gold teeth as I see him squeeze the trigger in my direction. I squeeze mine simultaneously and then roll to the ground and take cover from the metal bolted to the side of the ship. Once I have somersaulted to the railing, I raise the scope up over the edge of the ship to see if the shooter is still standing. I clearly missed with my first shot because he is still standing in the same spot, aiming for his next shot, straight at The Captain in the helm. I squint my eye and focus, aiming for the man's heart. He never sees my bullet coming for him, and it is precise.

"I got him," I relay to Oz as I drop down next to him.

He gives me a hint of a smile. He sputters the words,

"Guess yer not... such a bad penny... after all, Sharkbait...For Cap'n." His weak hand flops onto mine and releases his lucky coin into my hand as his body grows limp and his eyes close.

Lan's tear-filled eyes gaze into mine. They are full of hurt and longing. All I can do is put my arm around her body and allow her to collapse into me.

"We ain't got time fer all yer cuddlin'. There are more pirates over there readyin' their cannon, and another 'n has the rifle!" Shouts The Captain through the window of the helm.

Soarin and I jump to our feet immediately. He leaps over to the harpoon and fires off a shot. I watch as a cloud of smoke, shrapnel, and wood blasts in all directions as a result of the shot. As the smoke clears, it appears to have created quite a bit of damage to their ship, as well as to the pirates who have all taken to their dilapidated deck. A few appear injured, and a few get to their feet, ready to retaliate. I grab the can that Lan brought up from the hull and begin filling it with Einsteinium from the little vial. I only pour about a quarter of it into the can, just in case we need another one, and I am not sure how much it will take to blow up their ship. I hate to waste more if a small amount will do the trick.

CLANK!

Another cannonball must have slammed into the side of our ship. The jolting of the ship causes the vial in my hands to slip out of my grasp. The Einsteinium spills out all over the deck of the ship.

"NO!" I yell. Lan's eyes jump to me, and she sees that I have spilled the Einsteinium. I drop to my knees and do what I can to scoop up as much as possible back into the vile. But it is like sweeping fine-grained powder, and I am unable to save much. The thought of this highly unstable and explosive element sprinkled all over the deck ignites panic through my brain like wildfire.

"Whatever you do, don't let a cannonball, or anything flammable, near here!" I yell toward Lan and Marina, working together to use the water cannon to stop anyone or anything from reaching our ship. Lan nods with dire understanding.

"I need to get some wax to seal the can without igniting the Einsteinium," I say to Soarin.

"I will go get a candle from one of the lanterns below deck," Marina replies, overhearing my request. "Lan is much better with the water cannon than I am anyway. Let me go." She darts to the hatch. I see how Soarin watches her go below as his eyes smile. I shake my head and laugh to myself. I know that look. That is the same way I look at Lan when she doesn't know I am watching. I want to give him a brotherly fist-bump or grunt, but there isn't time for that now.

"They're shootin' another one," shouts The Captain, followed by another rattling blast. This time, there isn't a cannonball, but bits of metal flinging at us ferociously. We all duck and take cover from whatever is close by. The area around the harpoon gun is littered with chunks of what used to be silverware. After the sounds of plinking metal have ceased, I glance around the ship to survey the damage and make sure everyone is okay. Everything is still intact as I push back up to a standing position. Marina, in a strange, ducking chicken run, makes her way over to Soarin and me with a candle and matches in her hands.

"Here you go." She pants, her eyes darting back to the enemy pirate ship.

I light a match away from the Einsteinium and place it on the wick of the candle, using my other hand to block out the wind. However, the howling fierceness blows out the match almost instantly.

"I need you to try and help block the wind."

Both Soarin and Marina use their hands to block out as much wind as they can as I attempt to light another match. Luckily, with their help, I am able to light the wick.

"Keep blocking the wind. I need as much wax as we can get to seal this can closed."

I can hear Lan firing up the water cannon and shooting toward the other ship once again. I wish I could make this wax melt faster. A strong gust of wind and spritzing water from the cannon and waves douse the candle flame. I swipe another match against the box, light the wick again, and continue the process until we have enough wax melted along the lip of the can to seal in the Einsteinium. I use some nearby rope to tie it onto the harpoon, far enough away from the initial firing but close enough to the grenade so it will get ignited when it blows. I've only seen Einstein use similar can bombs at the Elementerprise station, so I'm not exactly sure if this will work, but we really don't have any other options at this point. Soarin loads the grenade into the harpoon gun and fires it straight away. We all hold our breath and watch as it flies directly at their ship, as if time is in slow motion. The blast is immense, and the wave of heat, smoke, and water causes us to all topple over. I pop my head up as soon as I am able. As the thick air begins to dissipate, we can see the remaining back end of their ship in flames just before it sizzles and sinks down into the wild ocean waves.

We all erupt into whooping and jumping up and down in triumph. But our celebration is short-lived as The Captain turns the wheel of the ship sharply, sending us all tipping over like drunken sailors. Our laughter continues, but the shouting Captain interrupts our joy.

"Soarin set the Mainsail. We need to get as close to the island as we can before that other ship gets 'round here." His finger points through the open helm window. Soarin jumps up to help the Mainsail catch the wind and move us in the correct direction for the island. Then, we all see the second ship sailing around the island toward us.

"I knew there were two ships," Marina whimpers. "I just thought that one sailed off."

"Looks like it was just waiting for their turn or for us to sail off," Lan adds with a deep sigh. "Here we go again."

"Dameon, get in the rowboat 'n get to that island 'fore they get 'round to us! We'll keep 'em distracted and make sure they don't get to that island after ya."

"But Captain…"

"No, buts. Get goin'. Hurry up now. Soarin will help ya put the charged DD on the rowboat to clear the path in the water, and I'll get ya as close as I can."

I recall that the DD stands for Deterrent Device. I'm afraid to even look at what might be lurking in the waters ahead of us if The Captain said I need the DD attached to the rowboat.

Soarin has already grabbed the device and climbed over the edge of the ship toward the rowboat before I have a chance to protest. I squint my eyes to see the small toy-looking pirate ship growing from behind the backend of the island and heading toward us.

"Keep the rope tied onto the rowboat, and we'll hopefully still be here to hook it to the crank engine ya fixed ta help pull ya' back in when yer done." The Captain's voice yells over the whipping sails and crashing waves.

"Fair winds, me boy." The Captain chants the same words Oz told him before he sailed off to the island. Oz! For a moment, I forgot about Oz. I think we all had forgotten in the commotion. I stick my hand into my pocket and pull out his lucky coin.

"I almost forgot. Captain, Oz wanted me to give this to you." I shout, holding up the gold coin, as the hint of sunlight peeking through the clouds glints a shining reflection onto The Captain's face.

"Keep it. Fer good luck." There is a quiver in his voice, and I know that this coin means everything to him. I need to do everything I can to make it back safely to this ship so I can give it to him. I nod as I turn to head to the rowboat. But out of the corner of my eye, I catch a glimpse of The Captain wiping a single tear from his brave, wrinkled, leathery face.

"Better hurry, or that ship will see you rowing to the island," Soarin recommends.

I nod.

Lan runs to me, wraps her arms around me, and then, she kisses me. For a moment, the world stops. The waves stop crashing, the wind stops blowing, and I forget about all the impending doom surrounding us. My legs would go limp if I let them, but I lock them tightly and press my lips against hers. I don't want to pull away, but she does instead.

"I will be ready to help pull you back here as soon as I see you in that boat." I can tell she is trying to put on a brave face for me, but her quivering chin gives her away.

"I will try to hurry back to you," I add, stealing one more quick kiss before I let her go.

Soarin is waiting for me at the edge of the ship. I swing my legs over and climb down the rope ladder. I grab hold of the ropes and unhook them. I can feel Soarin's brute strength take the weight of the boat from the ropes above as he helps to lower me down to the hungry, swirling waves below. The rowboat begins to rock and weave, making it impossible to stand as soon as it reaches the rough water's surface.

"Be sure to connect my line to the crank engine."

"Remember to use the DD if the swarm of creatures gets to be too much.

Fair winds, my brother," Soarin's voice calls after me, but I am already rowing as hard as I can toward the island.

I focus my gaze on the mountain ahead instead of the choppy, swarming waters directly in front of me. The fog is not as thick now, and I can see the outline of the erected rocks more clearly. The base of the mountain slopes up toward the clouds. Sitting on top of the sloped-cliff wings is a formation of rocks resembling the head of a majestic bird.

"Thunderbird Island," Nibi Ikwe's words whisper in my mind as I recall the name of the island shown on the map.

I watch as the bird grows larger and larger until I am too close to see its complete form. My rowboat slams hard against something in the water, causing me to slide off the center bench, nearly dropping one of the oars into the angry waves. Then, I realize it isn't just the ocean waves that are angry. I have crashed into a large, dark creature

384

bobbing below. An enormous tentacle erupts from the water and crashes down onto the rowboat, nearly pulling it down under the water with its force. My hand reaches over and slaps down onto the button of the DD, sending a strong pulse of electrical current through the creature and surrounding water. I can feel the tickle of each individual strand of hair on my head, reaching in every direction. The tentacle slowly slides off the edge of the boat and disappears into the waves. I watch as the dark mass sinks deeper and deeper beneath me. Careful not to touch the water, I ignore the burning in my shoulders and row even faster. My breath chugs out steady and heavy with each pump of the oars like I'm an unstoppable machine. I keep my eyes glued to the approaching shoreline. The firing of the sniper rifle rings out back at the ship, and I can't help but whip my head around to see what they are firing at. Not only has the pirate ship reached firing distance of the Scylla, but two pirates have clearly lowered their dinghy, and are rowing ferociously toward me and the island. Or should I say, one pirate now, since the other one slumps over and splashes into the water.

Keep rowing.
Keep rowing.

BANG!
I turn to watch as the other pirate in the dinghy collapses into the waves. A barrage of sharks attacks him instantly until there is nothing left but a puddle of foaming, red water.

Keep rowing and don't fall into the water.
Keep rowing and don't fall into the water.

The water below me is no longer swarming. It must be too shallow for the large creatures. A few more strokes, and I should hit land.
The scraping sand along the bottom of my boat would normally make me cringe, but it is the most glorious sound in the

world right now. As the waves retreat back into the ocean, I am finally able to jump out of the boat and onto the beach. I tug the rowboat as far as I can out of the water and pull the rope to tie it around a nearby dried trunk of a palm tree. My entire body is shaking with exhaustion, and I would love to just plop on the sand and relax for a few minutes to catch my breath. But I know there isn't time for that luxury. The sand under the weight of my feet shifts, causing my rubber boots to sink with each step. As the ground begins to shake with great ferocity, I am no longer able to stand. My wedged boots keep my lower half in place as my upper body propels forward. My arms swim through the air to keep my balance as the ground quakes.

> *The volcano seems to be getting more active. I'm not sure going inside that mountain is a good idea.*

I wiggle my boots loose from the caking sand and tromp forward toward the mountain. I don't know exactly how to get into what The Captain called the vault, but I know I watched him going and coming from this direction on the island. The sandy beach turns into a thick treed jungle of brown vines, like the area is tied off to keep visitors away. My hands are constantly pulling at the dried-out vegetation. It looks like this area was once a green, lush jungle. But now, with the constant whipping winds and cooler temperatures, there are only spots of green in the center of a few remaining leaves, and the rest is just entanglements of brown. I feel as though I'm stepping into a giant, tightly woven basket. The sound of rumbling penetrates from every direction like surround sound. I can't tell if it is coming from angry, hiding animals, gurgling up from deep within the ground, or from the mountain itself. All I know, is that I need to hurry.

Chapter 40

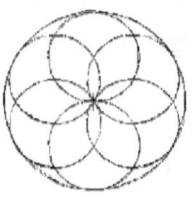

Ton

J look ahead to see where there are ebony boulders encased in the trunks and vines. I am pretty sure this must be the base of the mountain. Upon further investigation, and the removal of a few more vines and branches, there is a small opening to a cave. It wasn't noticeable from a distance because the black rocks are layered in a way that the mouth is set back between layers, disguising the entrance. I step behind the curtain of rock and squint ahead into the darkness. I instantly feel the shell around my neck levitate and hover straight in front of my clavicle. The shell attached to the leather is illuminating, and I am forced to steady my feet, so it doesn't propel me forward into the dark cave. Unfortunately, although it is glowing, it doesn't provide enough light to see what lies ahead in the echoing darkness. I didn't plan well for spelunking.

> *No! I left my wristband sitting on the ship after filling the bomb.*
> *There is no way I am going to walk into a pitch-black cave.*
> *Surely, The Captain didn't walk through the cave in the dark.*

My hands feel along the mouth of the cave, and sure enough, there is a lever that makes me think of Dr. Frankenstein. I grasp the lever and switch it to the up position.

Overhead lights zap on, and the snapping sound continues like dominoes for quite a long distance. With the cave lit, I am greeted by a large, lime green bird with a patch of sky blue on its head, and grey on its belly. His squawks echo deep into the cave. He flies around my head dizzyingly and pecks at my hair.

"Hey, shhhh. Cut that out." I swat at the bird like he is a giant menacing mosquito. "Let's not let all the animals on the island know I'm here okay."

To my surprise, the bird lands on my arm and lifts my sleeve with its beak as if it is attempting to raise my arm. Its dark, beady eyes stare into mine, trying to tell me something. The bird shrieks again and shakes its head. It flies to a metal box hanging on the cave wall. It pecks at the metal, trying to get at whatever is inside. There is a small touchpad exactly like the one on the E-Springs elevator. I lean down as a red light scans my eye. At least this time, I know what to expect. As the fingerprint image is revealed, I place my finger on the pad. Another light scans my fingerprint and turns green as the box pops open. Inside the box, there is a resealable mylar bag and a laminated paper. I pull out the paper and notice that the writing is Great Granddad's. The protected page looks to have been torn from one of his journals.

Feed Con a treat from the box.

(Con is the Green Conure. And, yes, he is a little thief, so watch your pockets.)

He will lead you through the maze of the caves to the vault. Do not attempt to find the vault without him. There are too many tunnels, many of which are extremely dangerous. If he screeches, turns around abruptly, and flies back the way you came, turn around and follow him. If he aborts, then there is either an animal or the air is not safe to breathe. Either way, run after him! If he leads you to the vault, he will wait patiently outside the vault door until you complete your mission. Once you have exited the vault, he will expect you to give him another treat from the box outside the vault door before he will guide you back through the maze of caves.

Good luck!

The bird continues to peck at the silver bag inside the box.

"Hey there, Con. So, you want a treat, huh?"

The bird bobs his head up and down. I can't help but smile. I am having a conversation with a bird. I reach my fingers up slowly and stroke the blue feathers on top of his head. He ruffles his feathers with approval. Then, he nudges my hand toward the bag.

"Alright."

I reach into the metal box and pull out the bag. Con swoops down off the box, following the shiny bag. Curious to see what he will do, I hesitate to open the top. He hovers for a moment in the air impatiently and then flaps to my shoulder. He side-steps toward my face and nuzzles the top of his head against my neck and cheek.

"Are you just being nice to me so I will give you a treat?" I ask.

He takes a step away from my face and maneuvers his head up and down again.

Chuckling to myself, I open the bag, and Con explodes off my shoulder with excitement as I place my hand inside the sack.

"Calm down," I say to the puff of feathers attacking the back of my hand.

"I refuse to pull a treat out of the bag until you sit. Sit!" I repeat the command as if I'm talking to a pet dog. To my astonishment, he flies back to the edge of the metal box, and he perches obediently.

"Good boy. Here you go." I pull one of the treats from the bag. It is a compressed ball of seeds and berries. I hold it out in front of him as he pecks at it with his beak until it is gone. I seal the bag and place it back in the metal box.

"Okay, you got your treat. Now show me how to get to the vault."

But Con just pecks at the bag. I shew him away from the bag and close the metal box.

"No more treats until you show me to the vault. Come on, let's go." I take a few steps deeper into the cave and motion for him to lead the way. He doesn't budge.

"Want another treat?" I ask, with an enticing inflection in my voice.

Con bobs his head in a nod.

"Then, let's go get a treat. Come on, boy."

Con dives from the box and leads me into the cave.

I practically need to run to keep up with him. Luckily, he does slow down if he gets too far ahead and hovers as he waits for me to catch up. It causes my heart to pound when he pauses because I fear he will turn around and dart back. At least the shell will continue to guide me if I get separated from the bird. My hand clasps around the illuminating shell, and I can feel it pull toward the left or the right in the same direction as Con's guidance. However, I don't think it can tell me if the air is unsafe or if there is danger ahead like Con can. Therefore, I hold on tightly to the shell around my neck and run after the sound of flapping wings. We twist and wind through the endless black rock tunnels. My head feels like we have already gone in ten circles. Perhaps we have. For all I know, this bird is purposefully getting me lost inside the mountain, but the shell reassures me that the bird is leading me to where I need to go. Con plunges ahead and lands on another metal box. We've made it to the vault door.

"Good boy, Con. Good boy!" I reach out to pet his head, and of course, he pushes my hand toward the pad on the metal box.

"Hang on, buddy. I have something important I need to do first."

Chapter 41

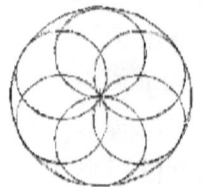

Operation Goldilocks

On the wall in front of the metal and stone vault door, there is an outlined depiction of an open hand and forearm. I place my hand and arm inside the lines as indicated. A blue beam of light scans my handprint and tattoo while a thin zing of pins pricks my pointer finger. The beam of light shining from under my hand switches to green. The ground beneath me begins to rumble as the impressive door slowly slides open. I hear the fluorescent lights zap and flicker on as the beam of light, now shining through the opening gap, grows to reach my impatient feet.

"I guess the security to get into this vault is a bit more extreme than it is to get to your treats. Hold up, how did Great Granddad get my fingerprint, or my tattoo print, and DNA, or whatever this one requires?"

Con just twists his head to look at me as if I'm odd for rambling to a bird. He then taps his beak against the metal box with urgency.

"Got it. You just want me to hurry up so I can get you another treat."

Con's head bobbles up and down.

"Alright, wait here." I signal with my hands for him to stay. He just continues bobbing.

Behind the sliding door is a square metal vault-like room. I step over the threshold of the cave door and onto the metal floor of the vault. As soon as I shift my weight forward onto the metal floor, the door behind me begins to slide closed. My heart begins to pound and worry flushes through my veins.

Should I get out now before it closes?
Will I get locked in?
Will Con still be there to guide me back when I finish?

But my feet can't move, and I am frozen with fear as I watch the closing gap shrink to nothing. A burst of cold, circulating air gushes around me. Goosebumps flood my arms as a shiver trickles down my spine.

"Okay, Great Granddad. I'm here. Now what?"

I wish more than anything he would appear in the shadows to help instruct me, but I am clearly alone.

"*Welcome to The Thunderbird Island Vault. You are cleared to proceed.*" A comforting woman's voice echoes from the walls.

"Ummm, okay. Thank you?" I reply, unsure if the voice is actually listening to me, like my devices do at home, or if the computerized room is just confirming I am cleared. I wait for further instructions, but I just find myself standing in the silence, rocking back and forth on my feet.

There is a giant machine in the center of the vault. Like an octopus, there are eight large metal tubes attached to it in a circle. At the end of each tube is an affixed canister.

What is this contraption? It looks even more
sophisticated than the generator time machine. But
what am I supposed to do with it?

"Siri?
Alexa?
Computer?
Whatever your name is, what am I supposed to do now?" I ask the female voice, but she doesn't respond.

I allow my eyes to focus on the various posters lining the walls for guidance. I walk to the nearest one and inspect it with great curiosity. It looks ancient and faded. I instantly notice the title,
OPTICKS: Or a Treatise of the Reflections, Refractions, Inflections, and Colours of Light
By Sir Isaac Newton, Knt.

I squint to try to make sense of the various lines drawn on the diagram below the title. It shows the lines entering a triangular prism, which spread and multiply, creating more lines, which then enter another triangular prism and, in turn, reflect three lines formed closely together.

> *So, what does Newton's light refraction diagram have to do with this machine?*

The next poster is a drawing done by Albert Einstein explaining his theory of *Stimulated Emission.*

The next poster is difficult to read as it appears to be an enlarged journal page belonging to Gordon Gould, where he explains the acronym for LASER as
"Light Amplification by Stimulated Emission of Radiation."
November 13, 1957.

> *Ah-ha, so this monstrous machine must be a giant laser.*
> *This is starting to make sense now, I think.*

I skim past the next posters on the wall because really, I don't want to know the history of lasers, I just want to figure out how to use this one. As I make it to the last wall of the vault, I take in the long rectangular stone altar. On the stone tabletop, there are five pedestals, each cradling a perfectly lit foot-long cylinder. The first is an astonishing iridescent metal, which makes it difficult to tell if it is more silver, pink, or green. The next cylinder is a glowing pale purple crystal, followed by a dazzling blue crystal. This one reminds me of the color of Great Granddad's, Dad's, and Jax's eyes. The next cylinder reflects a deep plum, and the last is a beautiful, brilliant red. The stone wall behind each cylinder glows and reflects a mural of a majestic rainbow of light.

> *Wow, this place went from a history museum to an art museum at the seam of the wall.*

Still shocked by the emanating colors, I am drawn into their exquisiteness, and my feet gravitate toward them. However, my fingers hover near the piercing blue cylinder, unable to bring myself to touch it, in fear of knocking it off the pedestal, loud alarms going off, or triggering the volcano to blow. Instead, I drop my hand onto the prominent journal placed below it. It lies open, and I instantly recognize the chicken-scratch handwriting.

> *Great Granddad wrote this, too!*

It explains the detailed instructions for the laser machine in the center of the room.

I close my eyes and exhale with relief, knowing that I don't have
to try and figure this out on my own.

> *I'm so glad there aren't codes and puzzles to figure out this time, just step-by-step instructions. I guess shooting lasers into the center of the earth isn't something to leave to chance.*

I read the instructions.

OPERATION GOLDILOCKS ACTIVATION SEQUENCE

WARNING! EVERYTHING IN THIS ROOM IS HIGHLY EXPLOSIVE, EXTREMELY REACTIVE, AND VERY DELICATE!
WATCH YOUR STEP!

Great, I was starting to feel more confident that I could do this safely until I read that.

Step 1 - Safety first — put on the goggles.

Check. I can handle this step.

I grasp a pair of goggles lying on the table, secure them around my eyes, and stretch the band around the back of my head. It is difficult to see through the obscured, dark glass, but I guess I will just have to be extra careful with what I am doing since it is difficult to see.

Step 2 — Initiate Sequential Approval from each Trigger Detonation Site

(You must flip each of the switches on the machine's control board. Then, if the light

above the switch turns on, it signifies detonation approval from that site and activates that portion of the trigger.)
*You MUST receive permission from ALL Trigger Detonation Sites in order to proceed.

I look over the detailed picture showing the switches of the control board on the machine.

Filling my lungs with the most bravery I can muster, I gulp down the impending dread building in my throat. I push my feet to shuffle toward the machine's control board. It looks identical to Great Granddad's drawing. I instantly recognize each of the locations listed under the line of switches. They are the same locations Great Granddad listed as the Trigger Detonation sites I read about in his other journal. I flip the first switch labeled Mount Weather Station, Virginia. I hold my breath and wait for the round bulb above it to light up.

How long will I need to wait before the site gives approval?

I could be here for weeks, months….

Great Granddad wrote, "You must receive permission from all Trigger Detonation Sites in order to proceed. I am not sure how accurate he is with punctuation. Does that mean that I need to wait for each detonation site in sequential order, meaning I shouldn't flip the next switch until I have permission from the site before or just that I need to have all of them approved before I can fire up the laser?

397

My heart begins to beat more rapidly against my chest as I contemplate the unclear set of directions. I decide to wait for approval from each site before flipping the next switch, just to be on the safe side. I run back to look over the instructions in the journal so I can be better prepared for the upcoming steps. But the thoughts in my brain can't concentrate and begin to swirl in my skull like I flipped the puree switch on a blender.

> *Wait, that first station is in Virginia. From the maps I've seen, Washington D.C. is underwater, but part of Virginia is still there. Could the President of The United States be residing at that location, and is he the person approving this? Assuming there still is a President. Who knows with Elementerprise in control at E-Springs, or Greenbrier, or whatever it's called now. Wait, surely The President isn't part of Elementerprise, right?*

A repeating buzzer sound shocks my heart like a defibrillator and forces me to spin around to look at the control board. Sure enough, the first light bulb above the first switch I flipped is now glowing red. Whoever is at that Mount Weather Station in Virginia has approved this laser detonation. Simultaneously, the outline of a world map begins to glow just below the switches.

Suddenly, my stomach fills with concrete and sinks to my feet, making it difficult to stammer back over to the machine, but I force my way over. I take a cleansing breath to clear my thoughts and flip the next switch: Cheyenne Mountain Station, Colorado. I've heard of this place. It is a top-secret military facility built into the Rocky Mountains. I've always wanted to see what it looks like inside. I figure I will most likely need to wait a while before the light blinks with approval, but almost immediately after I flip the switch, the red light signifies their affirmative response. It's almost as though someone at that location has been anxiously waiting for me to flip this switch.

As that red bulb above the switch flickers on, another small light, similar to a mini LED light, illuminates on the glowing map. My brows knit together, and I scratch my temple at the location.

> *Why did a light turn on the map to show the location of The Challenger Deep and illuminate the Pacific Ocean when the Cheyenne Mountain Site was approved? Cheyenne Mountain isn't even in The Pacific Ocean. It doesn't make sense.*

As if a lightbulb in my brain is triggered, I recall reading about the five ocean sites with the nuclear bomb symbols on them from the other journal. Each of these Trigger Detonation sites must be triggering the nuclear bombs placed in the deepest sites in each of the oceans. I decide to proceed and flick up the next switch titled Menwith Hill, England. As I turn to step toward the stone table to investigate some of the other pages of this new edition of Great Granddad's journal for answers, I am stopped once again by the instant flash of red in the corner of my eye as the red bulb illuminates above the last switch I flipped. I instantly notice another area of the map is now glowing. A new light ignites the location of The Molloy Deep, causing the entire Arctic Ocean to glow softly in the room's dim light.

I turn to move the next switch to the up position with a satisfying *CLICK*. The name under this switch is Porton Down, England.

> *Hmmm, I guess there are two Trigger Detonation sites in England.*

The red bulb above the switch as well as a new area on the map begin to glow just moments later. This time, The Puerto Rico Trench lights up on the map, which causes the Atlantic Ocean to radiate around it.

The next switch is labeled Pine Gap, Australia. I feel every second trudge by, waiting for a new area to spark on the map. I am tempted to take the time to look through Great Granddad's journal lying open to the directions for the laser machine, but it seems like every time I go to turn around, the light flickers on and I need to flip the next switch. So instead, I just hover over the dark bulb and chew the skin on my lower lip.

Come on! Come on, Australia! Let's just get this over with.
The less time I have to think about what I am actually about to do, the better.

My impatience spreads like the black plague through my body, and everything down to my feet bounces with sickening eagerness.

As if someone on the other end of that switch hears my thoughts, the light zaps on above the switch and on a new area on the map in The South Sandwich Trench and The Southern Ocean. My shaking fingers loiter over the last switch as I suck in as much air as I can through my nostrils.

"Alright, this is it, Mashabim, Israel, you are the last switch," I mutter under my breath, followed by a gulp as my fingers press the lever of the switch upward. I wait for the lightbulb to glow red. However, instead of it turning red, it lights up green, and not just this bulb is green, but the line of bulbs above the switches all change to green, including the newest site on the map, The Java Trench and the Indian Ocean. The entire control board now illuminates an eerie green glow as all the switches and oceans have been activated.

The familiar female voice from when I entered the room resonates once again.

"All detonation sites are sequentially triggered. You may now proceed with the laser assembly." The woman's voice reverberates off the metal walls and surrounds me with

reassurance. I leap over to the stone table to read the next step written in the journal. I know the voice just told me to assemble the laser; I'm just not sure how to accomplish that.

Step 3 – Activate each laser medium by pressing the blinking light on each tube in the proper sequence. The **gas** medium housing canisters should already be placed, sealed, and with their button blinking if you were successful in obtaining the approval from each trigger detonation site. However, the solid mediums (metal/crystal cylinders on the pedestals) must be placed and sealed in their proper housing canisters before their light will blink, indicating the medium is ready for activation. The following is the correct sequence for each laser medium housing canister:

1) Press the white blinking button on the housing canister containing **Carbon monoxide** (CO)

2) Press the white blinking button on the housing canister containing **Hydrogen Fluoride** (HF)

3) **Put on the safety gloves!** Carefully take the **Erbium cylinder** (iridescent, silvery, metal) from the first pedestal, and place it into the next housing canister, and press the raised button below the window to close and seal the canister. If placed/sealed correctly, the button at the base of the tube should begin blinking pink. Press the pink, blinking button.

4) Carefully take the **Neodymium cylinder** (light purple crystal) from the next pedestal, and place it into the next housing canister. Seal it using the raised button below the window. Press the purple blinking button.

5) Carefully take the **Titanium Sapphire cylinder** (dark blue crystal) from the next pedestal, and place it into the next housing canister, seal it, and press the blue blinking button.

6) Carefully take the **Alexandrite cylinder** (maroon crystal), place it in the next housing canister, seal it, and press the maroon blinking button.

7) Carefully take the **Ruby cylinder** (red crystal), place it, seal it into the next housing canister, and press the blinking red button.

8) The canister for **Krypton** (glowing white gas) should already be placed and sealed. Press the corresponding blinking white button at the end of its tube.

For each step, I am slow and overly cautious. I don't want to risk dropping or mishandling any of the elements. I follow each of the eight steps with precision, placing and sealing all the mediums into their housing canisters. After pressing the last white blinking button. I run back over to the journal.

Step 4 — Pull the lever labeled "conduit" near the entrance of the vault to open the venting conduit hatch.

I step over to the labeled lever near the door and use all my body weight to pull it down. The vault begins to shake once again as a large circle slides open above the laser machine, exposing the circular venting tube of the volcano. I shuffle my feet over to the new opening in the room's ceiling and look up to where the conduit is exposed. I imagine I will see all the way to the sky, but there is a metal plate closing off the top. I dart back to the journal.

Step 5 – Fire The Ozone Missile (large red button on top of the control board with the missile emblem – it should begin blinking once you open the conduit hatch).

*The next steps are time-sensitive and must be completed in a timely manner. The ozone will only remain open for a short period of time, making the sun clearly visible and strong enough to power the giant lasers. Therefore, time is of the essence! Hurry!

My heart begins to beat faster. I follow Great Granddad's instructions. I run over to the large blinking red button with the missile on it and press it. The heat radiating down the shaft of the conduit above me is intense, and I am forced to shield myself from its power with my arms. I feel my arm hairs singeing and melting. The overwhelming smell of kerosene blasts around me. Once I feel the pelting of small bits of rock and debris raining down on me cease, I squint one eye open to look up into the now completely open shaft. The metal sheet is no longer blocking the opening. Not only is it open, but I can also see there is not a single cloud in the sky, and I can see directly to the bright sun.

Cool!

I sprint back over to read the next step quickly.

Step 6 — Activate the self-adjusting mirror reflectors by pressing the blinking mirror button (light blue button with a mirror emblem, just under the missile launcher.)

*As the mirrors raise from the top of the machine toward the conduit, a protection barrier wall will also rise from the floor.

Stand behind the protection barrier wall and stay there until the firing of the lasers is completed!

I leap over to press the blinking blue mirror button. I watch as large mirrors rise from the machine, while a thick metal, circular wall emerges from the floor behind me. I run around to stand behind the newly revealed wall to read the next set of instructions.

Step 7 — On the backside of the protection barrier wall (where you should be standing now), there is a blinking button showing a magnifying glass.

Press it now to activate the magnifier.

Whatever you do, do **NOT** look around the protection barrier wall at this point. The sunlight will be too powerful, and it will cause you harm or death!

I decide to bring the journal with me behind the protective barrier wall this time so I don't waste any more time running back and forth. And, I don't want to risk it, or myself, getting damaged from the magnified sun. With the journal draped open over my left arm, I use my right finger to press the button with the magnifying glass on it. Even behind the protective barrier, I can feel the overwhelming light around me. It feels like being in a light oven as sweat pours down my back. I can barely open my eyes behind the protective goggles, but I squint just enough to read the next words in the journal.

Step 8 – The Einsteinium button (the button with the two arrows, the symbol for Einsteinium) on the backside of the protection barrier wall should now be blinking. This button will power and fire the lasers.

Press the button now and pray this works!

What?!? Pray this works?
Great Granddad, seriously?
Has this even been tested?
Is this safe?
Am I going to blow this volcano to smithereens?
Will this obliterate Earth?

"You have ten seconds of magnified sunlight remaining."
Echoes the female voice, just as calmly as if she is telling me a bedtime story.

"9...8...7...6..."

"Here goes nothing!" I force my shaking fingers to the outline of the Einsteinium symbol etched onto the button, squeeze my eyes closed and suck in as much breath as my lungs will hold as if these gestures will save me if this thing blows.

I press the button.

I am bathed in a rainbow of lights. The intense zapping sound shoots through my eardrums and feels like it makes them explode. I am blown back against the metal door of the vault in the explosion. Every bone in my body feels like they shatter on impact. A high-pitched squealing continues in my ears. But the machine and everything else in the vault is silent, as if dead. I reach up to feel the shell hanging limply against my chest. It is no longer glowing, and the magnetic force compelling it has ceased. I can't tell if everything around me is black because I am blind, or if all the lights in the vault have blacked out. I know I'm not dead because pain pierces through me as if every one of my muscles and bones has become a pincushion for hundreds of swords all at once.

Chapter 42

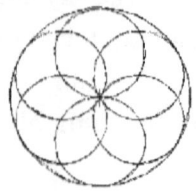

Fleeing

A red light and buzzer on top of the laser machine begins to flash.

"*Warning. Danger. Warning. Danger.*" The female voice repeats, with no more urgency than someone ordering their morning coffee.

With a few more breaths of searing pain, moving becomes manageable again. I can feel the heat radiating through the metal, shaking floor as the scorching temperature penetrates my clothes. I place my gloved hands on the large stone and metal door behind me, using it to balance my stance to standing, or should I say surfing. The constant quaking beneath my feet causes me to waver back and forth through the flashing darkness. Raining rocks and debris pelt against the now sealed metal ceiling and walls. I am grateful to be protected by a heavy-duty metal box as the sounds of the caves around me crumble.

> *What if the tunnels surrounding the vault cave in?*
> *Will I be able to get out of here, or is this my final tomb?*
> *Did the lasers successfully heat the core to maintain optimal rotation to sustain the planet?*

A red glow appears around the bottom of the machine in the center of the trembling room. Like a tube of radioactive cinnamon toothpaste, lava oozes up through the cracks surrounding the base of the laser machine. At least the glow of the oozing lava and flashing red warning light creates just enough radiance to see where I need to place my hand and forearm on the keypad to open the door. I rip the protective glove off my hand and place my arm in the indicated outline. The vault begins to rumble as the heavy door begins to slide open. However, it stops rumbling just as quickly as it started. It only opens a sliver before it gets stuck and stops moving. I place my arm back on the placement keypad and try again. This time, the sliver disappears as it closes. I try again to open it, but it only opens the same dismal amount before stopping.

"NO!
YOU HAVE TO OPEN!"
I shout at the door, but my demanding screams of frustration do nothing to free the door. However, Con's screeches squawk from the other side of the door.

He's still there waiting for me.

Flashes of the vault filling with lava with me still inside cause panic to surge through my body with my quickening heart. My eyes survey the vault for something to use as a lever. And then, I see the actual lever I used to open the conduit. I jump onto it, wrap my arms around it, and allow my body weight to pull it down. I can't tell if the rumbling in the vault is a result of the opening conduit or just more of the earth quaking, but I lean over and look up to see the metal plate of the conduit slide open once again to reveal the grey cotton clouds thickening above the opening. Not wanting to climb the rocks all the way up to the opening unless I am forced to, I feel better knowing that I at least have that option. However, I clasp my hands around the lever and begin unscrewing it from its position on the wall. Once it is unscrewed, I try to wedge it into the small open crack of the door. I push with all my strength to use it to force the door open, but it won't budge. I pull off the protective glove from my other hand so I have both hands free to get a better grip on the metal shaft. I place my foot onto the thick metal and stone making up the frame around the door and push against it while leaning my back against the lever. Another large rumble shakes around me and sends me flying to the scalding ground. A bubble erupts from the bottom of the laser machine and spurts more lava into the vault.

Con, now ballistic, screeches and pecks his head in through the open crack of the door.

"Get back, you crazy bird. Do you want to lose your head?" I push his frantic head back through the crack, but he is relentless and continues poking his head through. I get back to my feet and shove the lever back into the crack. This time, as I pull back, the door gives a bit and jerks open a tad more. Con comes squabbling into the vault, circling around my head, boisterously squealing.

"I know, bud. We need to get out of here." I respond to his alarms, and the female voice continues her repetitive warnings. Con begins to peck at the door as if he is going to be able to peck his way through the thick stone and metal, and I can't help but chuckle and shake my head at his naivety. The red oozing lava, like a monstrous blob, slowly gravitates toward me. I can see the metal floor around the machine melting and seeping into the red glowing excretion.

I puff my cheeks and let out a large puff of air through my tight lips as I pull back on the lever as hard as I can.

"Come on!" I yell through the grunt.

The floor beneath me rumbles, and I feel the door give away. It lurches open another foot before jolting to a halt. But that extra space blasts with cooler air and freedom. Con doesn't hesitate and dives through the opening. I squeeze my adrenaline-pumping body through the crack and sprint after him. My legs pump after being reborn with newfound hope. I don't even look back at the door. I hate to leave the magnificent vault and ingenious lasers behind, but the rumbling ground and raining rocks indicate I don't have a choice. I run after the bird, feeling a bit bad that I never gave him his treat for waiting, but he seems motivated enough to escape without it. My hands brace my head from the falling rocks as I run. Con instantly darts back toward my face suddenly as I look ahead to see the cave in front of us closed off with multiple boulders. He could have surely fit through the cracks, but there is no way I would. So, I turn and follow him down a different tunnel. We snake our way through each winding turn. I do my best to avoid the pelting debris and to stay erect over the shaking ground. Suddenly, Con begins cawing once again. He darts back over my head, turns, and flies back in front of me. As if pacing in the air. It is clear that our pathway is blocked. The lights overhead crash down and splatter around me, causing darkness to swallow the tunnel ahead. Luckily, the lights are still on in the tunnel behind me to show the silhouetted panting movement from a large beast as he approaches.

Seriously, a tiger? As if being forced out of a vault filling with lava and a collapsing volcanic mountain weren't enough. Now I am trapped, with boulders blocking my path ahead of me and I have a large tiger coming to eat me.
Fan-freaking-tastic.

I wipe the sweat from my brow but freeze mid-swipe as the tiger lets out an ostentatious roar. The cave around us thunders a similar rumble as rocks hail down. The massive animal crouches low to the ground and crawls toward me like a frightened kitten. I want more than anything to reach my hand out and stroke his velvety head, but the moment I even flinch in his direction, he snarls his large fangs back at me. Con lets out a disapproving shriek at the tiger in my defense. The tiger bats at him like he is a frustrated child, taking his wrath out on a toy. I seize the moment of the tiger's distraction to turn to the pile of boulders to see if I can push or pull them free. I am able to pull out a basketball-sized rock and roll it out of the way. I dig through the divot it left to find another similarly sized rock. This one I push, my legs scampering in the dirt behind me for force, and it rolls forward. Light from the other side of the pile pours through the hole, lighting the tiger in a debris-filled spotlight. Stunned, the tiger stops pawing at Con and leaps toward the light, knocking me out of the way. His giant claws dig at the rocks, boring his way through the opening. Con and I watch as the colossal creature combats the blockade. A moment of revolt from the cave as it dumps the top layer of rocks onto the tiger's head is no match for the determined beast. He simply shakes off the rubble and lunges out of the tunnel. Con and I exchange glances and then shoot through the new opening after the disappearing tiger.

Con leads me through a few more zigs and zags, but we don't ever see the tiger again. Euphoric laughter spews from me as I watch the bouncing light of the entrance grow ahead of us.

"Woohoo, Con! We did it! Good bird!" I shout as I burst through the opening into the dying trees of the jungle.

"Coo Coo," Con replies, pecking his beak at the metal box, begging for his treat.

"Haha. Alright, boy, you earned it. But let's hurry. I want to get away from this mountain as soon as possible." I pull off the goggles still wrapped around my face, allow the beam to scan my eye, and place my finger on the keypad. The lock clicks, and Con's head is in the box before I can get it open. I unroll the top of the bag and place it on a nearby branch, allowing Con to freely feast on the entirety of its bounty.

"I guess this is goodbye, buddy." I stroke my fingers along his back and down his tail a few times. He doesn't so much as turn to look at me. His head is buried in the bag.

"I don't think you will need to lead anyone back to the vault.

I'm guessing there is nothing left of it by now." I look back into the cave, but I am instantly forced to jump back as an earth-shattering rumble closes off the entrance.

"It truly was amazing Great Granddad. Let's just hope it worked," I add, petting Con one more time. This time, he reveals his teal feathered head from the bag and nuzzles my hand, still gnawing at the last bit of seeds.

"I am going to miss you." The corner of my mouth quivers upward.

Con's beady eyes double in size as he dive-bombs into the pocket of my pants and snatches Oz's lucky coin. My hand reaches out instantaneously and swipes it back.

"Oh, no, you don't, you little thief. Nice try." I clench my fingers around the coin tightly, securing it in my fist.

Con's beak clasps onto the now glowing shell against my chest and flies backward with eagerness. My free hand grasps at my now empty chest. Con was a split-second faster than me this time and got away. I watch as his eyes, reflecting his glowering triumph, turn back to laugh at me as he flies high and disappears into the clouds with my shell necklace dangling below him.

"Get back here, you little…" But I know he is gone, and he isn't coming back. He did his job, and now he has his reward. That shell led me to where I could access the core. It served its purpose. I don't imagine I will be needing it any longer anyway. I smile up at the swirling grey clouds as the ground shakes beneath me.

Suddenly, I feel thick, hot pulses of breath puffing behind me. The tiger is back. And this time, he isn't trying to flee from a collapsing cave. I turn around as his rancid breath attacks me, full force in a growl. A shiver of death scurries down my spine. I break off a nearby branch to use as a bat and take off running through the trees. The tiger sprints after me. The only advantage I have is being lean and limber. I can swerve in and out of the thick-lined trees where the tiger is too large to invade. However, we both know that eventually, the trees end, and I will need to run from their cover through the open beach to my boat. The tiger darts off ahead to wait for me to emerge from the trees. As the beach approaches, along with the pacing tiger, I stop to catch my breath. I lean against the trunk of a drying palm tree as my chest heaves and pants. The taste in my desert mouth is metallic, and I need water. But my thirst is nothing compared to my fear. I don't want to have come this far just to get eaten by a ravenous tiger. The thought of running back through the safety of the trees toward the mountain flashes in my mind, but it is stopped abruptly as I watch a plume of ash and burning lava rock explode, blasting the thunderbird's head in all directions. I know I don't have much time before rivers of lava erupt. I need to get off this island!

I hear a bird's cries chirping through the sound of the blast, and they aren't alone. An entire family of green conures shoots through the clouds like little green rockets. They shriek and attack the tiger with confusion from all directions.

They are helping me escape!

I sprint from the trees toward the rowboat, its backend now being attacked by the incoming tide. Hope pulses through my veins until out of the corner of my eye, I see the giant paw of the tiger slam against the smallest bird in Con's crew. The little bird crashes to the ground, and the tiger's large tongue laps it up and gulps it down. Con's cry pierces my heart, and before I know it, I have fled to his side and bashed the tiger's head with the branch clasped in my shaking hands.

That was stupid, Dameon. What were you thinking? You should have just run to the boat while the tiger was distracted.

But my thoughts of reasoning are too late. The tiger is livid, and it has turned its gaze to me. I watch as his bulky shoulder blades rise one at a time. He crouches low and springs toward me. His mammoth body bursts in attack, but my defensive instincts kick in as I roll to the ground beneath his soaring belly. His heavy momentum sends him sliding away as I push up and run toward the rowboat. He turns and paws at my heels as Con and the other birds attack him in protest. I'm afraid to waste a second by looking back, so I just randomly swing the thick branch in my hand behind me every once in a while, as I run. I feel the branch in my hand make contact with the tiger as he lets out an angry roar. Although the hit was successful, the force of the blow caused the branch to fly from my grip, and I now run unarmed. I do my best to zig and zag, but the ashy sand is thick like mud, making maneuvering from side to side difficult. My boot briefly gets stuck, but luckily, I am not the only one struggling. The tiger is also having a difficult time, as his front paws are wedged into what looks like quicksand. His fierce cries change from predatorial to cries for help. The large, helpless animal lets out a distressing wail as he uses his strong hind legs to free himself from the sand. However, he is now hesitant to continue through the concrete-like sand, knowing he can't get through the muck. Con and the surviving birds swirl around me as I shove the rowboat into the incoming waves and climb in. I watch the tiger pace back and forth with reluctance and frustration as he lets out a booming roar. As if the mountain replies to his cry, it too lets out a bellow even louder than the tiger's.

The intense shaking makes the waves surrounding me grow larger. I feel the tug of the rope tied to the back of the rowboat tighten and begin to thrust me backward toward the ship. I pump my arms, ferociously rowing, as I watch the thick ash snow down onto the island, blanketing everything with grey. Con and the other birds fly high above me, trying to free themselves from the invading ash. But they, too, are becoming grey blurs, struggling to fly through the thickening air. They become difficult to see, except for one familiar glowing light shining through the grey. Con still has the shell in his mouth. Before I can allow my heart to smile in response, I hear a loud explosion as the volcano blasts into a full eruption. I watch as a mushroom cloud of ash and lava swell into a monstrous entity. The blob cloud continues to grow in all directions as hot lava rocks shoot out like fireworks. The monstrous plumes chase toward me as I row with fury. I look up into the sky to search for Con and the birds, but the ash cloud is thicker than fog as it envelopes me. Luckily, by the time it reaches me, it is mostly just ash with bits of lava rocks and not waves of molten lava. The air becomes difficult to breathe, and I hold my breath and continue rowing. My lungs scream for oxygen as my head swims through the syrupy clouds. I am forced to close my eyes, cease rowing momentarily, and attempt to suck in a bit of ash-free air from under my shirt. With the fabric as a filter, I am able to squeeze enough oxygen into my lungs to hold my breath once again and continue rowing. Hot lava rocks streak through the clouds like bolts of lightning and shooting stars. The continuous rumbles from the island send my little boat scrambling through the revolting waves. I can no longer row as the front end of my boat suddenly shoots upward from the force of a wave pushing out from the island. My trembling hands grip onto the sides of the boat as I wrap my legs around the bench to keep me from sliding into the angry waters. One second later, the backend of the boat is pushed up from a wave forcing its way behind me toward the island and I am forced to stare into the face of the grey ocean. Confusing waves beat toward me from all directions, some toward the island, some away from the island, in a battle of stubborn rage. A strong hand grabs my shoulder and nearly causes me to skyrocket. I whip my head around to see Soarin reaching out to hold the boat steady. I pry my white knuckles from the edge of the boat and grab onto the dangling rope. I slide the loop over the hook at the end of the boat and pull it tightly.

"Don't lose the oar." His voice shouts over the cacophony of winds, waves, and rumbling.

I dive to grab the one remaining oar and secure it in the boat as he begins hoisting it out of the insane waves. I jump onto the rope and help him lift the boat. A large tsunami wave barrels toward me, filling my mouth with ashy water and slamming me up against the ship. The little rowboat is now full of water. It may as well be filled with lead with how heavy it is now as Soarin and I struggle to hoist it upward. My heart is filled with gratitude as I feel the motor kick in and the ropes begin rising rapidly, without us having to hoist them. As soon as the boat is as high as it can go, I lunge for the rope ladder. The feeling of the rope to freedom in my hands fills me with optimism. I climb quickly despite my shaking muscles. As soon as Soarin and I board the ship, Lan knocks me over in an embrace.

"You made it back! I thought you got swallowed by that cloud." Tears make lines down her grey-caked face.

"Did you succeed? Did you get to the core of the Earth, or whatever you needed to do?"

I smile and attempt to nod, but every muscle in my neck and shoulders is cramping.

"You look like a grey ghost." I wipe the tip of her nose with my wet fingers.

"Me? You should see yourself." She laughs as she licks her thumb and smudges it across my cheek, just the way my Mom used to.

The Captain yells, "Weigh anchor! Ready the sails to tack. Let's lose those pirates 'fore the sky clears."

"Wait, the other pirate ship is still here?" I ask, looking out into the grey sky, but I can't even see past the railing of the side of the ship. Instead, I watch as another gigantic wave pummels over the edge. We all slosh to the opposite side of the ship in the force of the incoming water.

"They were still there before the volcano erupted," Marina sputters as Soarin helps her to her feet.

I stand and help up Lan, her face washed clean by the wave, and I can see her beauty more clearly now.

"Full speed ahead!" The Captain's voice booms over the chaos. "You two get on that anchor rope and get it up as quickly as you can using the fixed engine. Dameon, you can help me with the mainsails."

My body springs into action without having to think about Soarin's orders. As if my muscles know exactly what to do on their own, we have the ship turned about and sailing in no time. The further we get from the island, the air becomes more clear and easier to breathe. All of us watch the grey clouds dissipate behind us over the aft, waiting to see if the pirate ship is following us. Fortunately, all we see are foaming waves of anger and swirling towers of grey cotton ash above them. There may not be sails cutting through the plumes behind us, but there is a slight movement. A set of grey wings and a glowing shell light.

"Con!" I shout and let out a whistle. The glowing light swoops down and lands on my shoulder. He is nearly unrecognizable, all camouflaged in grey. But his beady eyes are the same. He drops the shell into my hand and shimmies over to nuzzle his head against my neck.

"Thanks. Good boy." I stroke my fingers down his ash-covered back. I place the shell into my pocket and coax Con down into my hand. I use my soaked shirt to wipe his feathers clean. After a few wipes, his green color gleams against the grey sky. His azure head bows and snuggles against my hand. "There you go, buddy."

"He's beautiful." Lan gawks. She strokes his back with her finger and cleans off the remaining grey ash. The look on her face is priceless when he nuzzles her hand.

"I think he likes you, too." I smile.

Chapter 43

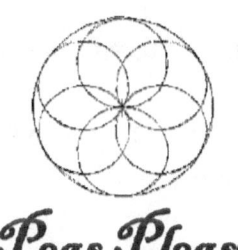

Peas Please

"I'll go give The Captain a break at the wheel. Why don't you go find us all something to eat," Soarin suggests.

Nodding, I lead the girls over to the hatch. Con revolts and refuses to go down below.

"Suit yourself. You are welcome to stay up here if you would rather." I say to the bird, but I leave the hatch open, just in case he decides to come down.

"Do either of you want to take a shower? Or I can find us something to eat first." I say to Lan and Marina.

"I'm starving," states Lan.

"I think I'm too tired to shower," Marina complains, sulking onto the bench at the table, her head plopping down onto her arms. A cloud of ash poofs around her.

I make my way to the cupboards lining the little kitchen. Cans come crashing out as I open the latched cupboard doors.

"There is a large can of dried peas," I say, referring to the one can that stayed put when I opened the door. "Or, we have a small can of green beans or some chili," I relay, reading the cans as I place them back into the cupboard.

"Peas? Green beans? Chili?" Marina's head has popped up from her arms and her eyes are wide.

"Any of those sound good?" I ask.

"They all sound good," Marina replies. "I haven't had any of those since I was a little girl."

"What are peas?" Lan asks.

Luckily, with the way the world is, Marina doesn't find Lan's question too bizarre.

"Mmmmm, you can boil them to make a soup. It is delicious," Marina answers.

I personally am not a big fan of pea soup. But right now, I am so hungry that anything sounds good.

I find a hand-crank can opener in one of the drawers and use it to remove the metal top. The can is large and contains too many dried peas for our small crew. I find a pot and pour in about a cup of peas per person. It takes me a minute to find a long lighter. I use it to light the strange gel fuel beneath the burner on the stove. I turn on the sink and add enough water to cover the peas. Again, I am not sure how to make pea soup, but I know that when I have seen the soup it is usually thick, lumpy, and not very liquidy. I think I can probably accomplish that. I search the cupboards for some salt. I am happy to discover there are multiple spices. Unfortunately, I don't know which ones taste good in pea soup.

"Ohhh, pea soup," The Captain states as he comes down off the stairs from the back of the ship. He takes off his ash-covered raincoat and hat and hangs them on a hook. "Be sure to add celery salt, garlic salt, 'n bay leaves," he adds. "Too bad we don't have a ham hock."

"You know how to cook?" Marina's face drops with shock.

"' Course. Do ya think I was always a cap'n on a ship? We all start out somewheres. I've swabbed many decks and cooked many meals in me younger days." He saunters over to me and pushes me out of the way. He fumbles around in the small galley kitchen, adding a dash of a few different spices into the pot. "The trick is keeping the pot centered on the stove in these waves." He lets out a boisterous laugh as he holds the handle of the pan in place, stirring the contents with his other hand. He has a slight bend in his knees, helping to steady his stance as the ship rocks back and forth.

"Now, tell me 'bout yer mission, son. Did you fire the lasers?"

"Yes, Captain."

"Was it 'mazin'? I always wanted to fire 'em, but I don't have clearance." I notice how child-like his expression is. He is like a big kid in a large, gruff man's body.

"I knew as soon as the volcano blew ya did it."

"You knew it would trigger the volcano, and you still let me do it?" I ask.

"I wasn't fer sure. But would ya still have done it if I told ya 'bout the dangers?"

I don't want to answer, because I knew I had to, no matter what.

"That's what I thought." The edge of his mouth grows into a smirk.

"I'm proud of ya, boy. That took some guts."

I'm not used to having anyone tell me they are proud of me, and his words catch me off-guard. I'm not quite sure how to respond.

"Lasers? Who are you people? Did you just blow up that island on purpose?" Marina's eyes nearly bug out of her head.

I almost forgot that Marina was here and that she doesn't understand what my purpose was on Thunderbird Island.

"Let's just say this young lad had a special mission, 'n he accomplished it. He just saved the world."

"Saved the world, how? Why is your pocket glowing?" Her questions begin to spew from her grey, ash-striped lips.

The Captain clicks his tongue, "Don't be askin' too many questions, las, or we'll have ta feed ya to the sharks."

Marina gulps, pursing her lips together, unsure if he is joking or not.

The Captain whistles a familiar tune as he continues to stir the peas.

"Wait, where did you hear that song, Captain?" I ask, realizing he is whistling the same tune the little music box plays from my wristband.

"Why it's the song of the sea. Sailors say it is the key that unlocks the gates to The Lost City of Atlantis."

"Really? Atlantis? Is that real?" The wheels in my head begin turning.

The Captain clicks his tongue again as he did to Marina's questions.

"Now, don't you be askin' too many questions, Sharkbait." He winks at me.

"These peas are gonna have to simmer and get soft fer a while. Why don't y'all go get cleaned up while ya wait."

"I can stir for a while, Captain. Why don't you go," I offer.

"Na, makin' ya some supper is the least I can do. Go on, now."

I pull Lan to her feet and help Marina up. "Are you sure you wouldn't like a warm shower, Marina?" I ask.

"I suppose it would be nice to wash all this ash off. Maybe just a quick one," She replies.

Lan and I decide to lay on my bunk while we wait for our turn in the shower. The tiny bed is much too small for one person, let alone two. Lan snuggles her back against me, and I wrap my arms around her to keep her from falling off the narrow bed.

"So, what did happen on the island?" She asks, with a drawn-out yawn.

I tell her all about how Con led me through the caves to the vault, and how I had to go through all the different steps to fire up the lasers, and then about the tiger. But I realize her steady breaths are heavy, and she is fast asleep in my arms. I'm unsure of how much of my story she heard, but it really doesn't matter. All I know is that she is safe and sound in my arms, and the world will hopefully be around tomorrow now so we can have more of these perfect moments.

"Shower is free." Marina pops her head into my cabin. "Oh, sorry." Her voice changes to a whisper as she realizes Lan is asleep in my arms.

Lan's body stirs, and her heavy eyes struggle to open.

"Do you want to go shower?" I whisper in her ear.

"You go first." Her sleepy voice disappears into a drunken mumble.

It takes a ninja-like maneuver to climb over her limp body in the small space of the bunk without dumping her on the floor, but I manage. I cover her with the wool blanket on the bed and take a moment to watch her coo in her sleep. I grab the clothes I hung on the hook to dry when I first got on the ship and rush to take the quickest shower of my life. I can't wait to come back to lie next to Lan.

After my shower, I scrape on the stiff, salty clothes Helen gave me and tie the shell back around my neck. I rush back to Lan. She is now taking up the entire bed and there is not a spare inch left for me to even attempt lying next to her. Instead, I decide to sit on the swaying floorboards and lay my head back on the bed next to Lan's back. Sleep overcomes my exhausted body instantly, and my nightmares are full of the dangers I encountered today. Just as I am about to get gobbled up by a lava-spewing tiger, I shout out,

"No, please.

Please."

"Peas." The Captain's voice calls.

"Mmmm, peas." Lan's voice repeats, half asleep.

We both rub the sleep out of our eyes and make our way to the rocking table where The Captain gives us both a bowl of steaming hot green soup.

"This smells delicious, thank you." Lan's eyes are suddenly wide awake.

"Yes, thank you, Captain," I add, scooping a bit onto my spoon and blowing on it momentarily before shoving it in my mouth. I clearly didn't blow long enough, and it may as well have been green lava scalding my tongue. I blow air repeatedly out of my mouth in an attempt to cool off the scorching bite. The flavor is surprisingly yummy, once my scorching taste buds are able to taste it.

"It's really good, but hot."

Lan is smart and continues blowing on her bite before she attempts to eat it.

"It's so good," she adds, blowing on another bite. "Where is Marina?" Lan asks.

"She took a bowl up ta Soarin." The Captain answers, blowing on a spoonful of his own.

"It's been a long day. I'm gonna take mine ta me quarters and go ta bed. 'Night, ya two."

"Good night. Thank you, Captain," I reply.

"No, thank you, me boy." He bows his head respectfully as he turns to head to the immaculately carved door to his quarters.

"So, how do we know if what you did worked?" Lan asks, with her mouth full of peas.

"I don't know. I guess we will have to wait and see."

"We might be waiting a long time," she giggles.

"Are we heading back to the time machine now?" Lan questions.

"I didn't ask, but I think so."

"What if the time machine is underwater, and we can't get to it? Will we be stuck here forever?" Her gold eyes flash with worry.

"I'm sure we'll find a way to get to it."

"Then, what is the plan? We go back to your time?" She asks.

"I need to check on Jax."

"I know. But then…" Her eyes look down as she swirls her spoon in her soup.

"We'll figure that out later." I hold her hand, and we eat our soup in silence.

I take our bowls to the sink as soon as we have scraped them clean. Lan helps me rinse out our bowls and the pan.

Lan's eyelids are drooping. "You look tired."

"I don't think I've ever been so tired," she replies. "I think I am going to take a quick shower and then go to bed.

"Yeah, I'm going to turn in as well. Do you need anything?" I ask.

"Nope, just to get this ash off and go to bed."

"Okay. Good night." I give her a little kiss on the forehead like we're an old married couple.

424

"Good night." She smiles back. I am not sure if it is exhaustion or worry, but something seems to be bothering her. I don't know if I should question her about it or just let her rest. I decide that maybe talking to her in the morning is a good idea, considering I can't keep my own eyes open. I stagger onto my bunk. I don't even have time to contemplate the day or the future before I'm taken over by slumber.

∞　　∞　　∞

I wake with my mind still in a hazy fog. I feel like I have been asleep for days. The boat is still swaying, but not as fiercely. I make my way out of my cabin and peek my head into the door across the hall. It is empty, but Lan and Marina's clothes and towels are hanging on the hooks.

I rush through the narrow hallway and through the kitchen and dining area to the hatch and climb up quickly. Green feathers instantly bombard my face. The sound of Con's familiar squealing is too obnoxious for my half-asleep brain.

"Good morning, Con," I say, petting his back as he lands on my arm. I am glad that he is still with us, but I worry that he left his family behind for my sake. Kind of like Lan. I search the deck and see Lan sitting by herself on a crate wrapped in a blanket, watching the bust of Scylla slice through the waves. Lan's glowing auburn tendrils of hair billowing behind her. I walk up behind her and wrap my arms around her shoulders. I feel her jump beneath my touch. Her body stiffens and then relaxes once she realizes it's me.

"Sorry, I didn't mean to startle you. I just wanted to say good morning."

"You mean afternoon," she laughs. "I was worried you weren't going to wake up."

"It's afternoon already? I guess I was really tired."

"I guess you deserve to sleep. I mean, you did save the world."

"I hope so."

"Me, too. Are you just sitting out here by yourself?" I ask.

"Yes. I heard The Captain go up in the middle of the night to relieve Soarin, and once he came down, Marina went to sleep next to him. They haven't come up yet. The waves are quite mesmerizing after a while, and Con has been keeping me company, haven't you, boy?"

Con squirms his way to her hands under her blanket and comes out, munching on a crumb.

"Oh, and he really likes the sea biscuits," she adds, ruffling his feathers. She reaches into her pocket and pulls out a biscuit and hands it to me. Con tries to steal it from her hand before I can grab it.

"Nu-uh, buddy. This one is mine," I say to him. But he just tilts his head and stares into my soul with his beady eyes. He flaps up onto my shoulder and nuzzles my neck. "Oh, alright. Just a little piece," I say, breaking off a small chunk and feeding it to him. His beak clicks repeatedly in my ear as he gobbles the biscuit.

Lan laughs. "He's hard to say no to, isn't he?"

"I can say no to him if I want to." I smile back at her, but we both know I'm lying.

A whistle comes from the open helm window and Con instantly swoops from my shoulder and flies to The Captain's shoulder. I squint to watch him pull a treat from his pocket and feed it to the bird. They both smile happily.

"I think that bird has learned how to manipulate everybody," I add with a shiver.

Lan opens her blanket, inviting me to sit with her as we snuggle below the itchy fabric.

"It's cold out, but not as cold as the first time we sailed."

"It was even colder in the woods with the snow," she points out.

"Maybe the world is fixing itself, or perhaps it just feels warmer because we aren't soaking wet."

426

"I know whatever you did with those lasers is working." She smiles. "I'm not sure how I know; I just know."

"Yeah, I think so, too." I agree. The shell, which I tied back around my neck last night after my shower, begins to glow warmly against my chest.

I place my fingers around the smooth ridges of the shell.

"I want you to have this," I say, untying the knot behind my neck. I slip the strands of leather around Lan's neck. As soon as the shell touches her neck it stops glowing.

"I can't. It only works for you." She tries to pull it from her neck. I place my hand on it and hold it to her chest. The shell fills with light and warmth again under my hands.

"Then, I guess you better stay close to me." I tie the leather tightly at the back of her neck. "Besides, it already served its purpose for me. It guided me to the vault. Ever since then, it only seems to light as more of a reminder so that I don't forget my purpose. And now, I don't need it. I only need you." Fire floods my emotions and the magnetic pull toward Lan is even stronger than ever before. My lips meet hers, and I feel I won't be able to pull away.

Ding! Ding!

The ringing of the ship's bell jerks us apart. My frantic eyes search the horizon for pirates, a storm, or other danger. Instead, I am greeted with The Captain's boisterous laugh, intermingling with Con's gleeful caws. As The Captain's laugh rolls to a stop, he points his two fingers at his eyes and then at me and Lan, signaling that he is watching us.

"Oh, he's worse than Einstein," Lan's face flushes.

"Only a few more hours 'til we arrive." The Captain's words carry on the whipping wind.

> *But what will Great Granddad's estate look like when we get there?*
> *Will it be completely submerged underwater?*

Chapter 44

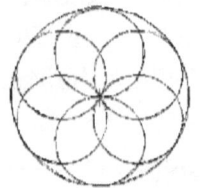

A Series of Goodbyes

The afternoon is full of eating, laughing, watching the waves, and The Captain even joins us for a round of cards. Boy, is he the world's biggest cheater! It is nice to enjoy spending time with Soarin, Marina, and The Captain, knowing that Lan and I will soon be leaving them behind, or is it ahead? At least, I hope we can. Who knows, maybe we will be stuck here forever, and these folks are our new family. I try to imagine a life at sea and going on adventures, perhaps finding Atlantis? It doesn't sound too bad. Especially on a beautiful day like today. The wind is blowing, but not biting. If the sun could shine through the thick afghan of clouds, it would feel somewhat pleasant. The angry towers of waves have calmed to what I would imagine would be gnarly surfing waves if I knew how to surf. Who knows, maybe one day I'll learn.

"Lettin' go!" Soarin's voice shouts as he pushes the lever down on the motor to let down the heavy anchor.

"Already?" I ask, searching the distant white-capped waves.

And then I see it. Great Granddad's house sits on a lone island, which I know used to be a mountaintop. A glimmering of sunlight peeks between an opening of thinning clouds just long enough to cast a ray of light, of hope, to glint off the cupula, transforming it into a golden dome. The two sturdy towers hold firm on both sides of the porch, sitting nervously about ten feet away from the taunting tides. As if the ocean itself is breathing in and out, I watch the tide wash closer to the estate and then further away in a steady pattern.

Lan stands at my side as we bask in its glory.

"Wow!" It truly is magnificent. "I would be fine living there forever. If it weren't surrounded by all this water," she smirks.

"Come on, let's get the bags." I pull her toward the hatch.

We climb down with eagerness, and I run to my cabin. I check in the pockets of the backpack and find where I secured the keyring for the estate.

"Few, they are still there." I toss the keyring in the air and catch it with a smile. I place it back into the front pocket. I proceed to check and make sure I have the journals and that they are secure in the satchel. My fingers scroll over the etchings of the metal box. I pull it out to gaze at its wonder.

"Should I leave this here with The Captain? He did a good job of protecting it before?" I ask for Lan's advice. "Or do we take it with us to protect it?" I bite my lip in contemplation.

"Well, the island is…. gone." She reminds me.

"That is true. But I'm sure The Captain can get it back to Great Granddad or knows of another location to keep it safe. Maybe we should ask him."

Lan nods in agreement.

I really don't want the responsibility of keeping the box and the serum safe. It would be one less thing to worry about if The Captain could hold on to it for me. I put it back in the backpack to bring it up to The Captain.

"We got everything?" I ask Lan.

She nods, taking the satchel from me and placing it over her shoulder.

We dart down the hall, scramble up the ladder, and squeeze out of the hatch to the deck. Soarin is standing with his arm around Marina's waist. They look like a beautiful couple already as Marina lays her head on his muscular upper arm.

Soarin clears his throat and states, "I guess this is goodbye. It has been a pleasure sailing with you." He reaches out his rough hand for me to shake. His grip is firm, and his grasp lingers longer than expected. "Thank you for getting me sailing again and especially for bringing me and Marina together." His gaze leaves my face, and he looks longingly at Marina. She melts into him, and her cheeks flush.

"I'm terrible at goodbyes." Marina's eyes begin to flood as she looks at Lan. Both girls wrap their arms around each other in an embrace.

"Think of this as a new beginning. I think you are going to be perfectly happy now," Lan whispers into Marina's ear.

Marina's grin lights up her face. She knows Lan is right. She is just beginning her new life with Soarin.

"I truly wish you two a life full of happiness," I say as Marina attacks my neck next. I pat her back awkwardly and look at Lan. I wasn't expecting a hug. Lan just sniggers at my discomfort. Thankfully The Captain rescues me.

"Time ta take these two back." The Captain puts his heavy hand on my shoulder. Con flitters around my head and then lands next to The Captain's gruff grasp.

"Ya sure ya want ta go back ta Doc's house? The weather does look like it's improvin', but we won't know for a while if what ya did was enough. Yer more than welcome to sail with us ya know." The Captain's dark eyes suddenly seem brighter and full of care.

"I need to go back. My little brother needs me." My sincerity quivers in my voice.

"But how will ya get back ta him? Wait, ya didn't come from the cellar, did ya?" The Captain looks over at Soarin and Marina's curious faces, and he pulls me aside.

"Doc told me he had a machine in the basement that can take 'im to different places, different times. But I just thought his brilliant mind was goin' a bit, *woo-woo*, ya know?" Con calls back to the *woo-woo* sound The Captain made in a mimicking manner.

"It's real, and it works. Or at least it did. Who knows now? The cellar flooded as soon as we got here, so we aren't sure if we can even get down to it now."

"Did you use the cellar pumps?"

"There are pumps?"

"Haha! Let's go see what we can do." The Captain slaps me on the back, nearly knocking the wind from my lungs.

"Well, take one last look at the face that saved the world," The Captain says to Soarin and Marina. They both look at each other with perplexed expressions taking over their faces.

"I'm happy to take them, Captain," Soarin offers as he sees The Captain begin to climb over the edge of the ship.

"Thank ya, but I think it's best if I take 'em." The wrinkles around his eyes scrunch together.

Soarin nods his head. "Best of luck."

"You, too," I respond as I help Lan climb over the edge of the ship to the rope ladder.

I watch Marina bury her head in Soarin's chest as my head lowers beneath the rails.

The Captain and I lower the rowboat down into the waves. I place my open hand on the worn wood of the ship one last time.

"Thank you for the ride, Scylla," I whisper to the beautiful schooner ship, patting my hand against her wood railing. "It's been a great adventure."

I jump down into the rowboat and pick up the one oar, remembering that I had lost the other one to the angry volcanic waves.

"I'll be rowin'" The Captain states, reaching out for the oar.

"No, Captain. I'll row."

"It's the least I can do fer the chosen one. I waited my entire life to meet ya. Ya saved the world. Now sit back and let me row ya home." He steals the oar from my hands. I really can't argue with The Captain. Lan and I huddle together on the bench and watch The Captain. His wiry whiskers catch the spritzing spray like a sponge. He rows our little boat forward with such pride as if this is his purpose in life coming to pass. I look over my shoulder and watch the magnificent serpent heads sprawling gloriously toward the sky disappear into the cottony clouds.

"Thank you, Captain," I say as the metal of our boat scrapes across the rocks and dirt.

I help Lan step out of the boat. The Captain tosses me the rope.

"Tie me on. I'll come in 'n help ya pump out the water."

"Thank you," Lan adds.

I tie the rope of the rowboat around one of the wind-worn pillars of the porch. The steps bow beneath my feet as I walk up them to the still-impressive front door. I turn my backpack around to my chest and dig out the ring of keys. Con circles around my head. The Captain and Lan join me at my sides as the lock clicks open. The door has swollen into place with moisture, but I lean my shoulder into it and thrust my weight forward. The door reluctantly budges free from its frame and swings open to reveal the comforting sight of the entryway. The grand staircase greets me like an old friend. Although the musty odor is relentless, I breathe in a refreshing breath of familiarity.

I'm home.

Bubbling with Giddiness, Lan and I race up the stairs. We pant at the top landing with smiles as wide as the Grand Canyon as we wait for The Captain to catch up. I fumble the skeleton key into the hidden lock in the wall panel and open it to reveal the hidden staircase to the observatory. The Captain follows us up the narrow, rickety staircase, his breath gasping behind us.

"You alright, Captain?" I ask, helping him up the last step.

"Scylla doesn't 'ave quite this many steps," he wheezes. His whiskers drop to his chest as he gazes around the observatory. "Why, the last time I was up here was at our first SOS meetin'." He shakes his head. "That was many years ago." He strokes his grey-streaked beard with wrinkled, leathery fingers.

"This place feels just like I'm back on me ship." He staggers over to stroke the beautifully stained wood of the pirate wheel used to magnify the glass. He stares out of the panoramic windows. Dirt and grime paint a layer of obscurity on the outside of the panes, but the view of the water in all directions is still immaculate.

Con lets out a chirp as he pecks at the coin in my pocket.

"Oh, thanks, buddy. I almost forgot. This belongs to you, Captain, and you can't say no this time.

Oz told me to give it to you." I pull the lucky coin from my pocket and hold it out to The Captain. He just stares down at the coin. Con flaps his wings wildly as if to say he is happy to take it. I take a step forward, place the coin in The Captain's hand, and secure his fist closed with my other hand. I watch as his lips purse together tightly. I can't tell if he is trying not to cry or holding back rebutting words.

"Thanks." He sniffs as he places the coin in the pocket of his shirt, right next to his heart.

"Well then, I thought we were here to get to the cellar." He wipes his nose and heads to a lever on the wall. "This is the lever for the pumps. It should work like the pumps on a submarine and have the cellar pumped out in no time."

"Pumps? All we had to do was turn on the pumps?" The color drains from Lan's face as she looks straight at me.

"Ya, I wish I would have known that, too." I give her a sideways glance as I watch The Captain press the lever down. The house gives a quick rumble and then fills with silence once again.

"Was that it?" Lan asks.

I drop to the middle of the floor, rattling the keyring, searching for the one with the matching symbol on the door in the floorboards. I find it, shove it into the lock, and twist. Lan helps me pull the door open, and a gurgle of water bubbles up over the edges of the floor. We all hold our breath and wait a moment for the water to recede, but the puddle on the floor around the door is growing.

"I don't think the pumps are working," Lan points out.

"I think Dr. Gardener said somethin' 'bout maybe needing ta secure the cellar walls first or somethin' like that. But I don't know which lever or button does that."

I search frantically for Great Granddad's journals in the satchel at Lan's side and pull them out.

"Help me look through these for something that might help us drain the cellar." I toss The Captain a journal. My fingers flip through the pages of the one in my hands with great urgency.

"Ah-ha! I think this is it," he shouts with a gleeful jump, shoving the open page under my nose. Sure enough, the pages show how the pump in the cellar works and, more importantly, which lever to pull to drop the metal walls all around the cellar to seal out the cracks. The cellar can become a metal vault, just like the one in Thunderbird Mountain.

"Of course," I cry. Con joins in with my burst of excitement. I dash to the indicated lever drawn in the picture and use my body weight to push it down toward the floor. A deep bellowing, grinding shakes the floorboards, followed by a shattering *THUMP!*

"Okay, let's try the pump lever again," I suggest.

Lan leaps over to the lever, pulls it back up, and jumps on it to push it down again. The same rumbling we heard before echoes below us, but this time, instead of stopping suddenly, it continues. We all burst into cheers as if we just saved the world again as we see the water drop below the trapdoor in the floor.

"It's working!" I hug Lan and swing her around in a circle. I grab the journals and place them back into the backpack on my back. I see the metal box still buried inside. I wrap my fingers around it and pull it out. We have a few minutes to wait before all the water is drained from the cellar, so I could ask The Captain what I should do with the box. The metal seems to vibrate with electricity in my grasp at my mental decision.

"Will you please keep the box safe for me, Captain?" I ask, doubting my decision the moment the words leak from my lips.

"I thought you were ta take it." The Captain's eyebrows bend toward the bridge of his crooked, sun-spotted nose.

"I don't know what I am supposed to do with it other than keep it safe and out of Elementerprise's hands. I don't have anywhere safe to keep it, and I thought maybe you might have an idea of a safe place to protect it for me." I raise the box and place it in The Captain's hands. Lan moves to my side, and as she does, the shell I tied around her neck begins to glow brightly, rising up from her chest toward the now glowing metal box. Warmth and light radiate from the grooves of the etched metal, surging energy in through the tattoo on my arm and jolt through my entire body. The metal box is bound to my fingers with a miraculous magnetic force. I can't let go of the box if I wanted to. The emanating glow reflects in The Captain's eyes and off his crooked teeth.

"I think we all can see who the box belongs to." The Captain pushes the box closer to me, and he removes his hands with ease. Still unable to remove my fingers, the answer is clear. The box and the shell have shown me that I am the keeper and protector of the box. As soon as revelation resonates through my body, the glowing power ceases, and the box and the shell return to their natural state. I place the sacred box back inside my backpack with great care.

I must keep the box and the serum safe. I know it is up to me now.

"It looks like the staircase has drained," Lan reveals.

I fasten my backpack and swing it onto my back. My head and body swirl as a result of the energy no longer being pulsed through my veins from the box. I take a breath and wait for the observatory to steady.

"After you," I say to The Captain.

His broad shoulders disappear down past the trapdoor. Lan enters the staircase next, and I follow her down.

I slowly step down into about four inches of water remaining on the cellar ground. Water drips and continues to pour off every surface in the cellar. The water hose floats on the surface of the water around our ankles like an anaconda. Wooden tools and odds and ends bob in the water nearby, rushing toward the multiple holes where the water continues to get pumped out.

"Let's see if we can get the generator working." I use my hand to wipe off the puddle left on top of the monstrous machine. I turn the wheel to open the drum as water comes rushing out.

"I guess we don't need to add any water." I try to make light of our soggy situation.

"Will it still light?" Lan asks. "The coals are soaked." She picks up one of the pieces of coal and mushes it in her hand like black clay.

"There is only one way to find out." I find my wristband in my bag, which I am grateful I remembered to find on the ship's deck, and I strap it over my tattoo. Remembering that I spilled most of the Einsteinium on the ship, I wince.

"I just hope this will be enough," I say, sliding the little vial from its strap and looking bleakly at the minuscule amount remaining. I don't want to waste the little bit I have, so I wait for the rest of the water to drain out from the ground. I grab a push-broom from the other side of the cellar and use it to push the remaining puddles away from the ground around the bottom of the time machine. I lean the broom against the wall, feeling slightly better being able to see enough ground where I can now sprinkle the elements. Hoping that the wet ground won't be an issue, I dump out the Einsteinium, the Europium, the Lanthanum, and the Neodymium. I know that the next step is to shovel fresh coal into the drum. There isn't any fresh coal, just the remaining black gunk caked on the lava rocks layering the bottom of the inside pan.

"Ummm, we need coal." I look around the room. There are a few black clumps scattered around the ground. We all grab as much as we can find and toss it into the drum like we are baking mud pies. With my black hands, I swing the door closed and twist the wheel. I set the date and time to when Lan and I left without even needing to refer to the note I made in the journal. I turn on the boiler and hold my breath as water sputters from all directions. It seems to die with one last spit. I try turning it on again. I can hear water and air pushing through the large metal pipes, and this time, after a few coughs, it ignites. Relief washes over me as I watch the temperature gauge begin to climb. I look at Lan and The Captain; they also seem relieved and full of adrenaline. Our chests pump with excitement. The needle on the gauge quivers much more slowly than it normally does. We should have already reached the needed 212 degrees, but it is still struggling to climb.

"Come on! Come on!" I chant. Con dives under The Captain's raincoat to hide, as if the machine may blow any second.

I wring my hands with anticipation.

Finally, the red button flashes and the buzzer begins to squeal. In response, Con shrieks and flies out from under The Captain's coat and flaps around in a panic.

"It's a'ight, Con. Come here. I'll keep ya safe." The Captain plucks the pinging green bird from the air and holds him tightly between his hands as I press the blinking red button. We all watch as the red specks and a bit of mud fly into the machine. I hold my breath.

The blue button begins to flash.

"Yes!" I cheer.

Con pokes his little head out between The Captain's fingers to see what I could possibly be happy about in this chaos. I can't help but laugh. Lan reaches her hand up to press the blue button and this one really makes me worried. I begin to pray.

"Please let there be enough, please!" I squeeze my eyes closed, too afraid to watch. I know that most of the Einsteinium was spilled on the ship.

I listen to the whooshing, sucking sounds and peek one eye open to watch the small amount of blue disappear into the machine. "Please!"

Euphoria erupts into the cellar as a yellow flashing light reflects off Lan's relieved face. Her arms flail around my neck, and her lips attack my cheek. We both reach up and press the yellow button together and squeal as the Lanthanum flies into the machine. The yellow light changes to purple, and we press the button with pure delight. The overwhelming hum, blaring silver light, and ear-piercing alarm are too much for Con. He escapes from The Captain's hands, and he whizzes up the stairs.

"Bye, Con. I will miss you, buddy." My words flutter after him, carrying with them, a little piece of my heart.

"Bye, Con." Lan's lips form a pout. "It's a shame he doesn't want to come with us."

"I'll take care of 'im, don't ya worry," the Captain responds.

And then it hits me like a load of bricks. I have to say goodbye to The Captain.

Why has my life turned into a series of goodbyes?
I meet incredible people, just to turn around and leave
them.

My blurry eyes lock onto The Captain's. He reaches his hand out to shake mine. I grab onto it but lean in for a full-forced hug. I wrap my other arm around him and don't want to let go.

"I will miss you the most. Thank you for everything, Captain."

The blur in my eyes becomes a flood.

"It's Hurley, son." His ungrasped arm wraps around me like a security blanket.

"My family doesn't call me Cap'n; they call me Hurley."

"Thank you, Hurley." My emotion begins to boil hot in my throat.

Lan jumps into our hug. Hurley and I let go of our handshake and use those arms to envelop her in our embrace.

"You want to come with us?" I ask Hurley.

"I can't leave me Scylla, and Soarin and his girl will be wonderin' what happened to me. You two take care of yourselves, though, ya hear? And that's an order."

"We will. Goodbye," Lan barely manages to squeak.

"Goodbye, las." Hurley kisses the top of her head. He then breaks away, clears his throat, and wipes at his eyes.

"Must've got some coal dust in me eyes."

Lan and I puff a spout of a laugh as we watch Hurley, the tough sea captain, cover up his big-hearted emotions.

I unstrap the little parts to the music box on my wristband and assemble it through watering eyes. I wind the box and allow the melody to plink through the cellar.

The familiar tune causes one side of Hurley's lips to curl up into a smile. He purses his lips together and whistles along. As the melody finishes, the latch opens, and the Terbium key slides into my awaiting hand.

"Well, if that's the key to The Lost City of Atlantis, I expect ya to come back to get me 'fore ya go there." He winks.

"I promise. Besides, I will need a ship, and a Captain, for that adventure."

We exchange smiles, adding to the warmth growing in the cellar.

Lan and I secure the backpack and satchels around our backs.

"Are you ready?" I ask Lan, holding the key toward the key slot.

She nods. We wrap our inside arms around each other's backs and clasp the key between our intertwined fingers of our outer arms.

"On three."

She nods.

"One...

Two...

Three!"

Chapter 45

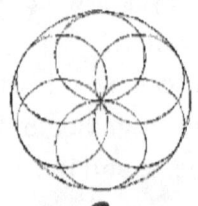

Home

"Lan? Are you okay?" I finally moan after the pain becomes tolerable.

"Yep, you?" Her voice echoes in the darkness, soothing the ringing in my ears.

It takes all the energy I have to reach up and flick the light on my wristband. As the column of light pans around us, we see that the cellar is just as it was: dry and the way we left it in my time. Lan rolls over to be at my side, and we lie with our chests heaving for air as we stare up at the dust dancing through the beam of light.

"Dameon? Son? You down there?" My dad's voice echoes from the top of the staircase.

Instantly pumped with adrenaline, I shove Lan over to hide her in the shadows in the corner of the cellar. I throw my backpack down in front of her body, hunched down as small as she can get. If Dad looks over here, there is no way he won't see her.

"Uh, yah, Dad. I'm coming."

I whisper to Lan. "I'll be back for you."

She nods.

I run toward the steps and plow into my Dad.

"Oooof, sorry," I blurt, trying to block the bottom of the staircase so my Dad can't step down off the last step.

"I just came down here looking for you, and you weren't here. I don't want you down here!" Dad's face contorts with anger, glowing in the narrow pillar of light coming from my wrist.

"And why didn't you just turn on the hanging light?" He asks with a snippy tone.

"Oh, ummm, the bulb burned out. I was just exploring one of the tunnels down here."

"I don't want you going into any tunnels. I'm sure they're not safe. I will get some of my guys down here to check them out and seal them up properly."

"Uhh, don't worry about that, Dad. I can seal them up. There isn't anything down them anyway. I already checked."

"No! I don't want you down here. Not after what happened to…" Dad stops mid-sentence, not wanting to say Jaxson, but it's too late. I already know. I look down at the rain boots on my feet. Realizing I probably look really bizarre in these old clothes, and I hope Dad doesn't notice. We both just stand here, drowning in the silence.

"So, you're okay? Just did some exploring around the house today?"

"Yep, pretty much," I lie.

"Is that a new watch? I don't think I've seen that one." He points to the wristband, clearly trying to change the heavy disposition swelling around us.

I look down and realize it has slid around my arm slightly, and a sliver of my tattoo is showing. I jerk it back into place nervously to hide my new mark.

"Oh, ya. I think it was Great Granddad's. I found it down here. Is it okay if I keep it?"

"Sure. I think you two would have had a lot in common. You would have really liked him. He was always tinkering around." Dad says as he turns to head back up the stairs to the observatory.

I know.
And is my Dad actually saying nice things about Great Granddad again?
He really must be trying to lighten the mood.

441

"I mean, wow! Just look at this room. In all my years here as a kid, I never once came up here. It's probably because Granddad kept it hidden by a secret panel door. How in the world did you find it anyway?" Dad asks, gawking out the massive, bayed windows of the observatory.

"Just poking around," I shrug.

Dad goes to turn the pirate wheel.

"Uh, I wouldn't touch that if I were you!" I lunge toward him to stop his hand from touching the wheel.

"There are all sorts of contraptions and things up here, but I think they might be broken, and I'm not sure how safe they are. I'm eager to see how they all work, but I don't want you breaking them further, you know…" I scramble to think of something to say that will keep Dad out of here.

Dad's hands shoot up in a surrendering gesture. "You're probably right. Knowing him, this room is probably booby-trapped." Dad winks at me like I'm five years old.

"But, I want the first tour after you figure it all out, okay?"

"Absolutely. So, you'll let me come up here to tinker? Can we keep it a secret from Mom for now? I don't want her coming up here to clean and messing things up, you know?"

"I totally understand," Dad laughs. "This can be your tinker-space for now, but no going down to the cellar. And just know that if we end up moving here, this is going to be my office," he says with a smile, gazing out at the incredible view.

"Deal. Thanks, Dad.

So, how is Jaxson?"

The long pause is torture.

"Well, I'm just going to treat you like a man and tell you what the doctors told us today."

Suddenly the somber, black curtain has dropped again. Dad looks for a place to sit and realizes there isn't anywhere, so he begins pacing.

"He isn't responding, at all. They are worried his body is shutting down, and he might not wake up." The veins in Dad's eyes pulse red, and they fill with tears despite him doing everything he can to keep them from crying in front of me. "I came to ask you if you want to come with me to see him tonight. They said it might be a good idea for all of us to spend as much time with him as we can."

A giant vacuum sucks all the air from the room, and I suddenly can't breathe. My heart shatters with physical pain, like I'm having a heart attack. I can't form words to respond to Dad. I can't think clearly. The world around me collapses. My legs give out underneath me, and my body slumps down to the floorboards. My shoulders shake with uncontrollable sobs. Dad rushes to my side and squats down next to me, placing his hand on my back.

"I'm not giving up. He is going to pull through. I know he is. I just wanted to let you know the situation before we go because I don't think Mom can handle seeing you like this." My lungs squeeze and I wipe away the snot dripping down my upper lip with my shirt.

"Son, look at me." Dad lifts my quivering chin, and I raise my eyes to look into his. They are like two dark storming seas. "It's going to be alright. No matter what happens, it will be okay."

Okay? How will this be, okay?

"What do you say you take a quick shower and get cleaned up." He says, noticing my odd clothes and hands smothered in black gunk. "Then, we will head out as soon as you're ready, okay? I'll even find somewhere to grab you a burger and fries on the way, alright?"

He says that as if fast food is magically going to make me feel better.

"Come on." He grabs my hands and helps me to my feet. He realizes his mistake after he looks down at his now grimy hands. "Maybe I should clean up a bit, too, huh?" He forces a smile.

I force a slight nod. That is all I can do.

I shower and get dressed in a blur. Everything feels numb, my mind, my body, everything.

> *What was the point of saving the world if I can't even save my little brother?*
> *Hold up. What if I can save Jaxson? I have the serum.*

"Dameon, you ready to go?" Dad's voice yells up from the entryway.

"Almost, just a minute," I shout, pulling on clean socks – who knew dry cotton socks could feel so good? I go to grab my wristband I had set down on my nightstand to get the music box key I need to open the metal box.

> *Wait, The Terbium key. I never found it after we came back. It must still be in the cellar with Lan.*

I dash to the landing at the top of the stairs, where I see a freshly showered Dad. The familiar smell of his aftershave wafts up the staircase.

"I'll be right down. I just need to go get something I want to bring for Jaxson," I say with probably too much enthusiasm than I should have. I don't want Dad getting suspicious. I run to the secret panel still cracked open along the wall, slide it open wide enough for me to squeeze through, and dash up, two stairs at a time. I slide on my way to the trapdoor, still open in the middle of the observatory floor, and jump down in. I force myself to slow down

444

enough to make sure I don't topple forward down the steps to the cellar.

"Lan?" I whisper, pulling on the string above my head to turn on the hanging lightbulb, remembering how I lied to Dad and said it was burned out.

Lan explodes from the same corner where I left her. She knocks me over in a hug. Her face is tear-stained, and her eyes are red and puffy.

"I heard," she sniffs. "I climbed up the stairs so I could hear your conversation with your Dad. I'm so sorry." She buries her head in my chest.

"It's okay." My fingers get tangled in her windblown red web of hair.

"I'm going to give Jaxson the serum. I need to hurry. My Dad is waiting for me."

I roll around her to search the ground for The Terbium key before I forget. Luckily, I see it straight away, glinting in the light of the dangling bulb. I grab it and place it in my pocket. Then, I reach for my backpack in the corner of the cellar, open the flap, and pull out the metal box. I insert the little music box key.

"Okay, what was the order of the maze again?" I ask Lan, not wanting to waste time searching through the journals for the order of the pictures in the prophecy.

"I know it was the turtle, then the swirling waters," I say, sliding the key through the maze of etched images.

"That one, the plant growing on the water," Lan points out. "Then that one."

"Then the fork-tongued snake," I continue, maneuvering the key. "The balance scale, and the two paths," I continue.

"And last, the infinity symbol," Lan and I say simultaneously as I slide the key in the figure-eight motion. Before I get around the last loop, my wrist instantly begins burning. This time, I know what I need to do. I take out the little key and secure it in my pocket. I place the tattooed symbol on my wrist over the matching symbol etched in metal. Heat pumps through my arm as it connects with the box, and a

445

pulse shoots through me like electricity. Every crease in the box begins to glimmer with red, radiating light as the lid of the box pops open. I lift the lid and stare down at the two remaining cradled syringes.

"I don't know if this is a good idea or not. What if it doesn't work and I waste one for nothing? What if Jaxson still doesn't make it? What if he does make it, and he hates me for the rest of his life because he becomes some crazed animal or something?"

"Don't you want to save your little brother? If you don't give him the serum, I will." She grabs one of the syringes from the dark protecting foam.

"You are right. I need to try. Give me that. I don't think I can explain you to my Dad right now. I'm sorry. I need to go to the hospital on my own. I will be back as soon as I can. Until then, feel free to shower, find some clothes, and eat whatever is in the kitchen."

"I wish I could come with you." Her eyes chase mine from side to side. "But, since I can't, a hot shower and a kitchen full of food sound like I might be able to survive here alone." Her smiling lips kiss mine. "Now go save your brother."

She doesn't need to tell me twice.

The car ride is brutally long and painfully silent. It gives me too much time to get entangled in my doubting web of thoughts. The plot of a book I had to read in school keeps plaguing me, *Tuck Everlasting*. In the story, the young girl wants to be able to live a normal life and decides not to drink from an everlasting spring. I can't help but think how the girl ultimately got to choose her fate.

Will this serum make us live forever?
Will Jaxson resent me for not letting him choose whether
or not he gets the serum?
Maybe I should wait to see if he gets better on his own.
I don't want to take his choice of living a normal life away
from him.

The thoughts storm through my head like a hurricane, contemplating if I am doing the right thing. Luckily, once we get closer to the city where the hospital is located, Dad makes good on his promise and stops to get me some food. The smell as we approach the drive-through is like heaven. You don't realize how much you miss things such as greasy fries until you haven't had them in a while. Or maybe my body really is more ravenously hungry after having the serum. Maybe this is why Lan enjoys food so much. Either way, I devour the food almost as quickly as Dad hands it to me.

"Wow, you must be growing. Didn't you eat lunch while I was gone?" Dad asks.

"Mmmmm, this just tastes so good," I mumble with my mouth overflowing.

"Oh, to have the metabolism of a teenager again." Dad chuckles as we pull into the gated parking lot. Dad shows his visitor's pass to the parking attendant, who then presses the button to raise the long arm. Dad doesn't even get the car into park before I am out of the car, stretching my cramped legs and ready to get to Jaxson. Dad does his best to keep up with me, but I have to wait on him at the hospital door because he has the badge, and they won't let me in without him.

As soon as we get to Jaxson's room, I see Mom's exhausted face. She looks like she hasn't eaten or showered in days, almost like she needs to be the one hooked up to all the machines. And then, I see Jaxson. His skin looks yellow and fake, like he is made of wax. The nauseating hospital smells flood my nose, and the heavy fast food suddenly doesn't sit well in my stomach. Maybe it is just the dizzying contemplation of the syringe weighing me down from inside my pocket.

"Hi, Mom. It is so good to see you." I wrap my arms around her frail, shivering body. Her eyes are bloodshot and sunken.

"Hey, Jax. I'm here for you, buddy." I clasp my fingers around his cold, chubby fingers.

"Can I maybe have a few minutes alone with him?" I ask my Mom and Dad. "Why don't you take a break and get something to eat, Mom. Please?"

Mom doesn't respond. She just stares at Jaxson's porcelain face.

"I think that's a great idea. Let's go get you a snack and give Dameon a few minutes alone with his brother. It will be good for both of you." Dad helps Mom to her shaking legs.

I can tell Mom wants to protest, but either she is too tired, or maybe she realizes Dad is right.

Dad nods at me and guides Mom to the door.

"We'll be back in a bit, son." His eyes are swimming. I can tell he doesn't want to leave either.

"Thank you." I choke back my own tears.

Seeing Jax like this and knowing that if I don't do something, he will most likely die, is so much harder than I thought it would be. I jump to the heavy hospital room door and close it as quietly as I can. Then, I leap back to Jaxson's side. I sit in the chair next to his bed, still warm from Mom's body heat.

"Hey, Jax. We don't have a lot of time. I have something for you that can help you, but I want it to be your decision, not mine. Please wake up. Give me a sign that you want me to help you. I don't really know how it will affect you. It might make you... different. But you won't be alone. I've had the serum, too.

Squeeze my hand or something.

I just... PLEASE," I beg, as tears leak from my eyes.

BEEEEEEEEEEEEEEEP.

I watch as the heart rate monitor flatlines.

"No!"

I rip the syringe from my pocket, knowing that the nurses will most likely be here any second, and I stab it into Jaxson's chest. But the continuous *BEEEEEEEEEEEEEEP* lingers. I toss the syringe in the trash, bury it in some paper towels, and open the door to the hallway.

"Help! Please! My brother…" I can't even get the words out through my bawling.

Two nurses push me out of the room and close the door, leaving me in the hallway to sob.

"Code blue, room 252. Code blue, room 252." The overhead announcement stabs at my heart as my back sinks down the wall.

I watch as two more nurses run toward the room. The male nurse is pushing the crash cart. The female stops to ask me some questions, but her words don't make sense. I see her lips moving, but it is like she is speaking in a different language that my raging brain can't comprehend. She tries to get me to stand and move to a different area, but I can't move. I refuse to move from this spot until I know that Jaxson is going to be alright.

I see Mom and Dad running toward the door, but the nurse by my side jumps to embrace Mom and stops her from opening the closed door. The look on Mom's face is something I will never forget. Total agony expels from every wrinkle, from every pore. It will haunt me for the rest of my life. Her silent screams and gasping for air are the worst sounds a child will ever hear. Dad takes over for the nurse, and he holds Mom up. Mom wraps her arms around his neck and collapses into him. If I thought Mom's broken-hearted face was gut-wrenching, Dad's is even worse. I am forced to look away from them, and my eyes drop down to the white square tiles on the floor. I can't handle seeing them like this. Jaxson's doctor comes barreling down the hallway and bursts past us like we aren't even here. But as soon as he opens the door, I hear the angelic voice of one of the nurses.

"He's stable and he's awake!"

Mom's head whips around faster than a bullet. She heard it, too. She erupts from Dad's arms, forces the door to the room open, and bursts in. I am right at her heels.

"Mom? Dad?" Jaxson's little squeaky voice is warm ambrosia for my senses.

"Jax!" I shout when I see his cheeks filling with color.

"Eon!" His face lights up.

The biggest, longest family hug in the history of family hugs ensues, and the doctors and nurses are forced to wait. But none of us want to let go.

"We need to run some tests." The doctor's voice brashly interrupts our moment.

"You are welcome to stay, but you need to let us do our work," he adds.

Dad pulls us back from Jaxson's bedside, allowing a nurse to draw some blood.

"Ow, stop it." Jaxson puts up quite a protest, and the other two nurses are forced to hold him down.

"Wow, I've never seen a patient emerge from a coma with so much strength." The doctor's raised eyebrows show that he is very impressed.

It worked.

Every fiber of my body zings with warmth.

The serum worked, and Jaxson is going to be okay.

Chapter 46

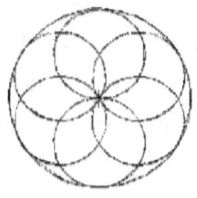

Secrets

J hear the sound of coffee streaming from the coffeemaker and then the aroma floods my nose. I sit up and free myself from the fluffy nest of bleached white sheets and blankets. Rubbing my eyes, I proceed to stretch my arms out wide in an intense yawn.

"Sorry to wake you so early, son, but I want to get back over to the hospital."

Oh yah, I remember they wouldn't let me and Dad stay in Jaxson's room with him because he is only allowed one overnight visitor, and well… Mom will obviously win that fight every time. So, Dad and I stayed as long as we could there before they kicked us out. We found this hotel across the street so we could get back to him first thing this morning.

"I can't believe that yesterday, Jaxson was fighting for his life and today they said he might get to come home. He truly is a medical miracle. Mom said the doctors have run every test and scan imaginable, and he is in perfect health. They can't explain it. They've moved him to a regular room and they want to keep him one more day to observe him, but Jaxson is getting a little feisty and says he just wants to go home." Dad laughs with excitement as he gulps his coffee. His face turns red, and he winces as he sticks his scalded tongue out of his mouth like an injured dog. "You want to come over with me now, or you can shower and walk across the street in a bit on your own if you would rather. We have the hotel room until tomorrow just in case they do make him stay one more night." Dad is talking a hundred miles per minute. He is even more excited now than when he heard he inherited Great Granddad's estate and company.

I sit up and realize I slept in my clothes.

"Looks like I'm already dressed. Can you wait long enough for me to use the bathroom?" I ask.

"Only if you hurry," Dad smirks.

I jump out of bed and scurry to use the restroom and rinse out my mouth.

Dad is waiting outside the bathroom door, handing me my shoes.

Sheesh, he is excited.

"I'll get you some breakfast at the hospital cafeteria, okay?" He asks, opening the door to a long corridor lined with brightly colored carpet smothered in geometric designs.

"Sounds good," I reply. This time, I am the one trying to stay caught up with Dad. We head to cross the street on foot. I guess getting in the car, trying to cross the street, and finding a place to park would take too much time. Dad doesn't even take the time to look before he darts into the busy road. He just runs for it. Cars blast their horns next to us as they slam on their breaks, but Dad's smiling face continues across.

I raise my hands up and do my best to apologize to the frantic drivers for my crazy Dad's behavior. Luckily, we make it to the hospital, and thankfully, we do not need a stretcher.

"My wife said my son has been moved to room 137." Dad flashes his visitor badge to the front desk. They make him sign in, which he does faster than a doctor, and they point us in the right direction.

"Jaxson! Look at you," Dad barks when he sees Jaxson walking down the hall in his gown, with Mom at his side. Jaxson runs to Dad and leaps into his arms. Dad spins him around with his gown flapping freely in the back, flashing Jaxson's cheeks to everyone in the hallway. Mom is mortified and chases them in the circle, failing to cover his backside. Jaxson's giggles are infectious, and I can't hold in the laughter bubbling inside me. It feels so good to laugh that it turns into a roar, and before we know it, we all have tears streaming down our cheeks. But this time, it's from pent-up laughter.

"Laughter truly is the best medicine," Mom states, wiping her cheeks.

As soon as Dad puts Jaxson back on the ground, he shuffles his little feet over to me and holds my hand. The smile on his face turns me into putty.

"This is my new room, but not for long," Jaxson says, walking through an open doorway and jumping up onto the adjustable bed. Using the remote attached to the bedframe, he flips on the television attached to the wall directly in front of him. He then pushes more buttons on the remote to adjust his bed in every position possible. In fact, I'm pretty sure he stops it in the exact position where he started, but he clearly enjoys playing with the buttons. He places his hands behind his head and crosses his feet as if he is basking in the life of luxury.

"Have you seen the doctor yet this morning?" Dad asks Mom.

"Yes, four different doctors. All of them are baffled. The Neurologist said his brain scans have completely cleared. There are no more signs of damage. The Cardiologist said his heart looks perfectly healthy. The Pulmonologist says he looks great. I forgot who the other doctor is, but they have cleared him to go. They can't find a reason to keep him. If his bloodwork comes back clear, they said we can fill out the discharge paperwork. He has quite a few follow-up appointments with some specialists just to watch his progress. But he seems like he is going to be just fine." Mom's words are filled with disbelief and joy.

"That's incredible," Dad responds.

"Excuse me." A woman knocks on the door and peeks her head into the room.

"I'm the discharge nurse. I'm here to go over the discharge packet with you if you would like to follow me to the nurse's station."

"You go, I'll stay," Dad says to Mom.

"You have all the new insurance information for your company. They were asking about that earlier, and I wasn't quite sure what to tell them," Mom states, trying to get Dad to go.

"Why don't you both go. Jax and I are just chilling and watching some TV."

"You can leave the door open. We are just going to the desk right there." The nurse points straight across the hall.

"Okay, we'll be right there if you need anything," Mom states with a hint of worry.

"We'll be fine," I promise.

As soon as Mom and Dad leave the room, I lean down and whisper to Jaxson.

"So, how are you feeling, bud?"

"Great!"

"I have a surprise for you when you get back to Great Granddad's house. But you have to promise to keep it a secret, okay?"

Jaxson's eyes light up and triple in size. "What is it?" He jumps up onto his knees. "Tell me, please," he pleads.

"First, you have to promise to keep the secret. It is something you CAN'T tell Mom and Dad."

"I promise!" He crosses his heart with his finger.

"Lan is at the house. She came back with us. I haven't told Mom and Dad yet, and I need to keep her a secret. Will you help me?"

"Really? Lan is here?" The pitch in Jaxson's voice jumps.

"Shhhh!" I lower my hands repeatedly as if I can physically lower his volume somehow.

"Oh, ya, shhhh." He smiles. "How did she get here?" He whispers.

"She touched my shirt when we left her time and it sent her back here with us," I whisper.

"I can't wait to see her."

"She is excited to see you, too. I really need you to keep another secret, too. You can't tell Mom and Dad about the time machine and our adventure. Okay? They would think we are crazy. And we can't have the world knowing about our secret time machine, right?" I realize I am asking a lot of my little brother. There is no way he is going to keep any of this a secret.

"It is our little secret. Pinky Promise." He shoves his little pinky toward me. I wrap my pinky around his, and we shake our pinkies up and down.

"Alright, you are all cleared to go." Dad cheers as he enters the room.

"Hooray!" Jaxson shouts, jumps off his bed, and runs toward the door.

"Not so fast. You need to put clothes on first." Mom blocks him from exiting and hands him a pair of folded pajamas from a bag. "Well, your Dad only brought pajamas for you, so here you go. Pajama day it is."

"Woohoo!" Jaxson snatches the pajamas and slams the bathroom door closed.

The car ride home is quiet. Mom is sleeping peacefully in the front seat, and Jaxson falls asleep on me almost instantly. With the rocking of the car, I can't help but join in,too.

"We're here." Dad's words wake us up.

Jaxson has his seatbelt off and is ready to take off into the house the moment his eyes open.

"Remember, shhhhh." I place my finger to my lip with one hand and hold up the pinky on my other hand as a reminder of our promise. Jaxson smiles and nods, mimicking my gestures.

I run up to the door, trying to get there first, being as loud as possible to let Lan know we are home.

"Isn't it great to be home?" I holler into the house, much louder than normal.

I peek into the entryway before fully opening the door.

I don't see or hear any sign of Lan.

"Okay, mister. I want you to take it easy today. You may play that old computer as long as you like." You would have thought Mom gave Jaxson the world.

"Really?"

She nods.

He darts off to the office.

"I need a shower," Mom huffs. "Can you keep an eye on him for a few minutes, Hun?" Mom asks Dad.

"Absolutely, I'll go get some work done in there next to him, you go shower."

I dash up the staircase and begin my search for Lan. I check my room first, because that is my initial instinct.

"Lan?" I whisper, closing my bedroom door behind me.

"Lan?" I ask, opening my closet door. And even though I kind of expected her to be here, I still jump when I see her.

She jumps up and embraces me. "Did I hear Jaxson? Is he here?"

I nod furiously. "I'll bring him up here to see you. I just had to find you first.

Sorry, my Dad got us a hotel room across from the hospital last night."

"I was so worried, but I'm just so glad you are both home. I can't wait to see him."

"I'll go get him. I'll be right back."

I run down the stairs to the office, where, unfortunately, Dad is sitting right next to Jaxson.

"Oh, hey, bud. I was wondering if you want to choose any book you want from the library, and I will read it to you." I hold up my pinky to where he can see it.

"Why would I want to read a book when…" His words stop immediately when he looks up at my wiggling pinky. I wink at him, and a wave of understanding washes over his pudgy cheeks.

"Yes, I would love for you to read me a book." His over-animated voice makes me cringe. There is no way Dad doesn't see through Jaxson's terrible acting, but he is too busy reading emails to notice.

"Hey, Dad, Jaxson and I are going up to my room to read for a bit, okay?"

"What, oh, sure. Great idea."

We race up the stairs to my bedroom and close the door behind us. I point to the closet.

Jaxson can't get to the door fast enough. He whips open the door and flies into Lan's arms. The reunion is enough to make me cry, but I am all out of tears after the last few days.

"It's so good to see you," Lan whispers. "I guess the medicine your brother gave you helped you get all better," she adds.

"What medicine?" Jaxson asks.

"You almost died, and I had to give you some special medicine to bring you back. But, again, you can't tell that to Mom and Dad. It came from the future. Mom, Dad, and the doctors today won't understand."

"Where did you get it, from Lan's time?" Jaxson asks.

"We had to go to a different time to get it for you," Lan responds.

I instantly see the hurt in Jaxson's eyes.

"You went on another adventure without me?" His chin quivers.

"I didn't have a choice bud; you were in a coma, and there was something I had to do to help save the world, and I had to get you the special medicine." But I can tell my words aren't helping Jaxson feel better. His face scrunches with betrayal.

"That's not fair. You should have waited for me."

"You would have died. I had to go without you."

"You still should have waited and taken me with you."

"We had to go. It was really important. He saved you." Lan's voice is soothing.

He doesn't respond. He just sits quietly, contemplation brewing in his blue eyes.

"I promise we won't go on any more adventures without you. In fact, I don't think it's safe to go on any more time-traveling adventures. I've done what I can to save the world. Let's just stay here and find adventures in our time together. Okay?" Jaxson just stares ahead at the back of the closet.

"We aren't going on any more time-traveling adventures, ever?" Lan asks.

"I don't think it's a good idea. We almost lost Jaxson."

"But I thought maybe you would take me back home."

"This can be your home now."

"What? You want me to live in your closet for the rest of my life?" Lan asks.

"No, I mean. We'll figure out where you can live."

"Tell me honestly. Are you ever going to be able to tell your parents about me? Or who I am? Or where I'm from? I had a lot of time to think while you were gone at the hospital, and I think I need to go back to my time. I need to check on *my* family. How do we know if what you did on that island worked unless we go to the future to see?"

"But we don't know if what I did will change you or your future. What if you go back and turn to dust or something because whatever we did made it so you aren't born? There are weird rules about time travel that we don't fully understand, even you said that."

"So, I'm just never going back?" For the first time, she looks at me with hurt in her eyes, and I am the cause of the pain.

"I think we just need to do some more research first. I'm sure Great Granddad has more information on the rules of time travel somewhere. I'm just saying it wouldn't hurt to wait until we are sure it is safe for you."

"And safe for me," Jaxson adds. "Because I'm coming with you."

"You can't go anywhere until we know that you are all better."

"I am all better. And I'm tired of everyone telling me what I can and can't do." He stands and stomps out of the closet.

"Wait, bud. You can do a lot of things. You are the best secret keeper, right? The secret keeper is the most important person on our team. Right, Lan?" Lan nods.

"I don't want to keep secrets. I want to go on adventures." He folds his arms across his chest.

"I'm going back down to play the computer," he pouts.

"Jaxson, wait," I shout after him. "Please, promise me you will still keep our secret."

"I already pinky-promised. I won't tell your stupid secret." He stomps out of the room.

"I'm dead if he blabs." I run my fingers through my hair and blow out a big stressed-out exhale.

Lan just stews next to me in silence.

"I'm sorry. I will take you back to your time if you want me to. I just can't live with myself if I lose you."

"I know. I just… I need to know. I can't live with myself, not knowing if they are okay."

"I get that. Can I please just have a little time to do some research first?"

She hesitates but finally nods.

"You hungry? Need something to eat? I'll go find you something." I want to do anything I can to make her feel better.

"No, thanks. I'm good," she states. "I actually started reading this book I found in that book room while you were gone, and I kind of want to finish it if that's okay."

"Yah, sure. Of course."

Oh no. She doesn't want food, and she wants to be left alone.
This is NOT good. I must've really made her mad.

I want to give her some space, so I close the door to the closet enough to block her from the line of sight of the door if Mom or Dad come in, but leave it open enough so she can still have enough light to read.

"This good? Do you need a flashlight or anything?"

"It's fine." Her words are cold and empty.

"You sure you're okay?" I ask.

"Really, I'm fine. I just want to be alone."

"Okay."

I look around and realize my backpack and satchel are now sitting in the corner of my room.

"Thanks for bringing these in here for me."

"You're welcome."

As soon as I see my wristband, I remember the keys in my pants pocket. I quickly snap both of them back into their proper places on the wristband.

"I guess I'm just going to see what I can find about time travel rules in the journals."

"You don't need to," she responds.

"I want to."

"You won't find anything else other than that page about The Grandfather Paradox telling us not to go to the past. I already searched."

"Then, we'll go search through Great Granddad's study, the library, the apothecary, and everywhere else when it's safe, until we find some answers. Okay?"

"Okay." She shrugs.

I find the journals sitting just under the flap of my backpack. I grab them and flop onto my bed to search through them. Not because I don't believe her that there isn't anything thing else about the rules of time travel in them, but because I really don't know what else to do.

The first page I open to, is, again, one I don't remember ever seeing before. It shows the A.T.H.P Serum recipe, The Elixir of Immortality.

Huh, would you look at that?

The recipe for the A.C.H.P. serum (The Elixir of Immortality) including sketches of the ingredients & symbols for Ambystoma (Axolotl), Tardigradas (Tardigrade), Homosapien Provectus (Evolved Human), White Sulphur Spring Water, Philosopher's Stone (Powder)

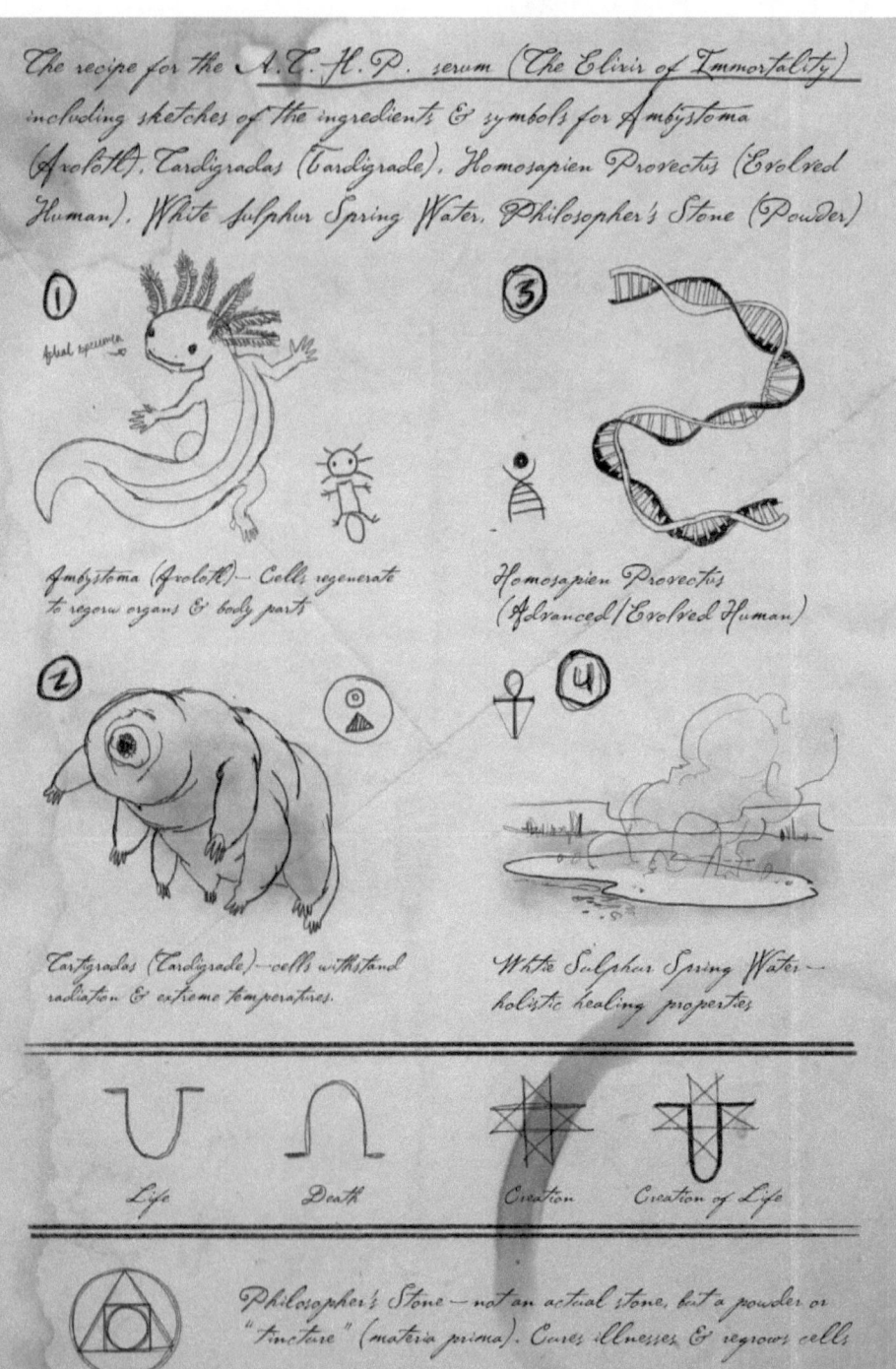

① Ambystoma (Axolotl) — Cells regenerate to regrow organs & body parts

② Tardigradas (Tardigrade) — cells withstand radiation & extreme temperatures.

③ Homosapien Provectus (Advanced/Evolved Human)

④ White Sulphur Spring Water — holistic healing properties

Life   Death   Creation   Creation of Life

Philosopher's Stone — not an actual stone, but a powder or "tincture" (materia prima). Cures illnesses & regrows cells

The Ambystoma, or Axolotl, makes it so our cells regenerate, and we can regrow body parts. That is so cool!

I can't help but think of the miracle of Lan's fingers regrowing. I look toward her peaceful body, hunched in the closet, and I hear her breathing heavily. I watch as her chest rises and falls methodically, and it puts me in a trance.

My eyes finally flutter open, but my room is now dark.

I must have fallen asleep. How long was I out? It's dark outside.

"Lan?" I whisper into the shadows, but she doesn't respond. I jump up and flip the light switch on the wall. I walk over and peek in the closet, but she isn't there.

Where did she go? Maybe she snuck her way out to the bathroom?

I instantly notice a piece of paper that looks like it has been torn out of one of the journals, sitting on my nightstand.

I know that wasn't there when I fell asleep. And I would never tear out a page from Great Granddad's journal.

I step to look at it and promptly realize it is definitely the same paper from the journal, but the handwriting is much neater than Great Granddad's.

Dear Dameon,

I have gone back to my time. I need to check on Einstein, Erb, and Neo to make sure they are okay. I will do everything I can to come right back to you. I know I can't live without you either. But you need to be with your family right now. You have all been through a lot. I borrowed some elements for the machine from the apothecary. I promise to replace them. I hope to see you soon. Who knows, maybe I will be back already by the time you read this.

Love, Lan

I goin wit her!
Jaxson

NO!

I sprint from my room and check the room where Jaxson has been sleeping. The bed looks slept in, but he isn't anywhere to be found.

"Jaxson?" I whisper, rummaging through his blankets.

I sprint downstairs.

"You okay, Dameon? You aren't sick, are you? You have been asleep all evening. We all just kind of did our own thing for dinner. I made noodle soup for Jaxson and put the leftovers in the fridge if you want some."

"Oh, I'm good. I can find some dinner. I just feel bad I missed out on time with Jaxson. Did you already put him to bed?" I ask, attempting to get more information.

"Yes, I put him to bed about an hour ago. He was all tuckered out. You don't mind listening for him tonight, do you?" I will be up to check on him every few hours, but just if you hear him call out or anything."

"Sure, Mom. I just slept for hours, so I will most likely be up all night. And don't worry, I'll check on him throughout the night, so you don't have to. You look tired. Why don't you go to bed."

"That would be amazing. Thank you. You are such a good kid." She reaches up to stroke my hair. "Wow, I think you have grown a good six inches in the last week. I'm not joking. It must have been the time away. Good night. Love you."

"Love you, too, Mom. Goodnight, Dad," I add, noticing my Dad is still working on his computer.

"Night."

NO! Jaxson is NOT in his bed.

My heart feels like it is going to pound out of my chest. I run up the stairs to the hidden panel in the wall. Luckily, they left it unlocked, and I am able to slide the door panel aside and rush up the stairs to the observatory. I pause and glance around, but there aren't any places to hide up here. No one is up here. The trapdoor is open in the middle of the floor, and I rush over and step down the stairs to the cellar.

"Lan? Jaxson?"

"Come on! Please, guys!"

I dash down the stairs to the cellar and dart over to look at the time dial on the machine. Using my finger, I wipe off the black dust covering the numbers. The dial is hot to the touch. The machine is still warm. It must have been used not long ago. The time shown on the dial screams back at me. It is set for the date we returned from when we brought Lan to our time. Lan has indeed gone back to her time, and Jaxson said he went with her.

Tracy Wilson grew up at the base of the mountains in Utah and now resides in sunny Florida. When she is not teaching or mentoring students and teachers, she can be found reading or writing young adult fiction novels. In her spare time, she loves to relax at the beach and travel with her family.

www.ingramcontent.com/pod-product-compliance
Lightning Source LLC
Chambersburg PA
CBHW030755260626
47169CB00001B/56

9 798991 238441